YEARS
of pure reading pleasure

100 Reasons to Celebrate

We invite you to join us in celebrating Mills & Boon's centenary. Gerald Mills and Charles Boon founded Mills & Boon Limited in 1908 and opened offices in London's Covent Garden. Since then, Mills & Boon has become a hallmark for romantic fiction, recognised around the world.

We're proud of our 100 years of publishing excellence, which wouldn't have been achieved without the loyalty and enthusiasm of our authors and readers.

Thank you!

Each month throughout the year there will be something new and exciting to mark the centenary, so watch for your favourite authors, captivating new stories, special limited edition collections...and more!

Raintree: Inferno
and
Loving Evangeline
LINDA HOWARD

MILLS & BOON®
Pure reading pleasure

First published in Great Britain 2008
by Harlequin Mills & Boon Limited,
Eton House, 18-24 Paradise Road, Richmond, Surrey TW9 1SR

The publisher acknowledges the copyright holders of the
individual works as follows:

Raintree: Inferno © Linda Howington 2007
Loving Evangeline © Linda Howington 1994

ISBN: 978 0 263 85942 3

46-0308

Printed and bound in Spain
by Litografía Rosés S.A., Barcelona

To Beverly Barton and Linda Winstead Jones,
for the years of friendship and all the fun
we had planning these books,
and to Leslie Wainger, for being everything
an editor should be, as well as a friend.

Dear Reader,

My friends Beverly, Linda and I have worked on the concept for these books for about four years, spent hours and hours discussing them, playing with ideas and laughing our heads off. Not that these books are funny, but after a while we got sort of punch-drunk and we'd go off on tangents. One such tangent was limericks (*There was a young man from Paducah...*), which of course had nothing to do with the Raintree books.

We loved working out the mythology behind the Raintree, extraordinary people trying to live in the ordinary world without being found out. We loved the characters. They are all very human, and at the same time they are...more than human. I hope you enjoy them, too.

Linda

Raintree: Inferno

Prologue

There have always been those among us who are more than human. At first they were few, but like always calls to like, and so it was from the beginning, when mankind was new and clumped together in fire-lit caves. Sometimes they were driven out by fear and fists wielding clubs. Sometimes they simply left, seeking others like them. And though they were few and the earth was large, they found each other, drawn by the very instinct and power and knowledge that set them apart from the very beginning—and by the will to survive, for only in numbers was there safety.

In time those numbers grew large, and there

was strife between those who wanted to use their powers, their *otherness*, to take what they wanted from the weaker humans, and those who wanted to live in harmony with the Ungifted. Over seven thousand years ago they split into what became two tribes, and then two kingdoms: the Raintree, and the Ansara.

The two kingdoms then locked into eternal war, and Earth in all her dimensions became the battleground.

So it was, and so it is.

Chapter 1

Dante Raintree stood with his arms crossed as he watched the woman on the monitor. The image was in black and white, to better show details; color distracted the brain. He focused on her hands, watching every move she made, but what struck him most was how uncommonly *still* she was. She didn't fidget, or play with her chips, or look around at the other players. She peeked once at her down card, then didn't touch it again, signaling for another hit by tapping a fingernail on the table. Just because she didn't seem to be paying attention to the other players, though, didn't mean she was as unaware as she seemed.

"What's her name?" he asked.

"Lorna Clay," replied his chief of security, Al Rayburn.

"Is that her real name?"

"It checks out."

If Al hadn't already investigated her, Dante would have been disappointed. He paid Al a lot of money to be efficient and thorough.

"At first I thought she was counting," said Al. "But she doesn't pay enough attention."

"She's paying attention, all right," Dante murmured. "You just don't see her doing it." A card counter had to remember every card played. Supposedly counting cards was impossible with the number of decks used by the casinos, but no casino wanted a card counter at its tables. There *were* those rare individuals who could calculate the odds even with multiple decks.

"I thought that, too," said Al. "But look at this piece of tape coming up. Someone she knows comes up to her and speaks, she looks around and starts chatting, completely misses the play of the people to her left—and doesn't look around even when the deal comes back to her, she just taps that finger. And damned if she didn't win. Again."

Dante watched the tape, rewound it, watched

it again. Then he watched it a third time. There had to be something he was missing, because he couldn't pick out a single giveaway.

"If she's cheating," Al said with something like respect, "she's the best I've ever seen."

"What does your gut say?" Dante trusted his chief of security. Al had spent thirty years in the casino business, and some people swore he could spot cheats as soon as they walked in the door. If Al thought she was cheating, then Dante would take action—and he wouldn't be watching this tape now if something hadn't made Al uneasy.

Al scratched the side of his jaw, considering. He was a big, bulky man, but no one who observed him for any length of time would think he was slow, either physically or mentally. Finally he said, "If she isn't cheating, she's the luckiest person walking. She wins. Week in, week out, she wins. Never a huge amount, but I ran the numbers, and she's into us for about five grand a week. Hell, boss, on her way out of the casino she'll stop by a slot machine, feed a dollar in and walk away with at least fifty. It's never the same machine, either. I've had her watched, I've had her followed, I've even looked for the same faces in the casino every time she's in here, and I can't find a common denominator."

"Is she here now?"

"She came in about half an hour ago. She's playing blackjack, as usual."

"Who's the dealer?"

"Cindy."

Cindy Josephson was Dante's best dealer, almost as sharp at spotting a cheater as Al himself. She had been with him since he'd opened Inferno, and he trusted her to run an honest game. "Bring the woman to my office," Dante said, making a swift decision. "Don't make a scene."

"Got it," said Al, turning on his heel and leaving the security center, where banks of monitors displayed every angle of the casino.

Dante left, too, going up to his office. His face was calm. Normally he would leave it to Al to deal with a cheater, but he was curious. How was she doing it? There were a lot of bad cheaters, a few good ones, and every so often one would come along who was the stuff of which legends were made: the cheater who didn't get caught, even when people were alert and the camera was on him—or, in this case, her.

It was possible for people to simply be lucky, as most people understood luck. Chance could turn a habitual loser into a big-time winner. Casinos, in fact, thrived on that hope. But luck itself wasn't habitual, and he knew that what passed for luck was often something else: cheating. Then there was the other kind of luck, the kind he himself possessed, but since it depended not on chance but on who and what he was, he knew it was an innate power and not Dame Fortune's erratic smiles. Since his power was rare, the odds made it likely the woman he'd been watching was merely a very clever cheat.

Her skill could provide her with a very good living, he thought, doing some swift calculations in his head. Five grand a week equaled two hundred sixty thousand dollars a year, and that was just from his casino. She probably hit all of them, careful to keep the numbers relatively low so she stayed under the radar.

He wondered how long she'd been taking him, how long she'd been winning a little here, a little there, before Al noticed.

The curtains were still open on the wall-to-wall window in his office, giving the impression, when one first opened the door, of stepping out onto a covered balcony. The glazed window faced west, so he could catch the sunsets. The sun was low now, the sky painted in purple and gold. At his home in the mountains, most of the windows faced east, affording him views of the sunrise. Something in him needed both the greeting and the goodbye of the sun. He'd always been drawn to sunlight, maybe because fire was his element to call, to control.

He checked his internal time: four minutes until sundown. He knew exactly, without checking the tables every day, when the sun would slide behind the mountains. He didn't own an alarm clock. He didn't need one. He was so acutely attuned to the sun's position that he had only to check within himself to know the time. As for waking at a particular time, he was one of those people who could tell himself to wake at a certain time, and he did. That particular talent had nothing to do with being Raintree, so he didn't have to hide it; a lot of perfectly ordinary people had the same ability.

There were other talents and abilities, however, that did require careful shielding. The long days of summer instilled in him an almost sexual high, when he could feel contained power buzzing just beneath his skin. He had to be doubly careful not to cause candles to leap into flame just by his presence, or to start wildfires, with a glance, in the dry-as-tinder brush. He loved Reno; he didn't want to burn it down. He just felt so damn *alive* with all the sunshine pouring down that he wanted to let the energy pour through him instead of holding it inside.

This must be how his brother Gideon felt while pulling lightning, all that hot power searing through his muscles, his veins. They had this in common, the connection with raw power. All the members of the far-flung Raintree clan had some power, some heightened form of ability, but only members of the royal family could channel and control the earth's natural energies.

Dante wasn't just of the royal family; he was the Dranir, the leader of the entire clan. "Dranir" was synonymous with "king," but the position he held wasn't ceremonial, it was one of sheer power. He was the oldest son of the previous Dranir, but he would have been passed over for the position if he hadn't also inherited the power to hold it.

Gideon was second to him in power; if anything happened to Dante and he died without a child who had inherited his abilities, Gideon would become Dranir—a possibility that filled his brother with dread, hence the fertility charm currently lying on Dante's desk. It had arrived in the mail just that morning. Gideon regularly sent them, partly as a joke, but mainly because he was doing all he could to insure that Dante had offspring—thus upping the chances that *he* would never inherit the position. Whenever they managed to get together, Dante had to carefully search every nook and cranny, as well as all his clothing, to make certain Gideon hadn't left one of his clever little charms in a hidden place.

Gideon was getting better at making them, Dante mused. Practice made perfect, after all, and God knows he'd made plenty of the charms in the past few years. Not only were they more potent now, but he varied his approach. Some of them were obvious, silver pieces meant to be worn around the neck like an amulet—not that Dante was an amulet kind of guy. Others were tiny, subtle, like the one Gideon had embedded in the newest business card he'd sent, knowing Dante would likely tuck the card into his pocket. He'd erred only in that the very power of the charm gave it away; Dante had sensed the buzz of its power, though he'd had the devil's own time finding it.

Behind him came Al's distinctive *knock-knock* on the door. The outer office was empty, Dante's secretary having gone home hours before. "Come in," he called, not turning from his view of the sunset.

The door opened, and Al said, "Mr. Raintree, this is Lorna Clay."

Dante turned and looked at the woman, all his senses on alert. The first thing he noticed was the vibrant color of her hair—a rich, dark red that encompassed a multitude of shades from copper to burgundy. The warm amber light danced along the iridescent strands, and he felt a hard tug of sheer lust in his gut. Looking at her hair was almost like looking at fire, and he had the same reaction.

The second thing he noticed was that she was spitting mad.

Chapter 2

Several things happened so closely together that they might as well have been simultaneous. With his senses already so heightened, the quick lash of desire collided with Dante's visceral reaction to fire, sending explosions of sensation cascading along all his neural pathways, too fast for him to control. Across the room, he saw all the candles leap with fire, the wicks burning too fast, too wild, so that the multiple little flames flared larger and more brightly than they should. And on his desk, Gideon's damn little fertility charm began to buzz with power, as if it had an on/off switch that had suddenly been pressed.

What the hell…?

He didn't have time to dissect and analyze everything that was going on; he had to control himself, and fast, or the entire room would be ablaze. He hadn't suffered such a humiliating loss of control of his powers since he'd first entered puberty and his surging hormones had played hell with everything.

Ruthlessly, he began exerting his will on all that leaping power. It wasn't easy; though he held himself perfectly still, mentally he felt as if he were riding a big, nasty-tempered bull. The natural inclination of energy was to be free, and it resisted any effort to tame it, to wrestle it back inside his mental walls. His control was usually phenomenal. After all, *having* power wasn't what made a Dranir; having it and *controlling* it *was*. Lack of control led to devastation—and ultimately to exposure. The Raintree had survived the centuries due in large part to their ability to blend with normal people, so it wasn't a matter to be taken lightly.

Dante had trained all his life to master the power and energies that ran through him, and even though he knew that as the summer solstice drew near his control was always stretched a bit, he wasn't accustomed to this degree of difficulty. Grimly he concentrated, pulling back, clamping down, exerting his will over the very forces of nature. He could have extinguished the candles, but with an even greater force of will he left them burning, for to make the tiny flames wink out now might draw even more attention than lighting them in the first place.

The only thing that evaded his control was that damn fertility charm on his desk, buzzing and throbbing and all but sending out a strobe effect. Even though he knew Al and Ms. Clay couldn't pick up on the energy the thing was sending out, not glancing at it took all his self-control. Gideon had outdone himself with this one. Just wait until the next time he saw his little brother, Dante grimly promised himself. If Gideon thought this was funny, they would both see how funny it was when the tables were turned. Gideon wasn't the only one who could make fertility charms.

All the wildfires once more under control, he returned his attention to his guest.

Lorna once again tried to twist her arm away from the gorilla holding her, but his grip was just strong enough to hold without applying undue pressure. While a small part of her appreciated that he was actively trying not to hurt her, by far the largest part of her was so furious—and, yes, scared—that she wanted to lash out at him with all her strength, clawing and kicking and biting, doing anything she could to get free.

Then her survival instinct kicked into high gear and her hair all but stood on end as she realized the man standing so silent and still in front of the huge windows was a far greater threat to her than was the gorilla.

Her throat closed, a fist of fear tightening around her neck. She couldn't have said what it was about him that so alarmed her, but she had felt this way only once before, in a back alley in Chicago. She was accustomed to taking care of herself on the streets and had normally used the alley as a shortcut to her place—a shabby single room in a run-down building—but one night when she had started down the alley, alarm had prickled her scalp and she'd frozen, unable to take another step. She couldn't see anything suspicious, couldn't hear anything, but she could *not* move forward. Her heart had been hammering so hard in her chest she could barely breathe, and she had abruptly been sick with fear. Slowly she had backed out of the alley's entrance and fled down the street to take the long way home.

The next morning a prostitute's body had been found in the alley, brutally raped and mutilated. Lorna knew the dead woman could have been her, if not for the sudden hair-raising panic that had warned her away.

This was the same, like being body-slammed by a sense of danger. The man in front of her, whoever he was, was a threat to her. She doubted—at least on a rational level—that he would murder and mutilate her, but there were other dangers, other destructions she could suffer.

She felt as if she were smothering, her throat so tight very little air could get past the constriction. Pinpricks of light flared at the edges of her vision, and in silent horror she realized she might faint. She didn't dare lose consciousness; she would be completely helpless if she did.

"Miss Clay," he said in a calm, smooth-as-cream voice, as if her panic were completely invisible to him and no one else in the room knew she was on the verge of screaming. "Sit down, please."

The prosaic invitation/command had the blessed effect of snapping her out of the trap of panic. Somehow she managed to take a breath without audibly gasping, then another. Nothing was going to happen. She didn't need to panic. Yes, this was mildly alarming and she probably wouldn't be coming back to the Inferno to gamble, but she hadn't broken any laws or casino rules. She was safe.

Those pinpricks of light flared again. What…? Puzzled, she turned her head and found herself staring at two huge pillar candles, each of them easily two and a half feet tall, one on the floor and the other perched on a slab of white marble that served as a hearth. Flames danced around the candles' multiple wicks.

Candles. She hadn't been about to faint. The flickers of light at the edge of her vision had come from those candles. She hadn't noticed them when she'd been literally dragged into the room, but that was understandable.

The candlelights were dancing and swaying, as if they stood in a draft. That too was understandable. She didn't feel any noticeable movement of air, but this was summertime in Reno, and the air-conditioning would be running full blast. She always wore long sleeves when she went to a casino anyway; otherwise she was too cold.

With a start she realized she was staring at the candles and had neither moved nor replied to the invitation to sit. She jerked her attention back to the man standing at the window, trying to recall what the gorilla had called him. "Who are you?" she demanded sharply. Once more she jerked her arm, but the gorilla merely sighed as he held her. "Let go!"

"You can let her go," the man said, sounding faintly amused. "Thank you for bringing her here."

The gorilla instantly released her, said, "I'll be in the security center," and quietly let himself out of the office.

Instantly Lorna began assessing her chance of

making a run for it, but for now she stood her ground. She didn't want to run; the casino had her name, her description. If she ran, she would be blacklisted—not just in the Inferno, but in every casino in Nevada.

"I'm Dante Raintree," the man said, then waited a beat to see if she gave any reaction to the name. It meant nothing to her, so she merely gave a slight, questioning lift of her brows. "I own the Inferno."

Crap! An owner carried serious weight with the gaming commission. She would have to tread very carefully, but she had the advantage. He couldn't prove she'd been cheating, because the simple fact was, she hadn't been.

"Dante. Inferno. I get it," she replied with a little edge of *so what?* in her tone. He was probably so rich he thought everyone should be awed in his presence. If he wanted to awe her, he would have to find something other than his wealth to do the job. She appreciated money as much as anyone; it certainly made life easier. Now that she had a little financial cushion, she was amazed at how much better she slept—what a relief it was not to worry where her next bite was coming from, or when. At the same time, she despised people who thought their wealth entitled them to special treatment.

Not only that, his name was ridiculous. Maybe his last name really was Raintree, but he'd probably chosen his first name for the drama and to fit the name of the casino. His real first name was probably something like Melvin or Fred.

"Please have a seat," he invited again, indicating the cream-colored leather sofa to her right. A jade coffee table sat between the sofa and two cushy-looking club chairs. She tried not to stare at the table as she took a seat in one of the chairs, which was just as cushy as it looked. Surely the table was just the color of jade and not actually made of the real stone, but it *looked* real, as if it were faintly translucent. Surely it was just glass. If so, the craftsmanship was superb.

Lorna didn't have a lot of experience with luxury items, but she did have a sort of sixth sense about her surroundings. She began to feel overwhelmed by the things around her. No, not overwhelmed; that wasn't the right word. She tried to nail down what she was feeling, but there was an alien, unknown quality to the very air around her that she couldn't describe. This was unfamiliar, and it definitely carried the edge of danger that had so alarmed her when she'd first become aware of it.

As Dante Raintree strolled closer, she realized that everything she was sensing centered on him. She'd been right; *he* was the danger.

He moved with indolent grace, but there was nothing slow or lazy about him. He was a tall man, about eight or nine inches taller than her own five foot five, and though his excellently tailored clothing gave him a lean look, there was no tailor skilled enough to completely disguise the power of the muscles beneath the fabric. Not a cheetah, then, but a tiger.

She realized she had avoided looking him full in the face, as if not having that knowledge would give her a small measure of safety. She knew better; ignorance was never a good defense, and Lorna had learned a long time ago not to hide her head in the sand and hope for the best.

He sat down across from her, and with an inward bracing she met his gaze full-on.

The bottom dropped out of her stomach.

She had a faint, dizzying sensation of falling; she barely restrained herself from gripping the arms of the chair to steady herself.

His hair was black. His eyes were green. Common colors, and yet nothing about him was common. His hair was sleek and glossy, falling to his shoulders. She didn't like long hair on men, but his looked clean and soft, and she wanted to bury her hands in it. She shoved *that* idea away and promptly became snagged by his gaze. His eyes weren't just green, they were *green*, so remarkably green that her first thought was that he was wearing colored contacts. A color that darkly rich and pure couldn't be real. They were just very realistic contacts, with tiny black striations in them like real eyes. She had seen ads for those in magazines. The only thing was, when the candles flared and his pupils briefly contracted, the color of his irises seemed to expand. Could contacts give that appearance?

He wasn't wearing contacts. Instinctively she knew that everything she saw, from the sleek blackness of his hair to that intense eye color, was real.

He was drawing her in. Some power she couldn't understand was tugging at her with an almost physical sensation. The candle flames were dancing wildly, brighter now that the sun had set and twilight was deepening outside the window. The candles were the only light in the now gloomy office, sending shadows slashing across the hard angles of his face, and yet his eyes seemed to glow brighter with color than they had only a few moments before.

They hadn't said a word since he'd sat down, yet she felt as if she were in a battle for her will, her force, her independent life. Deep inside, panic flared to candlelight life, dancing and leaping. *He knows*, she thought, and tensed herself to run. Forget the casinos, forget the very nice money she'd been reaping, forget everything except survival. *Run!*

Her body didn't obey. She continued to sit there, frozen…mesmerized.

"How are you doing it?" he finally asked, his tone still as calm and unruffled as if he were oblivious to the swirls and surges of power that were buffeting her.

Once again, his voice seemed to break through her inner turmoil and bring her back to reality. Bewildered, she stared at him. He thought *she* was doing all this weird stuff?

"I'm not," she blurted. "I thought you were."

She might have been mistaken, because in the dancing candlelight, reading an expression was tricky, but she thought he looked slightly stunned.

"Cheating," he said in clarification. "How are you stealing from me?"

Chapter 3

Maybe he didn't know.

His bluntness was a perverse relief. Lorna took a deep breath. At least now she was dealing with something she understood. Ignoring the strange undercurrents in the room, the almost physical sensation of being surrounded by…something…she lifted her chin, narrowed her eyes and gave him stare for stare. "I'm not cheating!" That was true— as far as it went, and in the normal understanding of the word.

"Of course you are. No one is as lucky as you seem to be unless he—excuse me, *she*—is cheating." His eyes were glittering now, but in her book glittering was way better than that weird glowing. Eyes didn't glow anyway. What was wrong with her? Had someone slipped a drug into her drink while her head was turned? She never drank alcohol while she was gambling, sticking to coffee or soft drinks, but that last cup of coffee had tasted bitter. At the time she'd thought she'd been unlucky enough to get the last cup in the pot, but now she wondered if it hadn't been pharmaceutically enhanced.

"I repeat. I'm not cheating." Lorna bit off the words, her jaw set.

"You've been coming here for a while. You walk away with about five grand every week. That's a cool quarter of a million a year—and that's just from my casino. How many others are you hitting?" His cool gaze raked her from head to foot, as if he wondered why she didn't dress better, taking in that kind of money.

Lorna felt her face getting hot, and that made her angry. She hadn't been embarrassed about anything in a very long time, embarrassment being a luxury she couldn't afford, but something about his assessment made her want to squirm. Okay, so she wasn't the best dresser in the world, but she was neat and clean, and that was what mattered. So what if she'd gotten her pants and short-sleeve blouse at Wal-Mart? She simply couldn't make herself spend a hundred dollars on a pair of shoes when a twelve-dollar pair fit her just as well. The eighty-eight dollar difference would buy a lot of food. And silk not only cost a lot, but it was difficult to care for; she would take a nice cotton/polyester blend, which didn't have to be ironed, over silk any day of the week.

"I said, how many other casinos are you hitting each week?"

"What I do isn't your business." She glared at him, glad for the anger and the surge of energy it gave her. Feeling angry was much better than feeling hurt. She wouldn't let this man's opinion matter enough to her that he could hurt her. Her clothes might be cheap, but they weren't ragged; she was clean, and she refused to be ashamed of them.

"On the contrary. I caught you. Therefore I should have Al warn the other security chiefs."

"You haven't *caught* me doing anything!" She was absolutely certain of that, because she hadn't *done* anything he could catch.

"You're lucky I'm the one in the driver's seat," he continued as if she hadn't spoken a word. "There's a certain element in Reno that thinks cheating is a crime deserving of capital punishment."

Her heartbeat stuttered. He was right, and she knew it. There were whispers on the street, tales of people who tried to tilt the odds their way—and who either disappeared completely or had assumed room temperature by the time they were found. She didn't have the blissful ignorance that would let her think he was merely exaggerating, because she had lived in the world where those things happened. She knew that world, knew the people who inhabited it. She had been careful to stay as invisible as possible, and she never used the ubiquitous players' cards that allowed the casinos to keep track of who was winning and who wasn't, but still she had done something wrong, something that called attention to herself. Her innocence wouldn't matter to some people; a word to the wrong person, and she was a dead woman.

Was he saying he didn't intend to turn her in, that he would keep the matter Inferno's private business?

Why would he do that? Only two possible reasons came to mind. One was the old sex-for-a-favor play: "Be nice to me, little girl, and I won't tell what I know." The other was that he might suspect her of cheating but had no evidence, and all he intended to do was maybe trick her into confessing or at the least bar her from the Inferno. If his reason was the former one, then he was a sleaze, and she knew how to deal with sleazes. If his reason was the latter, well, then he was a nice guy.

Which would be his tough luck.

He was watching her, really *watching* her, his

complete attention focused on reading every
flicker of emotion on her face. Lorna fought the
urge to fidget, but being the center of that sort of
concentration made her very uneasy. She preferred
to blend in with the crowd, to stay in the background; anonymity meant safety.

"Relax. I'm not going to blackmail you into
having sex with me—not that I'm not interested,"
he said, "but I don't need coercion to get sex when
I want it."

She almost jumped. Either he'd read her mind,
or she was getting really sloppy about guarding her
expression. She knew she wasn't sloppy; for too
long, her life had depended on staying sharp; the defensive habits of a lifetime were deeply ingrained.
He'd read her mind. *Oh, God, he'd read her mind!*

Full-blown panic began to fog her mind; then it
immediately dissipated, forced out by a sharply
detailed image of the two of them having sex. For
a disorienting moment she felt as if she were
standing outside her own body, watching the two
of them in bed—naked, their bodies sweaty from
exertion, straining together. His muscled body bore
her down, crushing her into the tangled sheets.
Her arms and legs, pale against his olive-toned
skin, were wrapped around him. She smelled the
scents of sex and skin, felt the heat and weight of
him on top of her as he pushed slickly inside, heard

her own quick gasp as she lifted into his slow, controlled thrusts. She was about to climax, and so was he, his thrusts coming harder and faster—

She jerked herself away from the scenario, suddenly, horribly sure that if she let it carry on to the end she would humiliate herself by climaxing for real, right in front of him. She could barely keep herself in the present; the lure of even imagined pleasure was so strong that she wanted to go back, to lose herself in the dream, or hallucination, or whatever the hell it was.

Something was wrong. She wasn't in control of herself but instead was being tossed about by the weird eddies of power surging and retreating through the room. Neither could she get a handle on anything long enough to examine it; just when she thought she was grounded, she would get tossed into another reaction, another wild emotion bubbling to the surface.

He spoke again, seemingly oblivious to everything but his own thoughts. How could he not *feel* everything that was going on? Was she imagining everything? She clutched the arms of the chair, wondering if she was having some sort of mental breakdown.

"You're precognitive." He tilted his head as if he were studying an interesting specimen, a slight smile on his lips. "You're also a sensitive, and maybe there's a little bit of telekinesis thrown in. Interesting."

"Are you crazy?" she blurted, horrified, and still struggling to concentrate. *Interesting?* He was either on the verge of destroying her life or she was going crazy, and he thought it was *interesting*?

"I don't believe so. No, I'm fairly certain I'm sane." Amusement flickered in his eyes, warming them. "Go ahead, Lorna, make the leap. The only way I could know if you were a precog is…?" His voice trailed away on a questioning lilt, inviting her to finish the sentence.

She sat as if frozen, staring fixedly at him. Was he saying he really *could* read minds, or was he setting some trap she couldn't yet see?

A sudden, freezing cold swept through the room, so cold she ached down to the bone, and with it came that same overwhelming sense of dread she'd felt when she'd first entered the room and seen him. Lorna hugged herself and set her teeth to keep them from chattering. She wanted to run and couldn't; her muscles simply wouldn't obey the instinct to flee.

Was he the source of this, .this *turmoil* in the room? She couldn't put a better description to it than that, because she'd never felt quite this way before, as if reality had become layered with hallucinations.

"You can relax. There's no way I can prove it, so I can't charge you with cheating. But I knew what you are as soon as you said you thought I was 'doing it.' Doing what? You didn't say, but the statement was an intriguing one, because it meant you're sensitive to the currents in the room." He steepled his fingers and tapped them against his lips, regarding her over them with an unwavering gaze. "Normal people would never have felt a thing. A lot of times, one form of psi ability goes hand in hand with other forms, so it's obvious, now, how you win so consistently. You know what card will turn up, don't you? You know which slot machines will pay off. Maybe you can even manipulate the computer to give you three in a row."

The cold left the room as abruptly as it had entered. She had been tensed to resist it, and the sudden lessening of pressure made her feel as if she might fall out of the chair. Lorna clenched her jaw tight, afraid to say anything. She couldn't let herself be drawn into a discussion about paranormal abilities. For all she knew, he had this room wired for both video and audio and was recording everything. What if one of those weird hallucinations seized control of her again? She might say whatever he wanted her to say, admit to any wild charge. Heck— everything she was feeling might be the result of some weird special effects he'd installed.

"I know you aren't Raintree," he continued softly. "I know my own. So the big question is…are you Ansara, or are you just a stray?"

Shock rescued her once again. "A *stray?*" she echoed, jerking back into a world that felt real. There was still an underlying sense of disorientation, but at least that sexually disturbing image was gone, the cold was gone, the dread was gone.

She took a deep breath and fought down the hot rush of anger. He'd just compared her to an unwanted mongrel. Beneath the anger, though, was the corrosive edge of old, bitter despair. *Unwanted.* She'd always been that. For a while, a wondrously sweet moment, she had thought that would change, but then even that last hope had been taken from her, and she didn't have the heart, the will, to try again. Something inside her had given up, but the pain hadn't dulled.

He made a dismissive gesture. "Not that kind of stray. We use it to describe a person of ability who is unaffiliated."

"Unaffiliated with *what?* What are you talking about?" Her bewilderment on this point, at least, was real.

"Someone who is neither Raintree nor Ansara."

His explanations were going in circles, and so were her thoughts. Frustrated, frightened, she made a sharp motion with her hand and snapped, "Who in hell is Aunt Sarah?"

Tilting his head back, he burst out laughing, the sound quick and easy, as if he did it a lot. The pit of her stomach fluttered. Imagining sex with him had lowered defenses she usually kept raised high, and the distant acknowledgment of his attractiveness had become a full-fledged awareness. Against her will she noticed the muscular lines of his throat, the sculpted line of his jaw. He was… *Handsome* was, in an odd way, too feminine a word to describe him. He was *striking*, his features altogether too compelling to be merely handsome. Nor were his looks the first thing she'd noticed about him; by far her first impression had been one of power.

"Not 'Aunt Sarah,' " he said, still laughing. "Ansara. A-N-S-A-R-A."

"I've never heard of them," she said warily, wondering if this was some type of mob thing he was talking about. She didn't suffer from the delusion that organized crime was restricted to the old Italian families in New York and Chicago.

"Haven't you?" He said it pleasantly enough, but with her nerve-endings stripped raw the way they were, she felt the doubt—and the inherent threat—as clearly as if he'd shouted at her.

She had to get her reactions under control. The weird stuff happening in this room had taken her by surprise, shocked her into a vulnerability she normally didn't allow, but now that she'd had a moment without any new assault on her senses, she began to get her composure back. Mentally she reassembled her internal barriers; it was a struggle, because concentration was difficult, but grimly she persisted. She might not know what was going on, but she knew protecting herself was vitally important.

He was waiting for her to respond to his rhetorical question, but she ignored him and focused on her shields—

Shields?

Where had that word come from? She never thought of herself as having shields. She thought of herself as strong, her heart weathered and toughened by hard times; she thought of herself as unemotional.

She never thought of herself as having *shields*.

Until now.

She was the most unshielded sensitive he'd ever seen, Dante thought as he watched her struggle against the flow and surge of power. She reacted like a complete novice to both his thoughts and his affinity for fire. He had his gift under strict control now, but to test her, he'd sent tiny blasts of it into the room, making the candles dance. She'd latched on to the arms of the chair as if she needed to anchor herself, her alarmed gaze darting around as if searching for monsters.

When he'd picked up on her expectation of

being blackmailed for sex—which hadn't exactly been hard to guess—he'd allowed himself a brief, pleasant little fantasy, to which she'd responded as if he'd really had her naked in bed. Her mouth had gotten red and soft, her cheeks flushed, her eyes heavy-lidded, while beneath that cheap sweater her nipples had become so hard their shape had been visible even through her bra.

Damn. For a moment there, she'd been in real danger of the fantasy becoming fact.

She might be Ansara, but if she was, she was completely untutored. Either that or she was skilled enough to *appear* untutored. If she *was* Ansara, he would bet on the latter. Being Raintree had a lot of advantages and one big disadvantage: an implacable enemy. The hostility between the two clans had erupted into a huge pitched battle about two hundred years ago, and the Raintree had been victorious, the Ansara almost destroyed. The tattered remnants of the once-powerful clan were scattered around the world and had never recovered to the point that they could again make concerted war on the Raintree, but that didn't mean that the occasional lone Ansara didn't try to make trouble for them.

Like the Raintree, the Ansara had different gifts of varying degrees of strength. The ones Dante had infrequently crossed paths with had all been trained as well as any Raintree, which meant none of them were to be taken lightly. While they weren't the threat they had been before, he was always aware that any one of them would love a chance to get at him in any way.

It would be just like an Ansara to get a kick out of stealing from him. There were bigger casinos in Reno, but stealing from the Inferno would be a huge feather in her cap—*if* she was Ansara.

He had some empathic ability—nothing in the same ballpark as his younger sister, Mercy, but enough that he could read most people as soon as he touched them. The exceptions, mainly, were the Ansara, because they had been trained to shield themselves in a way normal humans never were. Sensitives *had* to shield or be overwhelmed by the forces around them…much as Lorna Clay seemed to have been overwhelmed.

Maybe she was just a good actress.

The candlelight was magic on her skin, in her hair. She was a pretty woman, with finely molded bone structure, if a tad brittle and hostile in her attitude, but what the hell—if he'd been caught cheating, he would probably be hostile, too.

He wanted to touch her, to see if he could read anything.

She would probably run screaming from the room if he laid a hand on her, though. She was so tightly wound that she might throw herself back-ward in the chair if he said "Boo!" He thought about doing it, just for the amusement value.

He would have, if not for the very serious matter of cheating.

He leaned forward to hammer home a point, and—

A loud but not unpleasant tone sounded, followed by another, then another. A burst of adrenaline shot through his system, and he was on his feet, grabbing her arm and hauling her out of the chair before the recorded announcement could begin.

"What is it?" she cried, her face going white, but she didn't try to pull away from him.

"Fire," he said briefly, all but dragging her to the door. Once the fire alarm sounded all the elevators stopped responding to calls—and they were on the nineteenth floor.

Chapter 4

Lorna stumbled and almost went down on one knee as he dragged her through the doorway. Her hip banged painfully into the door frame; then she regained her balance, lurched upward and hurtled through so fast that she immediately crashed into the wall on the other side. Her arm, held tight in his iron grip, was wrenched as he ruthlessly pulled her onward. She didn't say a word, didn't cry out, almost didn't even notice the pain, because the living nightmare she was in crowded out everything else.

Fire!

She saw him give her a searing, comprehensive look; then he released her arm and instead clamped his left arm around her waist, locking her to his side and holding her up as he ran toward the stairs. They were alone in the hallway, but as soon as he opened the door marked Exit, she could hear the thunder of footsteps below them as people stampeded down the stairs.

The air in the hallway had been clear, but as the door clanged shut behind them, she smelled it: the throat-burning stench of smoke. Her heartbeat stuttered. She was afraid of fire, always had been, and it wasn't just the caution of an intelligent person. If she had to pick the worst way on earth to die, it would be by fire. She had nightmares about being trapped behind a wall of flame, unable to get to someone—a child, maybe?—who was more important to her than her own life, or even to save herself. Just as the flames reached her and she felt her flesh begin to sear, she would wake, trembling and in tears from the horror.

She didn't like any open flame—candles, fireplaces, or even gas cooktops. Now Dante Raintree was carrying her down into the heart of the beast, when every instinct she had screamed for her to go up, up into fresh air, as far away from fire as she could get.

As they made the turn at the first landing, the mental chaos of panic began to strengthen and grab at her, and she fought it back. Logically she knew they had to go down, that jumping off the roof wasn't a viable option. Clenching her teeth together to keep them from chattering, she concentrated on keeping her balance, making sure her feet hit each step squarely, though the way he was holding her, she doubted she could stumble. She didn't want to impede him or, God forbid, cause both of them to fall.

They caught up with a knot of people also going down the stairs, but the passage was clogged, and people were shouting at others to move out of the way. The uproar was confusing; no one could make themselves understood, and some were coughing now as the smoke thickened.

"You can't go up!" Raintree thundered, his voice booming over the pushing, yelling human logjam, and only then did Lorna realize that the uproar was caused by people trying to push their way up the stairs while others were just as focused on going down.

"Who the hell are you?" someone bellowed from below.

"The owner of the Inferno, that's who the hell I am," Raintree snapped. "I built this casino, and I know where I'm going. Now turn your ass around and go all the way down to the ground floor, that's the only way out."

"The smoke's worse that way!"

"Then take off your shirt and tie it over your nose and mouth. Everyone do that," he ordered, booming out the words again so all could hear him. He suited action to words, releasing Lorna to strip out of his expensive suit jacket. She stood numbly beside him, watching as he swiftly removed a knife from his pocket, flicked it open, and sliced the gray silk lining from the jacket. Then he just as swiftly ripped the lining into two oblong panels. Handing one panel to her, he said, "Use this," as he closed the knife and slipped it back into his pocket.

She expected some of the group to push on upstairs, regardless of what he said, but no one did. Instead, several men, the ones who wore jackets, were following his example and ripping out the garments' linings. Others were taking off their shirts, tearing them up and offering pieces to women who were reluctant to remove their blouses. Lorna hastily tied the silk over her nose and mouth, pulling it tight so it hugged her face like a surgical mask. Beside her, Raintree was doing the same.

"Go!" he ordered, and like obedient sheep, they did. The tangle of people began to unravel, then ribbon downward. Lorna found her own feet moving as if they weren't attached to her, taking her down, down, closer to whatever living, crackling hell awaited them. Every cell in her body was screaming in protest, her breath was coming in strangled gasps, but still she kept going down the stairs as if she had no will of her own.

His hand put pressure on her waist, moving her to one side. "Let us pass," he said. "I'll show you the way out." The people in front of them all moved to one side, and though Lorna heard several angry mutters, they were drowned out by others telling the mutterers to shut up, that it was his place and he'd know how to get out of the building.

More and more people were crowding into the stairwell ahead of them as the floors emptied, but they pressed to the side as Raintree moved Lorna and himself past them. The acrid smoke stung her eyes, making them water, and she could feel the temperature rising as they went down. How many floors had they descended? At the next landing she peered at the door and the number painted on it, but the tears in her eyes blurred the figures. Sixteen, maybe. Or fifteen. Was that all? Hadn't they gone farther than that? She tried to remember how many landings they had passed, but she had been too numb with terror to pay attention.

She was going to die in this building. She could feel the icy breath of Death as it waited for her, just on the other side of the flames that she couldn't see but could nevertheless feel, as if they were a great force pulling at her. *This* was why she had always been so afraid of fire; she had somehow

known she was destined to burn. Soon she would be gone, her life force seared or choked away—
—and no one would miss her.

Dante kept everyone moving downward, the mind compulsion he was using forcing them into an orderly evacuation. He had never tried this particular power, never even known he possessed it, and if they hadn't been so close to the summer solstice, he doubted he could have done it. Hell, he hadn't been sure he could make it work at all, much less on such a large group, but with fire threatening to destroy the casino he'd worked so hard to build, he'd poured all his will into the thought, into his words, and they had obeyed.

He could feel the flames singing their siren song, calling to him. Maybe they were even feeding his power, because the close proximity of fire was making his heart rate soar as adrenaline poured through him. Even though smoke was stinging his eyes and filtering through the silk tied over his nose and mouth, he felt so alive that his skin could barely contain him. He wanted to laugh, wanted to throw his arms wide and invite the fire to come to him, to do battle with him, so he could exert his will over it as he did over these people.

If it hadn't been for the level of concentration he needed to keep the mind compulsion in place, he would already have been mentally joined in battle. Everything in him yearned for the struggle. He *would* vanquish the flames, but first he had to get these people to safety.

Lorna kept pace beside him, but a quick glance at her face—what he could see of it above the gray silk—told him that only his will was keeping her going down the stairs. She was paper white, and her eyes were almost blank with terror. He pulled her closer to his side, wanting her within reach when they got to the ground floor, because otherwise her panic might be strong enough that she could break free of the compulsion and bolt. And he wasn't finished with her yet. In fact, with this damn fire, he thought he might have a good deal more to discuss with her than cheating at blackjack.

If she was Ansara, if she had somehow been involved in starting the fire, she would die. It was that simple.

He'd touched her, but he couldn't tell if she was Ansara or not. His empathic power was on the wimpy side anyway, and right now he couldn't really concentrate on reading her. Not picking up anything meant she was either a stray or she was Ansara, and strong enough to shield her real self from him. Either way, the matter would have to wait.

The smoke was getting thicker, but not drastically so. There was some talking, though for the most part people were saving their breath for getting down the stairs. There was, however, a steady barrage of coughing.

The fire, he sensed, was concentrated so far in the casino, but it was rapidly spreading toward the hotel portion of the building. Unlike most hotel/casinos, which were built in such a way that the guests were forced to walk through the casino on their way to anywhere else, thereby increasing the probability that they would stop and play, Dante had built Inferno with the guest rooms off to one side. There was a common area where the two joined and overlapped, but he also provided a bit of distance for the guest who wanted it. He'd been taking a chance, but the design had worked out. By concentrating on providing a level of elegance unmatched at any other hotel/casino in Reno, he'd made Inferno different and therefore desirable.

That offset design would save a lot of lives tonight. The guests who had been in the casino, though…he didn't know about them. Nor could he let himself dwell on them, or he might lose control of the people in the stairwell. He couldn't help the people in the casino, at least not now, so he let himself think only about his immediate charges. If these people panicked, if they started pushing and running, not only would some people fall and be trampled, but the crowd might well crush the exit bar and prevent the door from being opened. That had happened before, and would happen again—but not in his place, not if he could help it.

They reached another landing, and he peered through the smoke at the number on the door. Three. Just two more floors, thank God. The smoke was getting so thick that his lungs were burning. "We're almost there," he said, to keep the people behind him focused, and he heard people begin repeating the words to those stacked on the stairs above them.

He wrapped his arm around Lorna's waist and clamped her to his side, lifting her off her feet as he descended the remaining floors two steps at a time. The door opened not to the outside but into a corridor lined with offices. He held the door open with his body, and as people stumbled into the corridor, he said, "Turn right. Go through the double doors at the end of the hall, turn right again, and the door just past the soda machines will open onto the ground level of the parking deck. Go, go, go!"

They went, propelled by his will—stumbling and coughing, but moving nevertheless. The air here was thick and hot, his vision down to only a few feet, and the people who scrambled past him looked like ghosts and disappeared in seconds. Only their coughing and the sound of their footsteps marked their progress.

He felt Lorna move, trying to break his grip, trying to obey not only his mental command but the commands of her own panic-stricken brain. He tightened his hold on her. Maybe he could fine-tune the compulsion enough to exclude her right now…. No, it wasn't worth the risk. While he had them all under his control, he kept them there and kept them moving. All he had to do was hold Lorna to keep her from escaping.

He could feel the fire at his back. Not literally, but closer now, much closer. Everything in him yearned to turn and engage with the force of nature that was his to call and control, his to own. Not yet. *Not yet…*

Then no more smoke-shrouded figures were emerging from the stairwell, and with Lorna firmly in his grip he turned to the left—away from the parking deck and safety, and toward the roaring red demon.

"*Noooo.*"

The sound was little more than a moan, and she bucked like a wild thing in the circle of his arm. Hastily he gave one last mental shove at the stream of people headed toward the parking deck, then transferred the compulsion to a different command, this one directed solely at Lorna: "Stay with me."

Immediately she stopped struggling, though he could hear the strangled, panicked sounds she was making as he strode through the smoke to another door, one that opened into the lobby.

He threw the door open and stepped into hell, dragging her with him.

The sprinkler system was making a valiant effort, spraying water down on the lobby, but the heat was a monster furnace that evaporated the spray before it reached the floor. It blasted them like a shock wave, a physical blow, but he muttered a curse and pushed back. Because they were produced by the fire, were parts of the fire, he owned the heat and smoke as surely as he owned the flames. Now that he could concentrate, he deflected them, creating a protective bubble, a force field, around Lorna and himself that sent the smoke swirling and held the heat at bay, protecting them.

The casino was completely engaged. The flames were greedy tongues of red, great sheets of orange and black, transparent forks of gold, that danced and roared in their eagerness to consume everything within reach. Several of the elegant white columns had already ignited like huge torches, and the vast expanse of carpet was a sea of small fires, lit by the falling debris.

The columns were acting as candles, wicking the flames upward to the ceiling. He started there, pulling power from deep inside and using it to bend the fire to his will. Slowly, slowly, the flames licking up the columns began to die down, vanquished by a superior force.

Doing that much, while maintaining the bubble of protection around them, took every ounce of power he had. Something wasn't right. He realized that even as he concentrated on the columns, feeling the strain deep inside. His head began to hurt; killing the flames shouldn't take this much effort. They were slow in responding to his command, but he didn't let up even as he wondered if the energy he'd used on the group mind compulsion had somehow drained him. He didn't feel as if it had, but something was definitely wrong.

When only tendrils of smoke were coming from the columns, he switched his attention to the walls, pushing back, pushing back....

Out of the corner of his eye, he saw the columns burst into flame again.

With a roar of fury and disbelief, he blasted his will at the flames, and they subsided once again.

What the hell?

Windows exploded, sending shards of glass flying in all directions. Brutal streams of water poured through from the front, courtesy of the Reno Fire

Department, but the flames seemed to give a
hoarse laugh before roaring back brighter and
hotter than before. One of the two huge, glittering crystal chandeliers pulled loose from the
fire-weakened ceiling and crashed to the floor,
throwing up a glittering spray of lethal glass splinters. They were far enough away that few of the
splinters reached them, but one of the lovely
crystal hornets stung his cheek, sending a rivulet
of blood running down his face. Maybe they should
have ducked, he thought with distant humor.

He could feel Lorna pressed against him, shaking convulsively and making little keening sounds
of terror, but she was helpless to break the mind
compulsion he'd put on her. Had any of the glass
hit her? No time to check. With a great whoosh,
a huge tongue of fire rolled across the ceiling
overhead, consuming everything in its path as well
as what felt like most of the available oxygen; then
it began eating its way down the wall behind them,
sealing off any escape.

Mentally, he pushed at the flames, willing them
to retreat, calling on all his reserves of strength and
power. He was the Dranir of the Raintree; the fire
would obey him.

Except it didn't.

Instead it began crawling across the carpet,
small fires combining into larger ones, and those

joining with others until the floor was ablaze, getting closer, closer....

He couldn't control it. He had never before met a flame he couldn't bend to his will, but this was something beyond his power. Using the mind compulsion that way must have weakened him somehow; it wasn't something he'd done before, so he didn't know what the ramifications were. Well, yeah, he did; unless a miracle happened, the ramifications in this case were two deaths: his and Lorna's.

He refused to accept that. He'd never given up, never let a fire beat him; he wouldn't start with this one.

The bubble of protection wavered, letting smoke filter in. Lorna began coughing convulsively, struggling against his grip even though she wouldn't be able to run unless he released her from the compulsion. There was nowhere to run *to*, anyway.

Grimly, he faced the flames. He needed more power. He had thrown everything he had left at the fire, and it wasn't enough. If Gideon or Mercy were here, they could link with him, combine strengths, but that sort of partnership required close proximity, so he had only himself to rely on. There was no other source of power for him to tap—

—except for Lorna.

He didn't ask; he didn't take the time to warn

her what he was going to do; he simply wrapped both arms around her from behind and blasted his way past her mental shields, ruthlessly taking what he needed. Relief poured through him at what he found. Yes, she had power, more than he'd expected. He didn't stop to analyze what kind of power she had, because it didn't matter; on this level, power was power, like electricity. Different machines could take the same power and do wildly different things, like vacuuming the floor or playing music. It was the same principle. She had power; he took it, and used it to bolster his own gift.

She gave a thin scream and bucked in his arms, then went rigid.

Furiously he attacked the flames, sending out a 360-degree mental blast that literally blew out the wall of fire behind him and took the physical wall with it, as well. The rush of renewed oxygen made the fire in front of him flare, so he gathered himself and did it again, pouring even more energy into the battle, feeling his own reserves well up, renewed, as he took every ounce of power and strength from Lorna and blended it with his own.

His entire body was tingling, his muscles burning with the effort it took to contain and focus. The invisible bubble of protection around them began to shimmer and took on a faint glow. Sweating, swearing, ignoring the pain in his head, he blasted the energy of his will at the fire again and again, beating it back even while he tried to calculate how long he'd been standing there, how much time he needed to give the people in the hotel to escape. There were multiple stairwells, and he was certain not all evacuations had been as orderly as the one he'd controlled. Was everyone out by now? What about disabled people? They would have to be helped down the flights of stairs. If he stopped, the fire would surge forward, engulfing the hotel—so he couldn't stop. Until the fire was controlled, he couldn't stop.

He couldn't put it out, not completely. For whatever reason, whether he was depleted or distracted or the fire itself was somehow different, he couldn't put it out. He accepted that now. All he could do was hold the flames at bay until the fire department had them under control.

That was what he concentrated on, controlling the fire instead of extinguishing it. That conserved his energy, and he needed every bit he had, because the fierceness of the fire never stopped pushing back, never stopped struggling for freedom. Time meant nothing, because no matter how long it took, no matter how his head hurt, he had to endure.

Somewhere along the way he lost the line of division between himself and the fire. It was an enemy, but it was beautiful in its destruction; it danced for him as always, magic in its movement and colors. He felt its beauty like molten lava running through his veins, felt his body respond with mindless lust until his erection strained painfully against his zipper. Lorna had to feel it, but there wasn't a damned thing he could do to make it go away. The best he could do, under the circumstances, was not grind it against her.

Finally, hoarse shouts intruded through the diminished roar of the beast. Turning his head slightly, Dante saw teams of firefighters advancing with their hoses. Quickly he let the bubble of protection dissolve, leaving him and Lorna exposed to the smoke and heat.

With his first breath, the hot smoke seared all the way down to his lungs. He choked, coughed, tried to draw another breath. Lorna sagged to her knees, and he dropped down beside her as the first firefighters reached them.

Chapter 5

Lorna sat on the bumper of a fire-medic truck and clutched a scratchy blanket around her. The night was warm, but she was soaking wet, and she couldn't seem to stop shivering. She'd heard the fire medic say she wasn't in shock; though her blood pressure was a little high, which was understandable, her pulse rate was near normal. She was just chilled from being wet.

And, yet, everything around her seemed…muted, as if there were a glass wall between her and the rest of the world. Her mind felt numb, barely able to function. When the medic had asked her name, for the life of her, she hadn't been able to remember, much less articulate it. But she *had* remembered that she never brought a purse to a casino because of thieves and that she kept her money in one pocket and her driver's license in another, so she'd pulled out her license and showed it to him. It was a Missouri license, because she hadn't gotten a license here. To get a Nevada license, you had to be a resident and gainfully employed. It was the "gainfully employed" part that tripped her up.

"Are you Lorna Clay?" the medic had asked, and she'd nodded.

"Does your throat hurt?" he'd asked then, and that seemed as reasonable an explanation for her continued silence as any other, so she'd nodded again. He'd looked at her throat, seemed briefly puzzled, then given her oxygen to breathe. She should be checked out at the hospital, he'd said.

Yeah, right. She had no intention of going to a hospital. The only place she wanted to go was *away*.

And, yet, she remained right where she was while Raintree was checked out. There was blood on his face, but the cut turned out to be small. She heard him tell the medics he was fine, that, no, he didn't think he was burned anywhere, that they'd been very lucky.

Lucky, her ass. The thought was as clear as a bell, rising from the sluggish morass that was her brain. He'd held her there in the middle of that roaring hell for what felt like an eternity. They should be crispy critters. They should, at least, be gasping for breath through damaged airways, instead of being *fine*. She knew what fire did. She'd seen it, she'd smelled it, and it was ugly. It destroyed everything in its path. What it didn't do was dance all around and leave you unscathed.

Yet, here she was—unscathed. Relatively, anyway. She felt as if she'd been run over by a truck, but at least she wasn't burned.

She should have been burned. She should have been *dead*. Whenever she contemplated the fact that she not only wasn't dead, she wasn't even injured, her head ached so much she could barely stand to breathe, and the glass wall between her and reality got a little bit thicker. So she didn't think about being alive, or dead or anything else. She just sat there while the nightmarish scene revolved around her, lights flashing, crowds of people milling about, the firefighters still busy with their hoses putting out the remaining flames and making certain they didn't flare again. The fire engines rumbled so loudly that the noise wore on her, made her want to cover her ears, but she didn't do that, either. She just waited.

For what, she wasn't certain. She should leave. She thought a hundred times about just walking away into the night, but putting thought into action proved impossible. No matter how much she wanted to leave, she was bound by an inertia she couldn't seem to fight. All she could do was…sit.

Then Raintree stood, and, abruptly, she found herself standing, too, levered upward by some impulse she didn't understand. She just knew that if he was standing, she would stand. She was too mentally exhausted to come up with any reason that made more sense.

His face was so black with soot that only the whites of his eyes showed, so she figured she must look pretty much the same. Great. That meant she didn't have much chance of being able to slip away unnoticed. He took a cloth someone offered him and swiped it over his sooty face, which didn't do much good. Soot was oily; anything other than soap just sort of moved it around.

Determination in his stride, he moved toward a small clump of policemen, three uniforms and two plainclothes. Vague alarm rose in Lorna. Was he going to turn her in? Without any proof? She desperately wanted to hang back, but, instead, she found herself docilely following him.

Why was she doing this? Why wasn't she leaving? She struggled with the questions, trying to get her brain to function. He hadn't even glanced in her direction; he wouldn't have any idea where she'd gone if she dropped back now and sort of blended in with the crowd—as much as she could blend in anywhere, covered with soot the way she was. But others also showed the effects of the smoke; some of the casino employees, for instance, and the players. She probably could have slipped away, if she felt capable of making the effort.

Why was her brain so sluggish? On a very superficial level, her thought processes seemed to be normal, but below that was nothing but sludge. There was something important she should remember, something that briefly surfaced just long enough to cause a niggle of worry, then disappeared like a wisp of smoke. She frowned, trying to pull the memory out, but the effort only intensified the pain in her head, and she stopped.

Raintree approached the two plainclothes cops and introduced himself. Lorna tried to make herself inconspicuous, which might be a losing cause considering how she looked, plus the fact that she was standing only a few feet away. They all eyed her with the mixture of suspicion and curiosity cops just seemed to have. Her heart started pounding. What would she do if Raintree accused her of cheating? Run? Look at him as if he were an idiot? Maybe *she* was the idiot, standing there like a sacrificial lamb.

The image galvanized her as nothing else had. She would *not* be a willing victim. She tried to take a step away, but for some reason the action seemed beyond her. All she wanted to do was stay with him.

Stay with me.

The words resonated through her tired brain, making her head ache. Wearily, she rubbed her forehead, wondering where she'd heard the words and why they mattered.

"Where were you when the fire started, Mr. Raintree?" one of the detectives asked. He and the other detective had introduced themselves, but their names had flown out of Lorna's head as soon as she'd heard them.

"In my office, talking to Ms. Clay." He indicated Lorna without really looking in her direction, as if he knew just where she was standing.

They looked at her more sharply now; then the detective who had been talking to Raintree said, "My partner will take her statement while I'm taking yours, so we can save time."

Sure, Lorna thought sarcastically. She had some beachfront property here in Reno she wanted to sell, too. The detectives wanted to separate her from Raintree so she couldn't hear what he said and they couldn't coordinate their statements. If a business was going down the tubes, sometimes the owner tried to minimize losses by burning it down and collecting on the insurance policy.

The other detective stepped to her side. Raintree glanced at her over his shoulder. "Don't go far. I don't want to lose you in this crowd."

What was he up to? she wondered. He'd made it sound as if they were in a relationship or something. But when the detective said, "Let's walk over here," Lorna obediently walked beside him for about twenty feet, then abruptly stopped as if she couldn't take one step more.

"Here," she said, surprised at how raspy and weak her voice was. She had coughed some, sure, but her voice sounded as if she'd been hacking for days. She was barely audible over all the noise from the fire engines.

"Sure." The detective looked around, casually positioning himself so that Lorna had to stand with her back to Raintree. "I'm Detective Harvey. Your name is…"

"Lorna Clay." At least she remembered her name this time, though for a horrible split second she hadn't been certain. She rubbed her forehead again, wishing this confounded headache would go away.

"Do you live here?"

"For the moment. I haven't decided if I'll stay." She knew she wouldn't. She never stayed in one place for very long. A few months, six at the most, and she moved on. He asked for her address, and she rattled it off. If he ran a check on her, he would find the most grievous thing against her was a speeding ticket she'd received three years ago. She'd paid the fine without argument; no problem there. So long as Raintree didn't bring a charge of cheating against her, she was fine. She wanted to look over her shoulder at him but knew better than to appear nervous or, even worse, as if she were checking with him on what answers to give.

"Where were you when the fire started?"

He'd just heard Raintree, when asked the identical question, say he'd been with her, but that was how cops operated. "I don't know when the fire started," she said, a tad irritably. "I was in Mr. Raintree's office when the alarm sounded."

"What time was that?"

"I don't have a watch on. I don't know. I wouldn't have thought to check the time, anyway. Fire scares the bejesus out of me."

One corner of his mouth twitched a little, but he disciplined it. He had a nice, lived-in sort of face, a little droopy at the jowls, wrinkly around the eyes. "That's okay. We can get the time from the security system. How long had you been with Mr. Raintree when the alarm sounded?"

Now, there was a question. Lorna thought back to the episodes of panic she'd experienced in that office, to the confusing hallucinations, or whatever the disconcerting sexual fantasy was. *Nothing* in that room had been normal, and though she usually had a good grasp of time, she found herself unable to even estimate. "I don't know. It was sunset when I went in. That's all I can tell you."

He made a note of her answer. God only knew what he thought they'd been doing, she thought wearily, but she couldn't bring herself to care.

"What did you do when the fire alarm sounded?"

"We ran for the stairs."

"What floor were you on?"

Now, that, she knew, because she'd watched the numbers on the ride up in the elevator. "The nineteenth."

He made a note of that, too. Lorna thought to herself that if she intended to burn a building down she wouldn't go to the nineteenth floor to wait for the alarm. Raintree hadn't had anything to do with whatever had caused the fire, but the cops had to check out everything or they wouldn't be doing their jobs. Though...did detectives normally go to the scene of a fire? A fire inspector or fire marshal, whichever Reno had, would have to determine that a fire was caused by arson before they treated it as a crime.

"What happened then?"

"There were a lot of people in the stairwell," she said slowly, trying to get the memory to form. "I remember...a lot of people. We could go only a couple of floors before everyone got jammed up, because some of the people from the lower floors were trying to go up." The smoke had been heavy, too, because visibility had been terrible, people passing by like ghosts… No. That had been later. There hadn't been a lot of smoke in the stairs right then. Later— She wasn't certain about later. The sequence of events was all jumbled up, and she couldn't seem to sort everything out.

"Go on," Detective Harvey prompted when she was silent for several moments.

"Mr. Raintree told them—the people coming up the stairs—they'd have to go back, there was no way out if they kept going up."

"Did they argue?"

"No, they all turned around. No one panicked." Except her. She'd barely been able to breathe, and it hadn't been because of the smoke. The memory was becoming clearer, and she was amazed at how orderly the evacuation had been. No one had pushed; no one had been running. People had been hurrying, of course, but not being so reckless that they risked a nasty fall. In retrospect, their behavior had been damned unnatural. How could everyone have been so calm? Didn't they know what fire *did*?

But she hadn't run, either, she realized. She hadn't pushed. She had gone at a steady pace, held to Raintree's side by his arm.

Wait. Had he been holding her then? She didn't think he had been. He'd touched her waist, sort of guiding her along, but she'd been free to run. So…why hadn't she?

She had trooped along like everyone else, in an orderly line. Inside she'd been screaming, but outwardly she'd been controlled.

Controlled… Not self-controlled, but controlled like a puppet, as if she hadn't had a will of her own. Her mind had been screaming at her to run, but her body simply hadn't obeyed.

"Ms. Clay?"

Lorna felt her breath start coming faster as she relived those moments. Fire! Coming closer and closer, she didn't want to go, she wanted to run, but she couldn't. She was caught in one of those nightmares when you try to run but can't, when you try to scream but can't make a sound—

"Ms. Clay?"

"I— What?" Dazed, she stared up at him. From the mixture of impatience and concern on his face, she thought he must have called her name several times.

"What did you do when you got out?"

Shuddering, she gathered herself. "We didn't. I mean, we got to the ground floor and Mr. Raintree sent the others to the right, toward the parking deck. Then he…we…" Her voice faltered. She had been fighting him, trying to follow the others;

she remembered that. Then he'd said, *"Stay with me,"* and she had, with no will to do otherwise, even though she'd been half mad with terror.

Stay with me.

When he'd sat, she'd sat. When he'd stood, she'd stood. When he'd moved, that was when she had moved. Until then, she had been incapable of taking a single step away from him.

Just moments ago he'd said, "Don't go far," and she'd been able to leave his side then—but she hadn't gone far before she'd stopped as if she'd hit a brick wall.

A horrible suspicion began to grow. He was controlling her somehow, maybe with some kind of posthypnotic suggestion, though when and how he'd hypnotized her, she had no idea. All sorts of weird things had been happening in his office. Maybe those damn candles had actually given off some kind of gas that had drugged her.

"Go on," said Detective Harvey, breaking into her thoughts.

"We went to the left," she said, beginning to shake. She wrapped her arms around herself, hugging the blanket close in an effort to control her wayward muscles, but in seconds, she was trembling from head to foot. "Into the lobby. The fire—" The fire had leaped at them like a maddened beast, roaring with delight. The heat had been searing for the tiniest fraction of a second. She'd been choking on the smoke. Then…no smoke, no heat. Both had just gone away. She and Raintree should have been overcome in seconds, but they hadn't been. She'd been able to breathe. She hadn't felt the heat, even though she'd watched the tongues of fire hungrily lapping across the carpet toward her. "The fire sort of *w-whooshed* across the ceiling and got behind us, and we were trapped."

"Would you like to sit down?" he asked, interrupting his line of questioning, but considering how violently she was shaking, he probably thought sitting her down before she fell down was a good idea.

She might have thought so, too, if sitting down hadn't meant sitting on asphalt littered with the debris of a fire and running with streams of sooty water. He probably meant sit down somewhere else, which she would have liked, if she'd felt capable of moving a single step beyond where she was right now. She shook her head. "I'm okay, just wet and cold and shaken up some." If there was an award given out for massive understatement, she'd just won it.

He eyed her for a moment, then evidently decided she knew whether or not she needed to sit down. He'd tried, anyway, which relieved him of any obligation. "What did you do?"

Better not to tell him she'd felt surrounded by

some sort of force field; this wasn't *Star Wars*, so he might not understand. Better not to tell him she'd felt a cool breeze in her hair. She must have been drugged; there was no other explanation.

"There wasn't anything we *could* do. We were trapped. I remember Mr. Raintree swearing a blue streak. I remember choking and being on the floor. Then the firefighters got to us and brought us out." In the interest of believability, she had heavily condensed the night's events as she remembered them, but, surely, they couldn't have been in the lobby for very long, no more than thirty seconds. An imaginary force field couldn't have held off real heat and smoke. The firefighters must have been close to them all along, but she'd been too panic-stricken to notice.

There was something else, probably that worrisome niggle of memory, that she couldn't quite grasp. Something else had happened. She knew it; she just couldn't think what it was. Maybe after she showered and washed her hair—several times—and got twenty or thirty hours of sleep, she might remember.

Detective Harvey glanced over her shoulder then flipped his little notebook shut. "You're lucky to be alive. Have you been checked for smoke inhalation?"

"Yes, I'm okay." The medic had been puzzled by her good condition, but she didn't tell the detective that.

"I imagine Mr. Raintree will be tied up here for quite a while, but you're free to go. Do you have a number where you can be reached if we have any further questions for you?"

She started to ask, *Like what?* but instead said, "Sure," and gave him her cell-phone number.

"That local?"

"It's my cell." Now that cell numbers could be transferred, she no longer bothered with a landline so long as she had cell-phone service wherever she temporarily settled.

"Got a local number?"

"No, that's it. Sorry. I didn't see any point in getting a landline unless I decided to stay."

"No problem. Thanks for your cooperation." He nodded a brief acknowledgment at her.

Because it seemed the thing to do, Lorna managed a faint smile for him as he strolled back to the other detective, but it quickly faded. She was exhausted and filthy. Her head hurt. Now that Detective Harvey had finished interviewing her, she was going home.

She tried. She made several attempts to walk away, but for some reason she couldn't make her feet move. Frustration grew in her. She had walked over here a few minutes ago, so there was no reason why she shouldn't be able to walk now. Just to see if she could move at all, without turning around, she stepped back, moving closer to Raintree. No problem. All her parts worked just as they should.

Experimentally, she took a step forward, and heaved a sigh of relief when her feet and legs actually obeyed. She was beyond exhausted if the simple act of walking had become so complicated. Sighing, she started to take another step.

And couldn't.

She couldn't go any farther. It was as if she'd reached the end of an invisible leash.

She went cold with disbelief. This was infuriating. He must have hypnotized her, but how? When? She couldn't remember him saying, *"You are getting sleepy,"* and she was pretty certain hypnosis didn't work that way, anyway. It was supposed to be a deep relaxation, not a do-things-against-your-will type of thing, regardless of how stage shows and movies portrayed it.

She wished she'd worn a watch, so she could have noticed any time discrepancy from when she'd gone into Raintree's office and when the fire alarm had sounded. She had to find out what time that had been, because she knew roughly what time sunset was. She'd been in his office for maybe half an hour…she thought. She couldn't be certain. Those disconcerting fantasies could have taken more time than she estimated.

Regardless of how he'd done it, he was controlling her movements. She knew it. When he said, "Stay with me," she'd stayed, even when faced with an inferno. When he said, "Don't go far," she had been able to go only so far and not a step farther.

She turned her head to look at him over her shoulder and found him standing more or less alone, evidently having finished answering whatever questions the other detective had asked. He was watching her, his expression grim. His lips moved. With all the background noise she couldn't hear what he was saying, but she read his lips plainly enough.

He said, "Come here."

Chapter 6

She went. She couldn't stop herself. Her scalp prickled, and chills ran over her, but she went, her feet moving automatically. Her eyes were wide with alarm. How was he doing this? Not that the "how" mattered; what mattered was *that* he was doing it. Being unable to control herself, to have *him* in control, could lead to some nasty situations.

She couldn't even ask for help, because no one would believe her. At best, people would think she was on drugs or was mentally unstable. All sympathy would be with him, because he'd just lost his casino, his livelihood; the last thing he needed was a nutcase accusing him of somehow controlling her movements. She could just see herself yelling, "Help! I'm walking, and I can't stop! He's making me do it!"

Yeah, right. That would work—*not*.

He gave her a grim, self-satisfied little smile as she neared, and that pissed her off. Being angry felt good; she didn't like being helpless in any way. Too street-savvy to telegraph her intentions, she kept her eyes wide, her expression alarmed, though how much of her face he could see through all the soot and grime was anyone's guess. She kept her right arm close to her side, her elbow bent a little, and tensed the muscles in her back and shoulder. When she was close, so close she could almost kiss him, she launched an uppercut toward his chin.

He never saw it coming, and her fist connected from below with a force that made his teeth snap together. Pain shot through her knuckles, but the satisfaction of punching him made it more than worthwhile. He staggered back half a step, then regained his balance with athletic grace, snaking out his hand to shackle her wrist with long fingers before she could hit him again. He used the grip to pull her against him.

"I deserved one punch," he said, holding her close as he bent his head to speak just loud enough for her to hear. "I won't take a second one."

"Let me go," she snapped. "And I don't mean just with your hand!"

"You've figured it out, then," he said coolly.

"I was a little slow on the uptake, but being shoved into the middle of a freaking, big-ass fire was distracting." She laid on the sarcasm as thickly as possible. "I don't know how you're doing it, or why—"

"The 'why,' at least, should be obvious."

"Then I must be oxygen-deprived from inhaling smoke—gee, I wonder whose fault that is—because it isn't obvious to me!"

"The little matter of your cheating me. Or did you think I'd forget about that in the excitement of watching my casino burn to the ground?"

"I haven't been— Wait a minute. Wait just a damn minute. You couldn't have hypnotized me while we were going down nineteen stories' worth of stairs, and if you did it while we were in your office, then that was before the fire even started. 'Splain that, Lucy!"

He grinned, his teeth flashing whitely in his soot-blackened face. "Am I supposed to say 'Oh, Ricky!'?"

"I don't care what you say. Just undo the voodoo, or the spell, or the hypnotism, or whatever it is you did. You can't hold me here like this."

"That's a ridiculous statement, when I obviously *am* holding you here like this."

Lorna thought steam might be coming out of

her ears. She'd been angry many times in her life—
she'd even been enraged a couple of times—but
this was the most *infuriated* she'd ever felt. Until
tonight, she would have said that the three terms
meant the same thing, but now she knew that
being infuriated carried a rich measure of frustration with it. She was helpless, and she hated
being helpless. Her entire life was built around the
premise of not being helpless, not being a victim
ever again.

"Let. Me. Go." Her teeth were clenched, her
tone almost guttural. She was holding on to her
self-control by a gossamer thread, but only because
she knew screaming would get her exactly nowhere
with him and would make *her* look like an idiot.

"Not yet. We still have a few issues to discuss."
Completely indifferent to her temper, he lifted his
head to look around at the scene of destruction.
The stench of smoke permeated everything, and
the flashing red and blue lights of many different
emergency vehicles created a strobe effect that
felt like a spike being pounded into her forehead.
Hot spots still flared to crimson life in the smoldering ruins, until the vigilant firefighters targeted
them with their hoses. A milling crowd pressed
against the tape the police had strung up to cordon
off the area.

She saw the same details he saw, and the flashing lights reminded her of a ball of flame…no, not of flame…something else. She gasped as her head gave a violent throb.

"Then discuss them, already," she snapped, putting her hand to her head in an instinctive gesture to contain the pain.

"Not here." He glanced down at her again. "Are you okay?"

"I have a splitting headache. I could go home and lie down, if you weren't being such a jerk."

He gave her a considering look. "But I *am* being a jerk, so sue me. Now be quiet and stay here like a good girl. I'll be busy for a while. When I'm finished, we'll go to my house and have that talk."

Lorna fell silent, and when he walked off she remained rooted to the spot. Damn him, she thought as furious tears welled in her eyes and streaked down her filthy cheeks. She raised her hands and wiped the tears away. At least he'd left her with the use of her hands. She couldn't walk and she couldn't talk, but she could dry her face, and if God was really kind to her, she could punch Raintree again the next time he got within punching distance.

Then she went cold, goose bumps rising on her entire body. The brief heat of anger died away, destroyed by a sudden, mind-numbing fear.

What was he?

* * *

A man and a woman who had been standing behind the police cordon, watching the massive fire, finally turned and began trudging toward their car. "Crap," the woman said glumly. Her name was Elyn Campbell, and she was the most powerful firemaster in the Ansara clan, except for the Dranir. Everything they knew about Dante Raintree, and everything she knew about fire—aided by some very powerful spells—had been added together to form a plan that should have resulted in the Raintree Dranir's death and instead had accomplished nothing of their mission.

"Yeah." Ruben McWilliams shook his head. All their careful planning, their calculations, up in smoke—literally. "Why didn't it work?"

"I don't know. It *should* have worked. He isn't that strong. No one is, not even a Dranir. It was overkill."

"Then evidently he's the strongest Dranir anyone's ever seen—either that or the luckiest."

"Or he quit sooner than we anticipated. Maybe he chickened out and ran for cover instead of trying to control it."

Ruben heaved a sigh. "Maybe. I didn't see when they brought him out, so maybe he'd been standing somewhere out of sight for a while before I finally spotted him. All that damn equipment was in the way."

She looked up at the starry sky. "So we have two possible scenarios. The first is that he chickened out and ran. The second, and unfortunately the most likely, is that he's stronger than we expected. Cael won't be happy."

Ruben sighed again and faced the inevitable. "I guess we've put it off long enough. We have to call in." He pulled his cell phone from his pocket, but the woman put her hand on his sleeve.

"Don't use your cell phone, it isn't encrypted. Wait until we get back to the hotel, and use a land line."

"Good idea." Anything that delayed placing this call to Cael Ansara was a good idea. Cael was his cousin on his mother's side, but kinship wouldn't cut any ice with the bastard—and he meant "bastard" both figuratively and literally. Maybe this secret alignment with Cael against the current Dranir, Judah, wasn't the smartest thing he'd ever done. Even though he'd agreed with Cael that the Ansara were now strong enough, after two hundred years of rebuilding, to take on the Raintree and destroy them, maybe he'd been wrong. Maybe Cael was wrong.

He knew Cael would automatically go for the first scenario, that Dante Raintree had chickened out and run instead of trying to contain the fire, and completely dismiss the possibility that Raintree was stronger than any of them had imagined.

But what if Raintree really *was* that powerful? The attempted coup Cael had planned would be a disaster, and the Ansara would be lucky to survive as a clan. It had taken two centuries to rebuild to their present strength after their last pitched battle with the Raintree.

Cael wouldn't be able to conceive of being wrong. If the plan failed—which it had—Cael would see only two possibilities: either Ruben and Elyn hadn't executed the plan correctly, or Raintree had revealed a cowardly streak. Ruben *knew* they hadn't made any mistakes. Everything had gone like clockwork—except for the outcome. Raintree was supposed to be consumed by a fire he couldn't control, a delicious irony, because firemasters all had a strange love/hate relationship with the force that danced to their tune. Instead, he had emerged unscathed. Filthy, sooty, maybe singed a little, but essentially unhurt.

A bullet to the head would have been more efficient, but Cael didn't want to do anything that would alert the Raintree clan, which an overt murder would certainly do. Everything had to be made to look accidental, which of course made guaranteeing the outcome more problematic. The royal family, the most powerful Raintrees, had to be taken out in such a way that no one suspected murder. A fire— they would think losing their Dranir in a fire was tragic and a bitter finale, but they would completely understand that he would fight to the end to save his casino and hotel, especially the hotel, with all the guests in residence there.

Cael, of course, wouldn't allow for the fact that setting up incidents that *didn't* point to the Ansara wasn't an exact science. Things could go wrong. Tonight, something had definitely gone wrong.

Dante Raintree was still alive. That was about as wrong as things could get.

The big assault on the Raintree homeplace, Sanctuary, was planned for the summer solstice, which was a week away. He and Elyn had a week to kill Dante Raintree—or Cael would kill *them*.

Chapter 7

Dante grimly walked back to where he'd left Lorna, reluctant to leave but knowing there was nothing else he could do here. Once the police were finished questioning him, his only thought had been to check on his employees to find out if there had been any fatalities. To his deep regret and fury, the answer to that last question was yes. One body had already been pulled from the smoldering ruins of the casino, and the cops were working with the crowd to establish if there were any missing friends or relatives, which would take time. There might not be a final count for a couple of days.

He'd found Al Rayburn, hoarse and coughing

from smoke inhalation but refusing to go to a hospital, instead helping to keep order among the evacuated guests. The hotel staff was doing an admirable job. The hotel itself had suffered comparatively little damage, and most of that was to the lobby area that connected the hotel and casino, where Dante had made his stand. Everyone in the hotel, guests and staff, had safely evacuated. There were some minor injuries, sprained ankles and the like, but nothing major. There was smoke damage, of course, and the entire hotel would have to be cleaned to remove the stench. The good news, what there was of it, was that the parking deck hadn't been damaged, and the hotel had no structural damage. He could probably re-open the hotel within two weeks. The question was: why would anyone want to stay there without the casino?

The casino was a complete loss. About twenty vehicles in the parking lot outside the casino entrance had been damaged, and the parking lot itself was a mess right now. Twenty or thirty people had burns of varying degrees, and as many again were suffering from smoke inhalation; all of them had been transported to local hospitals.

The media had descended en masse, of course, their constant shouts and interruptions and requests/demands for interviews interfering with his attempts to organize his employees, arrange other lodging for his hotel guests, and arrange with Al for the guests to retrieve their belongings and at the same time secure the hotel from thieves posing as guests. He had his insurance provider to deal with. He had to call Gideon and Mercy, to let them know about the fire and that he was all right, before they saw all this on the news. They were both in the Eastern Time Zone, meaning he'd better get in touch with them damn soon.

Finally he'd accepted that there was little more he could do tonight; his staff was excellent, and they had matters well in hand, plus he could always be reached by phone. He might as well go home and take a much-needed shower.

And that left the problem of Lorna.

Tonight was a night of firsts. Before tonight, he'd never used mind compulsion, never known he could. He had no idea what the parameters were. At first he'd thought his own sense of urgency had provided the impetus, but even after the evacuation was over, he'd been able to control Lorna just with the words and a nudge from his mind, so adrenaline wasn't the catalyst. He had stepped into new territory, and he had to tread lightly because this particular power could be easily abused. Hell, he'd already abused it, hadn't he? Lorna would definitely say yes to that—when he let her speak.

Tonight was also the first time he'd brutally

overwhelmed someone else's mind and literally stolen all their available power. In the aftermath, she'd been dazed, lethargic, unable to remember even her name, all symptoms attributable to emotional shock. How extensive the amnesia was, and how temporary, was something that remained to be seen. She'd begun recovering fairly soon, but she still didn't remember vast portions of the experience—unless she'd recovered her memory in his absence, in which case he should probably find some body armor before he released her from the compulsion.

Was she Ansara? That was the burning question that had to be answered—and soon.

His thinking went both ways. Part of him said, no, she couldn't possibly be, or he wouldn't have been able to overpower her mind so easily, nor would she be so susceptible to mind compulsion. An Ansara, trained from birth to manage and control her unusual abilities, just as the Raintree were, would have automatically resisted mind compulsion. The power was rare, so rare that he'd never met anyone capable of exercising it, though the family history said that an aunt six generations back had been adept at it. Rare or not, because the power existed at all, he and every other Raintree had been taught how to construct mental shields. The Ansara basically mirrored the Raintree in their gifts, so undoubtedly they, too, taught their people how to shield, which meant that the completely unshielded Lorna could not be Ansara.

Unless…

Unless she was so gifted at shielding that he couldn't detect it. Unless she was merely pretending to be controlled by mind compulsion. He'd spoken his will aloud, so she knew what he wanted. If she also had the gift of controlling fire, she could have been bolstering the blaze, resurrecting the flames every time he managed to beat them down. No. He rejected that idea. If she'd been the one feeding the fire, he would have been able to extinguish it completely after he'd commandeered her power. Someone else must have been feeding the fire, but she could have been distracting him, deflecting some of his power.

Was she or wasn't she? He would know soon. If she wasn't…then he'd played some real hardball with a woman who might not be an innocent but was still far from being an enemy. He didn't know that he would have done anything differently, though. When he'd overwhelmed her mind, it had been an act of desperation, and he hadn't had the luxury of time to explain things to her. He might have to make amends, but he wasn't sorry he'd done it. He was just glad she'd been there, glad she was gifted and had a pool of mental energy for him to tap.

He rounded a fire engine, where the crew was laying out their hoses in preparation for recoiling them, and stepped up on a curb. Now he could see her. So far as he could tell, she was standing in the exact spot in which he'd left her, which at least was off to the side, so she wasn't in the way of any of the firefighters. She was filthy, her hair matted from the unhappy combination of smoke, soot and water, her posture shouting exhaustion. She still clutched a blanket around her, and she was literally swaying where she stood. He felt a quick spurt of impatience, mingled with sympathy. Why hadn't she sat down? He hadn't prevented her from doing that.

Looking at her, he gave a mental wince on behalf of his car seats, then immediately shrugged, because he was just as filthy. What did it matter, anyway? The leather could be cleaned.

When she saw him, pure temper flashed in her eyes, dispelling the fatigue. If he'd expected her to be cowed, he would have been disappointed. As it was, a little tinge of anticipation shot through him. Even after all she'd been through, she was still standing up for herself. Remembering the vast pool of power he'd found when he tapped her mind, he wondered if even she knew how strong she really was.

"Come with me," he said, and, obediently, she followed.

There was nothing obedient about the way she grabbed his arm, though, pulling him around. She glared furiously up at him, indicating her mouth with a brief, impatient gesture. She wanted to talk; she probably had a lot of things memorized to say.

Dante started to release the compulsion, then stopped and grinned. "I think I'll enjoy the quiet for a little longer," he said, knowing that would really twist her drawers in a knot. "There's nothing you need to say that can't wait until we're alone."

Al had arranged for one of his security people to fetch Dante's car from the parking deck, where he had a reserved slot next to a private elevator. He'd been discreet about it, because some of the guests, the ones without identification, weren't being allowed to take their vehicles from the deck. They were already sorting out that security problem for those guests who felt they absolutely had to have a car tonight, even though Dante was providing shuttles to take everyone to the various hotels where his people had found them lodging. He was doing everything possible to take care of his guests, but he knew there could still be a lot of resentment that formed over details like him getting his car when they couldn't.

The phantom-black Lotus Exige was idling, parking lights on, at the end of the huge casino parking lot, concealed from most of the crowd of onlookers by the huge knot of emergency vehicles with their flashing lights. Dante led Lorna along the edge of the lot; as they neared the car, the driver's door opened and one of the security men got out. "Here you go, Mr. Raintree."

"Thanks, Jose." Dante opened the passenger door. Lorna directed a lethal glare at him as she climbed into the car and somehow managed to dig an elbow into his ribs. He concealed a wince, then closed the door with a firm click and went around to the driver's side.

The Lotus was low-slung and not all that comfortable for his muscular six-two frame, but he loved driving it when he was in the mood for something with attitude. When he wanted more comfort, he drove his Jag. Tonight he would have liked to drive out into the desolate countryside and put the hammer down, to ease his anger and sharp edge of sorrow with sheer speed and aggression. The Lotus could go from zero to a hundred in eleven seconds, which was a rush. He needed to go a hundred miles an hour right now, needed to push the high-performance little machine to its limit.

Instead he drove calmly and deliberately, aware that he couldn't let go of the tight leash he was holding on his temper. The fact that it was night helped, but the date was too close to the summer solstice for him to take any chances. Hell—could *he* have started the accursed fire? Was *he* responsible for the loss of at least one life?

The fire marshal said preliminary interviews indicated that it had started in the back, where the circuit breakers were, but the scene was still too hot for the investigators to get in there to check. If the fire had started from an electrical problem, then he had nothing to do with it, but he brooded over the possibility that the fire would turn out to have been started by something completely different. His control had wavered when he'd first seen Lorna, with the last rays of the setting sun turning her hair to rich fire. He'd lit the candles without even thinking about them; had he lit anything else?

No, he hadn't done it. He was sure of that. If he'd been the cause, things would have been bursting into flame all over the hotel and casino, rather than in one distant spot. He'd contained his power, brought it under control. The casino fire had been caused by something else; the timing was just coincidence.

Almost half an hour had lapsed before he opened his gate with a remote control and guided the Lotus up a twisting, curving drive to his tri-level house tucked into an eastern-facing fold of the Sierra Nevadas. Another button on the remote raised his garage door, and he put the Lotus in its slot like an astronaut docking a shuttle with the Space Station, then closed the garage door behind him. The silver Jag gleamed in its place beside the Lotus.

"Come on," he told Lorna, and she got out of the car. She stared straight ahead as he stepped aside to allow her to precede him into his gleaming kitchen. He punched his code into the security system to stop its warning beep, then paused. He briefly considered taking her back to town after he'd finished talking to her, then discarded that idea. He was tired. She could stay here, and if he had to—as he undoubtedly would—he would use a compulsion to keep her here and out of trouble. If she didn't like it, tough; the last couple of hours had been a bitch, and he didn't feel like making the drive.

With that in mind, he reset the alarm and turned to her. She was standing with her back to him, not four feet away, her shoulders stiff and, judging by the angle of her head, her chin up.

Regretting the imminent loss of silence, he said, "Okay, you can talk now."

She whirled to face him, and he braced himself for a flood of invective as her fists clenched at her sides.

"Bathroom!" she bellowed at him.

Chapter 8

The change in his expression would have been comical if Lorna had been in any mood to appreciate humor. His eyes rounded with comprehension, and he rapidly pointed to a short hallway. "First door on the right."

She took one frantic step, and then froze. Damn it, he was still holding her! The searing look she gave him should have accomplished what the casino fire hadn't, namely singe every hair from his head. "Don't go far," he snapped, realizing he hadn't amended the compulsion.

Lorna ran. She slammed the bathroom door but didn't take time to lock it. She barely made it in

time, and the sense of relief was so acute she shook
with involuntary shudders. A Tom Hanks scene from
A League of Their Own ran through her mind, and
she bit her lip to keep from groaning aloud.

Then she just sat there, eyes closed, trying to
calm her jangled nerves. He'd brought her to his
home! What did he intend to do? Whatever he was,
however, he was controlling her, she was helpless
to break free. The entire time he'd been gone, she
had been willing herself over and over to take a
single step, to speak a word—and she couldn't. She
was scared half out of her mind, traumatized out of
the other half, and on top of it all, she was so angry
she thought she might have a screaming, out-of-
control, foot-stomping temper tantrum just to
relieve the pressure.

Opening her eyes, she started to flush, but she
heard his voice and went still, straining to hear
what he was saying. Was someone else here? Just
as she began to relax just a fraction, she realized
he was on the phone.

"Sorry to wake you." He paused briefly, then
said, "There was a fire at the casino. Could be
worse, but it's bad enough. I didn't want you to see
it on the morning news and wonder. Call Mercy
in a couple of hours and tell her I'm all right. I've
got a feeling I'm going to have my hands full for
the next few days."

Another pause. "Thanks, but no. You've got no business getting on an airplane this week, and everything here is fine. I just wanted to call you before I got so tied up in red tape I couldn't get to a phone."

The conversation continued for a minute, and he kept reassuring whoever was on the other end that no, he didn't need help; everything was fine— well, not fine, but under control. There had been at least one fatality. The casino was a total loss, but the hotel had suffered only minor damage.

He ended the call, and a moment later Lorna heard a savage, muttered curse, then a thud, as if he'd punched the wall.

He didn't seem like the wall-punching type, she thought. Then again, she didn't know him. He might be a serial wall-puncher. Or maybe he'd fainted or something, and the thud had been his body hitting the floor.

She liked that idea. She would seize the chance to kick him while he was down. Literally.

The only way to see if he was lying there unconscious was to leave the bathroom. Reluctantly, she flushed, then went to the vanity to wash her hands—a vanity with a dark, golden-brown granite top and gold fixtures. When she reached out to turn on the water, the contrast between the richness of the vanity and her absolutely filthy, blacksooted hand made her inwardly cringe as she lifted her head.

A grimy nightmare loomed in the mirror in front of her. Her hair was matted to her head with soot and water, and stank of smoke. Her face was so black only her eyes had any real definition, and they were bloodshot. With her red eyes, she looked like some demon from hell.

She shuddered, remembering how close the flames had gotten. Given that, she couldn't imagine how she had any hair left on her head at all, so she shouldn't complain about it being matted. Shampoo—a lot of it—would take care of that. The soot would scrub off. Her clothes were ruined, but she had others. She was alive and unharmed, and she didn't know how.

As she soaped her grimy hands, rinsed, then soaped again, she tried to reconstruct an exact sequence of events. Her headache, which had subsided, roared back so fiercely she had to brace her soapy hands on the edge of the bowl.

Thoughts whirled, trying to connect in a coherent sequence, but then the segments would whirl out of touch again.

—she should have been burned—

—hair singed off—

—bubble—

—no smoke—

—agony—

Whimpering from the pain in her head, she sank to her knees.

Raintree cursing.

Something about that reminded her of something. Of being held in front of him, his arms locked around her, while his curses rang out over her head and his...his—

The memory was gone, eluding her grasp. Pain made her vision swim, and she stared at the soap bubbles on her hands, trying to summon the energy to stand. Was she having a stroke? The pain was so intense, burning, and it filled her head until she thought her skull might explode from the pressure.

Soap bubbles.

The shimmery bubbles...something about them reminded her...there had been something around her....

A *shimmering bubble*. The memory burst into her aching brain, so clear it brought tears to her eyes. She'd *seen* it, surrounding them, holding the heat and smoke at bay.

Her head had felt as if it really were exploding then. There had been an impact so huge she couldn't compare it to anything in her experience, but she imagined the sensation was the same as if she'd been run over by a train—or struck by a meteor. It was as if all the cellular walls in her brain had dissolved, as if everything she had been, was, and would be, had been sucked out, taken over and used. She'd been helpless, as completely helpless as a newborn, to resist the pain or the man who had ruthlessly taken everything.

With a crash, everything fell back into place, as if that memory had been the one piece she needed to put the puzzle together.

She remembered it all: every moment of unspeakable terror, her inability to act, the way he had used her.

Everything.

"You've had enough time," he called from the kitchen. "I heard you flush. Come here, Lorna."

Like a puppet, she got to her feet and walked out of the bathroom, soap still clinging to her hands and her temper flaring. He looked grim, standing there waiting for her. With every unwilling step she took, her temper soared into another level of the stratosphere.

"You *jerk!*" she shouted, and kicked his ankle as she walked by. She could go only a couple of steps past him before that invisible wall stopped her, so she whirled around and stalked past him again. "You *ass!*" She threw an elbow into his ribs.

She must not have hurt him very much because he looked more astonished than pained. That infuriated her even more, and when the wall forced her to turn around yet again, she reached a whole new level of temper as she began marching back and forth within the confines of his will.

"You made me go into *fire*—" A snake-fast pinch at his waist.

"I'm *terrified* of fire, but did you *care?*" Another kick, this one sideways into his knee.

"Oh, no, I had to *stand there* while you did your mumbo jumbo—" On that pass, she leveled a punch at his solar plexus.

"Then you *brain-raped* me, you jerk, you gorilla, you freakin' *witch doctor*—" On the return trip, she went for a kidney punch.

"Then, to top it all off, the whole time you were *grinding your hard-on against my butt!*" She was so incensed that she shrieked that last bit at him, and this time put everything she had into a punch straight to his chin.

He blocked it with a swift movement of his forearm, so she stomped on his foot instead.

"Ouch!" he yelped, but the jerk was *laughing*, damn him, and in another of his lightning moves, he captured her in his arms, pulling her solidly against him. She opened her mouth to screech at him, and he bent his head and kissed her.

In contrast to the strong-arm tactics he'd used against her all night, the kiss was soft and feather-light, almost sweet. "I'm sorry," he murmured, and kissed her again. He stank as much as she did, maybe even more, but the body beneath his ruined clothing was rock solid with muscle and very warm in the air-conditioned coolness of the house. "I know it hurt… I didn't have time to explain—" Between phrases, he kept on kissing her, each successive touch of his lips becoming a little deeper, lingering a little longer.

Shock held her still: shock that he would be kissing her; shock that she would *let* him kiss her, after all the antagonism between them; after he'd done everything he'd done to her; after she'd subjected him to that battery of drive-by attacks. He wasn't forcing her to let him kiss her; this was nothing like wanting to walk and not being able to. Her hands were on his muscled chest, but she wasn't making any effort to push him away, not even a mental one.

His mouth slid to the soft hollow beneath her ear, deposited a gentle bite on the site of her neck. "I'd much rather have been grinding my hard-on against your front," he said, and went back to her mouth for a kiss that had nothing light or sweet about it. His tongue swept in, acquainting him with her taste, while his right hand went down to her bottom, slid caressingly over the curves, then pressed her hips forward to meet his.

He was doing exactly what he'd said he would much rather have been doing.

Lorna didn't trust passion. From what she had seen, passion was selfish and self-centered. She wasn't immune to it, but she didn't trust it—didn't trust men, who in her experience would tell lies just to get laid. She didn't trust anyone else to care about her, to look out for her interests. She opened herself to passion slowly, warily, if at all.

If she hadn't been so tired, so stressed, so traumatized, she would have had complete control of herself, but she'd been off balance from the minute his chief of security had escorted her into his office. She was off balance now, as dizzy as if the kitchen were rotating around her, as if the floor had slanted beneath her feet. In contrast, he was solid and so very warm, his arms stronger than any that had ever held her before, and her body responded to him as if nothing else existed beyond the simple pleasure of the moment. Being held against him felt good. His incredible body heat felt good. The thick length of his erection, pushing against her lower belly, felt good—so good that she had gone on tiptoe to better accommodate it, and she didn't remember doing so.

Belatedly alarmed by the no-show of her usual caution, she pulled her mouth from his and pushed against his chest. "This is stupid," she muttered.

"Brainless," he agreed, his breath coming a little fast. He was slow to release her, so she pushed again, and, reluctantly, he let his arms drop.

He didn't step back, so she did, staring around her at the kitchen so she wouldn't have to look at him. As kitchens went, it was nice, she supposed. She didn't like cooking, so in the general scheme of things, kitchens were pretty much wasted on her.

"You kidnapped me," she charged, scowling at him.

He considered that, then gave a brief nod. "I did."

For some reason his agreement annoyed her more than if he'd argued with her assessment. "If you're going to charge me with cheating, then do it," she snapped. "You can't prove a thing, and we both know it, so the sooner you make a fool of yourself, the better, as far as I'm concerned, because then I can leave and not see you—"

"I'm not making any charges against you," he interrupted. "You're right. I can't prove anything."

His sudden admission stumped her. "Then why drag me all the way up here?"

"I said I can't prove you did it. That doesn't mean you're innocent." He gave her a narrow, assessing look. "In fact, you're guilty as hell. Using your paranormal gifts in a game of chance is cheating, pure and simple."

"I don't have—" Automatically, she started to

deny that she was psychic, but he raised a hand to cut her off.

"That's why I did the 'brain-rape,' as you called it. I needed an extra reserve of power to hold off the fire, and I knew you were gifted—but I was surprised at *how* gifted. You can't tell me you didn't know. There was too much power there for you to pass yourself off as just being lucky."

Lorna hardly knew how to react. His cool acknowledgment of what he'd done to her raised her hackles all over again, but the charge that she was "gifted" made her so uneasy that she was already shaking her head before he finished speaking. "Numbers," she blurted. "I'm good with numbers."

"Bull."

"That's all it is! I don't tell fortunes or read tea leaves or anything like that! I didn't know 9/11 was going to happen—"

But the flight numbers of the downed flights had haunted her for days before the attack. If she tried to dial a phone number, the numbers she dialed were those flight numbers—in the order in which the planes had crashed.

That particular memory surfaced like a salmon leaping out of the water, and a chill shook her. She hadn't thought of the flight numbers since then. She had buried the memory deep, where it couldn't cause trouble.

"Go away," she whispered to the memory.

"I'm not going anywhere," he said. "And neither are you. At least, not right away." He sighed and gave her a regretful look. "Take off your clothes."

Chapter 9

"I will not!" Lorna yelped, backing as far away from him as she could get, which of course wasn't far.

"So will I, probably," he replied ironically, moving closer, looming over her. "Can't be helped. Look, I'm not going to assault you. Just take off your clothes and get it over with."

She retreated as he advanced, clutching at her blouse as if she were an outraged Victorian virgin and looking around for a weapon, any weapon. This was a kitchen, damn it; it was supposed to have knives sitting in a fancy block on the fancy countertop. Instead, there was nothing but a vast expanse of polished granite.

He took a deep breath, then heaved it out as if he were bored. "I can make you do it without even touching you. You know that, and I know that, so why do this the hard way?"

He was right, she thought impotently. Whatever it was that his mind did to her mind, he could make her do anything he wanted. "This isn't fair!" she shouted at him, curling her hands into fists. "How are you *doing* this to me?"

"I'm a freakin' witch doctor, remember?"

"Don't forget the rest of it! Jerk! Ass—"

"I know, I know. Now take off your clothes."

She shook her head, matted hair flying. Bitterly, she expected him to take control of her mind, but he didn't. He just inexorably advanced as she retreated, backing down the hallway past the powder room she'd used, through what she assumed was a very stylish den, though she didn't dare take her gaze from him long enough to look around.

He was herding her, she realized, as if she were a sheep, and she had no choice, but to do anything other than be herded. His bloodshot green eyes glittered in his grimy face, making him look completely uncivilized. Her heartbeat skittered wildly. Was he some sort of mad serial killer who left pieces of dismembered bodies scattered all over Nevada? A modern-day Rasputin? An escapee from some mental institution? He certainly didn't look or act like the millionaire owner of a top-notch casino/hotel. He acted like some sort of—of warlord, master of all he surveyed.

She backed into a door frame, briefly staggered off balance, then brought herself up short as she realized he'd maneuvered her into another bathroom, this one a full bath, and far more opulent than the half bath off the kitchen. No lights were on, but the illumination coming in the open door revealed their reflections in the gleaming mirror on her left.

He reached in and flipped on the lights, so bright and white that she lifted a hand to shield her eyes. "Now," he said, "no more stalling. Take off your clothes yourself, or we'll do this the hard way."

Lorna looked around. She was cornered. "Go to hell," she said, and did what cornered animals always do: she attacked.

For a short while he merely blocked her punches, deflected her kicks, avoided her bites, and the ease with which he did so made her that much angrier. She lost one shoe in the battle, the cheap sandal sailing across the room to clatter into the huge sunken tub. Then she felt a sudden wave of impatience emanating from him, and in three seconds flat he had her bent over the vanity with her hands pinned behind her.

He crowded in close, using his powerful legs to control her kicks, and gripped the neckline of her top. Three hard yanks brought the sound of several threads giving way, but the seams held. He cursed and yanked harder, and the left-side seam surrendered. Ruthlessly he tore at the garment until it was in rags, hanging from her right wrist. Her bra fastened in back, easy prey to the quick pinch of his fingers that released the hooks.

She squirmed like an eel, screaming until she was hoarse. He completely ignored everything she said, every insult and plea she hurled at him, silently and grimly concentrating on stripping her. She alternated between fury and sobs of panic as he opened the fastening of her pants, lowered the zipper, but stopped before pushing her pants and underwear down over her hips.

She went limp, sobbing, her face pressed against the cold stone of the vanity. He stopped pulling at her clothes, and instead the heat of his hand moved over her neck, lifting her matted hair aside for a moment, then tracing over her shoulders. He shifted his grip on her hands, instead pulling them up and over her head before resuming what felt like an inch-by-inch search of her skin. The sides of her breasts, her ribs, the indentation of her waist, the flare of her hips—he examined all of that, even pushing her pants lower to scrutinize the bottom curves of her buttocks. Mortified, she squirmed and sobbed, but he was inexorable.

Then he sighed and said, "I owe you another apology."

He released his grip on her hands and stepped back, freeing her from the pressure of his body. On his way out he said, "I'll bring you some clothes. Think about taking a shower, get your breath back and we'll talk afterward." He paused, added, "Don't leave this room," then quietly closed the door.

Sobbing, she slid from the vanity to the floor and curled in a vanquished heap. At first all she could do was cry and shake. After a while her temper resurrected itself and flashed over in a wordless shriek. She wept some more. Finally she sat up, wiped her face with the shreds of her blouse, yelled, "You bastard!" at the door, and felt marginally better for the invective.

Her eyes were swollen and her nose was clogged, but she felt calm enough to stand, though that wasn't easy with her pants around her knees. The indignity made her flush with humiliation, but there was no point in pulling them up. Instead she stripped completely naked and stood there in rare indecision.

The suggestion to take a shower, she discovered, had been just that: a suggestion. If she didn't want to, she didn't have to. She could take a long soak in the sunken tub, if she wished. She didn't have to bathe at all, though that was an option she immediately discarded.

Getting in the tub wouldn't be practical, because she would end up sitting in dirty water. A long—very long—hot shower was the only way to get clean.

The shower didn't have a door. The entrance was a curved wall of stone that led past a built-in shelf, stacked with thick, copper-colored towels, to three steps down into a five-foot-square stall with multiple showerheads. The controls were within easy reach, and when she turned the handle, water spurted out of three walls and from overhead. She waited until she felt the heat of the steam rising to her face, then stepped into the deluge.

Concentrating on getting clean, and nothing else, gave her nerves a much-needed respite. The hot water streaming over her body was a soothing, pulsating massage. She shampooed and rinsed, then did it again, and yet again, before her hair felt clean and untangled. She lathered and scrubbed with the fragrant bath gel, and found it didn't remove even half the soot and grime. A second scrubbing produced results that weren't much better, so she switched back to the shampoo; it had worked on her hair, so it should work on her skin.

Finally she realized that she'd been in the shower so long that her fingertips had wrinkled and the hot water should have long since been used up, though it wasn't—but enough was enough. She was waterlogged. Regretfully, she turned off the water, and the pulsating streams disappeared so suddenly that it was as if they'd been sucked back into the showerheads. Only the sounds of the vent fan overhead and the draining water came to her ears.

She hadn't turned on the vent fan. Unless it came on automatically when the humidity level reached a certain point, he'd come back into the bathroom.

Hurriedly, she went up the three steps, grabbed one of the fluffy towels and wrapped it around herself, then got another one and twisted it into a turban over her dripping hair. Following the curving wall, she moved until she could see into the main part of the bathroom. The mirrored wall behind the double sinks threw her reflection back at her, but hers was the only reflection. She was alone—now. The thick terry-cloth robe folded over the vanity stool told her that he *had* been there.

Lorna stared at the mirror. She looked pale, even to herself. The skin across her cheekbones was drawn tight, giving her a stark, shocked expression.

That was okay. She *felt* stark and shocked.

He'd said not to leave the bathroom. She was so soul-weary that she didn't even try, so she didn't know if that had been another suggestion or one of his weird mental orders that she couldn't disobey. At this point it didn't matter whether it was a suggestion or command. She was content to simply stay there, where there was nothing more complicated to do than dry her hair.

Rummaging in the drawers of the vanity, she found scented lotion, as well as a hair dryer and brush, which was all she needed right now. The shampoo had made her skin feel tight, so she rubbed in the lotion everywhere she could reach, then began the task of drying her hair.

Her motions with the brush became slower, then slower still. Exhaustion made her arms tremble. She was lucky that her hair was mostly straight, and had good body, because any attempt at styling it was beyond her. She just wanted her hair to be dry before she collapsed, that was all.

With that chore accomplished, she put on the robe, which was evidently his; the sleeves fell several inches past the tips of her fingers and the hem almost reached the floor. Funny, she thought fuzzily, he didn't seem like the robe-wearing type.

Then she waited, swaying on her feet, her bare toes clenching on the plush rug. She could have at least opened the door, but she wasn't in any rush to face him, or to find out that even with the door open, she was imprisoned in this room. Time enough for that. Time enough to engage the enemy again.

They would talk, he'd said. She didn't want to talk to him. She had nothing to say to him that didn't involve a lot of four-letter words. All she wanted was to go...well, not *home*, exactly, because she didn't have a home in that sense. She wanted to go back to where she was staying, to where her clothes were. That was close enough to home for her. For now, she just wanted to sleep in the bed she was accustomed to.

Without warning, the door opened and he stood there, tall and broad-shouldered, as vital as if the night hadn't been long and traumatic. He'd showered, too; his longish black hair, still damp, was brushed straight back to reveal every strong, faintly exotic line of his face. He'd shaved, too; his face had that freshly scraped look.

He was wearing a pair of very soft-looking pajama pants...and nothing else. Not even a smile.

His keen eyes searched her face, noting the white look of utter exhaustion. "We'll talk in the morning. I doubt you could form a coherent sentence right now. Come on, I'll show you where your room is."

She shrank back, and he looked at her with an unreadable expression. "*Your* room," he emphasized. "Not mine. I didn't make that a command, but I will if necessary. I don't think you'd be comfortable sleeping in the bathroom."

She was awake enough to retort, "You'll have to make it a command, otherwise I can't leave the bathroom, anyway."

She had decided that his command not to leave the bathroom had been meant to short-circuit her own will, and by his flash of irritation, she saw she'd been right.

"Come with me," he said curtly, a command that released her from the bathroom but sentenced her to follow him like a duckling.

He led her to a spacious bedroom with seven-foot windows that revealed the sparkling neon colors of Reno. "The private bath is through there," he said, indicating a door. "You're safe. I won't bother you. I won't hurt you. Don't leave this room." With that, he closed the door behind him and left her standing in the dimly lit bedroom.

He *would* remember to tack on that last sentence, damn him—not that she felt capable of making a run for it. Right now her capability was limited to climbing into the king-size bed, still wearing the oversize robe. She curled under the sheet and duvet, but still felt too exposed, so she pulled the sheet over her head and slept.

Chapter 10

Monday

"Are you okay?"

Lorna woke, as always, to a lingering sense of dread and fear. It wasn't the words that alarmed her, though, since she immediately recognized the voice. They were, however, far from welcome. Regardless of where she was, the dread was always there, within her, so much a part of her that it was as if it had been beaten into her very bones.

She couldn't see him, because the sheet was still over her head. She seldom moved in her sleep, so she was still in such a tight curl that the oversize robe hadn't been dislodged or even come untied.

"Are you okay?" he repeated, more insistently.

"Peachy keen," she growled, wishing he would just go away again.

"You were making a noise."

"I was snoring," she said flatly, keeping a tight grip on the sheet in case he tried to pull it down— like she could stop him if he really wanted to. She had learned the futility of that in the humiliating struggle last night.

He snorted. "Yeah, right." He paused. "How do you like your coffee?"

"I don't. I'm a tea drinker."

Silence greeted that for a moment; then he sighed. "I'll see what I can do. How do you drink your tea?"

"With friends."

She heard what sounded remarkably like a growl, then the bedroom door closed with more force than necessary. Had she sounded ungrateful? Good! After everything he'd done, if he thought the offer of coffee or tea would make up for it, he was so far off base he wasn't even in the ballpark.

Truth to tell, she wasn't much of a tea drinker, either. For most of her life she'd been able to afford only what was free, which meant she drank a lot of water. In the last few years she'd had the occasional cup of coffee or hot tea, to warm up in very cold weather, but she didn't really care for either of them.

She didn't want to get up. She didn't want to have that talk he seemed bent on, though what he thought they had to talk about, she couldn't imagine. He'd treated her horribly last night, and though he'd evidently realized he was wrong, he didn't seem inclined to go out of his way to make amends. He hadn't, for instance, taken her home last night. He'd imprisoned her in this room. He hadn't even fed the prisoner!

The empty ache in her stomach told her that she had to get out of bed if she wanted food. Getting out of bed didn't guarantee she would get fed, of course, but staying in bed certainly guaranteed she wouldn't. Reluctantly, she flipped the sheet back, and the first thing she saw was Dante Raintree, standing just inside the door. The bully hadn't left at all; he'd just pretended to.

He lifted one eyebrow in a silent, sardonic question.

Annoyed, she narrowed her eyes at him. "That's inhuman."

"What is?"

"Lifting just one eyebrow. Real people can't do that. Just demons."

"*I* can do it."

"Which proves my point."

He grinned—which annoyed her even more, because she didn't want to amuse him. "If you want to get up, this demon has washed your clothes—"

"What you didn't shred," she interjected sourly, to hide her alarm. Had he emptied her pockets first? She didn't ask, because if he hadn't, maybe her money and license were still there.

"—and loaned you one of his demon shirts. You'll probably have to throw your pants away, because the stains won't come out, but at least they're clean. They'll do for now. Your choices for breakfast are cereal and fruit, or a bagel and cream cheese. When you get dressed, come to the kitchen. We'll eat in there." He left then—really left, because she watched him go.

He was assuming she would share a meal with him. Unfortunately, he was right. She was starving, and if the only way she could get some food was to sit anywhere in his vicinity, then she would sit there. One of the first lessons she'd learned about life was that emotions didn't carry much weight when survival sat on the other end of the scale.

Slowly she sat up, feeling aches and twinges in every muscle. Her newly washed, stained-beyond-redemption pants lay across the foot of the bed, as well as her underwear and a white shirt made out of some limp, slinky material. She grabbed for the pants and dug her hand into each pocket, and her heart sank. Not only was her money gone, but so was her license. He either had them, or they had fallen out in the wash, which meant she had to find the laundry room in this place and search the washer and dryer. Maybe he had someone working for him who did the laundry; maybe that person had taken her money and ID.

She got out of bed and hobbled to the bathroom. After taking care of her most urgent business, she looked in the drawers of the vanity, hoping he was a good host—even if he was a lousy person—and had stocked the bathroom with emergency supplies. She desperately needed a toothbrush.

He was a good host. She found everything she needed: a supply of toothbrushes still in their sealed plastic cases, toothpaste, mouthwash, the same scented lotion she'd used the night before, a small sewing kit, even new hairbrushes and disposable razors.

The toothbrush manufacturer had evidently not intended for anyone without a knife or scissors to be able to use their product. After struggling to tear the plastic case apart, first with her fingers and then with her teeth, she got the tiny pair of scissors from the sewing kit and laboriously stabbed, sawed and hacked until she had freed the incarcerated toothbrush. She regarded the scissors thoughtfully, then laid them on the vanity top. They were too small to be of much use, but…

After brushing her teeth and washing her face, she dragged a brush through her hair. Good enough. Even if she'd had her skimpy supply of makeup with her, she wouldn't have put any on for Raintree's benefit.

Going back into the bedroom, she locked the door just in case he decided to waltz in again, then removed the robe and began dressing. The precaution was useless, she thought bitterly, because if he wanted in, all he had to do was order her to unlock the door and she would do what he said, whether she wanted to or not. She *hated* that, and she hated *him*.

She didn't want to put on his shirt. She picked it up and turned it so she could see the tag. She didn't recognize the brand name, but that wasn't what she was looking for, anyway. The tag with the care instructions read 100% Silk—Dry-clean Only.

Maybe she could smear some jelly on the shirt. Accidentally, of course.

She started to slip her arms into the sleeves, then paused, remembering how he'd phrased his last statement: *When you're dressed, come to the kitchen.* Once she was dressed, she probably wouldn't have a choice about going to the kitchen, so anything she wanted to do, she should do before putting on that shirt.

She dropped the shirt back on the bed and retrieved the tiny scissors from the bathroom, slipping them into her right pocket. Then she systematically searched both the bathroom and bedroom, looking for anything she might use as a weapon or to help her somehow escape. If she saw any opening, however small, she had to be prepared to take it.

One big obstacle was that she didn't have any shoes. She doubted the ones she'd been wearing could be saved, but at least they would protect her feet. Raintree hadn't brought them to the bedroom, but they might still be in the bathroom she'd used last night. She didn't want to run barefoot through the countryside, though she would if she had to. How far would she have to run before she was free? How far out did Raintree's sphere of influence reach? There had to be a distance at which his mind tricks wouldn't work—didn't there? Did she have to hear him speak the command, or could he just *think* it at her?

Uneasily, she hoped he had somehow simply hypnotized her, because otherwise she was so deep in *The Twilight Zone* doo-doo she might never get the weird crap off her shoes.

Other than the scissors, neither the bath nor the bedroom supplied anything usable. There were no pistols in the built-in drawers, no stray hammer she could use to bash him in the head, not even any extra clothes in the huge closet that she could have used to suffocate him. Regretfully, with no other option left, she finally put on the silk shirt. As she was rolling up the too-long sleeves, she wondered when the command stuff would kick in. The slippery material didn't roll up very well, so she redid the sleeves several times before she gave up and let the rolls droop over her wrists. Even then, she didn't feel an irresistible urge to go to the kitchen.

She was on her own. He hadn't put the command mojo on her.

Tremendously annoyed that, under her own free will, she was doing what he'd told her to do anyway, she unlocked the bedroom door and stepped out into the hallway.

Two sets of stairs opened before her, the one on the right going up to the next floor and leading to what appeared to be a balcony. The set on the left went down, widening to a graceful fan at the bottom. She frowned, not remembering any stairs from the night before. Had she been that out of it? She definitely remembered arriving at the house, remembered noticing that it had three separate levels, so of course there were stairs—she just didn't remember them. Having this kind of hole in her memory was frightening, because what else did she not remember?

She took the down staircase, pausing when she got to the bottom. She was in a spectacular…living room? If so, it wasn't like any living room she'd ever seen. The arched ceiling soared three stories above her head. At one end was an enormous fireplace, while the wall at the other end was glass. Evidently he was fond of glass, because he had a lot of it. The view was literally breathtaking. But she didn't remember this, either. Any of it.

A hallway led off to the side, and cautiously she followed it. Something about this seemed familiar, at least, and she opened one door to discover the bathroom in which she'd showered last night—and in which he'd ripped off her clothes. Setting her jaw, she went in and looked around for her shoes. They weren't there. Resigned to being barefoot, she walked through the den, past the powder room she'd used and into the kitchen.

He was sitting at the bar, long legs hooked around a stool, a cup of coffee in one hand and the morning newspaper in the other. He looked up when she entered. "I found some tea, and the water is boiling."

"I'll drink water."

"Because tea is what you share with friends, right?" He put down the newspaper and got up, opening a cabinet door and taking down a water glass, which he filled from the faucet. "I hope you don't expect designer water, because I think it's a huge waste of money."

She shrugged. "Water's water."

He gave her the glass, then lifted his brows—both of them. "Cereal or bagel?"

"Bagel."

"Good choice."

Only then did she notice a small plate with his own bagel on it, revealed when he'd put down the paper. Maybe it was petty of her, but she wished they weren't eating the same thing. She didn't wish it enough to eat cereal, though.

He put a plain bagel in the toaster and got the cream cheese from the refrigerator. While the bagel was toasting, she looked around. "What time is it? I haven't seen a clock anywhere."

"It's ten fifty-seven," he said, without turning around. "And I don't own a clock—well, except for the one on the oven behind you. And maybe one on the microwave. Yeah, I guess a microwave has to have a clock nowadays."

She looked behind her. The oven clock was digital, showing ten fifty-seven in blue numbers. The only thing was, she'd been blocking the oven from his view—and he hadn't turned around, anyway. He must have looked while he was getting the cream cheese.

"My cell phone has the time, too," he continued. "And my computers and cars have clocks. So I guess I do own clocks, but I don't have just *a* clock. All of them are attached to something else."

"If small talk is supposed to make me relax and forget I hate you, it isn't working."

"I didn't think it would." He glanced up, the green in his eyes so intense she almost fell back a step. "I needed to know if you were Ansara, and to get the answer I was rough in the way I handled you. I apologize."

Frustration boiled in her. Half of what he said made no sense to her at all, and she was tired of it. "Just who the hell are these Aunt Sarah people, and where the hell are my *shoes?*"

Chapter 11

"The answer to the second part of your question is easy. I threw them away."

"Great," she muttered, looking down at her bare feet, toes curling on the cold stone tiles.

"I ordered a pair for you from Macy's. One of my employees is on the way with them."

Lorna frowned. She didn't like accepting anything from anyone, and she especially didn't like accepting anything from *him*—but it seemed she was having to do a lot of it no matter how she felt. On the other hand, he had thrown away her shoes and destroyed her blouse, so replacing them was the least he could do.

"And the Aunt Sarah people?" She knew he'd said "Ansara"—not that *that* made any more sense to her—but she hoped mangling the word would annoy him.

"That's a longer explanation. But after last night, you're entitled to hear it." A little *ding* sounded, and the toaster spat up the bagel. Using the knife he'd got to spread the cream cheese, he flipped the two bagel halves out of the toaster slot and onto a small plate, then passed knife, plate and cream cheese to her.

She took the bar stool farthest from him and spread cream cheese on one slice of bagel. "So let's hear it," she said curtly.

"There are a few other things I'd like to get cleared out of the way. First—" He reached into the front pocket of his jeans, pulled out a wad of bills and slid them in front of her.

Lorna looked down. Her license was tucked amid the bills. "My money!" she said, grabbing both and putting them in her own pockets.

"My money, don't you mean?" he asked grimly, but he hadn't insisted on keeping it. "And don't tell me again that you didn't cheat, because I know you did. I'm just not sure even *you* know you cheated, or how you're doing it."

She focused her attention on her bagel, her expression shutting down. He was going off into *woo-woo* land again, but she didn't have to travel with him. "I didn't cheat," she said obstinately, because he'd told her not to.

"You don't know— Hold on, my cell phone's vibrating." He pulled a small cell from his pocket, flipped it open and said, "Raintree… Yeah. I'll ask her." He looked at Lorna and said, "How much did you say your new shoes cost?"

"One twenty-eight ninety," she replied automatically, and took a bite of the bagel.

He flipped the phone shut and slid it back into his pocket.

After a few seconds the silence in the room made her look up. His eyes were such a brilliant green, they looked as if they were glowing. "There wasn't a call on my cell," he said.

"Then why did you ask—" She stopped, abruptly realizing what she'd said when he'd asked about the shoes, and what little color she'd regained washed out of her face. She opened her mouth to tell him that he must have mentioned the price of the shoes to her, then shut it again, because she knew he hadn't. She had a cold, sick feeling in the pit of her stomach, almost the same feeling she had every morning when she woke up. "I'm not a weirdo," she said in a thin, flat voice.

"The term is 'gifted.' You're gifted. I just proved

it to you. I didn't need any proof, because I already knew. I'm even more gifted than you are."

"You're crazy, is what you are."

"I'm mildly empathic, just enough that I can read people very well, especially if I touch them, which is why I always shake hands when I go into a business meeting," he said, speaking over her as if she hadn't interrupted. "As you know very well, using just my mind, I can compel people to do things against their wishes. That's a new one on me, but what the hell. We *are* close to the summer solstice. That, added to the fire, probably triggered it. I can do a bunch of different things, but most of all, I'm a Class A Number One Fire-Master."

"Which means what?" she asked sarcastically, to cover the fact that she was shaken to the core. "That you moonlight at the circus as a fire-eater?"

He held out his hand, palm up, and a lovely little blue flame burst to life in the middle of his hand. He casually blew it out. "Can't do that for very long," he said, "or it burns."

"That's just a trick. Stunt people do that in movies all—"

Her bagel caught on fire.

She stared at it, frozen, as the thick bread burned and smoked. He picked up the plate and flicked the burning bagel into the sink, then ran water on it. "Don't want the fire alarm to go off," he explained, and slid the plate, with the other half of bagel on it, back in front of her.

Behind him, a candle flared to life. "I keep a lot of candles around," he said. "They're my equivalent of a canary in a coal mine."

A thought grew and grew until she couldn't hold it back. "You set the casino on fire!" she said in horror.

He shook his head as he slid back onto his stool and picked up his coffee. "My control is better than that, even this close to the solstice. It wasn't my fire."

"So you say. If you're a Class A Number One hotshot Fire-Master, why didn't you put it out?"

"That's the same question I've been asking myself."

"And the answer is…?"

"I don't know."

"Wow, that's enlightening."

His brilliant grin flashed across his face. "Has anyone ever told you you're a smart-ass?"

She barely kept herself from flinching back in automatic response. Yeah, she'd heard the comment before—many times, and always accompanied by, or even preceded by, a slap.

She didn't look up to see if he'd noted anything strange about her response, but concentrated on putting cream cheese on the remaining half of her bagel.

"Since I had never done mind control before last night, it's possible I drained myself of energy," he continued after a moment. She still refused to look up, but she could feel the intensity of his gaze on her face. "I didn't feel tired. Everything felt normal, but until I explore the parameters, I won't know what the effects of mind control are. Maybe I wasn't concentrating as much as I should have been. Maybe my attention was splintered. Hell, I *know* it was splintered. There were a lot of unusual factors last night."

"You honestly think you could have put out that fire?"

"I know I could have—normally. The fire marshal would have thought the sprinkler system did a great job. Instead—"

"Instead, you dragged me into the middle of a four-alarm fire and nearly killed both of us!"

"Are you burned?" he asked, sipping his coffee.

"No," she said grudgingly.

"Suffering from smoke inhalation?"

"No, damn it!"

"Don't you think you should have at least a few singed strands of hair?"

He was only saying everything she'd thought herself. She didn't understand what had happened during the fire, and she didn't understand anything that had happened since then. Desperately, she wanted to skate over the surface of everything, pretend nothing weird was going on, and leave this house with the pretense still intact, but he wasn't going to let that happen. She could feel his determination, like a force field emanating from him.

No! she told herself in despair. No force field, no emanating. Nothing like that.

"I threw a shield of protection around us. Then at the end, when I was using all your power combined with mine to beat back the fire, the shield solidified a bit. You saw it. I saw it. It shimmered, like a—"

"Soap bubble," she whispered.

"Ah," he said softly, after a moment of thought. "So that's what triggered your memory."

"Do you have any idea how much that *hurt*, what you did?"

"Taking over your power? No, I don't know, but I can imagine."

"No," she said flatly. "You can't." The pain had been beyond any true description. If she said it had felt as if an anvil had fallen on her head, that would be an understatement.

"Again, I'm sorry. I had no choice. It was either that, or we were both going to die, along with the people still evacuating the hotel."

"You have a way of apologizing that says you'd do the same thing again if the situation arose, so it's really hard to believe the 'sorry' part."

"That's because you're not only a precog, though an untrained one, you're also very sensitive to the paranormal energy around you."

Meaning he *would* do the same thing again, in the same circumstances. At least he wasn't a hypocrite.

"Yesterday, in my office," he continued, "you were reacting to energies you wouldn't have sensed at all if you weren't gifted."

"I thought you were evil," she said, and savagely bit into the bagel. "Nothing you've done since has changed my mind."

"Because you turned me on?" he asked softly. "I took one look at you, and every candle in the room lit up. I'm not usually that out of control, but I had to concentrate to rein everything in. Then I kept looking at you and thinking about having sex, and damned if you didn't hook into the fantasy."

Oh, God, he'd known *that?* She felt her face burn, and she turned her embarrassment into anger. "Are you coming on to me?" she asked incredulously. "Do you actually have the *nerve* to think I'd let you touch me with a ten-foot pole after what you did to me last night?"

"It isn't *that* long," he said, smiling a little.

Well, she'd walked into that one. She slapped the bagel onto the plate and slid off the stool. "I don't want to be in the same room with you. After I leave here, I never want to see your face again. You can take your tacky little fantasy and shove it, Raintree!"

"Dante," he corrected, as if she hadn't all but told him to drop dead. "And that brings us to the Ansara. I was looking for a birthmark. All Ansara have a blue crescent moon somewhere on their backs."

She was so angry that a red mist fogged her vision. "And while you were looking for this birthmark on my *back* you decided to check out my ass, too, huh?"

"It's a fine ass, well worth checking out. But, no, I always intended to check it out. 'Back' is imprecise. Technically, 'back' could go from the top of your head all the way down to your heels. I've seen it below the waist before, and in the histories there are reports of, in rare cases, the birthmark being on the ass cheek. Given the seriousness of the fire, and the fact that I couldn't put it out, I had to make sure you hadn't been hindering me."

"Hindering you how?" she cried, not at all mollified by his explanation.

"If you had also been a fire-master, you could have been feeding the fire while I was trying to put it out. I've never seen a fire I couldn't control—until last night."

"But you said yourself you'd never used mind control before, so you don't know how it affected you! Why automatically assume I had to be one of these Ansara?"

"I didn't. I'm well aware of all the variables. I still had to eliminate the possibility that you might be Ansara."

"If you're so good at reading people when you touch them, then you should have known I wasn't," she charged.

"Very good," he acknowledged, as if he were a teacher and she his star pupil. "But Ansara are trained from birth to manage their gifts and to protect themselves, just as Raintree are. A powerful Ansara could conceivably have constructed a shield that I wouldn't be able to detect. Like I said, my empath abilities are mild."

She felt as if she were about to explode with frustration. "If I'd had one of these shields, you idiot, you wouldn't have been able to brain-rape me!"

He drummed his fingers lightly on top of the bar, studying her with narrowed eyes. "I really, *really* don't like that term."

"Tough. I really, *really* didn't like the brain-rape itself." She threw the words at him like knives and hoped they buried themselves deep in his flesh.

He considered that, then nodded. "Fair enough. Back to the subject of shields. You have them, but not the kind I'm talking about. The kind you have develop naturally, from life. You shield your emotions. I'm talking about a mental shield that's deliberately constructed to hide a part of your brain's energy. As for keeping me out—honey, there's only one other person, at least that I know of, who could possibly have blocked me from taking over his mind, and you aren't him."

"Ooooh, you're so scary-powerful then, huh?"

Slowly he nodded. "Yep."

"Then why aren't you, like, King of the World or something?"

"I'm king of the Raintree," he said, getting up and putting his plate in the dishwasher. "That's good enough for me."

Strange, but of all the really weird things he'd said to her, this struck her as the most unbelievable. She buried her head in her hands, wishing this day was over. She wanted to forget she'd ever met him. He was obviously a lunatic. No—she couldn't comfort herself with that delusion. She had been through fire with him, quite literally. He could do things she hadn't thought were possible. So maybe—just maybe—he really was some sort of leader, though "king" was stretching things a bit far.

"Okay, I'll bite," she said wearily. "Who are the Raintree, and who are the Ansara? Is this like two different countries but inhabited only by weirdos?"

His lips twitched as if he wanted to laugh. "Gifted. *Gifted*. We're two different clans—warring clans, if you want the bottom line. The enmity goes back thousands of years."

"You're the weirdo equivalent of the Hatfields and the McCoys?"

He did laugh then, white teeth flashing. "I've never thought of it that way, but…yeah. In a way. Except what's between the Raintree and the Ansara isn't a feud, it's a war. There's a difference."

"Between a war and a feud, yeah. But what's the difference between the Raintree clan and the Ansara clan?"

"An entire way of looking at life, I guess. They use their gifts to cheat, to do harm, for their personal gain. Raintree look at their abilities as true gifts and try to use them accordingly."

"You're the guys with the white hats."

"Within the spectrum of human nature—yes. Common sense tells me some Raintree aren't that far separated from some Ansara when it comes to their attitudes. But if they want to remain in the Raintree clan, they'll do as I order."

"So all the Ansara might not be totally bad, but if they want to stay in *their* clan, with their friends and families, they have to do as the Ansara king orders."

He dipped his head in acknowledgment. "That's about it."

"You admit you might be more alike than you're different."

"In some ways. In one big way, we're poles apart."

"Which is?"

"From the very beginning, if a Raintree and an Ansara crossbred, the Ansara killed the child. No exceptions."

Lorna rubbed her forehead, which was beginning to ache again. Yeah, that was bad. Killing innocent children because of their heritage wasn't just an opportunistic outlook, it was bad with a capital *B*. Part of her own life philosophy was that there were some people who didn't deserve to live, and people who hurt children belonged in that group.

"I don't suppose there has been much intermarriage between the clans, has there?"

"Not in centuries. What Raintree would take the chance? Are you finished with that bagel?"

Thrown off track by the prosaic question, Lorna stared down at her bagel. She had eaten maybe half of it. Even though she'd been starving before, the breakfast conversation had effectively killed her appetite. "I guess," she said without interest, passing the plate to him.

He dumped the bagel remnants and put that plate in the dishwasher, too. "You need training," he said. "Your gifts are too strong for you to go around unprotected. An Ansara could use you—"

"Just the way you did?" She didn't even try to keep the bitterness out of her tone.

"Just the way I did," he agreed. "Only they would be feeding the fire instead of fighting it."

As she stood there debating the merits of what he'd said, she realized that gradually she had become more at ease with discussing these "gifts" and that somewhere during the course of the conversation she had been moved from denial to acceptance. Now she saw where he was going with all this, and her old deep-rooted panic bloomed again.

"Oh, no," she said, shaking her head as she backed a few steps away. "I'm not going to let you 'train' me in anything. Do I have 'stupid' engraved on my forehead or something?"

"You're asking for trouble if you don't get some training, and fast."

"Then I'll handle it, just like I always have. Besides, you have your own trouble to handle, don't you?"

"The next few weeks will be tough, but not as tough for me as they will be for the people who lost someone. Another body was pulled out just after dawn. That makes two fatalities." His expression went grim.

"I'm not talking about that. I'm talking about the cops. Something hinky is going on there, because otherwise, why would two detectives be

interviewing people before the fire marshal had
determined if the fire was arson or accidental?"

The expression in his eyes grew distant as he
stared at her. That little detail had escaped his all-
knowing, all-seeing gifts, she realized, but if there
was one thing a hard life had taught her, it was
how the law worked. The detectives shouldn't have
been there until it was clear there was something
for them to detect, and the fire marshal wouldn't
make that determination until sometime today,
probably.

"Damn it," he said very softly, and pulled out his
phone. "Don't go anywhere. I have some calls to
make."

He'd meant that very literally, Lorna discovered when she tried to leave the kitchen. Her feet
stopped working at the threshold.

"Damn you, Raintree!" she snarled, whirling on
him.

"Dante," he corrected.

"Damn you, Dante!"

"Much better," he said, and winked at her.

Chapter 12

Dante began making calls, starting with Al Rayburn. Lorna was right: something hinky was going on, and he was pissed that she'd had to point it out to him. He should have thought of that detail himself. Instead of answering the detectives' questions, he should have been asking them his own, such as: What were they doing there? A fire scene wasn't a crime scene unless and until the cause was determined to be arson or at the very least suspicious. Uniformed officers should have been there for crowd control, traffic control, security—a lot of reasons—but not detectives.

He didn't come up with any answers to his

questions, but he hadn't expected to. What he was doing now was reversing the flow of information, and that would take time. Now that questions were being asked—by Al, by a friend Dante had at city hall, by one of his own Raintree clan members who liked life a little on the rough side and thus had some interesting contacts—a lot of things would be viewed in a different light.

Whatever was going on, however those two detectives were involved, Dante intended to find out, even if he had to bring in Mercy, whose gift of telepathy was so strong that she had once, when she was ten and he was sixteen, jumped into his head at a very inopportune moment—he'd been with his current girlfriend—and said, "Eww! Gross!" which had so startled him he'd lost his concentration, his erection *and* his girlfriend. Sixteen-year-old girls, he'd learned, didn't deal well with anything they saw as an insult to their general desirability. That was the day when he'd started blocking Mercy from his head, which had infuriated her at the time. She'd even told their parents what he'd been doing, which had resulted in a very long, very serious talk with his father about the importance of being smart, using birth control and taking responsibility for his actions.

Faced with his father's stern assurance that Dante *would* marry any girl he got pregnant and stay married to her for the rest of his life, he had then become immensely more careful. The Raintree Dranir most definitely did *not* have a casual attitude about his heirs. A Raintree, any Raintree, was a genetic dominant; any children would inherit the Raintree gifts. The same was true of the Ansara, which was why the Ansara had immediately killed any child born of a Raintree and Ansara breeding. When two dominant strands blended, anything could be the result—and the result could be dangerous.

Mercy's gift had only gotten stronger as she got older. Dante didn't think her presence would be required, though; the Raintree had other telepaths he could call on. They might not be as strong as Mercy, but then, they wouldn't need to be. Mercy was most comfortable at Sanctuary, the homeplace of the Raintree clan, where she didn't have to almost shut down her gift because of the relentless emotional and mental assault by humans who had no idea how to shield. Occasionally she and Eve, her six-year-old daughter, would visit him or Gideon—Mercy was completely female in her love of shopping, and he and Gideon were always glad to keep Eve the Imp while her mother indulged in some retail therapy—but Mercy was the guardian of the homeplace. Sanctuary was her responsibility, hers to rule, and she loved it. He wouldn't call for her help if he had other options.

The whole time he was making calls, Lorna stood where he'd compelled her to stay, fuming and fussing and growing angrier by the minute, until he expected all that dark red hair to stand straight up from the pressure. He could have released her, at least within the confines of the house, but she would probably use that much freedom to attack him with something. As it was, he had to admit he rather enjoyed her fury and less-than-flattering commentary.

The fact was, he enjoyed *her*.

He'd never before been so charmed—or so touched. When he'd heard that pitiful little whimpering sound she made in her sleep, he'd felt his heart actually clench. What really, really got to him was that it was obvious she knew what sound she'd been making—she probably did it all the time—and yet she resolutely denied it. *Snoring* his ass.

She refused to be a victim. He liked that. Even when something bad happened to her—such as himself, for instance—she furiously rejected any sign of vulnerability, any hint of sympathy, any suggestion that she was, in any way, weaker than King Kong. She didn't bother defending herself; instead she attacked, with a ferocious valiance and sharp tongue, as well as the occasional uppercut.

He'd been rough on her—in more ways than one. Not only had he terrified her, mentally brutalized her, he'd humiliated and embarrassed her by tearing off her clothes and examining her the way he had. If she'd only cooperated… But she hadn't, and he couldn't blame her. Nothing he'd done last night would have inspired trust in her, not that trust appeared to come easily to her in any case. He couldn't even tell himself that he'd never intended her any harm. If the blue crescent birthmark of the Ansara had been on her back—well, her body would never have been found.

The sharpness of his relief at not finding the birthmark had taken him by surprise. He'd wanted to take her in his arms and comfort her, though unless he bound her with a compulsion not to harm him, she would likely have taken his eyeballs out with her fingernails, and as for his other balls— he didn't want to think what she would have done to them. By that time she hadn't wanted anything from him except his absence.

The way she'd been allowed to grow up was a disgrace. She should have been trained in how to control and develop her gifts, trained in how to protect herself. She had the largest pool of raw energy he'd ever seen in a stray, which meant there was enormous potential for her to abuse or to be abused.

Now that he thought about it, her gift probably wasn't precognitive so much as it was claircognitive. She didn't have visions, like his cousin Echo; rather, she simply "knew" things—such as which card would be played next, whether a certain slot machine would pay off, how much her new shoes cost. Why she chose to play at casinos instead of buying a lottery ticket he couldn't say, unless she had instinctively chosen to stay as invisible as possible. Certainly she had the ability to win any amount of money she wanted, since her gift seemed to be slanted toward numbers.

Above all else, two sharp truths stood out:

She annoyed the hell out of him.

And he wanted her.

The two should have negated each other, but they didn't. Even when she annoyed him, which was often, she made him want to laugh. And he not only wanted her physically, he wanted her to accept her own uniqueness, accept him in all his differences, accept his protection, his guidance in learning how to shape and control her gift—all of which she rejected, which circled right back around to annoyance.

The doorbell rang, signaling the arrival of Lorna's shoes. Leaving her fuming, he went to the door, where one of his hotel staff waited, box in hand. "Sorry I'm late, Mr. Raintree," the young man said, wiping sweat from his forehead. "There was a wreck on the interstate that had traffic backed up—"

"No problem," he said, easing the young man's anxiety. "Thanks for bringing this out." Since he was continuing to pay his staff's salaries, he thought they might as well make themselves useful in whatever manner he needed.

He took the shoe box to the kitchen, where Lorna was still rooted to the spot. "Here you go, try them on," he said, handing the box to her.

She glared at him and refused to take it.

Guess he couldn't blame her.

He took the shoes from the box, the wads of tissue paper from the toes, and went down on one knee. He expected her to stubbornly refuse to pick up her foot, but she let him lift it, wipe his hand over her bare sole to remove any grit, and slide the buttery-soft black flat on her foot. He repeated the process with her other foot, then remained on one knee as he looked up at her. "Do they fit? Do they pinch anywhere?"

The shoes were much like her ruined ones, he knew: simple black flats. But that was where the resemblance ended. This pair was made of quality leather, with good arch support and good construction. Her other pair had had paper-thin soles, and the seams had been starting to fray. She'd been carrying over seven thousand dollars in her pocket, and wearing fifteen-dollar shoes. Whatever she was spending all that money on, clothing wasn't it.

"They feel okay," she said grudgingly. "But not a hundred and twenty-eight dollars worth of okay."

He laughed quietly as he rose to his feet and looked down at her face for a moment, charmed all over again by her stubbornness. She was one of those women whose personality made her prettier than she actually was, if one considered only her features. Not that she wasn't pretty; she was. Not flashy, not beautiful, just pleasant to look at. It was that attitude, that sarcastic, sassy mouth, the damn-you-to-hell-and-back eyes, that made her sparkle with vitality. The one way Lorna Clay would never be described was *restful*.

He should release her from the compulsion that kept her here, but if he did, she would leave—not just this house, but Reno. He knew it with a certainty that chilled him.

Dante functioned very well in the normal, human world, but he was the Raintree Dranir, and within his realm, he was obeyed. He had been Dranir for seventeen years now, since he was twenty, but even before that, he hadn't led an ordinary life. He was of the Raintree Royal Family. He had been Prince, Heir Apparent and then Dranir.

"No" wasn't a word he heard very often, nor did he care to hear it from Lorna.

"You may go anywhere you wish within this house," he said, and silently added a proviso that in case of danger, the compulsion was ended. If the house caught fire, he wanted her to be able to escape. After last night, such things were very much on his mind.

"Why can't I leave?" Her hazel green eyes were snapping with ire, but at least she didn't punch, pinch or kick him.

"Because you'll run."

She didn't deny it, instead narrowed her eyes at him. "So? I'm not wanted for any crimes."

"*So* I feel responsible for you. There's a lot you need to know about your gifts, and I can teach you." That was as good a reason as any, and sounded logical.

"I don't—" She started to deny she had any gifts, but stopped and drew a deep breath. There was no point in denying the obvious. When he had first broached the subject to her, in his office, her denial had been immediate and absolute. At least now she was beginning to accept what she was.

How had she come to so adamantly deny everything she was? He suspected he knew, but unless she was willing to talk about it, he wouldn't pry.

After a moment she said obstinately, "I'm responsible for myself. I don't want or need your charity."

"Charity, no. Knowledge, yes. I think I was wrong when I said you're precognitive." He watched relief flare on her face, then immediately die when he continued. "I think you may be claircognitive. Have you ever even heard of that?"

"No."

"How about *el-sike*?"

"That's an Arab name."

He grinned. *El-sike* was pronounced *el-see-kay*—and she was right, it did sound Arab. "It's a form of storm control. My brother Gideon has that gift. He can call lightning to him."

She gave him a pitying look. "It sounds like a form of brain damage. What fool wants to be near lightning?"

"Gideon. He feeds off electricity. He also has electrical psychokinesis, which in a nutshell means he plays hell with electronics. He explodes streetlights. He fries computers. It isn't safe for him to fly unless I send him a shielding charm."

Her interest was caught, however reluctantly. He saw the quicksilver gleam of it in her eyes. "Why doesn't he make his own shielding charms?"

"That's kind of along the same lines of precogs not being able to see their own futures. Only those in the royal family can gift charms, but never for themselves. He's a cop, a homicide detective, so I keep him stocked in protection charms, and if he has to fly, I send him a charm that shields his electrical energy so he won't fry all the plane's computers."

"Electrical psychokinesis," she said slowly, trying out the words. "Sounds kinky."

"So I've heard," he said dryly. He'd also heard that Gideon sometimes glowed after sex—or maybe that was before. Or during. Some things a brother just didn't ask too many questions about. But if Lorna was at last interested in learning about the whole range of paranormal abilities, he didn't mind using some of the more exotic gifts to keep her intrigued.

"Tell you what," he said, as if he'd just thought of the idea, when in fact he'd been considering something of the sort all morning. "Why don't you agree to a short trial period—say, a week—and let me teach you some basic stuff to protect yourself? You're so sensitive to every passing wave of energy that I'm surprised you're able to go out in public. I can also set up some simple tests, get a ballpark idea of how gifted you are in different areas."

He saw the instant repudiation of that idea in her expression, a quick flash, then her curiosity rose to counter it. Almost immediately, caution followed;

she didn't easily put herself in anyone's hands. "What would I have to do?" she asked warily.

"You don't *have* to do anything. If you're absolutely dead set against the idea of learning more, then I'm not going to tie you to a chair and make you read lessons. But since you're going to be here for a few days anyway, you might as well use the time to learn something about yourself."

"I'll need my clothes," she said, which was as close to capitulation as he was likely to hear from her.

"Give me your address and I'll have them brought here."

"This is just for a few days. After that, I want your word you'll lift this stupid compulsion thing and let me go."

Dante considered that. He was the Dranir; he didn't, couldn't, give his word lightly. Finally he said, "After a week, I'll consider it. You're smart, you can learn a lot in a week. But I can't make a definite promise."

Chapter 13

"What, exactly, went wrong?"

Cael Ansara's tone was pleasant and even, which didn't fool Ruben McWilliams at all. Cousin or not, there had always been something about Cael that made Ruben tread very warily around him. When Cael was at his most pleasant, that was when it paid to be extra cautious. Ruben didn't like the son of a bitch, but there you go, rebellion made for strange bedfellows.

His intuition had told him to delay contacting Cael, so he hadn't called last night; instead, he'd put people in the field, asking questions, and his gamble had paid off—or at least provided an interesting variable. He didn't yet know exactly what they'd discovered, only that they'd found *something*.

"We don't know—not exactly. Everything went perfectly from our end. Elyn was connected to me, Stoffel and Pier, drawing our power and feeding the fire. She said they had Raintree overmatched, that he was losing ground—and fast. Then…something happened. It's possible he saw he couldn't handle the fire and retreated. Or he's more powerful than we thought."

Cael was silent, and Ruben shifted uneasily on the motel bed. He'd expected Cael to leap on the juicy possibility that the mighty Dante Raintree had panicked and run from a fire, but as usual, Cael was unpredictable.

"What does Elyn say?" Cael finally asked. "If Raintree ran, if he stopped trying to fight the fire, without his resistance it would have flashed over. She'd have known that, right? She'd have felt the surge."

"She doesn't know." He and Elyn had discussed the events from beginning to end, trying to pinpoint what had gone wrong. She *should* have felt a surge, if one had happened—but she not only hadn't felt a surge, she hadn't felt the retreat when the fire department beat back the flames. There *had* to have been some sort of interference, but they were at a loss to explain it.

"Doesn't know? How can she not know? She's a Fire-Master, and that was her flame. She should know everything about it from conception on."

Cael's tone was sharp, but no sharper than their own tones had been when he and Elyn had dissected the events. Elyn hadn't wanted the finger of blame pointed at her, of course, but she'd been truly perplexed. "All she knows is, just as she was drawing the fire into the hotel, she lost touch with it. She could tell it was still there, but she didn't know what it was doing." He paused. "She's telling the truth. I was linked to her. I could feel her surprise. She thinks there had to be some sort of interference, maybe a protective shield."

"She's making excuses. Shields like that exist only at homeplace. We've never detected anything like that on any of the other Raintree properties."

"I agree. Not about Elyn making excuses, but about the impossibility of there being a shield. She simply asked. I told her, no, I'd have known if one were there."

"Where were the other Raintree?"

"They were all accounted for." None of the other Raintree had been close enough for their Dranir to link to them and use their power to boost his own, as Elyn had done by linking to him and the others. They'd pulled in people to follow the various Raintree clan—members in Reno. There were only eight, not counting the Dranir, and none of them had been close to the Inferno.

"So, despite all your assurances to me, you failed, and you don't know why."

"Not yet." Ruben ever so slightly stressed the *yet*. "There's one other possibility. Another person, a woman, was with Raintree. None of us saw them being brought out because the fire engines blocked our view, but we've been posing as insurance adjusters and asking questions." They hadn't raised a single eyebrow; insurance adjusters were already swarming, and not just the ones representing Raintree's insurance provider. Multiple vehicles had been damaged. Casino patrons had lost personal property. There had been injuries, and two deaths. Add the personal injury lawyers to the mix, and there were a lot of people asking a lot of questions; no one noticed a few more people *or* questions, and no one checked credentials.

"What's her name?"

"Lorna Clay. One of the medics got her name and address. She wasn't registered at the hotel, and the address on the paperwork was in Missouri. It isn't valid. I've already checked."

"Go on."

"She was evidently with Raintree from the beginning, in his office in the hotel, because they evacuated the building together. They were in the west stairwell with a lot of other people. He directed everyone else out, through the parking deck, but he and this woman went in the other direction. Several things are suspicious. One, she wasn't burned—at all. Two, neither was Raintree."

"Protective bubble. Judah can construct them, too." Cael's tone went flat when he said Judah's name—Judah was his *legitimate* half brother and the Ansara Dranir. Envy of Judah, bitterness that he was the Dranir instead of Cael, had eaten at Cael all his life.

Ruben was impressed by the bubble. Smoke? Smoke had a physical presence; any Fire-Master could shield from smoke. But heat was a different entity, part of the very air. Fire-Masters, even royal ones, still had to breathe. To somehow separate the heat from the air, to bring in one but hold the other at bay, was a feat that went way beyond controlling fire.

"The woman," Cael prompted sharply, pulling Ruben from his silent admiration.

"I've seen copies of the statement she gave afterward. It matches his, and neither is possible, given what we know of the timetable. I estimate he was engaged with the fire for at least half an hour." That was an eternity, in terms of survival.

"He should have been overwhelmed. He should have spent so much energy trying to control the fire that he couldn't maintain the bubble. He's the hero type," Cael said contemptuously. "He'd sacrifice himself to save the people in the hotel. *This should have worked*. His people wouldn't have been suspicious. They would have expected him to do the brave and honorable thing. The woman has to be the key. She has to be gifted. He linked with her, and she fed him power."

"She isn't Raintree," said Ruben. "She has to be a stray, but they aren't that powerful. If there had been several of them, maybe there would have been enough energy for him to hold back the fire." He doubted it, though. After all, there had been four powerful Ansara, linked together, feeding it. As powerful as Dante undoubtedly was, adding the power of one stray, even a strong one, would be like adding a cup of water to a full bathtub.

"Follow your own logic," Cael said sharply. "Strays aren't that powerful, therefore she can't be a stray."

"She isn't Raintree," Ruben insisted.

"Or she isn't *official* Raintree." Cael didn't use the word "illegitimate." The old Dranir had recognized him as his son, but that hadn't given Cael precedence over Judah, even though he was the elder. The injustice had always eaten at him, like a corrosive acid. Everyone around Cael had learned never to suggest that maybe Judah was Dranir because of his power, not his birthright.

"She'd have to be of the royal bloodline to have enough power for him to hold the fire for that long against four of us," said Ruben dubiously, because that was impossible. The birth of a royal was taken far too seriously for one to go unnoticed. They were simply too powerful.

"So maybe she is. Even if the split occurred a thousand years ago, the inherited power would be undiminished."

As genetic dominants, even if a member of one of the clans bred with a human—which they often did—the offspring were completely either Ansara or Raintree. The royal families of both clans were the most powerful of the gifted, which was how they'd become royal in the first place; as dominants, their power was passed down intact. To Ruben's way of thinking, that only reinforced his argument that, no matter what, a royal birth wouldn't go unnoticed for any length of time, certainly not for a millennium.

"Regardless of what she is, where is she now?"

"At his house. He took her there last night, and she's still there."

Cael was silent, so Ruben simply waited while his cousin ran that through his convoluted brain.

"Okay," Cael said abruptly. "She has to be the

key. Wherever it comes from, her power is strong enough that he held the four of you to a draw. But that's in the past. You can't use fire again without the bastard getting suspicious, so you'll have to think of something else that'll either look accidental or can't be linked to us. I don't care how you do it, just do it. The next time I hear your voice, you'd better be telling me that Dante Raintree is dead. And while you're at it, kill the woman, too."

Cael slammed down the phone. Ruben replaced the receiver more slowly, then pinched the bridge of his nose. Tactically, killing the royal Raintrees first was smart. If you cut off the head of a snake, taking care of the body was easy. The comparison wasn't completely accurate, because any Raintree was a force to be reckoned with, but so were the Ansara. With the royals all dead, the advantage would be theirs and the outcome inevitable.

The mistake they'd made two hundred years ago was in not taking care of the royal family first, a mistake that had had disastrous results. As a clan, the Ansara had almost been destroyed. The survivors had been banished to their Caribbean island, where most of them remained. But they had used those two hundred years to secretly rebuild in strength, and now they were strong enough to once more engage their enemy. Cael thought so, anyway, and so did Ruben. Only Judah had held them back, preaching caution. Judah was a *banker*, for God's sake; what did he know about taking risks?

Discontent in the Ansara ranks had been growing for years, and it had reached the crisis point. The Raintree had to die, and so did Judah. Cael would never let him live, even in exile.

Ruben's power was substantial. Because of that, and because he was Cael's cousin, he'd been given the task of eliminating the most powerful Raintree of all—a task made more difficult because Cael insisted the death look accidental. The last thing he wanted was all the Raintree swarming to the homeplace to protect it. The power of Sanctuary was almost mystical. How much of it was real and how much of it was perceived, Ruben didn't know and didn't care.

The plan was simple: kill the royals, breach the protective shields around Sanctuary and take the homeplace. After that, the rest of the Raintree would be considerably weakened. Destroying them would be child's play.

Not destroying the Ansara homeplace two centuries ago, not destroying every member of the clan, was the mistake the Raintree had made. The Ansara wouldn't return the favor.

Ruben sat for a long time, deep in thought. Getting to Raintree would be easier if he was distracted. He and the woman, Lorna Clay, were evidently lovers; otherwise, why take her home with him? She would be the easier of the two to take out, anyway—and if she were obviously the target rather than Raintree, that wouldn't raise the clan's alarm.

Cael's idea had been a good one: kill the woman.

Chapter 14

Monday afternoon

"What happens if you die?" Lorna asked him, scowling as, car keys in hand, he opened the door to the garage. "What if you have a blowout and drive off the side of the mountain? What if you have a pulmonary embolism? What if a chicken-hauler has brake failure and flattens that little roller skate you call a car? Am I stuck here? Does your little curse, or whatever, hold me here even if you're dead or unconscious?"

Dante paused halfway out the door, looking back at her with a half amused, half disbelieving expression. "Chicken-hauler? Can't you think of a more dignified way for me to die?"

She sniffed. "Dead is dead. What would you care?" Then something occurred to her, something that made her very uneasy. "Uh—you *can* die, can't you?" What if this situation was even weirder than she'd thought? What if, on the *woo-woo* scale of one to ten, he was a thirteen?

He laughed outright. "Now I have to wonder if you're planning to kill me."

"It's a thought," she said bluntly. "Well?"

He leaned against the door frame, negligent and relaxed, and so damned sexy she almost had to look away. She worked hard to ignore her physical response to him, and most of the time she succeeded, but sometimes, as now, his green eyes seemed to almost glow, and in her imagination she could feel the hard, muscled framework of his body against her once more. The fact that, twice now, she'd felt his erection against her when he was holding her only made her struggle that much more difficult. Mutual sexual desire was a potent magnet, but just because she felt the pull of attraction, that didn't mean she should act on it. Sometimes she wanted to run a traffic light, too, because it was there, because she didn't want to stop, because she could—but she never did, because doing so would be stupid.

Having sex with Dante Raintree would fall into the same category: stupid.

"I'm as mortal as you—almost. Thank God. As much as mortality sucks, immortality would be even worse."

Lorna took a step back. "What do you mean, *almost?*"

"That's another conversation, and one I don't have time for right now. To answer your other question, I don't know. Maybe, maybe not."

She was almost swallowed by outrage. "What? *What?* You don't know whether or not I'll be stuck here if something happens to you, but you're going to go off and leave me here anyway?"

He gave it a brief thought, said, "Yeah," and went out the door.

Lorna leaped and caught the door before it closed. "Don't leave me here! Please." She hated to beg, and she hated him for making her beg, but she was suddenly alarmed beyond reason by the thought of being stuck here for the rest of her life.

He got into the Jaguar, called, "You'll be okay," and then the clatter of the garage door rising drowned out anything else she might have said.

Furious, she slammed the kitchen door and, in a fit of pique, turned both the lock on the handle and the dead bolt. Locking him out of his own house was useless, since he had his keys with him, but the annoyance value was worth it.

She heard the Jag backing out; then the garage door began coming down.

Damn him, damn him, *damn him!* He'd really gone off and left her stranded here. No, not stranded—*chained.*

Her clothes had been delivered earlier, and she'd changed out of the ruined pants—and out of his too-big silk shirt—so he wouldn't have had to wait for her to get ready or anything. He had no reason for leaving her here, given that he could easily prevent her from escaping with one of his damnable mind commands.

Impotently, she glared around the kitchen. Being a drainer—king—whatever the hell he'd said—had made him too big for his britches. He pretty much did whatever he felt like doing, without worrying about what others wanted. It was obvious he'd never been married and likely never would be, because any woman worth her salt would—

Salt.

She looked around the kitchen and spotted the big stainless steel salt and pepper shakers sitting by the cooktop. She began opening doors until she found the pantry—and a very satisfying supply of salt.

She'd noticed he put a spoonful of sugar in his coffee. Now she very carefully poured the salt out of the salt shaker, replaced it with sugar from the sugar bowl, then put the salt in the sugar bowl. He wouldn't much enjoy that first cup of coffee in the morning, and anything he salted would taste really off.

Then she got creative.

About an hour after he left, the phone rang. Lorna looked at the caller ID but didn't bother answering; she wasn't his secretary. Whoever was calling didn't leave a message.

She explored the house—well, searched the house. It was a big house for just one person. She had no frame of reference for estimating the square footage, but she counted six bedrooms and seven and a half baths. His bedroom took up the entire top floor, a vast expanse that covered more floor space than most families of four lived in. It was very much a man's room, with steel blue and light olive-green tones dominating, but here and there—in the artwork, in an unexpected decorative bowl, in a cushion—were splashes of deep, rich red.

There was a separate sitting area, with a big-screen television that popped out of a cabinet when a button was pushed and sank back into hiding afterward. She knew, because she found the remote and punched all the buttons, just to see what they would do. There was a wet bar with a small refrigerator and a coffeemaker in case he didn't want to bother going downstairs to make his coffee or get something to eat. She'd replaced the sugar with salt there, too—*and* mixed dirt from the potted plants in with his coffee.

Then she sat in the middle of his king-size bed, on a mattress that felt like a dream, and thought.

As big and comfortable as the house was, it wasn't what she would call a mansion. It wasn't ostentatious. He liked his creature comforts, but the house still looked like a place to be lived in, rather than a showcase.

She knew he had money, and a lot of it—enough to afford a house ten times the size of this one. Throw in the fact that he lived here alone, with no daily staff to take care of him and his home, and she had to draw the obvious conclusion that his privacy was more important to him than being pampered. So why was he forcing her to stay here?

He'd said he felt responsible for her, but he could feel that way wherever she stayed, and because of that damned newly discovered talent of his for making people do whatever he wanted, she couldn't have left if he'd commanded her to stay. Maybe he was interested in her untrained "power" and wanted to see what he could make of it just to satisfy his curiosity. Again, she didn't have to stay here for him to give her lessons or conduct a few experiments on her.

He wanted to have sex with her, so maybe that was what motivated him. He could compel her to come to him, to have sex, but he wasn't a rapist. He was possibly a lunatic, definitely a bully, but he wasn't a rapist. He wanted her to be willing, truly willing. So was he keeping her here in order to seduce her? He couldn't do that if he went off somewhere and left her here, not to mention doing so made her mad at him.

Somehow the sex angle didn't feel right, either. If he wanted to get her in bed, making her a prisoner wasn't the right way to win her over. Not only that, she wasn't a femme fatale; she simply couldn't see anyone going to such extraordinary lengths to have sex with her.

He had to have another reason, but damned if she could figure out what it was. And until she knew…well, there wasn't anything she could do, regardless. Unless she could somehow knock him out and escape, she was stuck here until he was ready to let her leave.

Last night, from the moment the gorilla had "escorted" her away from the blackjack table and manhandled her up to Raintree's office, had been a pure nightmare. One shock had followed so closely on the heels of another—each somehow worse than the one before—that she felt as if she'd lost touch with reality somewhere along the way.

Yesterday at this time she had been anonymous, and she liked it that way. Oh, people would come up and talk to her, the way they did to winners, and she was okay with that, but being alone was okay, too. In fact, being alone was better than okay; it was *safe*.

Raintree didn't know what he was asking of her, staying here, learning how to be "gifted." Not that he was asking—he wasn't giving her a choice.

He'd tricked her into admitting that she had a certain talent with numbers, but he didn't know how nauseated she got at the thought of coming out of the paranormal closet. She would rather remain a metaphysical garment bag, hanging in the very back.

He had grown up in an underground culture where paranormal talents were the norm, where they were encouraged, celebrated, trained. He had grown up a *prince*, for God's sake. A prince of weird, but a prince nonetheless. He had no idea what it had been like growing up in slums, skinny and unwanted and different. There hadn't been a father in her picture, just an endless parade of her mother's "boyfriends." He'd never been slapped away from the table, literally slapped out of her chair, for saying anything her mother could construe as weird.

As a child, she hadn't understood why what she said was weird. What was so wrong with saying the bus her mother took across town to her job in a bar would be six minutes and twenty-three seconds late? She had thought her mother would want to know. Instead she'd been backhanded out of her seat.

Numbers were her thing. If anything had a number in it, she knew what that number was. She remembered starting first grade—no kindergarten for her, her mother had said kindergarten was a stupid-ass waste of time—and the relief she'd felt when someone finally explained numbers to her, as if a huge part of herself had finally clicked into place. Now she had names for the shapes, meanings for the names. All her life she'd been fascinated with numbers, whether they were on a house, a billboard, a taxicab or anywhere else, but it was as if they were a foreign language she couldn't grasp. Odd, to have such an affinity for them but no understanding. She had thought she was as stupid as her mother had told her she was, until she'd gone to school and found the key.

By the time she was ten, her mother had been deep into booze and drugs, and the slaps had progressed to almost daily beatings. If her mother staggered in at night and decided she didn't like something Lorna had done that day or the day before—or the week before, it didn't matter—she would grab whatever was handy and lay into Lorna wherever she was. A lot of times Lorna's transition from sleep to wakefulness had been a blow—to her face, her head, wherever her mother could hit her. She had learned to sleep in a state of quiet terror.

Whenever she thought of her childhood, what she remembered most was cold and darkness and fear. She had been afraid her mother would kill her, and even more afraid her mother might not bother to come home some night. If there was one thing Lorna knew beyond doubt, it was that her mother hadn't wanted her before she was born and sure as hell didn't want her *after*. She knew because that had been the background music of her life.

She had learned to hide what numbers meant to her. The only time she'd ever told anyone—*ever*—had been in the ninth grade, when she had developed a crush on a boy in her class. He'd been sweet, a little shy, not one of the popular kids. His parents were very religious, and he was never allowed to attend any school parties, or learn how to dance, anything like that, which was okay with Lorna, because she never did any of that stuff, either.

They had talked a lot, held hands some, kissed a little. Then Lorna, summoning up the nerve, had shared her deepest secret with him: sometimes she knew things before they happened.

She still remembered the look of absolute disgust that had come over his face. "Satan!" he'd spat at her, and then he'd never spoken to her again. At least he hadn't told anyone, but that was probably because he didn't seem to have any buddies he *could* tell.

She'd been sixteen when her mother really did walk out and not bothered to come back. Lorna had come home from school—"home" changed locations fairly often, usually when rent was overdue—to find her mother's stuff cleared out, the locks changed and her own meager collection of clothes dumped in the trash.

Without a place to live, she had done the only thing she could do: she had contacted the city officials herself and entered the foster system.

Living in foster homes for two years hadn't been great, but it hadn't been as bad as her life had been before. At least she got to finish high school. None of her foster parents had beaten or abused her. None of them ever seemed to like her very much, either, but then, her mother had told her she wasn't likeable.

She coped. After she was eighteen, she was out of the system and on her own. In the thirteen years since then—for her entire life, actually—she had done what she could to stay below the radar, to avoid being noticed, to never, ever be a victim. No one could reject her if she didn't offer herself.

She had stumbled into gambling in a small way,

in a little casino on the Seminole reservation in Florida. She had won, not a whole lot, but a couple hundred dollars meant a lot to her. Later on she'd gone in some of the casinos on the Mississippi River and won some more. Small casinos were everywhere. She'd gone to Atlantic City but hadn't liked it. Las Vegas was okay, but too *too*: too much neon, too many people, too hot, too gaudy. Reno suited her better. Smaller, but not too small. Better climate. Eight years after that first small win in Florida, she regularly won five to ten thousand dollars a week.

That kind of money was a burden, because she couldn't bring herself to spend much more than she had always spent. She didn't go hungry now, or cold. She had a car if she wanted to pack up and leave, but never a new one. She had bank accounts all over the place, plus she usually carried a lot of cash—dangerous, she knew, but she felt more secure if she had enough cash with her to take care of whatever she might need. Unless and until she settled somewhere, the money was a problem, because how many savings books and checkbooks could she be expected to cart around the country?

That was her life. Dante Raintree thought all he had to do was educate her a little on her talent with numbers, and—well, what *did* he expect to happen? He knew nothing about her life, so he couldn't have any specific changes in mind. Was she supposed to become Little Mary Sunshine? Find other people like her, maybe develop their own little gated community, where, if you ran out of charcoal lighter fluid at the neighborhood barbecue, one of the neighbors could breathe fire on the briquettes to light them? Maybe she could blog about her experiences, or do talk radio.

Uh-uh. She would rather eat ground glass. She liked living alone, being alone and depending only on herself.

The phone rang again, startling her. She scrambled across the bed to look at the caller ID, though why she bothered, she had no idea; she wouldn't recognize the number of anyone calling Dante Raintree, anyway. She didn't answer that call, either.

She had sat on the bed, thinking, for so long that the afternoon shadows were beginning to lengthen, and she was drowsy. Thank goodness for that phone call, or she might have fallen asleep on his bed, and wouldn't that have been an interesting situation when he got home? She had no intention of playing Goldilocks.

But she *was* sleepy, as well as hungry. After a late breakfast, she hadn't had lunch. Why not eat a light dinner now and go to bed early? She couldn't think of any reason why she should wait for Raintree, since he hadn't had the courtesy to tell her when he might be back.

The least he could do was call—not that she would answer the phone, but he could always leave a message.

Definitely no point in waiting for him. She raided the refrigerator and made a sandwich of cold cuts, then looked at all the books in his bookshelves—he had a lot of books on paranormal stuff, but she chose a suspense novel instead—and settled down in the den to read for a while. By eight o'clock she was nodding over her book, which evidently wasn't suspenseful enough to keep her awake. The sun hadn't quite set yet, but she didn't care; she was still tired from the night before.

Fifteen minutes and one shower later, she was in bed, curled in a warm ball, with the sheet pulled over her head.

The flare of a lamp being turned on woke her. She endured the usual grinding fear, the panic, knowing that her mother wasn't there even though, all these years later, her subconscious still hadn't gotten the message. Before she could relax enough to pull the sheet from over her head, the covers were lifted and a very warm, mostly naked Dante Raintree slid into bed with her.

"What the hell are you doing?" she sputtered sleepily, glaring at him over the edge of the sheet.

He settled himself beside her and stretched one long, muscled arm to turn out the lamp. "There appears to be sand in my bed, so I'm sleeping here."

Chapter 15

"Don't be silly. I couldn't leave the house, so how would I get sand? It's salt." Maybe he expected her to deny any involvement, but that *would* be silly, given that she'd been the only person in the house after he left. Maybe he also expected her to get all indignant and starchy because he was in bed with her, but for some reason, she wasn't alarmed. Annoyed at being awakened, yes, but not alarmed.

"I stand corrected." He used his superior muscle and weight to shove her over in the bed. "Move over. I need more room."

He had already forced her out of her nice warm spot, which annoyed her even more. "Then why didn't you get in on the other side, instead of making me move?" she grumbled as she scooted to the other side of the bed, which was king-size, like every other bed in the house.

"You're the one who put salt in my bed."

The sheets were cold around her, making her curl in a tighter ball than usual. Even the pillow was cold. Lorna lifted her head and pulled the pillow from beneath her, tossing it on top of him. "Give me my pillow. This one's cold."

He made a grumbling sound, but pushed the warm pillow toward her and tucked the other pillow under his head. She snuggled down into the warmth; the soft fabric already had his scent on it, which wasn't a bad thing, she discovered. She had known him only a short time, but a lot of it had been spent in close contact with him. The primitive part of her brain recognized his scent and was comforted.

"What time is it?" she asked drowsily, already drifting back to sleep.

"You know what time it is. It's a number. Think about it." He sounded drowsy himself.

She had never thought of time as a number, but as soon as she did, the image of three numbers popped into her head. "One-oh-four."

"Bingo."

Mildly pleased, she went to sleep.

She woke before he did, which wasn't surprising, given how early she'd gone to bed and how late he'd gotten in. She lay there through the tense expectation of being hit, then slowly relaxed. The bed was toasty warm; he gave off so much heat that she could feel the warmth even though they weren't touching.

Sleepily curious to see if the time thing worked again, she thought of time as a series of numbers and immediately saw a four, a five and a one. She pulled the sheet from over her head; the room was getting a little brighter. Without any way to check—short of getting out of bed and going down to the kitchen, which she wasn't willing to do—she supposed four fifty-one was close enough. How handy was that, to not need a clock?

Dante was lying on his side, facing her, one arm bent under his head, his breathing slow and deep. The room was still too dim for her to make out many details, but that was okay, because she wasn't ready for details yet; the general impression was sexy enough as things were.

What was a woman supposed to think when a healthy, heterosexual man slept with her for the first time and didn't even try to cop a feel? That something was wrong with her? That he wasn't attracted to her?

She thought he was dangerously intelligent and intuitive.

Sex was definitely part of their relationship, if knowing someone for roughly thirty-six hours could be described as a relationship. Some of those thirty-six hours had seemed years long, especially the first four or five. She couldn't say that their time together had been quality time, either. On the other hand, since she hadn't seen him at his best, she thought she might know him better than someone who had known him for a much longer time but only in a social setting, so she wasn't surprised that he hadn't made a pass at her during the night.

She wasn't ready for sex with him, might never be ready, and he knew that. If he'd tried to storm the barricades, as it were, she would have stiffened her resistance. By simply sleeping with her and not making any overtly sexual moves, he was, in a way, counteracting those first terrible hours together and making sex a possibility, at least.

He wasn't even naked, though the boxers he'd worn to bed didn't cover much. She wasn't naked, either; he'd had *all* her clothes brought to her, so she was sleeping in her usual cotton pajamas. Perversely, because he *hadn't* tried to have sex, she began to wonder what it would be like if they did—then suspected that he'd known that would be her reaction.

Sex wasn't easy for her. She didn't trust easily; she didn't arouse easily. Voluntarily giving up her personal sense of privacy was difficult, and the payback was usually not worth the cost. She liked the feel of sex, and when she thought about it in the abstract, she wanted it. The reality, though, was that the execution didn't live up to the expectation. Regardless of what she was doing, she seldom relaxed completely, which she thought good sex probably required.

The thing was, she was more relaxed with Dante than she'd been in a long, long time. He knew what she was, knew she was different, and he didn't care—because he was even more different than she was. She didn't have to hide anything with him, because she didn't care if he liked her or not. She certainly hadn't tried to hide her temper or sweeten her tart tongue. Likewise, she had no soft-focus ideas about his character. She knew he was ruthless, but she also knew he wasn't mean. She knew he was autocratic, but that he tried to be considerate.

So maybe she could let herself go and really enjoy sex with him. She didn't have to worry about his ego; if he started going too fast, she could tell him to slow down, and if he didn't like that… tough. She wouldn't have to worry about his pleasure; he would see to that himself.

She wondered if he took his time, or if he liked to get down to business.

She wondered how big he was.

Maybe she could relax enough to enjoy it, and even if she didn't, at least she could satisfy her curiosity.

With a suddenness that startled her, he threw back the covers and got out of bed. "Where are you going?" she asked, surprised when he headed toward the door instead of the bathroom.

"It's sunrise," was all he said.

And? The sun rose every day. Did he mean he always got up at this time, even when he'd had only four hours' sleep? Or did he have an early appointment?

She didn't follow him. She had her own appointment—with the bathroom. She also wanted to give him enough time to have that first cup of coffee.

When she left her room forty-five minutes later, after having made the bed and put away her clothes, she went to the kitchen but found it empty. A pot of coffee had been made, however, and she smiled with satisfaction.

Where was he? In the shower?

She didn't intend to stand around waiting for him to make an appearance. She was in the living room, heading toward her bedroom, when he appeared on the balcony two floors above.

"Come up here," he called down. "I'll be outside."

His bedroom had a deck—or was it a balcony, too?—that faced east. She had looked at it yesterday, but hadn't gone out, because his damn command had kept her from stepping outside. There were two comfortable-looking chairs and a small table out there, and she'd thought it must be a comfortable place to sit in the afternoon when the sun had passed its apex and that side of the house was shaded.

She went up the two flights of stairs to his bedroom. His bed, she noticed, had been stripped; that gave her a sense of satisfaction. She could see him sitting in one of the chairs outside, so she went to the open French door. Coffee cup in hand, he sat with his head tilted back a little, his eyes almost closed against the brilliance of the bright morning sun, the expression on his face almost... blissful.

"You're handy with the salt, aren't you?" he said neutrally, sipping the coffee, but she sensed he wasn't angry. Of course, the coffee from the kitchen wasn't dirt-flavored. When he made the next pot of coffee in here, he might not be as sanguine about things.

"Payback."

"I guessed."

He didn't say anything else, and after a moment she shifted her weight. "Was that all you wanted, just to say that?"

He looked around, as if he'd drifted off into a

reverie and was faintly surprised by her presence. "Don't just stand there, come out here and sit down."

Just thinking about doing so gave her the sense of running into a wall. "I can't."

That got a quick smile from him as he realized she was still housebound. He didn't say anything, but immediately the mental wall disappeared.

"Crap," she said, stepping outside and going to sit beside him.

"What?"

"You didn't say anything, you just thought it. I'd hoped you had to speak the command out loud, that I had to *hear* it, before it would work."

"Sorry. All I have to do is think it. I was tempted to use the gift yesterday afternoon and tell a few people to go jump in the lake, but I restrained myself."

"You're a saint among men," she said dryly, and he gave her a quick grin.

"I was dealing with the media, so, considering the level of temptation, I tend to agree with you."

Media, huh? No wonder he had refused to take her with him.

"I called last night to tell you I wouldn't make it back until late, but you didn't answer the phone."

"Why would I? I'm not your secretary."

"The call was for *you*."

"I didn't know that, did I?"

"I left a message for you."

"I didn't hear it." The answering machine was in the kitchen; she'd been in his bedroom when the last phone call came in, which must have been him calling her.

"That's because you didn't bother to play it back." He sounded annoyed now.

"Why would I? I'm not—"

"My secretary. I know. You're a pain in the ass, you know that?"

"I try," she said, giving him a smile that was more a baring of her teeth than anything related to humor.

He grunted and sipped coffee for a while. Lorna pulled her bare feet up in the chair and looked out over the mountains and broad valleys, enjoying being outside after an entire day cooped up in the house. The morning was cool enough to make her wish she had on socks, but not so cool that she was forced to go inside.

"Do you want to go with me today?" he finally asked, with obvious reluctance.

"Depends. What are you doing?"

"Overseeing cleanup, talking to insurance adjusters, and I still don't have an answer to why two detectives were asking questions immediately after the fire, so I'm pursuing that by going directly to the source."

"Sounds like fun."

"I'm glad someone thinks so," he said wryly. "Get ready and we'll eat breakfast out. For some reason, I don't trust the food here."

Chapter 16

Tuesday morning, 7:30 a.m.

The man sitting concealed behind some scrub brush had been in place since before dawn, when he had relieved the unlucky fool who had been on surveillance duty all night. When he saw the garage door sliding up, he grabbed the binoculars hanging by a strap around his neck and trained them on the house. Red brake lights glowed in the dimness of the garage; then a sleek Jaguar began backing out.

He picked up a radio and keyed the microphone. "He's leaving now."

"Is he alone?"

"I can't tell—no, the woman is with him."

"Ten-four. I'll be ready."

His job done for the moment, he let the binoculars fall before the light glinting on the lenses gave him away. He could relax now. Following Raintree wasn't his job.

"Has the fire marshal said yet how the fire started?" Lorna asked as they drove down the steep, winding road. The air was very clear, the sky a deep blue bowl. The shadows thrown by the morning sun sharply delineated every bush, every boulder.

"Only that it started around a utility closet."

She settled the shoulder strap of the seat belt so the nylon wasn't rubbing against her neck. "So have one of your mind readers take a peek and tell you what the fire marshal thinks."

Dante had to laugh. "You seem to think there are a lot of us, that I have an army of gifted people I can call on."

"Well, don't you?"

"Scattered around the world. Here in Reno, there are nine, including myself. None of them are gifted with telepathy."

"You mean you can't call your strongest telepath, tell him—"

"Her."

"—*her* the fire marshal's name, and she could do it from wherever she is?"

"The telepath is my sister, Mercy, and she could do it only if she already knew the fire marshal. If she were meeting him in person, she could do it. But a cold reading, at a distance of roughly twenty-five hundred miles, on a stranger? Doesn't work that way."

"I guess that's good—well, unless you need a stranger's mind read from a few thousand miles away. I suppose this means mind reading isn't one of your talents." She hoped not, anyway. If he'd read her mind that morning…

"I can communicate telepathically with Gideon and Mercy, if we deliberately lower our shields, but we're more comfortable with the shields in place. Mercy was a nosy little kid. Then, when she got older, she wanted to make sure we couldn't pop into her head without warning, so she armored up, too."

"What all *can* you do? Other than play with fire and this mind-control thing."

"Languages. I can understand any language, which comes in handy when I travel. That's called xenoglossy. Um…you know I have a mild empathic gift. Something that's fun is that I can make cold light, psycholuminescence. That's usually called witch light."

"Bet that comes in handy when the electricity goes off."

"It has on occasion," he admitted, smiling. "It was especially fun when I was a kid, and Mom made me turn out the light and go to bed."

That sort of home life was as alien to her as if he'd grown up on Mars, and it made her feel vaguely uneasy. To get away from the subject, she asked, "Anything else?"

"Not to any great degree."

She lapsed into silence, mulling over all that information. There was so much she didn't know about this stuff. From the way Dante talked about himself and his family, their gifts had evolved with age, and their skills had grown like any other skill, through constant use. If she began learning more about what she could do, would she find more abilities within her power? She wasn't certain she wanted that. In fact, she was almost certain she didn't. Enough was enough.

Now that she was away from his house, she felt exposed and vulnerable. Though his autocratic way of keeping her there had been maddening, maybe he'd had the right idea. She had been insulated from the world there, able to more calmly think about being one of the gifted—albeit a lowly "stray" rather than a Raintree or Ansara, which she likened to being a Volkswagen as compared to, well, a Jaguar—because she hadn't had to guard herself. With every minute they drew closer to Reno, and with every minute she grew more and more anxious. By the time he sent the Jaguar prowling up the on-ramp to the interstate and they joined with heavy traffic, she was almost in a panic.

Old habits and patterns were very hard to break. A lifetime of caution and secrecy couldn't be easily changed. What was easy enough to contemplate while in seclusion seemed entirely different in the real world. Lorna's mother hadn't been the only person in her life to react so negatively to her ability. Dante could call it a gift all he wanted, but in her life it had been more of a curse.

She felt suddenly dizzy and sick at just the thought of getting deeper into this new world than she already was. Nothing would change. If she let anyone know, she would be leaving herself open for exploitation at the best, ridicule or persecution at the worst.

"What's wrong?" Dante asked sharply, glancing over at her. "You're almost hyperventilating."

"I don't want to do this," she said, teeth chattering from sudden cold. "I don't want to be part of this. I don't want to learn how to do more."

He muttered a curse, gave a quick look over his shoulder to check traffic, and slotted the Jaguar between a semi and a frozen-pizza truck. At the next exit, he peeled off the interstate. "Take a deep breath and hold it," he said, as he pulled into the parking lot of a McDonald's. "Damn it, I should have thought—this is why you need training. I told you that you're a sensitive. You're picking up all the energy patterns around you—has to be all the traffic—and it's throwing you into overload. How in *hell* did you ever function? How did you survive in a casino, of all places?"

Obedient to his earlier suggestion, Lorna sucked in the deepest breath she could and held it. *Was* she hyperventilating? she wondered dimly. She supposed she was. But she was cold, so cold, the way she'd been in Dante's office before the fire.

He put a calming hand on her bare arm, frowning a little when he felt how icy her skin was. "Focus," he said. "Think of your sensitivity as this shining, faceted crystal, picking up the sun and throwing rainbows all around you. Envision it. Or if you don't like crystals, make it something else fragile and breakable. Are you doing that? Can you see it in your imagination?"

She struggled to concentrate. "What shape crystal? Hexagonal? How many sides does it have?"

"What difference does it—never mind. It's round. The crystal is round and faceted. Got it?"

She formed a mental picture of a round crystal, only hers was mirrored. It didn't throw rainbows, it threw reflections. She didn't mention that, though. Concentrating helped dispel that debilitating coldness, so she was willing to think of crystals all day. "Got it."

"Okay. A hailstorm is coming. The crystal will be shattered unless you build a shelter around it. Later you can come back and build a really strong shelter around it, but right now you have to use whatever materials you have at hand. Look around. What do you see that you can use to protect the crystal?"

In her mind she looked around, but no handy bricks and mortar were nearby. There were some bushes, but they weren't sturdy. Maybe she could find some flat rocks and start stacking them in layers to form a barrier.

"Hurry," he said. "You only have a few minutes."

"There are some rocks here, but not enough of them."

"Then think of something else. The hailstones are the size of golf balls. They'll knock the rocks down."

In her mind she glared at him; then, desperate and unable to think of anything else, she mentally dropped to her knees and began scooping a hole in the sandy dirt. The sides of the hole were soft and kept caving in, so she scooped some more. She could hear the storm approaching with a thunderous roar as the hail battered everything in its

path. She had to get under shelter herself. Was the
hole deep enough? She put the crystal in the hole,
and hurriedly began raking dirt around and over
it. No, it was too shallow; the crystal ball wasn't
completely underground. She began raking dirt
from a wider circle, piling it on top of the crystal.
The first hailstone hit her shoulder, a blow like a
fist, and she knew the dirt wasn't going to do the
job. With no time left and no other choice, she
threw her own body over the dirt mounded over
the crystal, protecting it with her life.

She shook herself out of the image and glared
at him. "Well, that didn't work," she snapped.

He was leaning very close, his green eyes
intent on her face, his hand still on her arm.
"What did you do?"

"I threw myself on the hand grenade, so to speak."

"What?"

"I was trying to bury the damn crystal but I
couldn't get it deep enough, so I threw myself on
top of it and the hailstones beat me to death. No
offense, but your imagery sucks."

He snorted and released her arm, sitting back in
his seat. "That wasn't my imagery, it was yours."

"You thought of the stupid crystal."

"Yeah. It worked, too, didn't it?"

"What did?"

"The imagery. Are you still feeling—I don't

know how you were feeling, but I'd guess it was as if you were being attacked from all sides."

Lorna paused. "No," she said thoughtfully. "I'm not feeling that now. But it wasn't as if I were being attacked. It was more of an anxious feeling, a sense of doom. Then I got so cold, just the way I did in your office before the fire."

"Only then? You've never felt overwhelmed like that except in my office?" He considered the idea, frowning a little.

She rubbed the back of her neck, feeling the knots of tension. "Contrary to what you seem to think, I could pretty much go anywhere and do anything without feeling all those swirls and currents, or like the world was coming to an end. I thought you were the one doing all of it, remember?" Whatever this new stuff was, she didn't like it at all. She wasn't a happy-go-lucky person, never had been—it was tough to be Little Miss Sunshine when you were getting slapped every time you opened your mouth—but neither had she felt hopeless, overwhelmed by a dark despair that went way beyond depression.

"I'm not a sensitive," he said. "I've never felt what you're describing. I know I give off a force field of energy, because other sensitives have picked up on it, but no one has ever said I made them feel as if the world was coming to an end."

"Maybe they didn't know you the way I do," she said sweetly.

"You're right about that," he replied, smiling a little, and just that fast the air between them became heavy and hot, as if a summer thunderstorm were approaching. His gaze dipped down to her breasts, stroked over the curves with an almost physical sensation. He'd never touched her breasts, hadn't touched her sexually at all unless she counted the times she'd been able to feel his erection against her. Come to think of it, that was pretty damn sexual. With a jolt of self-honesty, she realized she'd liked knowing she could make him hard; thinking of how he'd felt made her abdominal muscles clench, low in her belly.

How could he do that, make her respond so fast? Her nipples beaded, so that every breath she took scraped them against her bra, which made them even harder. She almost hunched her shoulders to relieve the pressure, but she knew that would be a dead giveaway. Her bra was substantial enough that he couldn't see her excitement, which was a good thing. He might suspect, from the heightened color she could feel in her cheeks, but he couldn't *know*.

His gaze flashed up, caught hers. Slowly, but not at all hesitantly, he lifted his hand and rubbed the back of one finger over her left nipple, letting her know that she'd been wrong: he *knew*. Her cheeks got hotter, and she felt that delicious clenching again, the softening deep inside. If she hadn't been thinking about having sex with him...if she hadn't been thinking just a couple of hours ago about seeing him naked...maybe she wouldn't have responded so readily. But she had been, and she did.

"When you're ready," he said, holding her gaze a moment longer. Then he dropped his hand and nodded toward the fast-food restaurant. "Let's go get breakfast."

He had his door open and was getting out when, in tones of astonishment, she said, "You brought me to get breakfast at *McDonald's?*"

"It's those golden arches," he said. "They get to me every time."

Chapter 17

"They're going into McDonald's," one of the Ansara watchers reported.

"Sit tight," said Ruben McWilliams, sitting on the bed in his motel room. Why the hell didn't motels put the damn phone on the stupid little table so a man could sit in a chair when he talked on the phone, instead of sitting hunched over on an uncomfortable mattress? "Keep them in sight, but don't get any closer. Something spooked him. Let me know when they leave."

Something had prompted Raintree to abruptly cut across two lanes of traffic and take the exit ramp at seventy miles an hour, but Ruben doubted it was a sudden urge for a McMuffin. It wasn't as if he couldn't have gone another couple of exits and found another McDonald's, without the dangerous maneuver.

He didn't think it was anything his people had done that had caused the aberrant behavior, but he wasn't on-site, so he couldn't be certain. His people were supposed to watch and follow, that was all. Raintree wasn't a clairvoyant, so he shouldn't have picked up any warning that way, but he could have had a premonition. Premonition was such a common ability, even ordinary humans had it. Raintree might have felt a twinge of uneasiness, but because he was one of the gifted, he would never dismiss the warning; he would act on it, where most ordinary humans would not.

Since there had been no immediate danger— that would come later—maybe he'd sensed an accident in his immediate future if he stayed on the interstate, so he'd gotten off at the next exit. That was possible. There were always variables.

Staging the planned incident hadn't been possible on such short notice. They hadn't known when Raintree would leave his house, or where he would go when he did. Now that they had a tail on him, they could direct the *amigos* to him wherever he was; then they would fall back and let the *amigos* do their job.

* * *

Over a McMuffin, Dante said, "Tell me exactly what you felt when you were in my office."

Lorna sipped her coffee, thinking. After the weird feelings she'd had in the car, she'd wanted something hot to drink, even though Dante had dispelled all the physical chill. The heat of the coffee couldn't touch the remnant of mental chill she still felt, but it was comforting anyway.

She searched through her memory. It was normally excellent anyway, but everything had happened so recently that the details were still fresh in her mind. "You scared the crap out of me," she finally replied.

"Because you'd been caught cheating?" he prompted when she didn't immediately go on.

"I didn't cheat," she insisted, scowling at him. "Knowing something isn't the same as cheating. But, no, it wasn't that. Once, in Chicago, I was going home one night and was about to take a short-cut through an alley. I used the alley a lot—so did a bunch of people. But that night, I couldn't. I froze. Have you ever felt a fear so intense it made you sick? It was like that. I backed out of the alley and took another way home. The next morning a woman's mutilated body was found in that alley."

"Presentiment," he said. "A gift that saved your life."

"I felt the same way when I saw you." She saw by his expression that he didn't like that at all, but he'd asked, so she told him. "I felt as if this huge force just...*slammed* into me. I couldn't breathe. I was afraid I'd pass out. But then you said something, and the panic went away."

He sat back in the booth, frowning. "You weren't in any danger from me. Why would you have such a strong reaction?"

"You're the expert. You tell me."

"My first reaction to *you* was that I wanted you naked. Unless you're terrified of sex, and I don't think you are—" he gave her a hooded look that had her nipples tightening again "—you weren't picking up anything from me that would cause you to feel that way."

Heat again pooled low in her belly, and it wasn't from the coffee. Because they were in McDonald's and there was a four-year-old sitting in the booth behind her, she looked away and forcibly removed her thoughts from going to bed with him. "At least part of it was from you," she insisted. "I remember thinking that even the air felt different, alien, something I'd never felt before. When you got closer, I could tell the feeling came from you. You're a dangerous man, Raintree."

He just watched her, waiting for her to continue,

because he couldn't accurately deny that particular charge.

"I could feel you," she said, her voice low as she became mired in the memory. "Pulling at me, almost like a touch. The candles were going wild. I wanted to run, but I couldn't move."

"I *was* touching you," he said. "In my imagination, anyway."

Remembering how she'd been snagged by his sexual fantasy, drawn in, stole her breath. "I knew something was wrong," she whispered. "I wasn't in control. I felt as if I'd been caught in a power surge that kept blinking out, and then coming back, pushing me off balance. Then I got so *cold*, just like in the car. Not a normal cold, with chill bumps and shivering, but something so intense it made my bones hurt. Then that feeling of dread came back, the same feeling I had in the alley. You were talking about how I was sensitive to the currents in the room—"

"I was talking about sexual currents," he said wryly. "The summer solstice is in a few days, and control is more difficult when there's so much sunshine. That's why the candles were dancing. I was turned on, and my power kept flaring."

Lorna thought about that. She'd been attracted to him from the first moment she'd looked him in the eyes. Regardless of the fear and panic she'd felt at first, when she had met his gaze, she'd fallen headlong into lust. The debilitating coldness had come afterward and hadn't affected her physical response to him, because when the coldness left, the attraction remained—unchanged.

"The cold went away," she said. "Like something had been pressing me into the chair and then suddenly was gone. I thought I might fall out of the chair, because I'd been pushing back so hard, and all of a sudden the pressure was gone. That was it. We talked some more, and then the fire alarm went off. End of scene, beginning of even more weirdness."

"And you felt the same thing in the car?"

She nodded. "Exactly the same. Except for the sex. The farther we got from the house, the more anxious and depressed I felt, as if I were really exposed and vulnerable. Then I got really cold."

"You were definitely picking up on external negative energies, probably from the traffic around us. You never know who's in the car beside you. Could be someone you wouldn't want to meet even on a crowded street at high noon. What puzzles me is why you felt the same way in my office." He shook his head. "Unless you sensed the fire that was about to burn down the casino, which is possible, if you have some precognitive ability."

"I think I might, but only as things relate to numbers." She told him about the 9/11 flight numbers, and the fact that she hadn't had any visions of airplane crashes or buildings burning, just the flight numbers interjecting themselves into her subconscious. "What I felt before the fire was *different*. Maybe it's because I'm—"

She stopped and glared at him. He raised his eyebrows. "You're…what?"

"I have a hang-up about fire." He waited, and, exasperated, she finally said, "I'm afraid of it, okay?"

"Anyone with any intelligence is cautious of fire. *I'm* cautious with it."

"It isn't caution. I'm *afraid* of it. As in terrified. I have nightmares about being trapped in a burning building." He might be cautious with fire, she thought, but it still turned him on. He would make a jim-dandy firebug. Standing in the burning casino, she had felt his fascination and appreciation for the flames, felt his excitement, because he had expressed it very physically. "Anyway, maybe that's why I felt so panicked then, and so anxious. But why would I feel that way today—unless you're going to force me into another burning building in the next hour or so, in which case tell me now, so I can kill you."

He laughed as he gathered up the debris of their meal, loading it on the plastic tray. She slid from the booth, walking ahead of him as they left the restaurant. "Where to now?"

"The hotel."

They were back on the interstate within a minute. Dante slanted a glance at her. "Feeling okay?"

"I feel fine. I don't know what was going on."

She *did* feel fine. She was riding around in a Jag with the most unusual man she'd ever met, and she was thinking about going to bed with him. She glanced over at him, thinking of how he'd looked wearing just those boxers, and feeling the pleasant warmth of anticipation.

She liked watching him drive. Sunday night, going to his house, she hadn't been in any shape to appreciate the smoothness, the economy of motion, with which he handled a car. Good driving was very sexy, she thought. The play of muscles in his forearms, bared by the short-sleeved polo shirt he was wearing, was incredibly sexy. He had to work out somewhere, on a regular basis, to keep that fit.

They were cruising in the middle lane. A car with a loud muffler was coming up from the right, and she saw him glance in the rearview mirror. "Idiots," he muttered, smoothly accelerating into the left lane. Lorna turned her head to see what he was talking about. A battered white Dodge, gray smoke belching from its exhaust, was coming up fast. She could see several people inside it. What had prompted Dante to move over and give them plenty of room was the blue Nissan right on the bumper of the Dodge.

"That's an accident waiting to happen," she said, just as the blue Nissan swung into the middle lane, the one they had just vacated, and shot forward until it was even with the white Dodge. The Nissan swerved toward the Dodge, and the driver of the Dodge slammed on his brakes, setting off a chain reaction of squealing brakes and smoking tires behind him. The Nissan's motor was screaming as the car drew even with Dante and Lorna. Inside, she could see four or five Hispanics, laughing and pointing back at the Dodge.

Traffic on the interstate was fairly heavy, as usual, but not so heavy that the driver of the white Dodge wasn't now rapidly gaining on them.

"Gangs," Dante said in a clipped voice, braking to let the rolling disaster that was unfolding get ahead of him. He couldn't go faster, because there was a car ahead of him; he couldn't get around the car, because the blue Nissan was right beside them, boxing him in. No one in the Nissan seemed to be paying attention to them; they were all watching the Dodge. If anything, the Nissan's driver let up on the gas pedal, as if he *wanted* the Dodge to catch up.

"Shit!" Dante swerved as far as he could to the left as the Dodge pulled even with the Nissan. Lorna saw a blur as the left rear passenger in the

Dodge rolled down his window and stuck out a
gun; then Dante's right hand closed over her
shoulder in a grip that seemed to go to the bone,
and he yanked her forward and down as the
window beside her head shattered in a thousand
pieces. There were several deep, flat booms, punc-
tuated by lighter, more rapid cracks, then a soul-
jarring impact as Dante spun the steering wheel
and sent them skidding into the concrete barrier.

Chapter 18

Somehow Dante had pulled her shoulder free of the seat belt's shoulder strap, but the lap belt tightened with a jerk. Something grazed the right side of her head and hit her right shoulder so hard and fast it slammed her backward, and she ended up facedown, with her upper body lying across the console and twisted between the bucket seats. All the horrible screeching noises of tires and crushed metal had stopped, and a strange silence filled the car. Lorna opened her eyes, but her vision was blurred, so she closed them again.

She'd never been in a car accident before. The sheer speed and violence of it stunned her. She didn't feel hurt, just…numb, as if a giant had picked her up and body-slammed her to the ground. The hurting part would probably arrive soon enough, she thought fuzzily. The impact had been so ferocious that she was vaguely surprised she was alive.

Dante! What about Dante?

Spurred by that urgent thought, she opened her eyes again, but the blurriness persisted and she couldn't see him. Nothing looked familiar. There was no steering wheel, no dashboard….

She blinked and slowly realized that she was staring at the backseat. And the blurriness was… fog? No—*smoke*. She heaved upward in abrupt panic, or tried to, but she couldn't seem to get any leverage.

"Lorna?"

His voice was strained and harsh, as if he were having difficulty speaking, but it was Dante. It came from somewhere behind and above her, which made no sense.

"Fire," she managed to say, trying to kick her legs. For some reason she could move only her feet, which was reassuring anyway since they were the farthest away; if they could move, everything between there and her spine must be okay.

"Not fire—air bags. Are you hurt?"

If anyone would know whether or not there was

a fire, Dante was that person. Lorna took a deep breath, relaxing a little. "I don't think so. You?"

"I'm okay."

She was in such an awkward position that pain was shooting through her back muscles. Squirming, she managed to work her left arm from beneath her and push with her hand against the back floorboard, trying to lift herself up and around so she could slide back into her seat. "Wait," Dante said, grabbing her arm. "There's glass everywhere. You'll cut yourself to shreds."

"I have to move. This position is murder on my back." But she stopped, because the mental image of what sliding across broken glass would do to her skin wasn't a good one.

There were shouts from outside, coming nearer, as passersby stopped and ran to their aid. Someone beat on Dante's window. "Hey, man! You okay?"

"Yeah." Dante raised his voice so he could be heard. She felt his hand against her side as he tried to release his seat belt. The latch was jammed; he gave a lurid curse, then tried once more. On the third try, it popped open. Freed from its restraint, he shifted around, and she felt his hands running down her legs. "Your right foot's tangled in the air bag. Can you move..." His hand closed over her ankle. "Move your knee toward me and your foot toward your window."

Easier said than done, she thought, because she could scarcely maneuver at all. She managed to shift her right knee just a little.

The man outside Dante's window grabbed the door handle and tried to pull it open, shaking the car, but the door was jammed. "Try the other side!" she heard Dante yell.

"This window's busted out," said another man, leaning in the front passenger window—or where it had been—and asking urgently, "Are you guys hurt?"

"We're okay," Dante said, leaning over her and pushing on her right ankle while he turned her foot.

The trap holding her foot relaxed a little, which let her move her knee a bit more. "This proves one thing," she said, panting from the effort of that small shift.

"Point your toes like a ballerina. What does it prove?"

"I'm definitely—*ouch!*—not precognitive. I didn't see *this* coming."

"I think it's safe to say neither of us is a precog." He grunted, then said, "Here you go." With one last tug, her foot was free. To the man leaning in the window he said, "Can you find a blanket or something to throw over this glass so you can pull her out?"

"I don't need pulling," Lorna grumbled. "If I can shift around, I'll be able to climb out."

"Just be patient," Dante said, turning so he

could slide his right arm under her chest and shoulders and support her weight a little to give her muscles some rest.

They could hear sirens blasting through the dry air, but still some distance away.

A new face, red and perspiring, and belonging to a burly guy wearing a Caterpillar cap, appeared in the broken window. "Had a blanket in my sleeper," he said, leaning in to arrange the fabric over the seat, then folding the excess into a thick pad to cover the shards of glass still stuck in the broken window.

"Thank you," Lorna said fervently as Dante began levering her upright into the seat. Her muscles were screaming from the strain, and the relief of being in a more natural position was so intense that she almost groaned.

"Here you go," said the truck driver, reaching through once more and grasping her under the arms, hauling her out through the broken window before she could do it under her own steam.

She thanked him and everyone else who had reached out to help, then turned and got her first look at the car as Dante came out with the lithe grace of a race car driver, as if exiting through a window was something he did every day.

But as cool and sexy as he made his exit look, what stunned her to silence was the car.

The elegant Jaguar was nothing but crumpled and torn sheet metal. It had skidded almost halfway around, the front end crushed against the concrete barrier, the driver's side almost at a T to the oncoming traffic. If another car had plowed into them after they hit the barrier, Dante would be dead. She didn't know why no other vehicle had smashed into them; traffic had been heavy enough that it was nothing short of a miracle. She looked at the snarled pileup of cars and trucks and SUVs stopped at all angles, as if people had been locking down their brakes and skidding. There was a three-car fender bender in the right lane, about fifty yards down, but the people were out of their vehicles examining the damage, so they were okay.

She wasn't okay. The bottom had dropped out of her stomach, and her heart felt as if someone had punched her in the chest. She had a very clear memory of Dante spinning the steering wheel, sending the Jaguar into a controlled skid—turning the passenger side away from the spew of bullets and his side toward the oncoming traffic.

She was going to kill him.

He had no right to take that sort of risk for her. None. They weren't lovers. They'd met less than forty-eight hours before, under really terrible circumstances, and for most of that time she would gladly have pushed him into traffic herself.

How dare he be a hero? She didn't want him to be a hero. She wanted him to be someone whose absence wouldn't hurt her. She wanted to be able to walk away from him, whole and content unto herself. She didn't want to think about him afterward. She didn't want to dream about him.

Her father hadn't cared enough to stick around, assuming he'd even known about her. She had no real idea who he was—and neither had her mother. Her mother certainly wouldn't have risked a nail, much less her life, to save Lorna from anything. So what was this…this *stranger* doing, putting his own life in danger to protect her? She hated him for doing this to her, for making himself someone whose footprint would always be on her heart.

What was she supposed to do now?

She turned her head, searching for him. He was only a few feet away, which she supposed made sense, because if he'd moved any farther away than that she would have been compelled to follow him. He wouldn't lift that damned mind control he used to shackle her, but he'd risk his life for her—the jerk.

He normally kept his longish black hair brushed back, but now it was falling around his face. There was a thin line of blood penciling down his left cheek from a small, puffy cut high on his cheekbone. The skin around the wound was swelling and turning dark. His left arm looked bruised, too; the span from his wrist almost to his elbow was a dark red. He wasn't cradling his arm or swiping at his cheek, any of the things people instinctively did when they were hurt. His injuries might as well not exist for all the attention he paid them.

He looked in complete command of himself and the situation.

Lorna thought she might be sick, she was so angry. What he'd done wasn't fair—not that he'd seemed concerned about fairness before now anyway.

As if he were attuned to her thoughts, his head turned sharply and his gaze zeroed in on her. With two swift strides he was beside her, taking her arm. "You don't have any color at all in your face. You should sit down."

"I'm fine," she said automatically. A sudden breeze blew a curtain of hair across her face, and she lifted her hand to push it back. Two RPD patrol cars were approaching on the other side of the highway, sirens blaring, and she almost had to shout to make herself heard. "I'm not hurt."

"No, but you've had a shock." He raised his voice, too, turning his head to watch the patrol cars come to a stop on the other side of the barrier. The sirens died, but other emergency vehicles were approaching, and the din was getting louder again.

"I'm *okay!*" she insisted, and she was—physically, at least.

His hand closed on her arm, moving her toward the concrete barrier. "Come on, sit down. I'll feel better if you do."

"I'm not the one bleeding," she pointed out.

He touched his cheek, as if he'd forgotten all about the cut, or maybe had never noticed it in the first place. "Then come sit down with me and keep me company."

As it happened, neither of them got to sit down. The cops were trying to find out what had happened, get traffic straightened out and moving again, albeit very slowly, and get any injured people transported to a hospital to be checked out. Soon a total of seven patrol cars were on the scene, along with a fire engine and three medic trucks. The drivers of the damaged cars that were still drivable were instructed to move their vehicles to the shoulder.

There were several witnesses to what had happened. No one knew whether road rage had caused the shooting or if the whole thing had been a conflict between rival gangs, but everyone had an opinion and a slightly different version of events. The one thing they all agreed on was that the people in the white Dodge had been shooting at the Nissan, and the people in the Nissan had been shooting back.

"Did anyone get the plate number of either vehicle?" a patrolman asked.

Dante immediately looked at Lorna. "Numbers?"

She thought of the white Dodge and three numbers came into sharp focus. "The Dodge is 873." Nevada plates were three digits followed by three letters.

"Did you get the letters?" the patrolman asked, pen at the ready.

Lorna shook her head. "I just remember the numbers."

"This will narrow the search considerably. What about the Nissan?"

"Hmm…612."

He jotted that down, too, then turned away as he got on the radio.

Dante's cell phone rang. He fished it from the front pocket of his jeans and checked the caller ID. "It's Gideon," he said, flipping the phone open. "What's up?" He listened a moment, then said, "Royally screwed."

A brief pause. "I remember."

They talked for less than a minute when Lorna heard him say, "A glimpse of the future," which made her wonder what was going on. He had just laughed at something his brother said when she suddenly shivered, wrapping her arms around herself even though the temperature was rapidly climbing toward the nineties. That awful, bone-aching chill had seized her as suddenly as if she'd been dropped into a pool of ice water.

Dante's gaze sharpened, and he abruptly ended the call, tucking the phone back into his pocket.

"What's wrong?" he asked, keeping his tone low as he pulled her to the side.

She fought waves of dizziness, brought on by the intense cold. "I think the depraved serial killer must have followed us," she said.

Chapter 19

Dante put his arms around her, pulling her against the heat of his body. His body temperature was always high, she thought, as if he had a permanent fever. That heat felt wonderful now, warming her chilled skin.

"Focus," he said, bending his head so no one else could hear him. "Think of building that shelter."

"I don't want to build a damn shelter," she said fretfully. "This didn't happen before I met you, and I want it to stop."

He rubbed his cheek against her hair, and she felt his lips move as he smiled. "I'll see what I can do. In the meantime, if you don't want to build shelters, see if you can tell what's causing the problem. Close your eyes, mentally search around us, and tell me if you're picking up anything, like any changes in energy patterns from a particular area."

That suggestion seemed a lot more practical to her than building imaginary shelters for imaginary mirrored crystals. She would rather be doing something to stop these sudden sick feelings instead of merely learning how to handle them. She did as he said, leaning into him and letting him support part of her weight while she closed her eyes and began mentally searching for something weird. She didn't know what she was doing, or what she was "looking" for, but she felt better for doing it.

"Is this really supposed to work?" she asked against his shoulder. "Or are you just distracting me?"

"It should work. Everyone has a personal energy field, but some are stronger than others. A sensitive has a heightened awareness of these energy fields. You should be able to tell where a strong one is coming from, sort of like being able to tell from which direction the wind is blowing."

That made sense to her, put it in terms she could understand. The thing was, *if* she was a sensitive, why didn't she sense stuff like this on a regular basis? Other than the time in Chicago when she'd been suddenly terrified of what lurked in that alley, she'd never been aware of anything unusual.

Some are stronger than others, Dante had said. Maybe she had been around mostly normal people all her life. If so, these feelings must mean that there were now people near her who weren't normal and had very strong energy fields.

The strongest of all was holding her in his arms. Concentrating like this, she decided to use him as a sort of standard, a pattern, against which she could measure anything else she detected. She could physically *feel* the energy of his gifts, almost like static electricity surrounding her entire body. The sensation was too strong to call pleasant, but it wasn't *un*pleasant. Rather, it was exciting and sexual, like tiny pinpoints of fire reaching deep into her body.

Keeping a part of the feeling in the forefront of her consciousness, she began widening her awareness, looking for the places that had stronger currents. It was, she thought, like trout fishing.

At first there was nothing other than a normal flow of energy, albeit from many different people. She and Dante were surrounded by police officers, firemen, medics, people who had come to their aid. Their energy flow was warm and comforting, concerned, protective. These were good people; they all had their quirks, but their baseline was good.

She expanded her mental circle. The pattern here was slightly different. These were the onlookers, the rubberneckers, the ones who were curious but weren't moved to help. They wanted to talk about seeing the accident, about being stuck in traffic for X number of hours, as if it were a great hardship to endure, but they didn't want to put out any effort. They—

There!

She started, a little alarmed by what she felt.

"Where is it?" Dante whispered against her hair, his arms tightening. Probably the people around them thought he was comforting her, or that they were clinging to each other in gratitude that they'd been spared any harm.

She didn't open her eyes. "To my left. About…I don't know…a hundred yards out, maybe. Off to the side, as if he's pulled onto the shoulder."

"He?"

"He," she replied, very definitely.

"Our friends missed completely," the Ansara follower said in disgust, lowering the binoculars he held in one hand to concentrate on the phone call. "He wrecked the car, but they aren't hurt."

Ruben cursed under his breath. He guessed this just proved the old adage: *If you want something done right, do it yourself.*

"Call off surveillance," he said. "I have something else in mind."

Their plans had been too complex. The best plan was the simplest plan. There were fewer details that could go wrong, fewer people to screw things up, less chance of the target being warned.

Instead of trying to make Raintree's death look like an accident, the easiest thing to do was wait until the last minute, when it was too late for the clan to rally to Sanctuary, then simply put a bullet through his head.

Simple was always best.

"I see who you're talking about," Dante said, "but I can't tell anything from this distance. He doesn't seem to be doing anything, just standing outside his car like a bunch of other people."

"Watching," Lorna said. "He's watching us."

"Can you tell anything about his energy field?"

"He's sending out a lot of waves. He's stronger than anything else I'm sensing out there, but, um, I'd say nowhere near as strong as you." She lifted her head and opened her eyes. "He's the only unusual one as far as I can tell. Are you sure I'm not just imagining this?"

"I'm sure. You need to start trusting your senses. He's probably just—"

"Mr. Raintree," one of the policemen called, beckoning Dante over.

He gave Lorna a quick kiss on the mouth, then

released her and strode over to the cop. Willy-nilly, Lorna followed, though she stopped as soon as she was able, when the compulsion was no longer tugging her forward.

The accident scene was beginning to clear up; witnesses had given their statements, and more and more people were managing to maneuver their vehicles around the demolished Jag, the remains of the fender bender and all the rescue vehicles. Two wreckers had arrived, one to tow Dante's Jaguar, the other to get the center car in the fender bender, because it had a ruptured radiator. Before his poor car was taken away, Dante was getting his registration and insurance card from the glove compartment, as well as the garage door opener. Given how mangled the car was, finding anything and getting to it was a major undertaking.

From what Lorna could tell, he wasn't upset at all about the Jaguar. He didn't like the inconvenience, but the car itself didn't mean anything to him. He had already made arrangements for a rental car to be waiting for him at the hotel, and one of his many employees was on the way to the accident site to pick them up. As she had always suspected, money smoothed out many of life's bumps.

Thinking of money prompted her to casually brush her hand against her left front pocket. Her money was still there, and her driver's license and the tiny pair of scissors were in her right pocket. She had no idea what good those scissors would do in any truly dangerous situation, but she had them anyway.

She noticed she was feeling much better, that the ugly, cold sensation had gone away. She turned and looked over to where the watcher had been parked. He wasn't there any longer, and neither was his car. Coincidence, she wondered, or cause and effect?

And wasn't it odd that she'd had that sickening cold feeling both right before the casino fire, and right before she almost got mowed down in the crossfire of a gang shooting? Maybe she wasn't reacting to a person at all but to something that was about to happen. Maybe that coldness was a warning. Of course, she'd also gotten the feeling right before Dante fed her a McMuffin for breakfast, but the principle could still be holding true: Warning! McMuffin ahead!

She had almost come to terms with the clair-cognizance thing, because even though she'd spent a lifetime insisting she was simply good with numbers, she had always *known* it was more than that. She didn't want to discover yet another talent, particularly one that seemed to be useless. A warning was all well and good if you knew what you were being warned about. Otherwise, why bother?

"Our ride's here," Dante said, coming up behind

her and resting his hand on the curve of her waist.
"Do you want to go to the hotel with me, or go
back home?"

Home? He was referring to his house as her
home? She looked up, ready to nail him on his
mistake, and the words died on her lips. He was
watching her with a steady, burning intent; that
hadn't been a slip of the tongue but a warning of
a different kind.

"We both know where we're going with this,"
he said. "I have a suite at the hotel, and the electri-
cians got the power back on yesterday, so it's func-
tional. You can come with me to the hotel or go
home, but either way, you're going to be under
me. The only difference is that going home will
give you a little more time, if you need it."

She needed more than time, but standing on the
side of the interstate wasn't the place to have the
showdown she knew was coming.

"I haven't decided yet whether or not to sleep
with you, and I'll make the decision on my timetable,
not yours," she said. "I'll come to the hotel with you
because I don't want to spend another day cooped up
in that house, so don't get too cocky, Raintree."

The expression of intense focus faded, to be
replaced by wryness. Looking down at himself, he
said, "Too late."

Chapter 20

Lorna was too restless to just sit in Dante's suite while he was literally all over the hotel, directing the cleaning and repairs, touring with insurance adjusters, meeting with contractors. She dogged his steps, listening but not joining in. The behind-the-scenes details of a luxury hotel were fascinating. The place was hopping, too. Rather than wait until the insurance companies ponied up, he'd brought the adjusters in to take pictures; then he got on with the repairs using his own money.

That he was able to do so told her that he was seriously wealthy, which made his lifestyle even more of a statement about him. He didn't have an army of servants waiting on him. He lived in a big, gorgeous home, but it wasn't a mansion. He drove expensive cars, but he drove himself. He made his own breakfast, loaded his own dishwasher. He liked luxury but was comfortable with far less.

When it came to the hotel, though, he was unbending. Everything had to be top notch, from the toilet paper in the bathrooms to the sheets on the beds. A room that was smoke-damaged couldn't be cleaned and described as "good enough." It had to be perfect. It had to be better than it had been before the fire. If the smell of smoke wouldn't come out of the curtains, the curtains were discarded; likewise the miles of carpet.

Lorna found out that the day before had been a madhouse, with guests being allowed to go to their rooms and retrieve their belongings. Because the destroyed casino was attached to the hotel, for liability purposes guests had to be escorted to make certain their curiosity didn't lead them where they shouldn't go.

A casino existed for one reason only, and that reason was money. In a rare moment when he had time to talk, he told Lorna that over six million dollars a day had to go through the casino just for him to break even, and since the whole point of a casino was its generous profit margin, the amount of cash he actually dealt with on a daily basis was mind-boggling.

The acre of melted and charred slot machines held thousands upon thousands of dollars, so the ruins had to have around-the-clock security until the machines could be transported and as much as possible of their contents was salvaged. About half the machines had spewed printed tickets instead of belching out quarters, which saved both time and money. The coin vaults and the master vault were fireproof, thus saving that huge amount of cash, and his cashiers in the cages had refused to evacuate until they secured the money, which had been very loyal of them but not smart: the two fatalities had been from their ranks.

The fire marshal was wrapping up his investigation, so Dante cornered him. "Was it arson?" he demanded bluntly.

"All indications are that it was electrical in nature, Mr. Raintree. I haven't found any trace of accelerants at the source of the fire. The flames reached unusually high temperatures, so I was suspicious, I admit."

"So was I—when detectives were here questioning me immediately after the fire on Sunday night, when you hadn't even begun your investigation. This wasn't a crime scene."

The fire marshal rubbed his nose. "They didn't

tell you? A call came in about the time the fire started. Some nutcase claimed he was burning down the casino. When they tracked him down, turns out he'd been eating in one of the restaurants, and when the fire alarm went off, he pulled out his trusty cell phone and made a grab for glory. He'd had one too many adult beverages." He shook his head. "Some people are nuts."

Dante met Lorna's gaze; both were rueful. "We'd wondered what was going on. I was beginning to feel like a conspiracy theorist," he said.

"Weird things happen in fires. One of them is how you two are alive. You had no protection at all, but the heat and smoke didn't get to you. Amazing."

"I felt as if the smoke got to us," Dante said in a dry tone. "I thought I was coughing up my lungs."

"But your airways had no significant damage. I've seen people die who faced less smoke than you two dealt with."

Lorna wondered what he would think if he could see what was left of Dante's Jaguar, since the two of them were walking around without even a bruise.

No, that wasn't right. Frowning, she looked at Dante, really looked. He'd had a cut on his face where the impact of the air bag had literally split open the skin over his cheekbone. His cheekbone had been bruised and was swelling, and his left arm had been bruised.

Just a few hours later, his cheek looked fine. She couldn't see the cut at all. There was no swelling, no bruising. She knew she hadn't imagined it, because there had been blood on his shirt, and he had gone to his suite to change; instead of the polo shirt, he now wore a white dress shirt with his jeans, the sleeves rolled up to expose his unbruised left forearm.

She didn't have any bruises, either. After the way she'd been slammed around, she should at least have some stiff and sore muscles, but she felt fine. *What was going on?*

"That was a dead end," he remarked after the fire marshal had left and he was inspecting the damage done to the landscaping. "The stupidity of some people is mind-boggling."

"I know," she said absently, still mentally chasing the mystery of the vanishing cut. Was there any way to diplomatically ask a man, *Are you human?*

But what about her own lack of bruises? She knew *she* was human. Was this part of his repertoire? Had he somehow kept her from being injured?

"The cut on your face," she blurted, too troubled to keep the words in. "What happened to it?"

"I'm a fast healer."

"Don't pull that crap on me," she said, more annoyed than was called for. "Your cheekbone was bruised and swollen, and the skin was split open just a few hours ago. Now there isn't a single mark."

He gave her expression a lightning fast assessment, then said, "Let's go up to the suite so we can talk. There are a few things I haven't mentioned."

"No joke," she muttered as they went through the hotel offices to his private elevator, which went only to his suite. His office was on the same floor, but it was separate from the suite, on the other side of the hotel. When his chief of security had dragged her up here, he had used one of the public elevators. No wonder there hadn't been any other people on the floor when they evacuated, she thought; the entire floor was his.

The three-thousand-square-foot suite felt and looked like any luxury hotel suite: completely impersonal. He'd said the only time he spent the night there was if some complication kept him at the casino so late that driving home was ridiculous. The rooms were large and comfortable, but there was nothing of him there except the changes of clothing he kept for emergencies.

It was strange, she thought, that she already knew his taste in furnishings, his color choices, artwork he had personally chosen. Some interior designer specializing in hotels, not in homes, had decorated this suite.

He strolled down the two steps to the sunken living room and over to the windows. He had an affinity for windows, she'd noticed. He liked glass, and lots of it—but he liked being outside even more, which was why the suite had a sun-drenched balcony large enough to hold a table and chairs for alfresco dining.

"Okay," she said, "now tell me how bruises and cuts went away in just a few hours. And while you're at it, tell me why I'm not bruised, too. I'm not even sore!"

"That one's easy," he said, pulling a silver charm from his pocket and draping the cord over his hand so the charm lay flat on his palm. "This was in the console."

The little charm was some sort of bird in flight, maybe an eagle. She shook her head. "I don't get it."

"It's a protection charm. I told you about them. I keep Gideon supplied with them. He usually sends me fertility charms—"

Lorna jerked back, making a cross with her fingers as if to ward off a vampire. "Keep that thing away from me!"

He chuckled. "I said it's a protection charm, not a fertility charm."

"You mean it's like a rubber you hang around your neck instead of putting on your penis?"

"Not that kind of protection. This kind prevents physical harm—or minimizes the damage."

"You think that's why we weren't injured today?"

"I know it is. Since he's a cop, Gideon wears one

all the time. This one came in the mail on Saturday, which means he'd just made it. I don't know why he made a protection charm instead of a fertility charm, unless he now has a diabolical plot to eventually disguise a fertility charm as a protection charm, but this one is the real deal. This close to the solstice, his gifts can get away from him, just like mine sometimes do. He must have breathed one hell of a charm," he said admiringly. "I didn't wear it. I just put it in the glove box and forgot about it. Normally the charms are for specific individuals, but when neither of us was injured today…I guess it must affect anyone within a certain distance. It's the only explanation."

Actually, that was kind of cool. She even liked the way he'd phrased it: *Breathed one hell of a charm.* "Does it make you heal faster, too?"

Dante shook his head as he slipped the charm back in his pocket. "No, that's just part of being Raintree. When I say I'm a fast healer, I mean really, really fast. A little cut like that—it was nothing. A deeper cut might take all night."

"How terrible for you," she said, scowling at him. "What other unfair advantages do you have?"

"We live longer than most humans. Not a lot longer, but our average life expectancy is about ninety to a hundred years. They're usually good years, too. We tend to stay really healthy. For instance, I've never had a cold. We're immune to viruses. Bacterial infections can still lay us low, but viruses basically don't recognize our cellular composition."

Of all the things he'd told her, not ever having a cold seemed the most wonderful. That also meant never having the flu, and—"You can't get AIDS!"

"That's right. We run hotter than humans, too. My temperature is usually at or above a hundred degrees. The weather has to get really, really cold before I get uncomfortable."

"That's so unfair," she complained. "I want to be immune to colds and AIDS, too."

"No measles," he murmured. "No chicken pox. No shingles. No cold sores." His eyes were dancing with merriment. "If you really want to be Raintree and never have a stuffy nose again, there's a way."

"How? Bury a chicken by the dark of the moon and run backward around a stump seven times?"

He paused, arrested by the image. "You have the strangest imagination."

"Tell me! How does someone become Raintree? What's the initiation ritual?"

"It's an old one. You've heard of it."

"The chicken one is the only one I know. C'mon, what is it?"

His smile was slow and heated. "Have my baby."

Chapter 21

Lorna went white, then red, then white again. "That isn't funny," she said in a stifled tone, getting up to prowl restlessly around the room. She picked up a pillow and fluffed it, but instead of placing it back on the sofa, she stood with it clasped to her chest, her head bowed over it.

"I'm not joking."

"You don't…you shouldn't have babies as a means to an end. People who don't want babies for themselves should never, never have them."

"Agreed," he said softly, leaving his spot by the windows and strolling toward her as unhurriedly as if he had no destination, no agenda.

"It's nothing to be taken lightly." That was a dirty game of pool he was playing, saying *Have my baby* as if he meant it. He couldn't mean it. They had known each other two days. That was something men said to seduce women, because hundreds of centuries ago some cunning bastard had figured out most women were pushovers for babies.

"I'm taking this very seriously, I promise." His tone was gentle as he touched her shoulder, curving his palm over the slope before sliding his hand over her back. She felt the heat transferring from his skin to hers, burning through her clothes. His fingertips sought out her spine, stroking downward, gently rubbing out the tension thrumming beneath her skin.

She hadn't known she was so tense, or that the gentle massage would turn her to butter. She let him urge her against him, let her head nestle into his shoulder, because everything about what he was doing felt so good. Still… She looked up at him with narrowed eyes. "Don't think I haven't noticed how close that hand's getting to my butt."

"I'd be disappointed if you hadn't." A smile curved his mouth as he pressed a warm kiss, then another, to her temple.

"Don't let it get any lower," she warned.

"Are you sure?" Beginning at the waistband of her jeans, he traced a finger down the center seam—down, down, pressing lightly, while his hot palm massaged her bottom. That finger left a trail of fire in its wake, made her squirm and shudder and begin, at least ten times, to say *No*. He would stop if she said it; the decision to continue or not was hers—but the security of knowing that was what kept the single word unsaid. Instead, all she did was gasp with agonized anticipation, and arch, and cling—waiting, waiting, focusing entirely on the slow progression of the caress, as his hand slowly slid down to dip between her legs from behind. He pressed harder then, his fingers rubbing against her entrance through her jeans, so that the friction of the seam lightly abraded flesh that was soft and yielding.

He had been bringing her to this point for two days, since that first kiss in his kitchen, patiently feeding the spark of desire until it became a small flame, then keeping the flame going with fleeting touches and something even harder to resist: his open desire for her. She could recognize what he was doing, see the subtle progressions, and even appreciate the mastery of his restraint. Getting into bed with her last night—and then not touching her—had been diabolically intelligent. Since the moment they'd met, he had forced her to do a lot of things, but not once had he tried to force her response. She would have shut him down cold if he had. The spark would have gone out, and she wouldn't have let it be resurrected.

His warm mouth moved along the line of her jaw, leisurely nipping and tasting, as if he wanted nothing more than this and had all the time in the world in which to savor her. Only the rock-hard bulge in his jeans betrayed any urgency, and she was pressed so tightly to him that she could feel every twitch, every throb, that invited her to part her legs and let him get even closer.

Then his mouth closed over hers and the last shred of restraint dissolved. The kiss was hard and deep and hungry, his tongue taking her mouth. Desire sizzled along her nerves, turned her warm and yielding and boneless. His free hand moved to her breasts, found her nipples through the layers of cloth, gently pinched them awake. He had her now; she wasn't restraining him from any caress, and the clothing that kept his body from hers was suddenly maddening. She wanted the rest of it, all he had to give her, and with a burst of clarity, she knew she had to say what she wanted to say *now*. A minute from now would be too late.

The proof of how far gone she was came in the amount of willpower it took for her to tear her mouth from his. "We need to talk," she said, her voice strained and husky.

He groaned and laughed at the same time. "Oh,

God," he muttered, frustration raw in his tone. "The four words guaranteed to strike fear in any man. Can't it wait?"

"No—it's about this. Us. Now."

He heaved a sigh and pressed his forehead against hers. "Your timing is sadistic, you know that?"

Lorna slid her hands into the black silk of his hair, feeling the coolness of the strands, the heat of his scalp. "Your fault. I almost forgot." Her tongue felt a little thick, her speech slower than normal. Yes, this was definitely his fault, all of it.

"Let's have it, then." Resignation lay heavy in the words, the resignation of a simple male who just wanted to have sex. She would have laughed, if not for the heavy pull of desire that threatened to overwhelm everything else.

She swallowed, struggled to get the words lined up in her head so she could say them coherently. "My answer…to whether or not we do this…depends on you."

"I vote yes," he replied, biting her earlobe.

"This mind-control thing…you have to stop. I can be your prisoner or your lover, but I won't be both."

He lifted his head then, his gaze going cool and sharp. "There's no compulsion involved in this. I'm not forcing you." Anger clipped his words.

"I know," she said, drawing a shuddering breath.

"I can tell the difference, believe me. It's... I have to have the choice, whether to stay or go. The freedom has to be there. You can't keep moving me around like a puppet."

"It was necessary."

"At first. I hated it then, I hate it now, but you did have valid reasons *at first*. You don't now. I think you're too used to having your way in everything, *Dranir*."

"You would have run," he said flatly.

"My choice." She couldn't bend on this. Dante Raintree was a force of nature; dealing with him in a relationship would be challenging enough even without his ability to chain her with a thought. He had to bow to her free will or their only relationship could be jailer and prisoner. "We're equals...or we're nothing."

Reading him wasn't easy, but she could see he didn't like relinquishing control at all. Intuitively, she grasped his dilemma. On a purely intellectual basis, he understood. On a more primitive level, he didn't want to lose her, and he was prepared to be as autocratic and heavy-handed as necessary.

"All or nothing." She met his gaze, squaring up with him like fighters in a boxing ring. "You can't use mind control on me *ever again*. I'm not your enemy. At some point you have to trust me, and that point is now. Or were you planning to keep me pinned forever?"

"Not forever." He ground out the words. "Just until—"

"Until what?"

"Until you wanted to stay."

She smiled at that rough admission and gripped both hands in his hair. "I want to stay," she said simply, and kissed his chin. "But at some point I may want to go. You have to take that chance, and if that day does come, you have to let me go. I'm taking the same chance with you, that one day you may not want me around. I want your word. Promise me you'll never use mind control on me again."

She saw his fury and frustration, saw his jaw work as he ground his teeth. She knew what she was asking of him; giving up a power went against every instinct he had, as both a man and a Dranir. He lived in two worlds, both the normal and the paranormal, and in both he was boss. As understated as he kept things, he was still boss. If he hadn't been the Raintree Dranir, his natural dominance would have been reined in more, but reality was what it was, and he was a king in that world.

Abruptly he dropped his arms from around her and stepped back. His eyes were narrowed and fierce. "You may go."

Lorna barely controlled a protest at the loss of his touch, his heat. What was he saying? "Are you giving me your permission—or an order?"

"A promise."

Breathing was abruptly difficult. Her lips trembled, and she firmed them, started to speak, but he lifted a hand to stop her. "One thing."

"What?"

The green of his eyes almost glowed, they were so intent. "If you stay…the brakes are off."

Fair warning, she thought dizzily, shivering a little in anticipation. "I'm staying," she managed to say, taking half a step forward.

A half step was all she had time to take before he moved, an explosion of pent-up power that was now released from all constraint. If she was free, then so was he. He swung her off her feet and carried her into the bedroom, moving so fast her head swam. The slow, careful seduction was over, and all that was left was raw desire. He tossed her on the bed and followed her down, pulling at her clothes, his movements rough with urgency, even though she helped him, her own hands shaking as she dealt with buttons and zippers, hooks and laces. He jerked her shoes and jeans off as she fought to unbutton his shirt, peeled her underwear down her legs while she struggled to lower his zipper, hampered by the thrust of his erection.

He shoved his jeans and boxers down, and kicked them away. Lorna tried to reach for him, tried to stroke him, but he was a tidal wave that flattened her on the bed and crushed her under his heavy weight. His penetration wasn't careful, it was hard and fast and powerful, taking him deep.

She gave a choked cry, her body shocked by the impact even as she rose to meet it. His heat burned her, inside and out. He pulled out, thrust in again, then again. Her brain stuttered a warning of what that heat meant, and she managed to say, "Condom."

He swore, pulled out, and jerked open a drawer in the bedside table. He tore the first condom, rolling it on. Swearing even more, he slowed down, took more care with the second one. When he was safely sheathed, he pushed into her again, then held her crushed to him, their bodies straining together as relief shuddered through them. Tears rolled down her face. This wasn't an orgasm, it was…pure relief, as if unrelenting pain had suddenly vanished. It was completion—not a sexual one, but something that went deeper, as if some part of her had been missing and suddenly was there.

It was being filled, when she hadn't realized how empty she was; fed, when she hadn't known she was hungry.

He rose, supporting his weight on his arms as he pulled back, then eased forward in a slow, deep thrust. "Don't cry," he murmured, kissing the tears from her wet face.

"I'm not," she said. "It's just leakage."

"Ah."

He said it as if he understood, and maybe he did. He snagged her gaze and held it as he moved in and out, drawing her response to him, going deep to find more. She was both relaxed and tense at the same time: relaxed because she knew he wasn't going to leave her behind, and tense from the building pleasure.

It happened faster than she'd thought possible. Instead of hovering just out of reach, building slowly, she came hard in a rush of sensation that roared through her entire body. Dante slipped his own leash, driving fast and deep, and followed.

When she was able to breathe again, able to open her eyes, the first thing she saw was fire. Every candle in the room was flaming.

"Tell me why you denied your gift."

They were lying entwined, her head on his shoulder, barely recovered from what had felt so cataclysmic that neither of them had spoken for a long time. Instead they had been slowly stroking each other, touch replacing words, touches of re-assurance and comfort, of silent joy.

She sighed, for the first time in her life feeling

a little distance from the unhappiness of her childhood. "I think you already know. It's not an original story, or an interesting one."

"Probably not. Tell me anyway."

She smiled against his shoulder, glad he wasn't making any big deal of it, though the smile faded almost as fast as it had bloomed. Talking about her mother was difficult, even though it had been fifteen years since she'd last seen her. Maybe it would never be easy, but at least the pain and fear were less immediate.

"As bad as it was, a lot of kids have it worse. The only reason she didn't abort me was so she could get that monthly check. She told me that every month when it came. She'd shake the envelope at me and say, 'This is the only reason you're alive, you freak.' That check helped keep her in drugs and booze."

He didn't say anything, though his mouth tightened.

Her head found a more comfortable resting spot on his shoulder, and she nestled against him, soaking up his heat. She'd known he felt hot, but it was nice to know she hadn't been imagining things. "It was constant slaps, and she'd throw things at me—cups, empty wine bottles, a can opener. Whatever was near. Once she threw a can of chicken noodle soup, hit me in the head, and knocked me out. I had a headache for days. And she wouldn't let me have any of the soup."

"How old were you?"

"That time…six, I think. I'd started school and discovered numbers. Sometimes I was so excited I'd have to tell someone what I'd learned about the numbers that day, and she was the only someone I had. She told my teacher I'd fallen and hit my head on the curb."

"You'd have been better off in foster care," he growled.

"I ended up there when I was sixteen. She took off one day and never came back. I remember… even though she'd made it plain how much she hated me, when she left it was as if part of me was missing, because she was what I knew. By that time I wasn't helpless, but when I was little…no matter how bad it is, little kids will do anything to hold on to what passes for a family, you know?" She sighed. "I know I overreacted about the baby thing. I'm sorry. You said 'baby,' and that's one of my triggers."

A little smile curved his mouth. "Don't get upset again, but I wasn't joking. When a human mother gives birth to a Raintree baby, she becomes Raintree. No, I don't understand the science of it. Something to do with hormones and the mixing of blood, and the baby being a genetic dominant.

I'm not sure there *is* any science to explain it. Magic doesn't need to be logical."

The explanation intrigued her. Everything she'd learned about the Raintree intrigued her. It was such a different world, a different experience, and yet they existed normally within the regular world—not that the regular world knew about them, because if that ever came about, then their existence would not only not be normal but they might cease to exist at all. Lorna had few illusions about the world she lived in. "What about human men who have babies with Raintree women? What changes them?"

"Nothing," Dante said. "They stay human."

That didn't seem fair, and she said so. Dante shrugged. "Life isn't perfect. You deal with it."

Wasn't that the truth. She knew about dealing. She also knew that, right now, she was very happy.

The dozen or so candles in the room were putting out enough heat that she was beginning to be uncomfortable. Looking around at them, she realized that Dante and fire went hand in hand. She didn't like fire, would always be afraid of it, but…life wasn't perfect. You dealt with it.

"Can you put out those candles?" she asked.

He lifted his head from the pillow and looked at them, as if he hadn't realized they were burning.

"Damn. Yeah, no problem." Just like that, they went out, the wicks gently smoking.

Lorna climbed on top of him and kissed him, smiling as she felt a leap of interest against her inner thigh. "Now, big boy, let's see if you can light them again."

Chapter 22

Sunday morning

She had stayed.

Dante came back into the bedroom from the balcony where he'd met the sunrise, intense satisfaction filling him as he saw Lorna still peacefully asleep in his bed. Only the top half of her head was visible, dark red hair vivid against the white pillow, but he was acutely aware of what it meant for even that much to not be covered by the sheet.

She was feeling safer. Not completely safe, not yet, but safer. When he was in the bed with her, she slept stretched out, relaxed, cuddled against him. When he left the bed, though, within five minutes she was curled in a tight, protective ball. One day—maybe not this week or this month, or even this year, but one day—he hoped he could see her sprawled in sleep, head uncovered, maybe no covers at all. Then he would know she felt safe.

And when the day came that he didn't feel the need to constantly check on her whereabouts, he would know that he felt safe, too.

He *didn't* constantly check on her; his pride refused to let him do that to either her or himself, but the need, the anxiety, was always there.

On Wednesday she hadn't gone with him. He'd called the Jaguar dealership and had a new car sent over, and she had stayed there to accept it. The salesman had called his cell phone to let him know delivery had been made, but Dante had expected Lorna to also call and let him know. She hadn't. Since he had also had her own car—a dinged-up, slightly rusty red Corolla—delivered that morning, he'd been acutely aware that she was free, she had wheels, and she had cash in her pocket. If she wanted to leave, he couldn't stop her. He'd given his word.

He'd wanted to call, just to reassure himself that she was still there, but he hadn't. She could walk out as soon as the call ended, so talking to her at any given time was useless. The only thing he could do, *would* do, was hope. And pray.

He hadn't cut his work short. No matter what happened, whether she stayed or left, the work had to be done. Consequently, it was almost sunset when he drove up to see her car still parked in his garage, with his brand-new Jaguar sitting outside, exposed to the sun and blowing grit. As he'd zoomed the Lotus into its slot, all he'd been aware of was a relief so intense that he'd almost been weak with it. Let the Jaguar sit out; seeing her Corolla still there was worth more to him than any car, no matter how expensive.

She'd met him at the kitchen door, wearing a pair of cutoffs and one of his silk shirts, a scowl on her face. "It's eight-thirty. I'm starving. Do you work this late on a regular basis? Got any idea what we're going to do for dinner?"

He'd laughed and pounced, and showed her exactly what he wanted to eat for dinner. She hadn't said another word about food until after ten.

On Thursday, she'd gone to the hotel with him. Work was continuing at a frantic pace. He'd gotten the okay to bulldoze the charred ruins of the casino so he could begin rebuilding, and things were so hectic he'd actually delegated some authority to her, because he couldn't be in two places at once. On a perverse level, he'd enjoyed watching her give orders to Al Franklin. Al, being Al, was sanguine about everything, but Lorna got a great deal of satisfaction from the arrangement, and he'd got a great deal of enjoyment from her satisfaction.

At lunch, they'd gone to his suite and lit candles. Twice.

On Friday, she didn't go with him, and he'd sweated through that day, too. When he got home, his relief at seeing her car still there had been as acute as it had been on Wednesday, and that was when he faced the truth.

He loved her. This wasn't just sex, just a brief affair, or *just* anything. It was the real deal. He loved her courage, her gallantry, her grumpiness. He loved the snarky comments, the stubbornness and the vulnerability she hated for anyone to see.

Gideon would laugh his ass off when he found out, not just because Dante had fallen so far, but out of sheer relief that at long last, and if the angels smiled, he might soon lose his position as heir apparent.

The bottom dropped out of Dante's stomach and his gut clenched. Last night he'd been rolling on a condom when abruptly he knew that he didn't want to wear protection. Lorna had been watching him, waiting, and she'd noticed his long hesitation. Finally, without a word, he'd pulled off the condom and tossed it aside, then steadily met her gaze. If she wanted him to put on another one, he would; the choice was hers.

She had reached out and pulled him down and

into her. Just remembering the intense half hour that had followed turned him on so much that the candle beside the bed flared to life.

Today was the solstice, and he felt as if he could set the world on fire, as if his skin would burst from all the power boiling inside him. He wanted to pull her under him and ride her until he was completely empty, until she had taken everything he had to give. First, though, they had to have a very serious talk. Last night they'd done something that was too important for them to let drift along.

As he sat down on the edge of the bed, he extinguished the candle, because a candle that was already lit was useless as a barometer of his control. This conversation might be emotionally charged, so he would have to be very careful.

He slid his hand under the sheet and touched her bare thigh. "Lorna. Wake up."

He felt her tense, as always; then she relaxed, and one sleepy hazel eye blinked open and glared at him over the edge of the sheet. "Why? It's Sunday, the day of rest. I'm resting. Go away."

He tugged the sheet down. "Wake up. Breakfast is ready."

"It is not. You're lying. You've been on the balcony." She grabbed the sheet and pulled it over her head.

"How do you know that, if you've been asleep?"

"I didn't say I was sleeping, I said I was resting."

"Eating isn't considered work. Come on. I have fresh orange juice, coffee, the bagels are already toasted, and the sunrise is great."

"To *you*, maybe, but it's *five-thirty* on Sunday morning, and I don't want to eat breakfast this early. I want one day a week when you don't drag me out of bed at the crack of dark-thirty."

"Next Sunday you can sleep, I promise." Rather than fight her for custody of the sheet, he slid his hand under the covers, found her thigh again and swiftly reached upward to pinch her ass.

She squeaked and bolted out of bed, rubbing her backside. "Payback will be hell," she warned, as she pushed her disheveled hair out of her face and stalked off to the bathroom.

He imagined it would be. Dante grinned as he returned to the balcony.

She came out five minutes later, wrapped in his thick robe and still scowling. She wasn't wearing anything under the robe, so he enjoyed glimpses as she plopped into a chair across from him. It also gaped at the neck, revealing the gold chain from which hung the protection charm he'd given her on Wednesday night. He'd made it specifically for her, out here on the balcony, and let her watch. She'd been enthralled at the way he cupped the charm and held it up so his breath warmed it as he murmured a few words in Gaelic. The charm had taken on a gentle green glow that quickly faded. When he slipped the chain over her head she had fingered the charm, looking as if she might cry. She hadn't taken it off since.

As grumpy as she was when she first woke, she didn't stay that way for long. By the time she'd had her second bite of bagel she was looking much more cheerful. Still, he waited until she'd finished the bagel and her juice glass was empty before he said, "Will you marry me?"

She had much the same reaction as when he'd mentioned a baby. She paled, then turned red, then jumped out of her chair and went to stand at the railing with her back to him. Dante knew a lot about women, but more specifically, he knew Lorna, so he didn't leave her standing there alone. He caged her with his arms, putting his hands on top of hers on the railing, not holding her tightly but giving her his warmth. "Is the question that hard to answer?"

He felt her shoulders heave. Alarmed, he turned her around. Tears were streaking down her face. "Lorna?"

She wasn't sobbing, but her lips were trembling. "I'm sorry," she said, swiping at her face. "I know this is silly. It's just—no one has ever wanted me before."

"I doubt that. Probably you just didn't notice them wanting you. I wanted you the minute I saw you."

"Not that kind of wanting." Another tear leaked down. "The other kind, the staying-around kind."

"I love you," he said gently, mentally cursing the bitch who had given birth to her for not nurturing the sense of security that every child should have, the knowledge that, no matter what, someone loved her and wanted her.

"I know. I believe you." She gulped. "I sort of figured it out when you deliberately wrecked your Jaguar to protect me."

"I knew I could buy another car," he said simply.

"That's when I knew that you'd ruined me, that I wouldn't be able to leave unless you threw me out. I kept hoping it was just old-fashioned lust I was feeling, but I knew better, and it scared me to death." She gave a shaky laugh, despite the slow roll of yet another tear. "In just two days, you'd ruined me."

He rubbed the side of his nose. "We hadn't had much time together, but it was quality time."

"Quality!" She gaped at him, mouth open. Indignation dried her tears. "You manhandled me, dragged me into a fire, tore open my head and smashed my brain flat, tore off my clothes and kept me a prisoner!"

"I didn't say it was good quality. You have a

way with words, you know that? 'Tore open your head,' my ass."

"You don't like it when I call it 'brain-rape,'" she said sourly. "And I think I have a better grasp of how it felt than you do."

"I guess you do, at that. When you voluntarily link with someone, it doesn't—"

"Good God." She looked horrified. "Some of you actually do that *willingly?*"

"I told you, it doesn't hurt when it's done right. If someone needs to boost their power, they find someone else who is willing to link. Every so often Gideon and I go home to Sanctuary, and we link with Mercy to perform a protection spell over the homeplace. Doing it right takes time, but it doesn't hurt. Will you answer the—"

"I hope you have some kind of law against doing it without permission."

"Uh—no."

She looked horrified. "You mean you Raintree people can just go around breaking into people's heads, and nobody does anything about it?"

He was beginning to feel frustrated. Would the woman never answer his question? "I didn't say that. Very few of us are strong enough to over-power someone else's brain unless they cooperate."

"And you're one of those few," she said sarcastically. "Right. Lucky me."

"Specifically, only the royal family. Which I've asked you to join, I'd like to point out, if you'll answer the damn question!"

She smiled, and it was like a ray of sunshine breaking across her lively, mobile face. "Of course I will. Did you really doubt it?"

"I never know which way you'll jump. I thought you might love me, because you stayed. Then, last night—" He flicked a finger over her chin. "Not telling me to wear a condom was a dead giveaway."

She stared at him, a peculiar expression stealing over her face.

He straightened, instantly alert. "What's wrong?" Just that quickly she looked sick, as if she were going to throw up.

She rubbed her arms, frowning. "I'm cold. It's that same—" She broke off, her eyes widening with horror, and before he could react she threw herself bodily at him, catching him unprepared for the impact of her weight. He caught her, staggering back, then lurching to the side as he tried to catch his balance and failed. They fell to the floor of the balcony in a tangle of arms, legs and bathrobe as the French door behind him shattered. Hard on the explosion of glass came a sharp, flat retort that echoed through the mountains.

Rifle fire.

Dante wrapped his arms around Lorna, got his feet under him and lunged through the shattered door just as another shot spatted into the side of the house where they had been. Then he rolled with her, getting her away from the wall, before finally lunging to his feet and dragging her out into the hall. "Stay down!" he yelled at her when she tried to stand, pushing her flat again.

His mind was racing. The fire. The gang shooting when he and Lorna so conveniently happened to be boxed in the kill zone. Now someone was shooting at him again. These weren't a series of accidents; they were all related. The fire marshal hadn't found any evidence of arson, which meant—

A Fire-Master didn't need accelerants to start a fire, or to keep it going. Someone, or several some-ones, had been feeding the fire; that was why he hadn't been able to extinguish it. If he hadn't used mind control for the first time just minutes before trying to control the fire and hadn't known how it would affect him, if he hadn't suspected Lorna might be Ansara, he would have figured it out right away.

Ansara! He snarled his rage. It had to be them. Several of them must have gotten together and de-cided to try burning him out. They'd known he would engage the fire, that he wouldn't give up until it overwhelmed him. If Lorna hadn't been there, the plan would have worked, too, but they hadn't counted on her.

The cold, sick feeling she kept getting—that was when any Ansara were nearby.

"There was a red dot on your forehead," she said, though her teeth were chattering so hard she could barely speak, or maybe that was because he was practically kneeling on her back to keep her down.

A laser targeting system, then. This wasn't simply seizing an opportunity, but actively planning and pursuing.

The sniper had failed. What would they try next? He had to assume there was more than one Ansara out there, had to assume there was a backup plan. They wouldn't try to burn him out again, since the first effort had failed; they would think he had sufficient power to handle any flame they could muster. But what *would* they do?

Whatever it was, he couldn't let them succeed, not with Lorna here.

"Stay here," he commanded, getting to his feet.

She scrambled after him. The woman didn't obey worth a damn. "I said stay here!" he roared, whirling back and catching her arm, pushing her down once more. He started to stick her ass to the floor with a mental command, but he'd promised her—damn it, he'd *promised* her—and he couldn't do it.

"I was going to call the cops!" she shouted at

him, so furious at his rough handling that she was practically levitating.

"Don't bother. This isn't something the cops can handle. Stay here, Lorna. I don't want you caught between us."

"Who is *us?*" she yelled at his back as he charged down the stairs. "What are you going to do?"

"Fight fire with fire," he said grimly.

Dante had a tremendous advantage. This was his home, his property, and he knew every inch of it. Because he was Raintree, because he was the Dranir and took precautions, he went out through the tunnel he'd built under his house. He knew where he'd been standing when the laser scope had settled the telltale dot on his forehead, so he had a good idea where the shooter had been standing, too.

There was only one. He hadn't found signs of any others.

He had no intention of trying to capture the bastard or engaging him in any sort of face-to-face battle. He prowled up the ravine like a big cat, death in his eyes. The shooter's position must have been just around this cut, maybe in that big cluster of rocks. A sniper needed a stable shooting platform, and those rocks would be convenient. This ravine provided good cover, too, for approaching.

And for leaving.

Dante slid around the cut and came face-to-face with a man wearing desert camo and toting a rifle. He didn't hesitate at all. The man had barely moved, bringing the rifle up to fire, when Dante set him aflame.

The screams were raw and terrified. The man dropped the rifle and threw himself to the ground, frantically rolling, but Dante ruthlessly kept the fire going. This bastard had come close to killing Lorna, and there was no mercy in his heart for anyone who harmed her. In seconds the screams became howls, taking on an inhuman quality—and then silence.

Dante extinguished the flame.

The man lay smoldering, barely recognizable as human.

Dante used his foot to roll the man onto his back. Incredibly, hate-filled eyes glared up at him from the charred face. The hole that had been the man's mouth worked, and a ghostly sound tore from a throat that shouldn't have worked.

"Toooo late. Toooo late."

Then he died, massive shock stopping his heart. Dante stood frozen, his thoughts working furiously.

Too late? Too late for what?

He'd touched the Ansara. The man had been in

agony, his hate projected like a force field, and
Dante had read him.

Too late.

He could warn Mercy, but it would be too late.
"Oh, shit," he said softly, and ran.

Lorna had obeyed him, and stayed put. She was
in the kitchen, crouched by the refrigerator, when he
charged in and grabbed the nearest phone. His first
phone call was to Mercy. His second was to Gideon,
who could get to Mercy much faster than he could.

Because it was the solstice, because Gideon's
personal electrical field played hell with all electronics, when Gideon answered the phone almost
all Dante could hear was static.

"Get to Mercy!" he roared, hoping Gideon
would understand anyway. "The Ansara are attacking Sanctuary!" Then he slammed down the
phone and tore open the door to the garage, his
mind racing.

The corporate jet would get him to the airport
nearest Sanctuary in about four hours. He could try
Gideon again from the plane.

Two hundred years ago the Ansara had tried to
destroy the Raintree and had failed. Now they
were trying again, and, damn it, this time they
might succeed in destroying Sanctuary—where
Mercy was, with Eve.

"Where are you going?" Lorna shrieked as he got in the Lotus.

"Stay here!" he ordered one last time, and reversed out of the garage. He didn't want Lorna anywhere near Sanctuary. He didn't know if he would make it back alive, but no matter what, he had to know she was safe.

"I don't think so," Lorna muttered furiously as she changed clothes. Dante Raintree wasn't the only person who knew how to get things done. If he thought he could leave her behind while he went to fight some sort of supernatural battle, well, he would soon find out he was wrong.

* * * * *

Turn the page for a special preview of the final two titles in the Raintree trilogy,
Raintree: Haunted *by national bestselling author Linda Winstead Jones and*
Raintree: Sanctuary *by New York Times bestselling author Beverly Barton.*

Look for Raintree: Haunted
in April 2008
and
Raintree: Sanctuary
in May 2008
only from Mills & Boon® Intrigue.

Raintree: Haunted

by

Linda Winstead Jones

Monday Morning, 3:37 a.m.

When Gideon's phone rang in the middle of the night, it meant someone was dead. "Raintree," he answered, his voice rumbling with the edges of sleep.

"Sorry to wake you."

Surprised to hear his brother Dante's voice, Gideon came instantly awake. "What's wrong?"

"There's a fire at the casino. Could be worse," Dante added before Gideon could ask, "but it's bad enough. I didn't want you to see it on the morning news without some warning. Call Mercy in a couple of hours and tell her I'm all right. I'd call her myself, but I'm going to have my hands full for the next few days."

Gideon sat up, wide awake. "If you need me, I'm there."

"No, thanks. You've got no business getting on an airplane this week, and everything here is fine. I just wanted to call you before I got so tied up in red tape I couldn't get to a phone."

Gideon ran his fingers through his hair. Outside his window, the waves of the Atlantic crashed and rolled. He offered again to go to Reno and help. He could drive, if necessary. But once again Dante told him everything was fine, and they ended the call. Gideon reset his alarm for five-thirty. He would call Mercy before she started her day. The fire must have been a bad one for Dante to be so certain it would make the national news.

Alarm reset, Gideon fell back onto the bed. Maybe he'd sleep, maybe not. He listened to the ocean waves and let his mind wander. With the solstice coming in less than a week, his normal electric abnormalities were really out of whack. The surges usually spiraled out of control only when a ghost was nearby, but for the past few days—and for the week to come—it didn't take the addition of an electrically charged spirit to make appliances and electronics—or planes—in his path go haywire. There was nothing he could do but be cautious. Maybe he should take a few days off, stay away from the station altogether and lie low. He closed his eyes and fell back asleep.

She appeared without warning, floating over the end of the bed and smiling down at him, as she always did. Tonight she wore a plain white dress that touched her bare ankles, and her long dark hair was unbound. Emma, as she said she would one day be called, always came to him in the form of a child. She was very much unlike the ghosts who haunted him. This child came only in dreams and was untainted by the pain of life's hardships. She carried with her no need for justice, no heartbreak, no gnawing deed left undone. Instead, she brought with her light and love, and a sense of peace. And she insisted on calling him Daddy.

"Good morning, Daddy."

Gideon sighed and sat up. He'd first seen this particular spirit three months ago, but lately her visits had become more and more frequent. More and more real. Who knew. Maybe he had been her father in another life, but he wasn't going to be anyone's daddy in this one.

"Good morning, Emma."

The spirit of the little girl drifted down to stand on the foot of the bed. "I'm so excited." She laughed, and the sound was oddly familiar. Gideon liked that laugh. It made his heart do strange things. He convinced himself that the sense of warm familiarity meant nothing. Nothing at all.

"Why are you excited?"

"I'm coming to you soon, Daddy."

He closed his eyes and sighed. "Emma, honey, I've told you a hundred times, I'm not going to have kids in this lifetime, so you can stop calling me Daddy."

She just laughed again. "Don't be silly, Daddy. You always have me."

The spirit who had told him that her name would be Emma in this lifetime did have the Raintree eyes, his own dark brown hair and a touch of honey in her skin. But he knew better than to trust what he saw. After all, she only showed up in dreams. He was going to have to stop eating nachos before going to bed.

"I hate to tell you this, sweetheart, but in order to make a baby there has to be a mommy as well as a daddy. I'm not getting married and I'm not having kids, so you'll just have to choose someone else to be your daddy this time around."

Emma was not at all perturbed. "You're always so stubborn. I am coming to you, Daddy, I am. I'm coming to you in a moonbeam."

Gideon had tried romantic relationships before, and they never worked. He had to hide so much of himself from the women in his life; it would never do to have someone that close. And a family? Forget it. He already had to answer to the new chief, the rest of his family and a never-ending stream of ghosts. He wasn't about to put himself in a position where he would be obligated to answer to anyone else. Women came and went, but he made sure none ever got too close or stayed too long.

It was Dante's job to reproduce, not his. Gideon glanced toward the dresser, where the latest fertility charm sat ready to be packaged up and mailed. Once Dante had kids of his own, Gideon would no longer be next in line for the position of Dranir, head of the Raintree family. He couldn't think of anything worse than being Dranir, except maybe getting married and having kids of his own.

Big brother had his hands full at the moment, though, so maybe he would hold off a few days before mailing that charm. Maybe.

"Be careful," Emma said as she floated a bit closer. "She's very bad, Daddy. Very bad. You have to be careful."

"Don't call me Daddy," Gideon said. As an afterthought he added, "Who's very bad?"

"You'll know soon. Take care of my moonbeam, Daddy."

"On a moonbeam," he said softly. "What a load of…"

"It's just begun," Emma said, her voice and her body fading away.

* * * * *

Turn the page
for your first look at
RAINTREE: SANCTUARY
by New York Times *bestselling author*
Beverly Barton

Raintree: Sanctuary

by

Beverly Barton

Mercy Raintree sat on the firm, grassy ground, her eyes closed, her hands resting in her lap. Whenever she was troubled, she came to Amadahy Pointe to meditate, to collect her thoughts and renew her strength. The sunshine covered her like an invisible robe, wrapping her in light and warmth. The spring breeze caressed her tenderly, like a lover's soft touch. With her eyes closed and her soul open to the positive energy she drew from this holy place, this sanctuary within a sanctuary, she focused on what was most important to her.

Family.

Mercy sensed impending danger. But from

whom or from what, she did not know. Although her greatest talents lay in being an empath and a healer, she possessed latent precognitive powers, less erratic than her cousin Echo's, but not as strong. She had also been cursed with the ability to sense the emotional and physical condition of others from a distance. *Clairempathy*. As a child, she'd found her various empathic talents maddening, but gradually, year by year, she had learned to control them. And now, despite both Dante and Gideon blocking her from intercepting their thoughts and emotions, she could still manage to pick up something on the outer fringes of each brother's individual consciousness.

Dante and Gideon were in trouble. But she did not know why. Perhaps it was nothing more than stress from their chosen professions. Or it could even be problems in their personal lives.

If her brothers thought she could help them, they would ask her to intervene. That knowledge reassured her that their problems were within the realm of human reality and not of a supernatural nature. Her brothers were, as they had pointed out to her on numerous occasions, grown men, perfectly capable of taking care of themselves without the assistance of their baby sister.

Past experience had taught her that when their souls needed replenishing, their spirits nurtured, her brothers came home, here to the Raintree land, deep in the North Carolina mountains. The homeplace was protected by a powerful magic that had been established by their ancestors two centuries ago after The Battle. Within the boundaries of these secure acres, no living creature could intrude without alerting the resident guardian. Mercy Raintree was that guardian, protector of the homeplace, as her great-aunt Gillian had been until her death at a hundred and nineteen, and like Gillian's mother, Vesta, the first keeper of the Sanctuary in the early eighteen hundreds.

Taking a deep, cleansing breath, Mercy opened her eyes and looked at the valley below, spread out before her like a banquet feast. Late springtime in the mountains. An endless blue sky that went on forever. Towering green trees, the ancient, the old and the young growing together, reaching heavenward. Verdant life, thick and rich and sweet to the senses. A multitude of wildflowers blooming in abundance, their perfume tantalizing, their colors pleasing to the eye.

Mercy wasn't sure exactly what was wrong with her, but she felt a nagging sense of unease that had nothing to do with her brothers or with anyone in the Raintree tribe. No, the restlessness was within her, a yearning she was forced to control because of who she was, because of her duty to her family and to her people. Whenever these strange emotions unsettled her, she climbed the mountain to this sacred peak and meditated until the uncertainty subsided. But today, for some unknown reason, the anxiety clung to her.

Was it a warning?

Seven years ago, she had allowed that hunger inside her to lead her into dangerous territory, into a world she had been ill prepared for, into a relationship that had altered her life. She would not—could not—succumb to fear. And except for brief visits to Dante and Gideon, she would not leave the safety of the Raintree Sanctuary. Not ever again.

Loving Evangeline

Chapter One

Davis Priesen didn't think of himself as a coward, but he would rather have had surgery without anesthesia than face Robert Cannon and tell him what he had to tell him. It wasn't that the majority stockholder, CEO and president of Cannon Group would hold him responsible for the bad news; Cannon had never been known to shoot the messenger. But those icy green eyes would become even colder, even more remote, and Davis knew from experience that he would feel the frigid touch of fear along his spine. Cannon had a reputation for scrupulous fairness, but also for unmatched ruthlessness when someone tried to screw him. Davis couldn't think of anyone he respected more than Robert Cannon, but that didn't relieve his dread.

Other men in Cannon's position, with his power, insulated themselves behind layers of assistants. It was a measure of his own control and personal remoteness that only Cannon's personal assistant guarded the gates to his inner sanctum. Felice Koury had been Cannon's PA for eight years and ran his office with the precision of a Swiss watch. She was a tall, lean, ageless woman with iron-gray hair and the smooth complexion of a twenty-year-old. Davis knew that her youngest child was in his mid-twenties, putting Felice at least in her mid-forties, but it was impossible to guess her age from her appearance. She was cool under fire, frighteningly efficient and had never shown a hint of nervousness around her boss. Davis wished he had a little of that last ability.

He had called beforehand to make certain Cannon could see him, so Felice wasn't surprised when he entered her office. "Good morning, Mr. Priesen." She reached immediately for the phone and punched a button. "Mr. Priesen is here, sir." She replaced the receiver and stood. "He'll see you now." With the smooth efficiency that always intimidated him, she was at the door of the inner office before he could reach it, opening it for him, then firmly closing it when he was inside. There was nothing subservient in Felice's attention; rather, he felt as if she controlled even his entrance into Cannon's office. Which, of course, she did.

Cannon's office was huge, luxurious and exquisitely decorated. It was a tribute to his taste that the effect was relaxing, rather than overwhelming, even though original oil paintings hung on the walls and a two-hundred-year-old Persian rug was underfoot. To the right was a large sitting area, complete with entertainment center, though Davis doubted that Cannon ever used the large-screen television or VCR for anything other than business. Six Palladian windows marched along the wall, framing the matchless views of New York City as if they were six paintings. The windows were works of art in themselves, beautifully fashioned panes of cut glass that took the light streaming through them and splintered it into diamonds.

Cannon's massive desk was another antique, a masterpiece of carved black wood that supposedly had belonged to the eighteenth-century Romanovs. He looked very at home behind it.

He was a tall, lean man, with the elegant grace and power of a panther. There was something pantherish about his coloring, too, with his sleek black hair and pale green eyes. One might even think of Robert Cannon as indolent. One would be dangerously mistaken.

He rose to his feet to shake hands, his long, well-shaped fingers gripping Davis's with surprising strength. Davis was always taken aback by the steeliness of that grip.

On some occasions Cannon had invited him to the sitting area and asked if he would like coffee. This was not one of those occasions. Cannon hadn't reached his position by misreading people, and his eyes narrowed as he examined the tension in Davis's face. "I would say it's good to see you, Davis," he remarked, "but I don't think you're here to tell me something I'm going to like."

His voice had been easy, almost casual, but Davis felt his tension go up another ten notches. "No, sir."

"Is it your fault?"

"No, sir." Then, scrupulously honest, he admitted, "Though I probably should have caught it sooner."

"Then relax and sit down," Robert said gently as he reseated himself. "If it isn't your fault, you're safe. Now, tell me what the problem is."

Davis nervously took a seat, but relaxing was out of the question. He perched on the edge of a soft leather chair. "Someone in Huntsville is selling our software for the space station," he blurted.

Cannon was never a restless man, but now he became even more still, and those green eyes took on the glacial look that Davis dreaded. "Do you have proof?" he asked.

"Yes, sir."

"Do you know who?"

"I think so, sir."

"Fill me in." With those abrupt words, Cannon leaned back, his gaze focused on Davis like a pale green laser.

Davis did, stumbling several times as he tried to explain how he had become suspicious and done a bit of investigating on his own to verify his suspicions before he accused anyone. Cannon listened in silence, and Davis wiped the sweat from his brow as he described the results of his sleuthing. The Cannon Group company, PowerNet, located in Huntsville, Alabama, was currently working on highly classified software developed for NASA. That software was definitely showing up in the hands of a company affiliated with another country. This wasn't just industrial espionage, which would have been enough; this was treason.

His suspicions had centered on Landon Mercer, the company manager. Mercer had divorced the year before, and his style of living had gone noticeably upward. His salary was very good, but not good enough to support a family and live the way he had been living. Davis had discreetly hired an investigation service that had discovered large deposits into Mercer's bank account. After following him for several weeks, they had reported that he regularly visited a marina in Guntersville, a small town nearby, situated on Guntersville Lake, an impoundment of the Tennessee river.

The owner/operator of the marina was a woman named Evie Shaw; the investigators hadn't yet been able to find out anything substantive from her bank accounts or spending habits, which could mean only that she was smarter than Mercer. On at least two occasions, however, Mercer had rented a motorboat at the marina, and shortly after he had left in the boat, Evie Shaw had closed the marina, gotten into her own boat and followed him. They had returned separately, some fifteen minutes apart. It looked as if they were meeting somewhere on the big lake, where they would find it very easy both to conceal their actions, and to see and hear anyone approaching them. It was much safer than trying to conduct clandestine business in the busy marina; in fact, the popularity of the marina made it all the odder that she would close it down in the middle of the day.

When Davis had finished and sat nervously cracking his knuckles, Cannon's face was hard and expressionless. "Thank you, Davis," he said calmly. "I'll notify the FBI and take it from here. Good work."

Davis flushed as he got to his feet. "I'm sorry I didn't catch it sooner."

"Security isn't your area. Someone was falling down on the job. I'll take care of that, too. We're lucky that you're as sharp as you are." Robert made a mental note to both increase Davis's salary, which was already healthy, and begin grooming him for more responsibility and power. He had shown a sharpness and initiative that shouldn't go unrewarded. "I'm sure the FBI will want to speak with you, so stay available for the rest of the day."

"Yes, sir."

As soon as Davis had left, Robert used his private line to call the FBI. The bureau maintained a huge force in the city, and he had had occasion to work with them before. He was put through immediately to the supervisory agent. His control was such that none of his rage was revealed in his voice as he requested that the two best agents come to his office as soon as possible. His influence was such that no questions were asked; he was simply given the quiet assurance that two agents would be there within the half hour.

That done, he sat back and considered all the options open to him. He didn't allow his cold fury to cloud his thinking. Uncontrolled emotion was not only useless, it was stupid, and Robert never allowed himself to do anything stupid. He took it personally that someone at one of his companies was selling classified computer programs; it was a blemish on his own reputation. He had nothing but contempt for someone who would sell out his own country merely for the money involved, and he would stop at nothing to halt the theft and put the perpetrator behind bars. Within fifteen minutes, he had formulated his plan of action.

The two agents arrived in twenty minutes. When Felice buzzed him, he told her to send them in, and that he wanted no interruptions of any kind until the gentlemen had left. A perfect secretary to the bone, she asked no questions.

She ushered the two conservatively dressed men into his office and firmly closed the door behind them. Robert stood to welcome them, but all the while he was assessing them with his cool, unreadable gaze. The younger man, about thirty, was immediately recognizable as a midlevel civil servant, but there was also a certain self-assurance in the man's eyes that Robert approved of. The older man, perhaps in his early fifties, had light brown hair that had gone mostly gray. He was not quite of average height, and was stocky of build. The blue eyes, behind metal-framed glasses, were tired, but nevertheless sparkled with intelligence and authority. No junior agent, this.

The older man held out his hand to Robert. "Mr. Cannon?" At Robert's nod, he said, "I'm William Brent, senior agent with the Federal Bureau of Investigation. This is Lee Murray, special agent assigned to counterespionage."

"Counterespionage," Robert murmured, his eyes cool. The presence of these two particular agents meant that the FBI had already been investigating PowerNet. "Good guess, gentlemen. Please sit down."

"It wasn't much of a guess," Agent Brent replied ruefully, as they took the offered seats. "A corporation such as yours, which handles so many government contracts, is unfortunately a prime target for espionage. I'm also aware that you have some experience in that area yourself, so it followed that you might need our particular talents, so to speak."

He was good, Robert thought. Just the type of person to inspire trust. They wanted to know if he knew anything, but they weren't going to tip their own hand if he didn't mention PowerNet. That little charade was a screen of innocence, behind which they could exhibit surprise and consternation if he informed them that he had discovered a leak at the company, or hide their own knowledge if he didn't mention the matter.

He didn't let them get away with it. "I see you've picked up some disquieting information yourselves," he said remotely. "I'm interested in knowing why you didn't contact me immediately."

William Brent grimaced. He had heard that nothing got by Robert Cannon, but still, he hadn't expected the man to be so acute.

Cannon was looking at him with a slight, cool lift of his eyebrow that invited explanations, an expression most people found difficult to resist.

Brent managed to control the inclination to rush into speech, mingling explanation with apology; he was astonished that the impulse even existed. It made him study Robert Cannon even more closely. He already knew a lot about the man, as he had made it his business to find out. Cannon came from a cultured, moneyed background, but had made himself much wealthier with his own astute business sense, and his reputation was impeccable. He also had a lot of friends in both the State and Justice departments, powerful men in their own right, who held him in the greatest respect. "Look, here," one of those men had said. "If something crooked is going on with any of the Cannon Group companies, I'd take it as a personal favor if you'd let Robert Cannon know about it before you do anything."

"I can't do that," Brent had replied. "It would compromise the investigation."

"Not at all," the man had said. "I would trust Cannon with the country's most sensitive intelligence. As a matter of fact, I already have, on several occasions. He's done some...favors for us."

"It's possible he could be in on it," Brent had warned, still resisting the idea of briefing a civilian outsider on the situation developing down in Alabama.

But the other man had shaken his head. "No. Not Robert Cannon."

After learning something about the nature and magnitude of the "favors" Cannon had done, and the dangers involved, Brent had reluctantly agreed to apprise Cannon of the situation before they put any plans into operation. Cannon had derailed that by calling first, and they hadn't been certain if he already knew, or not. The plan had been to keep quiet until they found out why he had called. It hadn't worked. He'd seen through them immediately.

Brent was used to reading men, but he couldn't read Cannon. His persona was that of a wealthy, cultured, sophisticated man, and Brent supposed he was all that, but nevertheless, it was only the first layer. The other layers, whatever they were, were so well hidden that he only sensed their existence, and even that was due only to his own access to privileged information. Watching Cannon's leanly handsome face, he couldn't catch so much as a flicker of expression; there were only those remote eyes watching him with unlimited patience.

Making a swift decision, William Brent leaned forward. "Mr. Cannon, I'm going to tell you a lot more than I had originally planned. We have a definite problem at one of your companies, a software company down in Alabama—"

"Suppose I tell you what I know?" Robert interrupted in an even tone. "Then you can tell me if you have anything to add."

With calm, precise sentences, he recounted what Davis Priesen had told him. The two agents shared one startled, involuntary glance that revealed they hadn't discovered as much as Davis had, which upped that young man's stock with Robert even more.

When he had finished, William Brent cleared his throat and

leaned forward. "Congratulations. You're a bit ahead of us. This will help us considerably in our investigation—"

"I'm flying down there tomorrow morning," Robert said.

Brent looked disapproving. "Mr. Cannon, I appreciate your desire to help, but this is best handled by the bureau."

"You misunderstand. I don't intend to *help*. This is my company, my problem. I'll take care of it myself. I'm merely apprising you of the situation and my intentions. I don't have to take the time to set up a cover and get inside the operation, because I own it. I will, of course, keep you informed."

Brent was already shaking his head. "No, it's out of the question."

"Who better? I not only have access to everything, my presence wouldn't be as alarming as that of federal investigators." He paused, then said gently, "I'm not a rank amateur."

"I'm aware of that, Mr. Cannon."

"Then I suggest you talk this over with your superiors." He glanced at his watch. "In the meantime, I have arrangements to make."

He had no doubt that when Brent took this to his superiors, he would be surprised and chagrined to be told to back off and let Robert Cannon handle this problem on his own. They would provide every assistance, of course, and have backup in place if he needed it, but Agent Brent would find that Robert was calling the shots.

He spent the rest of the day clearing his calendar. Felice made the open-ended flight arrangements and his hotel reservation in Huntsville. Just before leaving that night, he checked his watch and took a chance. Though it was eight o'clock in New York, it was only six in Montana, and the long summer daylight hours meant ranch work went on for much longer than during the winter.

To his delight, the phone was picked up on the third ring and his sister's lazy drawl came over the line. "Duncans' Madhouse, Madelyn speaking."

Robert chuckled. He could hear in the background the din his two young nephews were making. "Had a busy day, honey?"

"Robert!" Pleasure warmed her voice. "You might say that. Would you be interested in having your nephews for a prolonged visit?"

"Not until they're housebroken. I won't be at home, anyway."

"Where are you off to this time?"

"Huntsville, Alabama."

She paused. "It's hot down there."

"I'm aware of that."

"You might even *sweat,*" she warned him. "Think how upset you'd be."

His firm mouth twitched at the amusement in her voice. "That's a chance I'll have to take."

"It must be serious, then. Trouble?"

"A few glitches."

"Take care."

"I will. If it looks as though I'll be down there for any length of time, I'll call you and give you my number."

"All right. Love you."

"Love you, too." He smiled a bit as he hung up. It was typical of Madelyn that she hadn't asked questions but had immediately sensed the seriousness of the situation awaiting him in Alabama. In six words she had given him her blessing, her support and her love. Though she was actually only his stepsister, the affection and understanding between them were as strong as if they had been connected by blood.

Next he called the woman he had been escorting rather regularly lately, Valentina Lawrence. The relationship hadn't progressed far enough that he would expect her to wait until his return, so the easiest thing for both of them was if he made it clear that she was free to see anyone she wished. It was a pity; Valentina was too popular to remain unattached for long, and he suspected he would be in Alabama for several weeks.

She was just the sort of woman Robert had always been most attracted to: the thoroughbred racehorse type—tall, lean, small-breasted. Her makeup was always impeccable and understated, her clothing both stylish and tasteful. She had a genuinely pleasant personality, and enjoyed the theater and opera as much as he did. She would have been a wonderful companion, if this problem hadn't interfered.

It had been several months since he had ended his last relationship, and he was feeling restless. He much preferred living with a woman to living alone, though he was perfectly content with his own company. He deeply enjoyed women, both mentally and physically, and he normally preferred the steadiness of a long-term relationship. He didn't do one-nighters and disdained those who were so stupid. He refrained from making love to a woman until she had committed herself to a relationship with him.

Valentina accepted the news of his prolonged absence with grace; after all, they weren't lovers and had no claim on each other. He could hear the gentle regret in her voice, but she didn't ask him to call when he returned.

That final piece of business concluded, he sat for several minutes, frowning as he allowed himself to think about the relationship that hadn't quite developed into intimacy, and how long it would be before he had time to attend to the sexual part of his life again. He wasn't pleased at the prospect of a long wait.

He wasn't casual about sex in any way. His intense sexuality was always under strict control; with the difference between a man's strength and a woman's, a man who *wasn't* in control could easily brutalize a woman, something that disgusted him. He tempered both his sexual appetite and his steely strength, reining them in with the icy power of his intellect. He never pressured a woman, though he always made it clear when he was attracted, so she would know where she stood. But he let his lady set the pace, let the intimacy progress at her speed. He respected a woman's natural caution about opening her tender, vulnerable body to a much bigger, stronger male. When it came to sex, he treated women gently and took his time so they could become fully aroused. Such control was no hardship; he could spend hours caressing soft, feminine skin and intriguing curves. Lingering over the lovemaking helped satisfy his own hunger, while intensifying his partner's.

There was nothing like making love that first time with a new partner, he mused. Never again was the experience so intense and hungry. He always tried to make it special for his lady, to make *her* feel special. He never stinted on the little details that made a woman feel treasured: romantic dinners for two, candlelight, champagne, thoughtful gifts, his complete attention. When the time finally came to retire to the bedroom, he would use all of his skill and control to satisfy her again and again before he allowed release for himself.

Thinking about what the problem in Alabama was causing him to miss made him irritated.

He was roused by a knock on his door. He looked up as Felice stuck her head in. "You should have gone home," he reproved. "You didn't have to stay."

"A messenger brought this envelope for you," she said, approaching to place it on his desk. She ignored his comment. No matter how late, she seldom left before he did.

"Go home," he said calmly. "That's an order. I'll call you tomorrow."

"Do you need anything before I go? A fresh pot of coffee?"

"No, I won't be staying much longer myself."

"Then have a good trip." She smiled and left the room. He could hear her in the outer office gathering together her possessions and locking everything up for the night.

He doubted that anything about the trip would be good. He was in a vengeful mood and out for blood.

He noticed that the manila envelope had no return address. He opened it and slid several pages out. There was one grainy, photostated picture, a recap of the situation and what they already knew about it, and a brief message from Agent Brent, identifying the woman in the picture and informing Robert that the bureau would cooperate with him in all matters, which was only what he had expected.

He picked up the reproduced photograph and studied it. It was of very poor quality, but pictured a woman standing on a dock, with motorboats in the background. So this was Evie Shaw. She was wearing sunglasses, so it was difficult to tell much about her, other than she had blondish, untidy hair and seemed to be rather hefty. No Mata Hari there, he thought, his fastidious taste of-

fended by her poor choice of clothes and her general haysee
appearance. She looked more like a female mud wrestler, a coars
hick who was selling out her country for greed.

Briskly he returned the papers to the envelope. He looked forward to bringing both Landon Mercer and Evie Shaw to justice.

Chapter Two

It was a typically hot, sultry Southern summer day. The sky overhead was a deep, rich blue, dotted with fat white clouds that lazily sailed along on a breeze so slight it barely rippled the lake's surface. Gulls wheeled overhead and boats bobbed hypnotically in their slips. A few diehard fishermen and skiers dotted the water, ignoring the heat, but most of the fishermen who had gone out that morning had returned before noon. The air was heavy and humid, intensifying the odors of the lake and the surrounding lush, green mountains.

Evangeline Shaw looked out over her domain from the big plate-glass windows at the rear of the main marina building. Everyone on earth needed his own kingdom, and hers was this sprawling skeletal maze of docks and boat slips. Nothing within these few square acres escaped her attention. Five years ago, when she had taken over, it had been run-down and barely paying expenses. A sizable bank loan had been required to give it the infusion of capital it had needed, but within a year she had had it spruced up, expanded and bringing in more money than it ever had before. Of course, it took more money to run it, but now the marina was making a nice profit. With any luck she would have the bank loan paid off in another three years. Then the marina would be completely hers, free and clear of debt, and she would be able to expand even more, as well as diversify her holdings. She only hoped business would hold up; the fishing trade had slacked off a lot, due to the Tennessee Valley Authority's "weed management" program that had managed to kill most of the water plants that had harbored and protected the fish.

But she had been careful, and she hadn't overextended. Her

debt was manageable, unlike that of others who had thought the fishing boom would last forever and had gone deeply into debt to expand. Her domain was secure.

Old Virgil Dodd had been with her most of the morning, sitting in the rocking chair behind the counter and entertaining her and her customers with tales of his growing-up days, back in the 1900s. The old man was as tough as shoe leather, but almost a century weighed on his inceasingly frail shoulders, and Evie was afraid that another couple of years, three at the most, would be too much for him. She had known him all her life; he had been *old* all her life, changing little, as enduring as the river and the mountains. But she knew all too well how fleeting and uncertain human life was, and she treasured the mornings that Virgil spent with her. He enjoyed them, too; he no longer went out fishing, as he had for the first eighty years of his life, but at the marina he was still close to the boats, where he could hear the slap of the water against the docks and smell the lake.

They were alone now, just the two of them, and Virgil had launched into another tale from his youth. Evie perched on a tall stool, occasionally glancing out the windows to see if anyone had pulled up to the gas pump on the dock, but giving most of her attention to Virgil.

The side door opened, and a tall, lean man stepped inside. He stood for a moment before removing his sunglasses, helping his eyes adjust to the relative dimness, then moved toward her with a silent, pantherish stroll.

Evie gave him only a swift glance before turning her attention back to Virgil, but it was enough to make her defenses rise. She didn't know who he was, but she recognized immediately *what* he was; he was not only a stranger, he was an outsider. There were a lot of Northerners who had retired to Guntersville, charmed by the mild winters, the slow pace, low cost of living and natural beauty of the lake, but he wasn't one of them. He was far too young to be retired, for one thing. His accent would be fast and hard, his clothes expensive and his attitude disdainful. Evie had met his kind before. She hadn't been impressed then, either.

But it wasn't just that. It was the other quality she had caught that made her want to put a wall at her back.

He was dangerous.

Though she smiled at Virgil, instinctively she analyzed the stranger. She had grown up with bad boys, daredevils and hell-raisers; the South produced them in abundance. This man was something different, something...more. He didn't embrace danger as much as he *was* danger. It was a different mind-set, a will and temperament that brooked no opposition, a force of character that had glittered in those startlingly pale eyes.

She didn't know how or why, but she sensed that he was a threat to her.

"Excuse me," he said, and the deepness of his voice ran over her like velvet. A strange little quiver tightened her belly and ran up her spine. The words were courteous, but the iron will behind them told her that he expected her to immediately attend to him.

She gave him another quick, dismissive glance. "I'll be with you in a minute," she said, her tone merely polite, then she turned back to Virgil with real warmth. "What happened then, Virgil?"

No hint of emotion showed on Robert's face, though he was a bit startled by the woman's lack of response. That was unusual. He wasn't accustomed to being ignored by anyone, and certainly not by a woman. Women had always been acutely aware of him, responding to the intense masculinity he kept under ruthless control. He wasn't vain, but his effect on women was something he largely took for granted. He couldn't remember ever wanting a woman and not having her, eventually.

But he was willing to wait and use the opportunity to watch this woman. Her appearance had thrown him a little off balance, also something unusual for him. He still hadn't adjusted his expectations to the reality.

This was Evie Shaw, no doubt about it. She sat on a stool behind the counter, all her attention on an old man who sat in a rocking chair, his aged voice gleeful as he continued to recount some tall tale from his long-ago youth. Robert's eyes narrowed fractionally as he studied her.

She wasn't the thick-bodied hayseed he had expected. Or

rather, she wasn't thick-bodied; he reserved judgment on the hay seed part. The unflattering image he'd formed must have bee caused by the combination of bad photography and poorly fittin clothes. He had walked in looking for a woman who was coars and ill-bred, but that wasn't what he'd found.

Instead, she…glowed.

It was an unsettling illusion, perhaps produced by the brillian sunlight streaming in through the big windows, haloing her sunny hair and lighting the tawny depths of her hazel eyes. The ligh caressed her golden skin, which was as smooth and unblemishe as a porcelain doll's. Illusion or not, the woman was luminous.

Her voice had been surprisingly deep and a little raspy, bringing up memories of old Bogie and Bacall movies and making Robert's spine prickle. Her accent was lazy and liquid, as melodious as a murmuring creek or the wind in the trees, a voice that made him think of tangled sheets and long, hot nights.

Watching her, he felt something inside him go still.

The old man leaned forward, folding his gnarled hands over the crook of his walking cane. His faded blue eyes were full of laughter and the memories of good times. "Well, we'd tried ever way we knowed to get John H. away from that still, but he weren't budging. He kept an old shotgun loaded with rat shot, so we were afeard to venture too close. He knowed it was just a bunch of young'uns aggravating him, but *we* didn't know he knowed. Ever time he grabbed that shotgun, we'd run like jackrabbits, then we'd come sneakin' back…."

Robert forced himself to look around as he tuned out the rest of Virgil's tale. Ramshackle though the building was, the business seemed to be prospering, if the amount of tackle on hand and the number of occupied boat slips were any indication. A pegboard behind the counter held the ignition keys to the rental boats, each key neatly labeled and numbered. He wondered how she kept track of who had which boat.

Virgil was well into his tale, slapping his knee and chortling. Evie Shaw threw back her head with a shout of pure enjoyment, her laughter as deep as her speaking voice. Robert was suddenly aware of how accustomed he had become to carefully controlled ocial laughter, how shrill and shallow it was compared to her unabashed mirth, with nothing forced or held back.

He tried to resist the compulsion to stare at her, but, to his surprise, it was like resisting the need to breathe. He could manage it for a little while, but it was a losing battle from the start. With a mixture of fury and curiosity, he gave in to the temptation and let his gaze greedily drink her in.

He watched her with an impassive expression, his self-control so absolute that neither his posture nor his face betrayed any hint of his thoughts. Unfortunately, that self-control didn't extend to those thoughts as his attention focused on Evie Shaw with such intensity that he was no longer aware of his surroundings, that he no longer heard Virgil's cracked voice continuing with his tale.

She wasn't anything like the women he had always found most attractive. She was also a traitor, or at least was involved in industrial espionage. He had every intention of breaking her, of bringing her to justice. Yet he couldn't take his eyes off her, couldn't control his wayward thoughts, couldn't still the sudden hard thumping in his chest. He had been sweating in the suffocating heat, but suddenly the heat inside him was so blistering that it made the outer temperature seem cool in comparison. His skin felt too tight, his clothing too restrictive. A familiar heaviness in his loins made the last two sensations all too real, rather than products of his imagination.

The women he had wanted in the past, for all the differences in their characters, had shared a certain sense of style, of sophistication. They had all looked—and been—expensive. He hadn't minded, and had enjoyed spoiling them more. They had all been well dressed, perfumed, exquisitely turned out. His sister Madelyn had disparagingly referred to a couple of them as mannequins, but Madelyn herself was a clotheshorse of the highest order, so he had been amused rather than irritated by the comment.

Evie Shaw, in contrast, evidently paid no attention to her clothes. She wore an oversize T-shirt that she had knotted at the waist, a pair of jeans so ancient that they were threadbare and almost colorless, and equally old docksiders. Her hair, a sunstreaked blond that ranged in color from light brown to the palest flax, and included several different shades of gold, was pulled back and confined in an untidy braid that was as thick as his wrist and hung halfway down her back. Her makeup was minimal and probably a waste of time in this humidity, but with her complexion, she didn't really need it.

Damn it, how could she glow like that? It wasn't the sheen of perspiration, but the odd impression that light was attracted to her, as if she forever stood in a subtle spotlight. Her skin was lightly tanned, a creamy golden hue, and it looked like warm, living satin. Even her eyes were the golden brown hazel of dark topaz.

He had always preferred tall, lean women; as tall as he was himself, he had felt better matched with them on the dance floor and in bed. Evie Shaw was no more than five-four, if that. Nor was she lean; rather, the word that came to mind was *luscious,* followed immediately by *delicious.* Caught off guard by the violence of his reaction, he wondered savagely if he wanted to make love to her or eat her, and the swift mental answer to his own question was a flat, unequivocal "yes." To both choices.

She was a symphony of curves, not quite full-figured, but sleek and rounded, the absolute essence of femaleness. No slim, boyish hips there, but a definite flare from her waist, and she had firm, round buttocks. He had always adored the delicacy of small breasts but now found himself entranced by the soft globes that shaped the front of the annoyingly loose T-shirt. They weren't big, heavy breasts, though they had a slight bounce that riveted his attention whenever she moved; they weren't exactly voluptuous, but were just full enough to be maddeningly tempting. Their soft, warm weight would fill his hands, hands that he tightened into fists in an effort to resist the urge to reach out and touch her.

Everything about her was shaped for a man's delight, but he wasn't delighted by his reaction. If *he* could respond to her like this, maybe Mercer was her pawn rather than the other way around. It was a possibility he couldn't ignore.

Not only was she nothing like the women he had previously desired, he was furious with himself for wanting her. He was down here to gather evidence that would send her to prison, and he couldn't let lust make him lose sight of that. This woman was wading hip-deep in the sewer of espionage, and he shouldn't feel anything for her except disgust. Instead he was struggling with a physical desire so intense that it was all he could do to simply stand there, rather than act. He didn't want to court her, seduce her; he wanted to grab her and carry her away. His lair was a hideously expensive Manhattan penthouse, but the primitive instinct was the same one that had impelled men to the same action back when their lairs were caves. He wanted her, and there was nothing civilized or gentle about it. The urge made a mockery of both his intellect and his self-control.

He wanted to ignore the attraction, but he couldn't; it was too strong, the challenge too great. Evie Shaw was not just ignoring him, she was totally oblivious to the pure male intent that was surging through him. He might as well have been a post for all the attention she was paying to him, and every aggressive cell in his body was on alert. By God, he *would* have her.

The door behind him opened, and he turned, grateful for the interruption. A young woman, clad in shorts, sandals and a T-shirt, smiled at him and murmured, "Hello," as she approached. Both the smile and the look lingered for just a moment before she turned her attention to the two people behind the counter. "Have you enjoyed your visit, PawPaw? Who all has been in today?"

"Had a good time," Virgil said, slowly getting to his feet with a lot of help from the cane. "Burt Mardis spent some time with us, and both of the Gibbs boys came by. Have you got the young'uns rounded up?"

"They're in the car with the groceries." She turned to Evie. "I hate to run, but it's so hot I want to get the food put up before it spoils."

"Everything I can, I put off until night," Evie said. "Including buying groceries. Bye, Virgil. You take care of that knee, all right? And come back soon."

"The knee feels better already," he assured her. "Getting old ain't no fun, but it's better than dying." He winked and steadily made his way down the aisle, using the cane but otherwise not making much allowance for his noticeable limp.

"See you later, Evie," the young woman said as she turned to go. She gave Robert another smile in passing.

When the old man and young woman had left and the door had closed behind them, Robert leaned negligently against the counter and said in a mild tone, "I assume she's his granddaughter."

Evie shook her head and turned away to check the gas pumps again. She was too aware of being alone with him, which was ridiculous; she was alone with male customers several times a day and had never felt the least hint of uneasiness—until now. She had felt a subtle alarm the second he had walked in the door. He hadn't said or done anything untoward, but still, she couldn't shake that feeling of wariness. "Great-granddaughter. He lives with her. I apologize for making you wait, but I'll have other customers, while Virgil is ninety-three, and he may not be around much longer."

"I understand," he said calmly, not wanting to antagonize her. He held out his hand, a gesture calculated to force her to look at him, truly acknowledge him, *touch* him. "I'm Robert Cannon."

She put her hand in his, just slowly enough to let him know that she was reluctant to shake hands with him and did it only to be polite. Her fingers were slim and cool and gripped his with surprising strength. "Evie Shaw," she said. He made certain his own grip was firm, but not enough to hurt, and promptly released her. The contact was brief, impersonal...and not enough.

Immediately she turned away and said briskly, "What is it you need, Mr. Cannon?"

He came up with several graphic ideas but didn't give voice to them. Instead he thoughtfully eyed her slim back, rapidly adjusting his impressions. He had thought her oblivious to him, but she was too studiously ignoring him for that; no, quite the contrary, she was very aware of him, and very on edge. In a flash, all of his plans changed.

He had entered the marina wanting only to look around a little, get an idea of the security and layout of the place, maybe buy a fishing license or map, but all of that had changed in the past few minutes. Rather than shadow Mercer, he now intended to stick to Evie Shaw like glue.

Why was she so wary of him? She had been, right from the beginning, even before he had introduced himself. The only explanation that came to mind was that she had already known who he was, had somehow recognized him, and she could only have done that if she had been briefed. If so, this operation was more sophisticated than he had expected. It wouldn't be beyond his capabilities, but it would certainly be more of a challenge. With one of his lightning-fast decisions, he changed the base of his investigation from Huntsville to Guntersville. Before the fall of the Soviet Union, he had, on a couple of memorable occasions, found himself attracted to female operatives; taking them to bed had been a risk, but a delightful one. Danger certainly added to the excitement. Bedding Evie Shaw, he suspected, would be an event he would never forget.

"First, I need information," he said, irritated because she still wasn't looking at him, but not a hint of it sounded in his voice. He needed to lull her suspicions, make her comfortable with him. Gentling women had never been difficult for him before, and he didn't expect it to be now. As far as anyone outside a few government officials knew, he was nothing more than a very wealthy businessman; if she was as smart as he now suspected her to be, she would soon see the benefits in becoming close to him, not only for what he could give her but for the information she could get from him. A summer fling would be perfect for her needs, and he intended to give her just that.

"Perhaps you should go to the Visitors' Center," she suggested.

"Perhaps," he murmured. "But I was told that you can help me."

"Maybe." Her tone was reluctant. She certainly wasn't committing herself to anything. "What kind of information do you need?"

"I'm taking a long vacation here, for the rest of the summer," he said. "My second reason for coming here is to rent a boat slip, but I also want someone to show me around the lake. I was told that you know the area as well as anyone.''

She faced him, her gaze hooded. ''That's true, but I don't guide. I can help you with the boat, but that's all.''

She had thrown up a wall as soon as she had seen him, and she had no intention of being cooperative about anything. He gave her a gentle smile, one that had been soothing nervous women for years. ''I understand. You don't know me.''

He saw the involuntary reaction to that smile in the way her pupils flared. Now she looked uncertain. ''It isn't that. I don't know a lot of my customers.''

''I believe the going rate for guides is a hundred a day, plus expenses. I'm willing to pay twice that.''

''It isn't a matter of money, Mr. Cannon. I don't have the time.''

Pushing her now wouldn't accomplish anything, and he had a lot to get in place before he could really pursue her. He had made certain she wouldn't forget him, which was enough for a first meeting. ''Can you recommend a guide, then?'' he asked, and saw her relax a little.

She reeled off several names, which he committed to memory, for he fully intended to learn the river. Then she said, ''Would you like to look at the boat slips that are available now?''

''Yes, of course.'' It would give him a chance to inspect her security arrangements, too.

She picked up a portable phone and clipped it to a belt loop, then came out from behind the counter. Robert fell into step slightly behind her, his heavy-lidded gaze wandering over her curvy hips and heart-shaped bottom, clearly outlined by the snug jeans. Her sun-streaked head barely reached the top of his shoulder. His blood throbbed warmly through his veins as he thought of cupping her bottom in his hands. It was an effort to wrench his attention away from the image that thought provoked.

''Do you just leave the store unattended?'' he asked as they walked down the dock. The sunlight was blinding as it reflected off the water, and he slipped his sunglasses into place again. The heat was incredible, like a sauna.

"I can see from the docks if anyone drives up," she replied.

"How many others work here?"

She gave him a curious glance, as if wondering why he would ask. "I have a mechanic, and a boy who works mornings for me during the summer, then shifts to afternoons during the school year."

"How many hours a day are you open?"

"From six in the morning until eight at night."

"That's a long day."

"It isn't so bad. During the winter, I'm only open from eight until five."

Four of the docks were covered, and most of the slips were occupied. A variety of crafts bobbed in the placid water: houseboats, cabin cruisers, pontoon boats, ski boats, sailboats. The four covered docks were on the left, and the entrance to them was blocked by a locked gate. To the right were two uncovered docks, for use by general traffic. The rental boats were in the first row of boat slips on the secured dock closest to the marina building.

Evie unlocked the padlock that secured the gate, and they stepped onto the floating dock, which bobbed gently on the water. Silently she led him down the rows of boats, indicating which of the empty slips were available. Finally she asked, "What size boat do you have?"

He made another instant decision. "I intend to buy a small one. A speedboat, not a cabin cruiser. Can you recommend a good dealership in the area?"

She gave him another of those hooded looks, but merely said in a brisk tone, "There are several boat dealerships in town. It won't be hard to find what you want." Then she turned and started back toward the marina office, her steps sure and graceful on the bobbing dock.

Again Robert followed her, enjoying the view just as much as he had before. She probably thought she was rid of him, but there was no way that would happen. Anger and anticipation mingled, forming a volatile aggression that made him feel more alert, more on edge, than he ever had before. She would pay for stealing from him, in more ways than one.

"Will you have dinner with me tonight?" he asked, using a totally unaggressive tone. She halted so abruptly that he bumped into her. He could have prevented the contact, but deliberately let his body collide with hers. She staggered off balance, and he grabbed her waist to steady her, easing her back against him before she regained control. He felt the shiver that ran through her as he savored the heat and feel of her under his hands, against his thighs and loins and belly. "Sorry," he said with light amusement. "I didn't realize having dinner with me was such a frightening concept."

She should have done a number of things. If reluctant, she should have moved away from the subtle sexuality of his embrace. If compliant, she should have turned to face him. She should have hastened to assure him that his invitation hadn't frightened her at all, then accepted to prove that it hadn't. She did none of those things. She stood stock-still, as if paralyzed by his hands clasping her waist. Silence thickened between them, growing taut. She shivered again, a delicately sensual movement that made his hands tighten on her, made his male flesh quiver and rise. Why didn't she move, why didn't she say something?

"Evie?" he murmured.

"No," she said abruptly, her voice raspier than usual. She wrenched away from him. "I'm sorry, but I can't go out to dinner with you."

Then a boat idled into the marina, and he watched her golden head turn, her face light with a smile as she recognized her customer. Sharp fury flared through him at how easily she smiled at others, but would scarcely even glance at him.

She lifted her left arm to wave, and with shock Robert focused on that slim hand.

She was wearing a wedding ring.

_____ *Chapter Three*

Evie tried to concentrate on the ledgers that lay open on her desk, but she couldn't keep her mind on posting the day's income and expenses. A dark, lean face kept forming in her mind's eye, blotting out the figures. Every time she thought of those pale, predatory eyes, the bottom would drop out of her stomach and her heart would begin hammering. Fear. Though he had been polite, Robert Cannon could no more hide his true nature than could a panther. In some way she could only sense, without being able to tell the exact nature of it, he was a threat to her.

Her instincts were primitive; she wanted to barricade herself against him, wall him out. She had fought too long to put her life on an even keel to let this dark stranger disrupt what she had built. Her life was placid, deliberately so, and she resented this interruption in the even fabric of days she had fashioned about herself.

She looked up at the small photograph that sat on the top shelf of her old-fashioned rolltop desk. It wasn't one of her wedding photos; she had never looked at any of those. This photo was one that had been taken the summer before their senior year in high school; a group of kids had gotten together and spent the whole day on the water, skiing, goofing off, going back on shore to cook out. Becky Watts had brought her mother's camera and taken photos of all of them that golden summer day. Matt had been chasing Evie with an ice cube, trying to drop it down her blouse, but when he finally caught her, she had struggled and made him drop it. Matt's hands had been on her waist, and they had been laughing. Becky had called, ''Hey, Matt!'' and snapped the photo when they both automatically looked over at her.

Matt. Tall, just outgrowing the gangliness of adolescence and putting on some of the weight that came with maturity. That shock of dark hair falling over his brow, crooked grin flashing, bright blue eyes twinkling. He'd always been laughing. Evie didn't spare any looks for the girl she had been then, but she saw the way Matt had held her, the link between them that had been obvious even in that happy-go-lucky moment. She looked down at the slim gold band on her left hand. *Matt.*

In all the years since, there hadn't been anyone. She hadn't wanted anyone, had been neither interested nor tempted. There were people she loved, of course, but in a romantic sense her emotional isolation had been so complete that she had been totally unaware if any man had been attracted to her...until Robert Cannon had walked into her marina and looked at her with eyes like green ice. Though his expression had been impassive, she had felt his attention focus on her like a laser, had felt the heated sexual quality of it. That, and something else. Something even more dangerous.

He had left immediately after looking at the boat slips, but he would be back. She knew that without question. Evie sighed as she got up and walked to the French doors. She could see starlight twinkling on the water and stepped out onto the deck. The warm night air wrapped around her, humid, fragrant. Her little house sat right on the riverfront, with steps leading down from the deck to her private dock and boathouse. She sat in one of the patio chairs and propped her feet on the railing, calmed by the peacefulness of the river.

The summer nights weren't quiet, what with the constant chirp of insects, frogs and night birds, the splash of fish jumping, the rustle of the trees, the low murmur of the river itself, but there was a serenity in the noise. There was no moon, so the stars were plainly visible in the black bowl of the sky, the fragile, twinkling light reflected in millions of tiny diamonds on the water. The main river channel curved through the lake not sixty feet from her dock, the current ruffling the surface into waves.

Her nearest neighbors were a quarter of a mile away, out of sight around a small promontory. The only houses she could see from her deck were on the other side of the lake, well over a mile away. Guntersville Lake, formed when the TVA had dammed the Tennessee River back in the thirties, was both long and wide, irregularly shaped, curving back and forth, with hundreds of inlets. Numerous small, tree-covered islands dotted the lake.

She had lived here all her life. Here was home, family, friends, a network of roots almost two hundred years old that spread both wide and deep. She knew the pace of the seasons, the pulse of the river. She had never wanted to be anywhere else. The fabric of life here was her fortress. Now, however, her fortress was being threatened by two different enemies, and she would have to fight to protect herself.

The first threat was one that made her furious. Landon Mercer was up to no good. She didn't know the man well, but she had a certain instinct about people that was seldom wrong. There was a slickness to his character that had put her off from the start, when he had first begun renting one of her boats, but she hadn't actually become suspicious of him for a couple of months. It had been a lot of little things that had gradually alerted her, like the way he always carefully looked around before leaving the dock; it would have made sense if he'd been looking at the river traffic, but instead he'd looked at the parking lot and the highway. And there was always a mixture of triumph and relief in his expression when he returned, as if he'd done something he shouldn't have and gotten away with it.

His clothes were wrong, somehow. He made an effort to dress casually, the way he thought a fisherman would dress, but never quite got it right. He carried a rod and reel and one small tackle box, but from what Evie could tell, he never used them. He certainly never came back with any fish, and the same lure had been tied onto the line every time he went out. She knew it was the same one, because it was missing the back set of treble hooks. No, Mercer wasn't fishing. So why carry the tackle? The only logical explanation was that he was using it as a disguise; if anyone saw him, they wouldn't think anything about it.

But because Evie was alert to anything that threatened her domain, she wondered why he would need a disguise. Was he seeing a married woman? She dismissed that possibility. Boats were noisy and obvious; using them wasn't a good way to sneak around. If his lover's house was isolated, a car would be better, because then Mercer wouldn't have to worry about the vagaries of the weather. If the house had neighbors within sight, then a boat would attract attention when it pulled up to the dock; river people tended to notice strange boats. Nor was an assignation in the middle of the lake a good idea, given the river traffic.

Drugs, maybe. Maybe the little tackle box was full of cocaine, instead of tackle. If he had a system set up, selling in the middle of the river would be safe; the water patrol couldn't sneak up on him, and if they did approach, all he had to do was drop the evidence over the side. His most dangerous time would be before he got out on the water, while he could be caught carrying the stuff. That was why he never examined the parking lot when he returned; the evidence was gone. For all intents and purposes, he had just been enjoying a little fishing.

She had no hard evidence. Twice she had tried to follow him, but had lost him in the multitude of coves and islands. But if he was using one of her boats to either sell or transfer drugs, he was jeopardizing her business. Not only could the boat be confiscated, the publicity would be terrible for the marina. Boat owners would pull out of the slips they rented from her; there were enough marinas in the Guntersville area that they could always find another place to house their boats.

Both times Mercer had headed toward the same area, the island-dotted area around the Marshall County Park, where it was easy to lose sight of a boat. Evie knew every inch of the river; eventually she would be able to narrow down the choices and find him. She didn't have any grandiose scheme to apprehend him, assuming he *was* doing something illegal. She didn't even intend to get all that close to him; she carried a pair of powerful binoculars with her in the boat. All she wanted to do was satisfy her suspicions; if she was correct, then she would turn the matter over to the sheriff and let him work it out with the water patrol. That way, she would have protected both her reputation and the marina. She might still lose the boat, but she didn't think the sheriff would confiscate it if she were the one who put him onto Mercer to begin with. All she wanted was to be certain in her own mind before she accused a man of something as serious as drug dealing.

The problem with following Mercer was that she never knew when to expect him; if she had customers in the marina, she couldn't just drop everything and hop in a boat.

But she would handle that as the opportunity presented itself. Robert Cannon was something else entirely.

She didn't want to handle him. She didn't want anything to do with him—this man with his cold, intense eyes and clipped speech, this stranger, this Yankee. He made her feel like a rabbit facing a cobra: terrified, but fascinated at the same time. He tried to hide his ruthlessness behind smooth, cosmopolitan manners, but Evie had no doubts about the real nature of the man.

He wanted her. He intended to have her. And he wouldn't care if he destroyed her in the taking.

She touched her wedding ring, turning it on her finger. Why couldn't Matt have lived? So many years had passed without him, and she had survived, had gotten on with her life, but his death had irrevocably changed her. She was stronger, yes, but also set apart, isolated from other men who might have wanted to claim her. Other men had respected that distance; *he* wouldn't.

Robert Cannon was a complication she couldn't afford. At the very least, he would distract her at a time when she needed to be alert. At the worst, he would breach her defenses and take what he wanted, then leave without any thought for the emotional devastation he left behind. Evie shuddered at the thought. She had survived once; she wasn't sure she could do it again.

Today, when he had put his hands on her waist and pulled her against his lean, hard body, she had been both shocked and virtually paralyzed by the exquisite pleasure of the contact. It had been so many years since she had felt that kind of joy that she had forgotten how enthralling, how potent, it was to feel hard male flesh against her. She had been startled by the heated strength of his hands and the subtle muskiness of his scent. She had been swamped by the sensations, by her memories. But her memories were old ones, of two young people who no longer existed. The hands holding her had been Matt's; the eager, yearning kisses had been from Matt's lips. Time had dulled those memories, the precious ones, but the image of Robert Cannon was sharp, almost painful, in its freshness.

The safest thing would be to ignore him, but that was the one thing she was sure he wouldn't allow.

Robert strolled into the offices of PowerNet the next morning and introduced himself to the receptionist, a plump, astute woman in her thirties who immediately made a phone call and then personally escorted him to Landon Mercer's office. He was in a savage mood, had been since he'd seen the wedding ring on Evie Shaw's hand, but he gave the receptionist a gentle smile and thanked her, making her blush. He never took out his temper on innocents; in fact, his self-control was so great that the vast majority of his employees didn't know he even *had* a temper. The few who knew otherwise had learned it the hard way.

Landon Mercer, however, was no innocent. He came swiftly out of his office to meet Robert halfway, heartily greeting him. "Mr. Cannon, what a surprise! No one let us know you were in Huntsville. We're honored!"

"Hardly that," Robert murmured as he shook hands with Mercer, deliberately modifying his grip to use very little strength. His mood deteriorated even further to find that Mercer was tall and good-looking, with thick blond hair and a very European sense of style. Expertly Robert assessed the cost of the Italian silk suit Mercer was wearing, and mentally he raised his eyebrows. The man had expensive tastes.

"Come in, come in," Mercer urged, inviting Robert into his office. "Would you like coffee?"

"Please." The acceptance of hospitality, Robert had found, often made subordinates relax a little. Landon Mercer would be edgy at his sudden appearance, anyway; it wouldn't hurt to calm him down.

Mercer turned to his secretary, who was making herself very busy. "Trish, would you bring in two coffees, please?"

"Of course. How do you take yours, Mr. Cannon?"

"Black."

They went on into Mercer's office, and Robert took one of the comfortable visitors' chairs, rather than automatically taking Mercer's big chair behind the desk to show his authority. "I apologize for just dropping in on you without warning," he said calmly. "I'm in the area on vacation and thought I'd take the opportunity to see the operation, since I've never personally been down here."

"We're pleased to have you anytime," Mercer replied, still in that hearty tone of voice. "Vacation, you say? Strange place to take a vacation, especially in the middle of summer. The heat is murderous, as I'm sure you've noticed."

"Not so strange." Robert could almost hear Mercer's furiously churning, suspicious thoughts. Why was Robert here? Why now? Were they on to Mercer? If they were, why hadn't he been arrested? Robert didn't mind Mercer being suspicious; in fact, he was counting on it.

There was a light knock on the door; then Trish entered with two cups of steaming coffee. She passed Robert's to him first, then gave the other cup to Mercer. "Thank you," Robert said. Mercer didn't bother with the courtesy.

"About your vacation?" Mercer prompted, when Trish had closed the door behind her.

Robert leaned back in the chair and indolently crossed his legs. He could feel Mercer sharply studying him and knew what he would see: a lean, elegantly dressed man with cool, slightly bored eyes, certainly nothing to alarm him, despite this unexpected visit. "I have a house on the lake in Guntersville," he said in a lazy, slightly remote tone. It was a lie, but Mercer wouldn't know that. "I bought it and some land several years ago. I've never been down here before, but I've let several of my executives use the place, and they've all returned with the usual exaggerated fishing stories. Even allowing for that, they've all been enthusiastic about coming back, so I thought I'd try out the fishing for myself."

"I've heard it's a good lake," Mercer said politely, but the mental wheels were whirling faster than before.

"We'll see." Robert allowed himself a slight smile. "It seems like a nice, quiet place. Just what the doctor ordered."

"Doctor?"

"High blood pressure. Stress." Robert shrugged. "I feel fine, but the doctor insisted that I needed a long vacation, and this seemed like the perfect place to avoid stress."

"That's for sure," Mercer said. Suspicion still lingered in his eyes, but now it was tempered with relief at the plausible explanation for Robert's presence.

"I don't know how long I'll stay," Robert continued in an indifferent tone. "I won't be dropping in on you constantly, though. I'm supposed to forget about work for a while."

"We'll be glad to see you anytime, but you really should listen to your doctor," Mercer urged. "Since you're here, would you like a tour of the place? There isn't much to see, of course, just a lot of programmers and their computers."

Robert glanced at his watch, as if he had somewhere else to go. "I believe I have time, if it wouldn't be too much trouble."

"No, not at all." Mercer was already on his feet, anxious to complete the tour and send Robert on his way.

Even if he hadn't already known about Mercer, Robert thought, he would have disliked him; there was a slickness to him that was immediately off-putting. Mercer tried to disguise it with a glib, hearty attitude, but the man thought he was smarter than everyone else, and the contempt slipped through every so often. Did he treat Evie with the same attitude? Or was she, despite her relative lack of sophistication, cool and discerning enough that Mercer watched his step with her?

They were probably lovers, he thought, even though she was married. When had marital vows ever prevented anyone from straying, if they were so inclined? And why would a woman involved in espionage hesitate at cheating on her husband? Odd that her marital status hadn't been included in the information he'd received on her, but then, why would it be, unless her husband was also involved? Evidently he wasn't, but nevertheless, as soon as Robert had returned to his hotel room in Huntsville the afternoon before, he had called his own investigative people and asked for information concerning the man. He was coldly furious; he had never, under any circumstances, allowed himself to become involved with a married woman, and he wasn't going to lower his standards now. But neither had he ever wanted another woman as violently as he wanted Evie Shaw, and knowing that he had to deprive himself made his temper very precarious.

Mercer was all smooth bonhomie as he escorted Robert through the offices, pointing out the various features and explaining the work in progress. Robert made use of the tour to gather information. Calling on his ability to totally concentrate on one thing at a time, he pushed Evie Shaw out of his mind and ruthlessly focused on the business at hand. PowerNet was housed in a long, one-story brick building. The company offices were in front, while the real work, the programming, was done in the back, with computer geniuses working their peculiar magic. Robert quietly noted the security setup and approved; there were surveillance cameras, and motion and thermal alarms. Access to the classified material could be gained only by a coded magnetic card, and the bearer still had to have the necessary security clearance. No paperwork or computer disks were allowed to leave the building. All work was logged in and placed in a secure vault when the programmers left for the day.

For Robert, the security measures made things simple; the only way the system could have been breached without detection was by someone in a position of authority, someone who had access to the vault: Landon Mercer.

He made a point of checking his watch several times during the tour, and as soon as it was completed, he said, "I've enjoyed this very much, but I'm supposed to meet with a contractor to do a few repairs on the house. Perhaps we could get together for a round of golf sometime."

"Of course, anytime," Mercer said. "Just call."

Robert allowed himself a brief smile. "I'll do that."

He was satisfied with the visit; his intention hadn't been to do any actual snooping but rather to let Mercer know he was in town and to see for himself the security measures at PowerNet. He had the security layout from the original specs, of course, but it was always best to check out the details and make certain nothing had been changed. He might have to slip into the building at night, but that wasn't his primary plan, merely a possibility. Catching Mercer on-site with classified data didn't prove anything; the trick was to catch him passing it to someone else. Let his presence make Mercer nervous. Nervous people made mistakes.

An envelope from his personal investigators was waiting for him at the desk when he returned to the hotel. Robert stepped into the empty elevator and opened the envelope as the car began moving upward. He quickly scanned the single sheet. The information was brief. Matt Shaw, Evie's husband, had been killed in a car accident the day after their wedding, twelve years before.

He calmly slid the sheet back into the envelope, but a savage elation was rushing through him. She was a widow! She was available. And, though she didn't know it yet, she was his for the taking.

Once in his hotel room, he picked up the phone and began making calls, sliding the chess pieces of intrigue into place.

Chapter Four

Evie stuck her head out the door. "Jason!" she bellowed at her fourteen-year-old nephew. "Stop horsing around. *Now!*"

"Aw, okay," he grudgingly replied, and Evie pulled her head back inside, though she kept an eye on him, anyway. She adored the kid but never forgot that he *was* just a kid, with an attention span that leaped around like a flea and all the ungovernable energy and awkwardness that went with early adolescence. Her niece, Paige, was content to sit inside with her, in the air-conditioning, but a couple of Jason's buddies had come by, and now they were out on the docks, clowning around. Evie expected any or all of the boys to fall into the water at any time.

"They're so jerky," Paige said with all the disdain a thirteen-year-old could muster, which was plenty.

Evie smiled at her. "They'll improve with age."

"They'd better," Paige said ominously. She pulled her long, coltish legs up into the rocking chair and returned to the young-adult romance she was reading. She was a beautiful girl, Evie thought, studying the delicate lines of the young face, which still wore some of the innocence of childhood. Paige had dark hair, like her father, and a classic bone structure that would only improve with age. Jason was more outgoing than his sister, but then, Jason was more outgoing than just about everyone.

A boat idled into the marina and pulled up to the gas pumps. Evie went outside to take care of her customers, two young couples who had already spent too much time on the water, judging by their sunburns. After they had paid and left, she checked on Jason and his friends again, but for the time being they were ambling along one of the docks and refraining from any rough horseplay. Knowing teenage boys as she did, she didn't expect that state of affairs to last long.

The day was another scorcher. She glanced up at the white sun in the cloudless sky; no chance of rain to cool things off. Though she had been outside for only a few minutes, she could already feel her hair sticking to the back of her neck as she opened the door to the office and stepped inside. How could the boys stand even being outside in this heat, much less doing anything as strenuous as their energetic clowning around?

She paused as she entered, momentarily blinded by the transition from bright sunlight into relative dimness. Paige was chatting with someone, her eager tone unusual in a girl who was normally quiet except with family members. Evie could see a man standing in front of the counter, but it was another minute before her vision cleared enough for her to make out his lean height and the width of his shoulders. She still couldn't see his features clearly, but nevertheless a tiny alarm of recognition tingled through her, and she drew a controlled breath. "Mr. Cannon."

"Hello." His pale green gaze slipped downward, leisurely examined her legs, which were exposed today, because the heat had been so oppressive that she had worn shorts. The once-over made her feel uncomfortable, and she slipped behind the counter to ring up the gas sale and put the money in the cash drawer.

"What may I do for you?" she asked, without looking at him. She was aware of Paige watching them with open interest, alerted perhaps by the difference in Evie's manner from the way she usually treated customers.

He ignored the distance in her tone. "I've brought my boat." He paused. "You *do* still have an available slip?"

"Of course." Business was business, Evie thought. She opened a drawer and pulled out a rental agreement. "If you'll complete this, I'll show you to your slip. When you were here the other day, did you see any particular location that you'd like?"

He glanced down at the sheet in his hand. "No, any one of them will do," he absently replied as he rapidly read the agreement. It was straightforward and simple, stating the rental fee and outlining the rules. At the bottom of the sheet was a place for two signatures, his and hers. "Is there an extra copy?" he asked, the businessman in him balking at signing something without keeping a record of it.

She shrugged and pulled out an extra copy of the rental agreement, took the one he held from his hands and slipped a sheet of carbon paper between the two sheets. Briskly she stapled them together and handed them back to him. Controlling a smile, Robert swiftly filled out the form, giving his name and address and how long he intended to rent the slip. Then he signed at the bottom, returned the forms to her and pulled out his wallet. The small sign taped to the counter stated that the marina accepted all major credit cards, so he removed one and laid it on the counter.

She still didn't look at him as she prepared a credit-card slip. Robert watched her with well-hidden greed. In the three days since he'd first met her, he had decided that she couldn't possibly have been as lovely as he had first thought or have such an impact on his senses. He had been wrong. From the moment he had entered the marina and watched her through the plate-glass window as she pumped gas, tension had twisted his guts until he could barely breathe. She was still as sleek and golden and sensual as a pagan goddess, and he wanted her.

He had accomplished a lot in those three days. In addition to making the first chess move with Mercer, he had bought a boat, a car and a house on the river. It had taken two days for the dealership to rig the boat, but he had taken possession of the house faster than that, having moved in the afternoon before. The Realtor still hadn't recovered from his blitzing style of decision making. But Robert wasn't accustomed to being thwarted; in record time the utilities had been turned on, the paperwork completed, a cleaning service from Huntsville dragooned into giving the place a thorough cleaning, and new furniture both selected and delivered. He had also put another plan into progress, one that would force Evie Shaw and Landon Mercer into a trap.

Silently Evie handed him the credit-card slip to sign. He scrawled his signature and returned it to her just as shouts from outside made her whirl.

Robert glanced out the window and saw several teenage boys

roughhousing on the docks. "Excuse me," Evie said, and went over to open the door.

"They're going to get it now," Paige piped up with obvious satisfaction, getting to her knees in the rocking chair.

Just as Evie reached the door, Jason laughingly pushed one of his buddies, who immediately returned the shove, with interest. Jason had already turned away, and the motion propelled him forward; his sneakers skidded on a wet spot perilously close to the edge of the dock. His gangly arms began windmilling comically as he tried to reverse direction, but his feet shot out from under him and he flew into the air, over the water.

"Jason!"

He was too close to the dock. Evie saw it even as she raced through the door, her heart in her mouth. She heard the sickening crack as his head hit the edge of the dock. His thin body went limp in midair, and a half second later he hit the water, immediately slipping beneath the surface.

One of the boys yelled, his young voice cracking. Evie caught only a glimpse of their bewildered, suddenly terrified faces as she fought her way through the thick, overheated air. The dock looked so far away, and she didn't seem to be making any progress, even though she could feel her feet thudding on the wood. Frantically she searched the spot where Jason had gone under, but there was nothing, nothing....

She hit the water in a long, flat dive, stroking strongly for where she had last seen him. She was dimly aware of a distant splashing, but she ignored it, all her attention on reaching Jason in time. Don't let it be too late. Dear God, don't let it be too late. She could still hear the sodden *thunk* of his head hitting the dock. He could already be dead, or paralyzed. No. Not Jason. She refused to lose him; she couldn't lose him. She couldn't go through that again.

She took a deep breath and dived, pushing her way through the water, her desperately searching hands reaching out. Visibility in the river wasn't good; she would have to locate him mostly by touch. She reached the muddy bottom and clawed her way along it. He had to be here! There was the dark pillar of the dock, telling her that she wasn't too far away from where he had gone in.

Her lungs began to ache, but she refused to surface. That would use precious seconds, seconds that Jason didn't have.

Maybe the wave motion had washed him *under* the dock.

Fiercely she kicked, propelling herself into the darker water under the dock. Her groping hands swept the water in front of her. *Nothing.*

Her lungs were burning. The need to inhale was almost impossible to resist. Grimly she fought the impulse as she forced her way down to feel along the bottom again.

Something brushed her hand.

She grabbed, and clutched fabric. Her other hand, groping blindly, caught an arm. Using the last of her strength, she tugged her limp burden out of the shadow of the docks and feebly kicked upward. Progress was frustratingly, agonizingly slow; her lungs were demanding air, her vision fading. Dear God, had she found Jason only to drown with him, because she lacked the strength to get them to the surface?

Then strong hands caught her, gripping her ribs with bruising force, and she was propelled upward in a mighty rush. Her head broke the surface, and she inhaled convulsively, choking and gasping.

"I have you," a deep, calm voice said in her ear. "I have both of you. Just relax against me."

She could hardly do anything else. She was supported by an arm as unyielding as iron as he stroked the short distance to the dock. The boys were on their knees, reaching eager hands down toward him. "Just hold him," she heard Cannon order. "Don't try to pull him out of the water. Let me do it. And one of you go call 911."

"I already have," Evie heard Paige say, the girl's voice wavery and thin.

"Good girl." His tone changed to brisk command, the words close by her ear. "Evie. I want you to hang on to the edge of the dock. Can you do that?"

She was still gasping, unable to talk, so she nodded.

"Let go of Jason. The boys are holding him, so he'll be okay. Do it now."

She obeyed, and he placed her hands on the edge of the dock. Grimly she clung to the wood as he heaved himself out of the water. She pushed her streaming hair out of her eyes with one hand as he knelt down and slipped both hands under Jason's arms. "He might have a spinal-cord injury," she croaked.

"I know." Robert's face was grim. "But he isn't breathing. If we don't get him up here and do CPR, he won't make it."

She swallowed hard and nodded again. As gently as possible, Robert lifted Jason out of the water, the muscles in his arms and shoulders cording under the wet shirt. Evie took one agonized look at Jason's still, blue face, and then she hauled herself out of the water, using strength she hadn't known she still possessed. She collapsed on the dock beside Jason, then struggled to her knees. "Jason!"

Robert felt for a pulse in the boy's neck and located a faint throb. Relieved, he said, "He has a heartbeat," then bent over the sprawled, limp body, pinching the boy's nostrils shut and using his other hand to press on his chin, forcing his mouth open. He placed his own mouth on the chill blue lips and carefully, forcefully, blew his breath outward. The thin chest rose. Robert lifted his mouth, and the air sighed out of the boy, his chest falling again.

Evie reached out, then forced herself to draw back. She couldn't do anything that Robert wasn't already doing, and she was still so weak and shaky that she couldn't do it nearly as well. She felt as if she were choking on her pain and desperation, on the overwhelming need to do *something,* anything. Her ears were buzzing. She would rather die herself than helplessly watch someone else she loved slowly die before her eyes.

Robert repeated the process again and again, silently counting. Fiercely he focused on what he was doing, ignoring the terrified kids grouped around them, not letting himself think about Evie's silence, her stillness. The kid's chest was rising with each breath forced into him, meaning oxygen was getting into his lungs. His heart was beating; if he didn't have a serious head or spinal injury, he should be okay, if he would just start breathing on his own. The seconds ticked by. One minute. Two. Then abruptly the boy's chest heaved, and he began choking. Quickly Robert drew back.

Jason suddenly convulsed, rolling to his side and knocking against Evie as he choked and gagged. She lurched sideways, off balance, unable to catch herself. Robert's hand shot out across Jason to steady her, the lean fingers catching her arm and preventing her from going into the water a second time. With effortless strength, he dragged her across Jason's legs, pulling her to him.

Water streamed from Jason's nostrils and open mouth. He gulped and coughed again, then abruptly vomited up a quantity of river water.

"Thank God," Robert said quietly. "No paralysis."

"No." Evie pulled loose from his grip. Tears burned her eyes as she crouched once again by Jason's side. Gently she touched the boy, soothing him, and noticed that the back of his head was red with blood. "You'll be okay, honey," she murmured as she examined the cut. "Nothing that a few stitches won't fix." She glanced up and saw Paige's white, tear-streaked face. "Paige, get a towel for me, please. And be careful! Don't run."

Paige gulped and headed back toward the marina. She didn't exactly run, but it was close.

Jason's coughing fit subsided, and he lay exhausted on his side, gulping in air. Evie stroked his arm, repeating that he was going to be all right.

Paige returned with the towel, and gently Evie pressed it to the deep cut, stanching the flow of blood. "A-aunt Evie?" Jason croaked, his voice so hoarse it was almost soundless.

"I'm here."

"Can I sit up?" he asked, beginning to be embarrassed by the attention.

"I don't know," she replied neutrally. "Can you?"

Slowly, cautiously, he eased himself into a sitting position, but he was weak, and Robert knelt down to support him, shifting so that one strong thigh was behind Jason's back. "My head hurts," Jason groaned.

"I imagine so," Robert said in a calm, almost genial voice. "You hit it on the edge of the dock." Sirens wailed, swiftly coming closer. Jason's eyes flickered as he realized a further fuss was going to be made.

Gingerly he reached back and touched his head. Wincing, he let his hand fall to his side. "Mom's going to be peed off," he said glumly.

"Mom isn't the only one," Evie replied. "But we'll settle that between ourselves later."

He looked abashed. He tried to move away from Robert's support but didn't quite make it. Then the paramedics were there, hurrying down the dock, carrying their tackle boxes of medical equipment. Robert drew back and pulled Evie with him, giving the paramedics room to work. Paige sidled over and slipped her arms around Evie's waist, burrowing close and hiding her face against Evie's wet shirt in a child's instinctive bid for reassurance. It was a simple thing for Robert to put his arms around both of them, and Evie was too tired, too numb, to resist. She stood docilely in his embrace. His strength enfolded her; his heat comforted her. He had saved Jason's life, and maybe even her own, because she wasn't certain she could have gotten Jason to the surface without his help. If so, she would simply have drowned with him rather than let him go and try to save her own life at the expense of his.

Jason was quickly checked; then the paramedics began preparations to transport him to the hospital. "That cut will have to be stitched," one of them said to Evie. "He probably has a concussion, too, so I wouldn't be surprised if they keep him overnight, at least."

Evie stirred in Robert's embrace. "I have to call Rebecca," she said. "And I want to ride with him to the hospital."

"I'll drive you," he said, releasing her. "You'll need a way back."

"Rebecca can bring me," she said as she hurried to the office, Robert and Paige both following her inside. She reached for the phone, then halted, rubbing her forehead. "No, she'll stay with Jason. Never mind. I can drive myself."

"Of course you can," he said gently. "But you won't, because I'm driving you."

She gave him a distracted look as she dialed her sister's number. "That isn't necessary—Becky. Listen, Jason slipped on the dock and cut his head. He's going to be okay, but he needs stitches, and the paramedics are taking him to the hospital. They're leaving now. I'll meet you there. Yes, I'm bringing Paige with me. Okay. Bye."

She hung up, then lifted the receiver and dialed another number. "Craig, this is Evie. Can you take over the marina for a couple of hours? Jason's had an accident, and I'm going with him to the hospital. No, he'll be okay. Five minutes? Great. I'm leaving now."

Then, moving swiftly, she got her purse from under the counter and fished out her keys. Like lightning, Robert caught her hand and calmly removed the keys from her grasp. "You're too shaky," he said in a gentle, implacable tone. "You came close to drowning yourself. Don't fight me on this, Evie."

It was obvious that she lacked the strength to physically fight him for the keys. Frustrated, she gave in rather than waste more time. "All right."

She drove a sturdy, serviceable four-wheel-drive pickup, handy for pulling boats up a launch ramp. Paige raced ahead to scramble inside, as if afraid she would be left behind if she didn't beat them to the vehicle. Evie was only grateful that the child automatically slid to the middle of the seat, positioning herself between Evie and Robert and hastily buckling herself in.

"It's a straight shift," she blurted unnecessarily as she buckled her own seat belt.

He gave her a gentle smile as he started the engine. "I can manage."

Of course, he did more than manage. He shifted gears with the smooth expertise of someone who knew exactly what he was doing. Evie's heart gave a little thump as she tried to imagine Robert Cannon being awkward at anything.

She forced herself to watch the road, rather than him, as she gave directions to the hospital. She didn't want to look at him, didn't want to feel that primal pull deep inside her. He was dripping wet, of course, his black hair plastered to his head and his white silk shirt clinging to his muscled torso like a second skin. His leanness was deceptive; the wet shirt revealed the width of his shoulders and chest, and the smooth, steely muscles of his abdomen and back. She thought the image of him, the outline of his body, was probably branded on her mind for all eternity, as was everything else that had happened in the last fifteen minutes. Only fifteen minutes? It felt like a lifetime.

He drove fast, pulling into the hospital parking lot right behind the ambulance. The hospital was small but new, and he couldn't fault the staff's response. Jason was whisked into an examining room before Evie could reach his side to speak to him.

Firmly Robert took her arm and ushered both her and Paige to seats in the waiting area. "Sit here," he said, and though his voice was mild, that implacable tone was in it again. "I'll get coffee for us. How about you, sweetheart?" he asked Paige. "Do you want a soft drink?"

Dumbly Paige nodded, then shook her head. "May I have coffee, too, Aunt Evie?" she whispered. "I'm cold. Or maybe hot chocolate."

Evie nodded her agreement, and Robert strode to the vending machines. She put her arm around Paige and gathered her close, knowing that the girl had suffered a shock at seeing her brother almost die. "Don't worry, honey. Jason will be home by tomorrow, probably, griping about his headache and driving you up the wall."

Paige sniffed back tears. "I know. I'll get mad at him then, but right now I just want him to be okay."

"He will be. I promise."

Robert returned with three cups, one filled with hot chocolate and the other two with coffee. Evie and Paige took theirs from him, and he settled into the chair on Evie's other side. When she sipped the hot brew, she found that he had liberally dosed it with sugar. She glanced at him and found him watching her, gauging her reaction. "Drink it," he said softly. "You're a little shocky, too."

Because he was right, she obeyed without argument, folding her cold fingers around the cup in an effort to warm them. Her wet clothes were uncomfortably chilly here in the air-conditioned hospital, and she barely restrained a shiver. He should be cold, too, she thought, but knew that he wasn't. His arm touched hers, and she felt heat radiating through his wet clothing.

As slight as it was, he felt the shiver that raced through her. "I'll get a blanket for you," he said, rising to his feet.

She watched him approach the desk and speak to the nurse. He was courteous, restrained, but in about thirty seconds he was returning with a blanket in his hands. He had an air of natural command, she thought. One look into those icy green eyes and people scurried to do his bidding.

He bent over her to tuck the blanket around her, and she let him. Just as he finished, the emergency room doors swung open and her sister, Rebecca, hurried inside, looking tense and scared. Seeing Evie and Paige, she changed her direction to join them. "What's happening?" she demanded.

"He's in the treatment room now," Robert answered for Evie, his deep voice as soothing as when he'd talked to Paige. "He'll have a few stitches in the back of his head, and a bad headache. They'll probably keep him overnight, but his injuries are relatively minor."

Rebecca turned her shrewd brown eyes on him and bluntly demanded, "Who are you?"

"This is Robert Cannon," Evie said, making an effort to appear calm as she made the introductions. "He dragged both Jason and me out of the water. Mr. Cannon, this is my sister, Rebecca Wood."

Rebecca took in Robert's wet clothes, then looked at Evie, seeing the strain on her sister's pale face. "I'll see about Jason first," she said in her usual decisive manner. "Then I want to know exactly what happened." She turned and marched toward a nurse, identified herself and was directed to the treatment room where Jason was located.

Robert sat down beside Evie. "What branch of the military

was your sister in?'' he asked, provoking a nervous giggle from Paige.

"I think it's called motherhood," Evie replied. "She began practicing on me at an early age."

"She's older, I presume."

"Five years."

"So you've always been 'baby sister' to her."

"I don't mind."

"I'm sure you don't. Drink your coffee," he admonished, lifting the cup himself and holding it to her lips.

Evie drank, then gave him a wry glance. "You aren't bad at the mother-hen routine yourself."

He allowed himself a slight smile. "I take care of my own." The words were a subtle threat—and a warning, if she were astute enough to hear it.

She didn't make the obvious retort, that she wasn't "his"; instead she withdrew, sinking back in her chair and staring straight ahead. Jason's close call had brought too many old memories to the surface, making it difficult for her to deal with anything just now, much less Robert Cannon. Right now, what she wanted most of all was to crawl into bed and pull the covers over her head, shutting out the world until she felt capable of facing it again. Maybe by the time night came, certainly by tomorrow, she would be all right. Then she would worry about the way he had taken over and about the gentle possessiveness that she couldn't fight. With Cannon, Evie was beginning to link gentleness with an implacable force of will that let nothing stand in his way. He would be tender and protective, but he would not be thwarted.

They sat in silence until Rebecca came out of the treatment room to rejoin them. "They're keeping him overnight," she said. "He has a slight concussion, a big shaved spot on the back of his head and ten stitches. He also won't say exactly what happened, other than mumbling that he fell. What's he trying to hide from me?"

Evie hesitated, trying to decide exactly what to tell Rebecca, and that gave Paige enough time to pipe up. "Scott and Jeff and

Patrick came by the marina, and they were all acting silly out on the docks. Aunt Evie yelled at Jason to settle down, but they didn't. Jason pushed Patrick, and Patrick pushed him back, and Jason slipped and fell, and hit his head on the dock, then went into the water. Aunt Evie went in after him, and she was under forever and ever, and Mr. Cannon tried to find both of them. Then Aunt Evie came up, and she had Jason, and Mr. Cannon pulled them to the dock. Jason wasn't breathing, Mom, and Aunt Evie nearly drowned, too. Mr. Cannon had to do that artificial breathing stuff on Jason, and then Jason started coughing and puking, and the paramedics came. I called 911,'' she finished in a rush.

Rebecca looked a bit bemused at this flood of words from her quiet child but heard the fear still lurking under the loquaciousness. She sat down beside Paige and hugged her. "You did exactly right," she praised, and Paige gave a little sigh of relief.

Rebecca examined Evie's pale, drawn face. "He's all right," she said reassuringly. "At least for now. As soon as he's recovered, I'm going to kill him. Better yet, I think I'll ground him for the rest of the summer. *Then* I'll kill him."

Evie managed a smile. "If he lives through all that, I want a turn at him."

"It's a deal. Now, I want you to go home and get out of those wet clothes. You look worse than Jason does."

The smile, this time, was easier. "Gee, thanks." But she knew that Rebecca's sharp eyes had seen below the surface and recognized the strain that she was under.

"I'll see to her," Robert said, standing and urging Evie to her feet. She wanted to protest, she really did, but she was so tired, her nerves so strained, that it was too much effort. So she managed to say goodbye to Rebecca and Paige, and tell them to kiss Jason for her; then she gave in and let him usher her out of the building and across the parking lot to the truck. She had left the blanket behind, but the searing afternoon heat washed over her like a glow, and she shivered with delight.

Robert's arm tightened around her waist. "Are you still cold?"

"No, I'm fine," she murmured. "The heat feels good."

He opened the truck door and lifted her onto the seat. The strength in his hands and arms, the ease with which he picked her up, made her shiver again. She closed her eyes and let her head rest against the window, as much from a desire to shut him out as from an almost overpowering fatigue.

"You can't go to sleep," he said as he got in on the driver's side, amusement lacing his tone. "You have to give me directions to your house."

She forced herself to open her eyes and sit up, and gave him calm, coherent directions. It didn't take long to get anywhere in Guntersville, and less than fifteen minutes later he stopped the truck in her driveway. She fumbled with the door but was so clumsy that he was there before she managed it, opening it and supporting her with a firm hand under her elbow. She got out, reluctant to let him inside her house but accepting the inevitable. Best just to go shower and change as fast as she could, and get it over with.

He entered right behind her. "Have a seat," she invited automatically as she headed toward her bedroom. "I'll be out in about fifteen minutes."

"I'm still too wet to sit down," he said. "But take your time. I'll go out on the deck, if that's okay with you."

"Of course," she said, giving him a polite smile without really looking at him, and escaped into the privacy of her bedroom.

Robert eyed the closed door thoughtfully. She was so wary of him that she wouldn't even look at him if she could help it. It wasn't a response he was accustomed to from a woman, though God knew she had reason to be wary, given his assumption that she knew of his connection to PowerNet. She couldn't have acted any more guilty if he had caught her red-handed. He could opt for patience and let time disarm her, but he already had plans in motion that would force the issue, so he decided to allay her suspicions in another manner, by making a definite, concerted effort to seduce her. He had planned to seduce her, anyway; he would simply intensify the pressure.

He heard the shower start running. He couldn't have asked for a better opportunity to look around, and he took advantage of it.

The house was probably forty years old, he thought, but had been remodeled so the interior was open and more modern, with exposed beams and gleaming hardwood floors. She had a green thumb; indoor plants of all sizes occupied every available flat surface. He could see into the kitchen from where he stood in the living room, and beyond that was the deck, with double French doors opening onto it. A dock led from the deck down to a boathouse.

Her furnishings were neat and comfortable, but certainly not luxurious. Without haste, he went over to the big, old-fashioned rolltop desk and methodically searched it, unearthing nothing of any great interest, not that he had expected to find anything. It wasn't likely she would have been fool enough to leave him in the room with an unlocked desk if the desk contained anything incriminating. He looked through her bank statement but found no unusually large deposits, at least at this particular bank or on this particular statement.

There was a small, framed photograph on the desk. He picked it up and examined the two people pictured. Evie, definitely—a very young Evie, but already glowing with seductiveness. The boy, for he was nothing more than that, was probably her husband, dead now for twelve years. Robert studied the boy's face more closely, seeing laughter and happiness and yes, devotion. But had the boy any idea how to handle the sensual treasure that the girl in his arms represented? Of course not; what teenage boy would? Still, Robert felt an unexpected and unpleasant twinge of jealousy for this long-dead boy, for the riches that had so briefly been his. Evie had loved him, enough that she still wore his wedding ring after all these years.

He heard the shower shut off and replaced the photograph, then quietly walked out onto the deck. She had a nice place here, nothing extravagant, but cozy and homey. There was plenty of privacy, too, with no houses visible except for those on the far side of the lake. The water was very blue, reflecting both the green of the mountains and the deep blue bowl of the sky. The afternoon was slipping away, and the sun was lower now, but still white and searing. Soon it would begin to turn bronze, and the lush scents of the heavy greenery would grow stronger. By the time purple twilight brought a respite from the heat, the air would be redolent with honeysuckle and roses, pine and fresh-cut grass. Time was slower here; people didn't rush from one occupation to another. He had actually seen people sitting on their front porches, reading newspapers or shelling peas, occasionally waving to passersby. Of course, people from New York and other large cities would say that the locals here had nothing to rush *to,* but from what he'd seen they stayed busy enough; they just didn't get in any great hurry.

He heard Evie come to the open French door. "I'm ready," she said.

He turned and looked at her. Her newly washed hair was still wet, but she had braided it and pinned the braids up so they wouldn't get her shirt damp. She had exchanged the shorts for jeans, and had on a pink T-shirt that made her golden skin glow. But her cheeks were still a bit pale, and her expression was strained.

"You have a nice place," he said.

"Thanks. I inherited it from my in-laws."

Though he knew the answer, now was the time to ask for information; it would be odd if he didn't. "You're married?" he asked.

"Widowed." She turned and retreated into the house, and Robert followed her.

"Ah. I'm sorry. How long has it been?"

"Twelve years."

"I saw the picture on the desk. Is that your husband?"

"Yes, that's Matt." She stopped and looked toward the photograph, and an ineffable sadness darkened her eyes. "We were just kids." Then she seemed to gather herself and walked briskly to the door. "I need to get back to the marina."

"My house is about five miles from here," he said. "It won't take long for me to shower and change."

She carried a towel out to the truck and dried the seat before she got inside. She didn't even bother protesting his continued possession of her keys; it would be pointless, though she was now obviously calm enough to drive safely.

His clothes had dried enough that they were merely damp now, rather than dripping wet, but she knew they had to be uncomfortable. Hers certainly had been. Her conscience twinged. He had not only saved Jason's life but likely hers, as well, and had put himself to a great deal of trouble to see that she was taken care of. No matter how he alarmed her, she knew that she would never forget his quick actions or his cool decisiveness.

"Thank you," she said softly, staring straight ahead. "Jason and I probably wouldn't have made it without you."

"The likelihood was unnerving," he said, his tone cool and even. "You'd pushed yourself so far that you couldn't have gotten him out of the water. Didn't it occur to you to let go of him and come up for another breath?"

"No." The single word was flat. "I couldn't have done that."

He glanced at her profile, saw the deepening strain in her expression and deftly changed the subject. "Will your sister really ground him for the rest of the summer?"

Evie was startled into a laugh, a rusty little sound that went right to his gut. "I'd say he'll be lucky if that's all she does. It isn't that he was fooling around, but that I'd already told him to stop and he disobeyed me."

"So he broke a cardinal rule?"

"Just about."

Robert intended to have a few words with the young man himself, about acting responsibly and the possible consequences of reckless actions, but he didn't mention it to Evie. She was obviously very protective of her niece and nephew, and though she couldn't say that it wasn't any of his business, she wouldn't like it. His conversation with Jason would be private.

When he stopped in the driveway of his new house, Evie looked around with interest. "This place has been on the market for almost a year," she said.

"Then I'm lucky no one beat me to it, aren't I?" He got out and walked around the truck to open the door for her. Though she hadn't waited for him to perform the service at the hospital, that had been an emergency; nor would she have waited when they had reached her house, if she had been able to get the door open in time. He'd had the strong impression then that she had wanted to bolt inside and lock him out. Now, however, she waited with the natural air of a queen, as if he were only doing what he should. She might be dressed in jeans, sneakers and a T-shirt, but that didn't lessen her femininity one whit; she *expected* that male act of servitude. Robert had always preferred to treat women with the small courtesies but hadn't insisted on them when his partner had protested. He was both amused and charmed by Evie's rather regal, very Southern attitude.

He mused about this subtle signal as he ushered her into the house. Though she was still very wary of him, obviously on some level her resistance had weakened. Anticipation tightened his muscles, but he deliberately resisted it. Now was not the time. Not quite yet.

"Make yourself at home while I shower," he invited, smiling faintly as he walked toward his bedroom, which was down the hallway to the right. He had no doubt that she would do exactly as he had done, take full advantage of the opportunity to do a quick search.

Evie stood in the middle of the living room after he had gone, too tense to "make herself at home." She looked around, trying to distract herself. The house was sprawling and modern, one story of brick and redwood, easily three times the size of her own. A huge rock fireplace dominated the left wall, the chimney soaring upward to the cathedral ceiling. Twin white ceiling fans stirred a gentle breeze. The furniture was chic but comfortable-looking, sized to fit a man of his height.

The living room was separated from the dining room by a waist-high planter in which luxurious ferns flourished. Huge double windows revealed a deck, furnished with comfortable chairs, an umbrella table and even more plants. Hesitantly she walked into the dining room for a better view. The kitchen opened up to the right, an immaculate oasis gleaming with the most modern appliances available. Even the coffeemaker looked as if the user would need a degree in engineering to work the thing. There was a breakfast nook on the far side of the kitchen, occupied by a smallish table with a white ceramic tile top. She could see him sitting there in the mornings, reading a newspaper and drinking coffee. Double French doors, far more ornate and stylish than her own, led from the breakfast nook onto the deck. She would have liked to explore further but felt too constrained here on his territory. Instead she retreated to the living room once more.

Robert took his time showering and dressing. Let her look around all she wanted; the fact that she wouldn't find anything alarming would help allay her suspicions. She would begin to relax, which was exactly what he wanted.

A lot of men, maybe most of them, would have made a move while they had been at her house; she had been more off-balance, vulnerable. He had even had the opportunity, had he chosen to take it, of walking in on her while she was unclothed. But he had elected to wait, knowing she would be more at ease now that the most provocative and dangerous circumstances were past. He hadn't made a pass at her then, so she wouldn't be expecting him to do so now. And since she wouldn't be mentally prepared to handle an advance, her response would be honest, unguarded.

Finally he stopped dawdling and returned to the living room. To his surprise, she was still standing almost exactly where he had left her, and little of the strain had faded from her face. She turned to watch him. Her lovely golden brown eyes were still dark with some inner distress that went far deeper than the episode with Jason, traumatic as that had been.

Robert paused while still several feet from her, studying those somber eyes. Then he simply moved forward with a graceful speed that gave her no time to evade him, and took her in his arms. He heard her instinctive intake of breath, saw the alarm widening her eyes as she lifted her head to protest, a protest that was smothered when his mouth covered hers.

She jerked in his arms, and he gently controlled the action, pulling her even more firmly against him. He took care not to hurt her but deepened the insistent pressure of his mouth until he felt her own mouth yield and open. The sweetness of her lips sent an electrical thrill along his nerves, tightening his muscles and swelling his sex. He took her mouth with his tongue, holding her still for the imitative sexual possession, repeating the motion again and again, until she shivered and softened in his arms, her lips beginning to cling to his.

Her tentative response made his head swim, and to his surprise he had to struggle to maintain his control. But she felt perfect in his arms, damn her, all those soft, luscious curves molding to the hard, muscled planes of his body. Her mouth was sweeter than any he had ever tasted before, and the simple act of kissing her was arousing him to an unbelievable degree.

He didn't want to stop. He hadn't planned to do more than kiss her, but he hadn't expected the intensity of his own response. His mouth crushed fiercely down on hers, demanding even more. He heard the soft, helpless sound she made in her throat; then her arms lifted around his neck, and she pressed full length against him. Pure, primitive male triumph roared through him at this evidence of her own arousal. He could feel her breasts, round and firm, the nipples hard against his chest, and he slipped his hand under her shirt to cup one of them, his thumb rubbing across the peaked nipple through the thin lace of her bra. Her body arched, her hips pressing hard against his...and then suddenly she was fighting, panicked, trying to squirm free.

He let her go, though every cell in his body was screaming for more. "Easy," he managed to say, but the word was low and rough and his breath was uneven. He tried for a more controlled reassurance. "I won't hurt you, sweetheart."

Evie had backed away from him, her face pale but her lips swollen and red from his kisses. She forced herself to stop retreating, to stand her ground and face him. The sensual pull of his masculinity was almost overwhelming, tempting her to go back into those arms, to yield to that fierce domination. She felt a sense of doom; he was far more dangerous to her than she had first suspected.

"Yes, you will," she whispered. Her teeth were chattering. "Why are you doing this? What do you want from me?"

Chapter Five

She looked ready to bolt. To soothe her, he moved back a few paces and let his hands relax at his sides. His eyes gleamed with faint irony. "You're a lovely woman, sweetheart. Surely you aren't surprised that I'm attracted to you? As for what I want from you, I was holding you closely enough that the answer to that question should have been obvious."

She didn't respond to his gentle teasing. Instead her somber gaze remained locked on his face, trying to probe beneath that smooth, urbane sophistication. He was very cosmopolitan, beyond a doubt, but he used that slick surface as a shield to hide the real man, the man who had kissed her with such ruthless passion. There were many hidden layers to him, his motives complex and unfathomable. Yes, he was attracted to her, as she was to him. It would be foolish to deny her own participation, and Evie wasn't a foolish woman. But she always had the feeling that he was studying her, manipulating her in some subtle manner. From the very first she had sensed his determination to force himself into her life, and he was doing exactly that with a calm force of will that refused to be denied. Whatever his motive, it was something that went beyond the physical.

"I don't have casual sex," she said.

He almost smiled. It was merely an expression in those pale eyes, rather than an actual movement of his mouth. "My dear, I promise you there wouldn't be anything *casual* about it." He paused. "Are you involved with someone else?"

She shook her head. "No."

He wasn't surprised that she had denied any involvement with

Mercer. "Then we don't have a problem, do we? You can't say that you aren't attracted to me, too."

She lifted her chin, and his pale eyes gleamed at that proud motion. "That velvet glove covers an iron fist, doesn't it?" she commented neutrally. "No, I can't say that I'm not attracted to you."

Her perception disturbed him, a reaction that he didn't allow to surface. "I can be determined when I want something...or someone."

She made an abrupt motion, as if tiring of the verbal jousting. "I phrased it wrong. I don't have affairs, either."

"A wise decision, but in this case too restrictive." He approached her now, and she didn't retreat. Gently he cupped her face with one long-fingered hand, his fingers stroking over the velvety texture of her cheek. God, she was lovely, not classically beautiful, but glowing with an intensely female seductiveness that made him think her name was very apt indeed. So must Eve have been, glorious in her nudity. No wonder Adam had been so easily led, a weakness he wouldn't allow himself, though he intended to fully enjoy Evie's sensuality. Her sweet, warm scent wafted up to him. "I won't force you," he murmured. "But I will have you."

"If you won't use force, how do you intend to go about it?" she asked.

His eyebrows lifted. "You think I should warn you?"

"Yes."

"An interesting notion, but one I'm going to leave untried." He rubbed his thumb over her lower lip. "For now, sweetheart, we'd better get back to the marina. You have a business to run, and I have a boat to get into a slip."

He let his hand drop as he spoke, and Evie turned from him with relief, as if she had been released from a force field. Her face tingled where he had touched her, and she remembered the electric sensation when he had put his hand on her breast. His boldness spoke of vast experience and self-confidence with women, something that put her at a disadvantage.

They were both silent on the drive back to the marina. She was vaguely surprised to see how late it was, the sun dipping low even for these long summer days. The sultry heat hadn't abated, though there was a hint of purple on the horizon that gave the promise of a cooling rain shower.

Robert's speedboat, a sleek, dark eighteen-footer, was still where he had left it, hitched to a black Jeep Renegade. Thank heavens it hadn't been blocking the launch ramps, or Craig would have had a mess on his hands. She hurried into the marina office, and Craig looked up from the sports magazine he was reading. "Is everything okay?" he asked, getting to his feet. "The kids said that Jason nearly drowned."

"He has a concussion, but he'll go home tomorrow," she said. "Thanks for coming in. I'm sorry for wrecking your day."

"No problem," he said cheerfully. He was seventeen, a tall, muscular, dark-haired kid who would be a senior when the new school year started. He had been working part-time for her for almost two years and was so steady that she had no qualms about leaving him in charge. "Say, what about that new boat outside?"

"It's mine," Robert said, stepping inside. "I'll be renting a slip here." He held out his hand. "I'm Robert Cannon."

Craig took his hand with a firm grip. "Craig Foster. Glad to meet you, Mr. Cannon. You must be the guy who pulled Evie and Jason out of the water. The kids said it was a tall Yankee."

"I'm the guy," Robert affirmed, amusement in his eyes.

"Thought so. Want me to help you get the boat into a slip?"

"I can do it," Evie said. "I've taken enough time out of your day."

"You pay me for it," Craig replied, grinning. "I might as well, since I'm already here. Mom won't be expecting me back until supper, anyway." He and Robert left, chatting companionably.

Kids seemed to like Robert, Evie thought, watching them from the window. Even shy Paige had been at ease with him. He didn't treat kids as equals—he was the adult, his was the authority—but at the same time he didn't dismiss them. Authority and responsibility sat easily on those broad shoulders, she mused. He was obviously accustomed to command.

For her own sake, her own protection, she had to hold him at bay, and she didn't know if she could. Today, with a few kisses and frightening ease, he had shown her that he could arouse her beyond her own control. She could love him, and that was the most terrifying prospect of all. He was a strong man, in mind and soul as well as body, a man worthy of love. He would steal her heart if she weren't careful, if she didn't keep her guard up at all times.

She turned away from the window. Twelve years ago, love had almost destroyed her, leaving only a forlorn heap of ashes from which she had laboriously rebuilt a controlled, protected life. She couldn't do that again; she didn't have the strength to once more live through that hell and emerge victorious. She had already lost too many people to believe that love, or life, lasted forever. She couldn't do anything about the people she already loved, the ones already in her heart: her family, old Virgil, a very few close friends, but she hadn't allowed anyone new to stake a claim on her emotions. She had already paid out too much in pain and had precious little reserve of spirit left. She had almost lost Jason today, and the pain had been overwhelming. Rebecca knew, had realized that if Evie hadn't been able to find Jason, she would now be mourning a sister as well as a son. That was the real basis for her sister's fury with Jason.

And Evie knew that Robert Cannon planned to force his way into her life. He would be here for the summer, he'd said; he wouldn't be looking for anything more than a pleasant affair, companionship during the long, lazy weeks. If she fell in love with him, that would make the affair sweeter. But at the end of summer he would go back to his real life, and Evie would have to continue here, with one more wound on a heart that had barely survived the last blow. Emotionally, she couldn't afford him.

There were always a hundred and one things to be doing around the marina, but suddenly she couldn't think of a single one. She felt oddly disoriented, as if the world had been turned upside down. Maybe it had.

She called the hospital and was put through to Jason's room. Her sister answered the phone on the first ring. "He's grouchy and has a throbbing headache," Rebecca cheerfully announced when Evie asked his condition. "I have to wake him every couple of hours tonight, but if he does okay, then he can go home in the morning. Paul left just a few minutes ago to take Paige to his mother's, then he's coming back here. How about you? Nerves settled down yet?"

"Not quite," Evie said truthfully, though Jason's close call wasn't all that had unsettled her. "But I'm over the shakes."

"Are you at home, I hope?"

"You know better than that."

"You should have taken it easy for the rest of the day," Rebecca scolded. "I had hopes that Mr. Cannon would take you in hand. He seems good at giving orders."

"World-class champion," Evie agreed. "I'll come by to see Jason after the marina closes. Do you want me to bring you anything? A pillow, a book, a hamburger?"

"No, I don't need anything. Don't come here. Jason's okay, and you need to go home and rest. I mean it, Evie."

"I'm okay, too," Evie calmly replied. "And I want to see Jason, even if just for a few minutes—" She cried out in surprise as the phone was plucked from her hand. She whirled as Robert lifted the receiver to his ear.

"Mrs. Wood? Robert Cannon. I'll see that she goes straight home. Yes, she's still a little wobbly."

"I am not," Evie said, narrowing her eyes at him. He reached out and gently stroked her cheek. Deliberately she stepped back, out of his reach.

"I'll take care of her," he firmly assured Rebecca, never moving his gaze from Evie's face. "On second thought, I'll take her out to dinner before I take her home. I think so, too. Goodbye."

As he hung up, Evie said in a cold voice, "I despise being treated as if I'm a helpless idiot."

"Hardly that," he murmured.

She didn't relent. "I suppose you thought that I would feel safe and protected, to have you take over and make my decisions for me. I don't. I feel insulted."

Robert lifted an inquisitive brow, hiding his true reaction. He had indeed hoped to provoke exactly that response from her and felt an uneasy surprise that she had so easily gone straight to the truth of the matter. She was proving to be uncomfortably astute. "What I think," he said carefully, "is that you were in more danger than you want your sister to know, and that you're still shaky. If you go to the hospital again, you'll have to put up a front to keep from scaring both her and Jason, and that will put even more strain on you."

"What *I* think," she replied, standing with her fists clenched at her sides, "is that I'm in far more danger from you than I ever was from the water." Her golden brown eyes were cool and unwaveringly level.

Again he felt a twinge of discomfort at her insight. Still, he was certain he could soften her stand, and his tone turned gently cajoling. "Even if I offer you a truce for tonight? No kisses, not even any hand-holding. Just dinner, then I'll see you safely home, and you can get a good night's rest."

"No, thank you. I won't have dinner with you, and I can get home by myself."

He gave her a considering look. "In that case, the offer of a truce is null and void."

His tone was so calm that she listened to it first, rather than to the actual words. She hesitated only a split second, but that was enough for him to have her in his arms again, and again she felt overcome by his steely, deceptive strength. His body was unyielding, his grip careful but unbreakable. The male muskiness of his clean, warm skin made her head swim. She had the dizzy impression that his mouth was lowering to hers and quickly ducked her head to rest it against his chest. It was disconcerting to hear a quiet chuckle over her head.

"Such a cowardly act, from one who isn't," he murmured, the words rich with amusement. "But I don't mind simply holding you. It has its own compensations."

She *was* a coward, though, Evie thought. She was terrified of him, not in a physical way, but emotional fear was just as weighty a burden to carry. She was handling him all wrong; he wouldn't be accustomed to rejection, so every time she turned him down it made him just that much more determined to have his way. If she had played up to him from the beginning, gushed over him, he would have been bored and left her alone. Hindsight, though, despite its acuity, was depressingly useless.

His hand moved soothingly over her back, subtly urging her closer. It was so easy to let him take more of her weight, so easy to give in to the strain and fatigue she had been successfully fighting until now. She resisted the urge to put her arms around him, to feel the heated vibrancy of his body under her hands, but she could hear the strong, steady thumping of his heartbeat beneath her ear, feel the rise and fall of his chest as he breathed, and that was enough to work its own seduction. The forces of life were strong in him, luring women to that intense strength. She was no different from all those countless, nameless others.

"Robert," she whispered. "Don't." A cowardly, shameless, useless plea.

That hand stroked up to her shoulder blades, rubbed the sensitive tendons that ran from her neck to her shoulders, massaged her tender nape. "Evie," he whispered in return. "Don't what?" He continued without waiting for a reply. "Is Evie your real name, or is it a nickname for Eve? Or possibly Evelyn? No matter, it suits you."

Her eyes drifted shut as his warmth and strength continued to work their black magic on her nerves, her will. Oh God, it would be so foolishly easy just to give in to him. His skill was nothing short of diabolical. "Neither. It's short for Evangeline."

"Ah." The short sigh was one of approval. He truly hadn't known her full name; none of the reports he had seen had called her anything except Evie. "Evangeline. Feminine, spiritual, sensual...sad."

Evie didn't respond outwardly to that analysis of her name, but the last word shook her. Sad...yes. So sad that for several long, bleak years she couldn't have said if the sun ever shone or not, because with her heart she had seen only gray. She could see the sunshine now; the relentless current of life as a whole had swept her out of the darkness, but there was never a day when she didn't realize how closely the shadows lurked. They were always there, a permanent counterpoint to life. If there was light, there had to be darkness; joy was balanced by pain, intimacy by loneliness. No one sailed through life untouched.

He was subtly rocking her with his body, a barely perceptible swaying that nevertheless urged her deeper and deeper into his embrace. He was aroused again; there was no mistaking that. She thought she should move away, but somehow in the past few minutes that had ceased to be an option. She was so tired, and the gentle motion of his body was soothing, like the swaying of a boat at anchor. The ancient rhythms were difficult to resist, linked as they were to instincts aeons beyond her control.

After several minutes he murmured, "Are you going to sleep?"

"I could," she replied, not opening her eyes. Beyond the danger, there was deep comfort in his embrace.

"It's almost six-thirty. Under the circumstances, I'm sure your customers would understand if you closed a little early."

"An hour and a half isn't a 'little' early. No, I'll stay until eight, as usual."

"Then so will I." He stifled his surge of annoyance. He himself let very few things interfere with his work—in actuality, only Madelyn and her family—but he didn't like the idea of Evie pushing herself into exhaustion at the marina.

"It isn't necessary."

"I rather believe it is," he replied thoughtfully.

"I still won't go out to dinner with you."

"Fair enough. I'll bring dinner to you. Do you have any preferences?"

She shook her head. "I'm not very hungry. I was going to have a sandwich when I got home."

"Leave it all to me."

She said against his chest, "You take charge very naturally. I suppose this is normal behavior for you."

"I'm decisive, yes."

"Don't forget autocratic."

"I'm sure you'll remind me if I forget."

She heard the undertone of amusement in his voice. Damn him, why couldn't he be nasty in his bullying, rather than relentlessly, gently cosseting? She never allowed herself to rely on anyone, though Rebecca had been trying to take care of her for years, but Robert simply ignored her resistance.

"I realize I'm rushing you," he murmured into her hair. "Today is only the second time we've met. I'll back off, sweetheart, and give you time to get to know me better and feel more comfortable around me. Okay?"

Her head moved up and down. She didn't want to agree to have anything to do with him, but right now she would grasp at any offer to cool down the situation. He had knocked her off balance, and she still hadn't regained it. Yes, she needed time, a lot of it.

Robert cupped her chin in his hand and forced her to lift her head away from the shelter of his chest. His pale green eyes were glittering with intensity. "But I won't go away," he warned.

Evie slept heavily that night, exhausted by the stress of the day. When she woke at dawn at the far-off roar of an early fisherman's outboard motor, she didn't rise immediately as was her habit but lay watching the pearly light spread across the sky.

For twelve years she had kept herself safe inside her carefully constructed fortress, but Robert was storming the walls. *Had* stormed them, if she was honest with herself. He was already in the inner court, though he hadn't yet managed to breach the defenses of the keep. Since Matt's death, she hadn't really *seen* any man, but Robert had forced her to see him. She was attracted to him, mentally as well as physically; it was only with effort that she had kept her emotions still safely locked away. She didn't want to love him and knew she risked doing exactly that if she continued to see him.

But she *would* see him, time and again. He had warned her— or was it a promise?—that he wasn't going to leave her alone, and he wasn't a man who could be easily distracted from his purpose.

He would kiss her, hold her, caress her. Eventually, she knew, all of her caution would vanish under the sheer force of physical desire, and she wouldn't be able to stop him—or herself.

She closed her eyes and relived the way he had kissed her the afternoon before, the way he had tasted, the calm expertise with which he had deepened the kiss. She thought of his lean fingers on her breast, and her nipples throbbed. For the first time since Matt, she wondered about making love in relation to herself. She thought of the feel of Robert's hard weight pressing down on her, of his hands and mouth moving over her bare skin, of his muscled thighs spreading hers apart as he positioned himself to take her. The appeal of her fantasy was strong enough to make her entire body clench with desire. Yes, she wanted him, as much as she feared the pain he would leave behind when he walked out of her life.

A prudent woman would immediately see a doctor about birth control, and Evie was a prudent woman. She could protect herself in that way, at least.

Chapter Six

Evie slid two food-filled plates onto the table, one in front of Rebecca and the other in front of her own seat, then refilled their coffee cups. "Thanks." Rebecca sighed, picking up her fork. Her eyes were dark-circled after the long, sleepless night spent with Jason in the hospital.

Evie sat down. After making a doctor's appointment for the next day, she had called the hospital to check on Jason. He was fine, but Rebecca had some definitely frayed edges. Not only had she been awake all night to keep watch on him and wake him regularly, evidently Jason had become as fractious and ill-tempered as he'd been as a baby whenever he was ill. He had complained about everything, griping about being woken every hour, even though both the doctor and Rebecca had explained the reason for it. In short, his mother's wrath was about to come down hard on his sore head.

So Evie had gone up to the hospital to take care of the myriad details involved in releasing Jason. Then she'd followed them home, helped get the restless teenager settled, pushed Rebecca into a chair and set about making breakfast for them all. She knew her way around Rebecca's kitchen as well as she did her own, so the work went smoothly, and in no time at all they were digging into scrambled eggs, bacon and toast. Jason was enthroned on the couch with a tray on his lap and the television blaring.

The coffee revived Rebecca enough that her big-sister instincts kicked in. She gave Evie a shrewd look over the rim of her cup. "Where did you have dinner last night?"

"At the marina. Sandwiches," Evie clarified.

Rebecca sat back, looking disgruntled. "He said he would take you out to dinner, then make sure you got home okay."

"I didn't want to go out."

"Really," Rebecca grumbled, "I'd thought the man was made of stronger stuff than that."

If he'd been any stronger, Evie thought wryly, she would have slept in *his* bed last night. "I was too tired to go out, so he brought sandwiches there. It was kind of him to do everything he did yesterday."

"Especially hauling both you and my brat out of the river," Rebecca said judiciously as she demolished a slice of bacon. "I need to thank him again for you. I'm reserving judgment on the wisdom of saving Jason."

Evie chuckled at Rebecca's sardonic statement. A sharp turn of phrase was a family trait that she shared with her sister, and even Paige had been exhibiting it for some time now.

"However," Rebecca continued in the same tone, "I know a man on the hunt when I see one, so don't try to throw me off the subject by telling me how *kind* he was. Kindness was the last thing on his mind."

Evie looked down at her eggs. "I know."

"Are you going to give him a chance, or are you going to look straight through him, like all the others?"

"What others?" Evie asked, puzzled.

"See what I mean? They were invisible to you. You've never even noticed all the guys who would have liked to go out with you."

"No one's ever asked me out."

"Why would they, when you never notice them? But I'll bet Robert asked you out, didn't he?"

"No." He'd *told* her that she was going out to dinner with him, and he had told her that he intended to make love to her, but he'd never actually asked her out.

Rebecca looked disbelieving. "You're pulling my leg."

"I am not. But he'll probably ask the next time he comes to the marina, if that's any consolation to you."

"The real question," her sister said shrewdly, "is if you'll go with him."

"I don't know." Evie propped her elbows on the table, the coffee cup cradled in her palms as she sipped the hot liquid. "He excites me, Becky, but he scares me, too. I don't want to get involved with anyone, and I'm afraid I wouldn't be able to stop myself with him."

"This is bad?" asked her sister with some exasperation. "Honey, it's been twelve years. Maybe it's time you became interested in men again."

"Maybe," Evie said in qualified agreement, though privately she didn't think so at all. "But Robert Cannon isn't the safest choice I could make, not by a long shot. There's something about him... I don't know. I just get the feeling that he's coming on to me for another reason besides the obvious. There's a hidden agenda there somewhere. And he puts up a good front, but he's *not* a gentleman."

"Good. A gentleman would probably take you at your word and never bother you again, after a hundred or so refusals. I have to admit, though, he struck me as being both gentle and protective."

"Possessive," Evie corrected. "And ruthless." No, he wasn't a gentleman. That cold force of will in his green diamond eyes was the look of an adventurer with a predator's heart. A hollow look of fear entered her own eyes.

Rebecca leaned forward and touched Evie's arm. "I know," she said gently. And she did, because Rebecca had been there and seen it all. "I don't want to push you into doing something you'll regret, but you never know what's going to happen. If Robert Cannon is someone you could love, can you afford to pass up that chance?"

Evie sighed. Rebecca's arguments to the contrary, could she afford to *take* that chance? And was she going to have the choice?

To her relief, Robert wasn't at the marina when she arrived to relieve Craig. Huge, black-bellied clouds were threatening overhead, and a brisk, cool wind began to blow, signaling one of the tempestuous thunderstorms so common during summer. Both pleasure-boaters and fishermen began coming in off the lake, and for an hour she didn't have a moment's rest. Lightning forked downward over the mountains, a slash of white against the purplish black background. Thunder boomed, echoing over the water, and the storm broke with blinding sheets of rain blowing across the lake.

With all of the fishermen who had put in at the marina safely off the water and the other boats snugly in their slips, Evie gladly retreated to the office where she could watch the storm from behind the protection of the thick, Plexiglass windows. She hadn't quite escaped all the rain, though, and she shivered as she rubbed a towel over her bare arms. The temperature had dropped twenty degrees in about ten minutes; the break from the heat was welcome, but the abrupt contrast was always chilling.

She loved the energy and drama of thunderstorms, and settled contentedly into her rocking chair to watch this one play out against the background of lake and mountains. Listening to the rain was unutterably soothing. Inevitably she became drowsy and got up to turn on the small television she kept to entertain Paige and Jason. A small logo at the bottom of the television screen announced "T'storm watch."

"I'm watching, I'm watching," she told the television, and returned to the rocking chair.

Eventually the violence of the storm dissipated, but the welcome rain continued, settling down to a steady soaker, the kind farmers loved. The marina was deserted, except for the mechanic, Burt Mardis, who was contentedly working on an outboard motor in the big metal building where he did all the repairs. She could see him occasionally through the open door as he moved back and forth. There wouldn't be any more business until the weather cleared, which it showed no signs of doing. At the top of the hour the local television meteorologist broke in on the normal programming to show the progression of the line of thunderstorms that were marching across the state, as well as the solid area of rain they had left behind, stretching all the way back into Mississippi. Rain was predicted well into the night, tapering off shortly before midnight.

It looked like a long, lazy afternoon ahead of her. She always kept a book there for such times and pulled it out now, but so much time had lapsed since she had started the thing that she didn't remember much about it, so she had to start over. Actually, this was the third time she had started over; she would have to carry it home if she ever hoped to finish it.

But she was already fighting drowsiness and after ten minutes she knew that reading was going to tip the scales in favor of sleep. Regretfully she put the book aside and looked around for some chores to do. Craig, however, had cleaned up that morning; the floors were freshly swept and mopped, the merchandise impeccably straight on the shelves or hanging on pegboard hooks.

She yawned and desperately turned the television channel to rock music videos. That should jar her awake.

When Robert walked in half an hour later, she was standing in front of the television, watching with a sort of amazed disbelief. Turning to him, she said in bemusement, "I wonder why bird-legged, sunken-chested musicians feel compelled to show their bodies to the audience?"

He was startled into a deep chuckle. He almost never laughed aloud, his amusement normally expressed, at most, by a twinkle in his eyes. This was twice, though, that Evie had charmed him into laughter. No one would ever suspect her of espionage, he thought suddenly, perhaps because of that very charm. It would be almost impossible for anyuone who knew her at all to think ill of her. Even he, who was well aware of her activities, couldn't keep himself from wanting her with a violence that both angered him and made him uneasy, because he couldn't control it.

He pushed those thoughts away as he walked toward her. If he let himself think about it now he would become enraged all over again, and Evie was so astute that he might not be able to hide it from her. When he reached her, though, and encircled her with his arms, forgetting about the other was laughably easy.

She blinked up at him, startled. Automatically she put her hands against his chest in a defensive movement. "You said you were going to back off and give me time," she accused.

"I am," Robert replied, lifting her left hand and pressing his warm, open mouth to the tender flesh on the inside of her wrist. Her pulse fluttered and raced beneath his lips. The scent of her skin was fresh and elusively, lightly fragrant, teasing him far more than if she had dabbed herself with perfume, no matter how expensive. He touched the tip of his tongue to the delicate blue veins that traced just under her skin and felt the throb of her blood beneath his touch.

Evie trembled at the subtle caress, her knees weakening. He felt that betraying quiver and gathered her more firmly against him, then lightly bit the pad at the base of her thumb. She swallowed a gasp; dear God, she hadn't known that could be so erotic.

"Will you go out to dinner with me tonight?" he murmured as his lips traveled on to her palm. Again his tongue flicked out, tasting her. Her hand trembled at the sensation.

"No, I can't." The instinctive denial was out before she could stop it, the habits of a dozen years firmly ingrained. Stunned, she realized that she *had* wanted to accept, much as a moth yearned toward the flame.

"Do you have another date?"

"No. It—it's difficult." He had no idea how difficult. She took a deep breath. "I haven't dated since my husband died."

Robert lifted his head, a slight frown drawing the black wings of his eyebrows together. "What did you say?"

She flushed and tugged her hand free. She started to wipe her palm against her jeans but instead tightly closed her fingers to hold the feel of his kiss. "I haven't gone out with anyone since Matt died."

He was silent, digesting this information, weighing it for truth. It was difficult to believe of anyone, but especially of a woman who looked like Evie. It was possible, of course, that she wasn't having an affair with Mercer after all, but to have lived like a nun for twelve years just didn't seem feasible. Still, he wasn't about to infuriate her by suggesting she was a liar.

Instead he gently stroked the underside of her jaw with the

back of one finger and was immediately absorbed with the velvety texture of her skin. "Why is that?" he murmured a bit absently. "I know all the men down here can't be blind."

She bit her lip. "It was my choice. I...wasn't interested, and it didn't seem fair to waste a man's time under those circumstances."

"Reasonable, for a while. But twelve years?"

Restlessly she tried to pull away from him, but he stilled the movement, tightening the arm that remained around her. They were pressed firmly together from waist to knees, his muscled thighs hard and warm against hers. A man's strength was wonderful, she thought, inviting a woman to relax against him. Until Robert had taken her in his arms, she hadn't realized how very much she needed to be held. But not by just any man; only by him. In that moment Evie knew for certain that she had lost the battle. There was no use trying to evade him; not only would he refuse to let her get away with it, but she didn't *want* to get away with it, not any longer. For better or worse, and with dizzying speed, she had gotten herself involved with Robert Cannon. Dear God, she didn't know if she had the strength to do this, but she knew she had to try.

She didn't try to explain those twelve years. Instead she said, to his chest, "All right. I'll go out with you. Now what?"

"For starters, you could raise your head."

Slowly she did, mentally bracing herself as she met his crystalline eyes. She had expected to see amusement in them, but it was triumph glittering there rather than mirth. She shivered, more from sudden alarm than from the coolness brought by the steady rain.

"Cold?" he asked softly, rubbing his warm hands up the length of her arms.

"No. Afraid," she admitted, with painful candor. "Of you, of getting involved with you." Her eyes were deep and mysterious with shadows as she looked up at this man who had so inexplicably forced himself into her life. If he insisted on establishing some kind of romantic relationship with her, he should know up front how she felt about a few things. "I'm not good at games,

Robert. Don't kiss me unless it's for real. Don't come around unless you mean to stay."

"Do you mean marriage?" he asked coolly, his expressive eyebrows lifting.

Her cheeks burned at his tone. Of course it was ridiculous to think of marriage; that wasn't at all what she had meant. At least, not the legality of marriage, the institution itself. Mentally she shied from the notion, unable to even think of it. "Of course not! I never want to get married again. But the stability, the emotional security, what I had with Matt...well, I won't settle for anything less than that, so if you're looking for a summer affair, I'm not your woman."

His mouth twisted as an unreadable expression crossed his face. "Oh, but you are. You just haven't admitted it to yourself yet."

She shivered again, but her gaze didn't waver. "I want emotional commitment. Under those terms, if you're still willing to get involved with me, I'll go out with you. I'm not comfortable with you, but I expect that will change as we get to know each other. And I don't want to sleep with you. That would just be too risky." He probably thought she meant physically, but for her the emotional risk was by far more dangerous.

He studied her face for a long moment before saying calmly, "All right, we'll take our time and get to know each other. But I *do* want to make love with you, and I'm not going to take a vow of chastity." He cupped her face in his hands, and the glitter in his eyes became more pronounced as his head began to slowly descend. "All you have to do to stop me, at any time," he whispered as his mouth touched hers, "is say no."

Her breath sighed out of her, as soft as a night breeze. The freedom to enjoy him was glorious; it felt as if she had long been frozen and was now thawing, growing warm with life again. For the first time her mouth opened welcomingly beneath his, and he took it with a calm mastery that liquefied her bones. He could give lessons in kissing, she thought hazily. His tongue probed and stroked, enticing her into a like response, so that their tongues touched and curled and petted. It was surprisingly sweet, and totally erotic.

It seemed as if he kissed her like that for a long time, simply holding her face between his palms, her body still pressed full against his. The play of his lips and tongue was both lulling and arousing. Her anxiety faded even as warmth slowly spread through her breasts and loins, making her feel as soft as butter. Her left hand was closed around his right wrist, but her right hand was leisurely stroking his back, feeling the firm, hard layers of muscle, the hollow of his spine, instinctively learning some of the details of how he was made.

The television played on unnoticed. No one came to the door on this rainy day; they stood alone in the office, oblivious to the music and the steady patter of the rain, hearing only each other's breathing and the soft, unconscious sounds of pleasure. Like a morning glory opening its shy face to the sun, Evie slowly bloomed in his arms, her golden sensuality growing in confidence. He was painfully aroused but held himself under strict control, ignoring his own condition so that she didn't feel pressured. She felt...safe, free to relax, and let herself feel the new sensations, explore the limits of her own desire. It was very different from the way it had been with Matt. She had been a girl then, and now she was a woman, with a woman's deeper and richer passion.

Though he had kissed her before, she had been distracted by the dangerous desire she felt for this man. Now, having given in, she could concentrate on the little details. She reveled in his taste, as the coolness of his lips rapidly became warm, then hard and hot. She measured the broadness of his shoulders, her palms smoothing over the curve of the joint and feeling the hardness of his solid bones covered by pads of muscle. She touched his hair, feeling it thick and silky and cool, warmer underneath, where it lay close to his skull. She felt the rasp of his five o'clock stubble against her cheeks. She inhaled the clean, musky scent of his maleness, a faint odor of soap, the fresh smell of rain on his clothes and skin.

"God." Abruptly he drew away, letting his head fall back as he drew in a deep breath. Her response had been hesitant at first, but then she had come alive in his arms, and he felt singed, as if he had been holding the sweetest of fires. His own response to her shook him with its violence. It was difficult to think of anything but taking her, and only their present location kept him from trying. "I'm the one calling a halt this time, sweetheart. We either have to stop or find a more private place."

She felt bereft, suddenly deprived of his touch. Her heart was pounding, and her skin felt as if it glowed with heat. Still, he was right. This wasn't the place for making out like teenagers. "There isn't a more private place," she said as she reached out to turn the television from rock to a country video station. The music abruptly changed from rap to a hauntingly passionate love song, and that was even more jarring to her nerves. She punched the Off button, and in the sudden quiet the rain sounded heavier than before. She looked out the window at the gray curtain that veiled the lake, obscuring the far bank.

"No one will be using their boats for the rest of the day," Robert said. "Why don't you close early and we'll go to Huntsville for dinner."

She considered how his questions and suggestions sounded like statements and demands. Had no one before her ever said no to this man? "I can't close early."

"The rain is supposed to last halfway through the night," he said reasonably.

"But that won't stop people from coming in to buy tackle. Granted, there probably won't be many, maybe not any, but the sign says that I'm open until eight."

And she would be, he thought, exasperated by the difficulty of courting a woman who refused to make time for him. He had certainly never had that problem before. In fact, he couldn't say that he'd ever had a problem with a woman at all—until Evie. Getting close to her presented him with as many obstacles as a mine field. Ruefully he thought that if he was going to spend any time with her, most of it would obviously be here at the marina.

Rather than become angry, which would only make her more obstinate, he said, "Could Craig swap shifts with you occasionally, if we give him advance notice?"

A tiny smile lifted the corners of her mouth, telling him that he was learning. "I suppose he could. He's generally accommodating."

"Tomorrow?"

This time she almost laughed aloud. "I can't tomorrow." She had an appointment with her doctor at ten in the morning. Though she had told Robert that she didn't want to sleep with him, he had said only that he would stop if she told him to. The "if" told her that she should be prudent, because his physical effect on her was potent. Of course, she wasn't going to tell Robert that she was arranging birth control; he would consider it a green light to making love.

He sighed. "The day after tomorrow?"

"I'll ask him."

"Thank you," he said with faint irony.

Robert received two phone calls the next morning. He was out on the deck, reading a sheaf of papers that Felice had faxed to him; it was remarkably easy, he'd found, to keep abreast of things by way of phone, computer and fax. The first call was from Madelyn. "How are things in Alabama?"

"Hot," he replied. He was wearing only gym shorts. The rain of the day before had made everything seem even more green and lush, the scents more intense, but it hadn't done anything to ease the heat. If anything, the heat was worse. The morning sun burned on his bare chest and legs. Luckily, with his olive complexion, he didn't have to worry about sunburn.

"The weather is perfect here, about seventy-five degrees. Why don't you fly up for the weekend?"

"I can't," he said, and realized how much he sounded like Evie. "I don't know how long I'll be down here, but I can't leave until everything is tied up."

"The invitation stands," Madelyn said in her lazy drawl. A funny pang went through him as he realized how similar Madelyn's accent was to Evie's. "If you do happen to find a couple of days free, we'd love to see you."

"I'll try to get up there before I go back to New York," he promised.

"Try really hard. We haven't seen you since spring. Take care."

The phone rang again almost immediately. This time it was the man he had hired to keep watch on Landon Mercer. "He had a visitor last night. We followed the visitor when he left, and we're working on identifying him. There hasn't been anything of interest on the phones."

"All right. Keep watching and listening. Has he spotted his tail yet?"

"No, sir."

"Anything in his house?" Robert was briefly thankful that he was a civilian and didn't have to follow the same tortuous rules and procedures that cops did, though it could have been sticky if his men had been caught breaking and entering. They hadn't seized any evidence, merely looked for it. Information was power.

"Clean as a whistle. Too clean. There's not even a bank statement lying around. We found out that he has a safety deposit box, so he might keep his paperwork in it, but we haven't been able to get into it yet. I'm working on getting a copy of his bank statement."

"Keep me informed," Robert said, and hung up. In a few days Mercer would start feeling a slight squeeze. He wouldn't think much of it at first, but soon it would become suffocating. Robert's plans for Evie, both personal and financial, were moving along nicely, too.

Chapter Seven

Robert didn't intend to see Evie at all that day. He was an expert strategist in the eternal battle between men and women; after his determined pursuit of her, she would be expecting him to either call or come to the marina, and the lack of any contact with him would knock her slightly off balance, further weakening her defenses. He had often thought that seduction was similar to chess, in that the one who could keep the other guessing was the one in control of the game.

He was in control of the seduction. His instincts in that part of the game were infallible. It might take him a few weeks of gentling, but Evie would end up in his bed. Not long after that, he would have this entire mess cleaned up; Mercer and Evie would be arrested, and he would go back to New York.

Damn.

That was the problem, of course. He didn't want Evie in jail. He had been furious when he had come down here, determined to put both her and her lover away for a very long time. But that was before he had met her, before he had held her and tasted the heady sweetness of her. Before he had seen the underlying sadness in those golden brown eyes, and wondered if he would cause that expression to deepen. The thought made him uneasy.

Was she even guilty? At first he had been convinced that she was; now, even after such a short acquaintance, he was no longer certain. No criminal was untouched by his deeds. There was always a mark left behind, perhaps in a certain coldness in the eye, a lack of moral concern in certain matters. He hadn't been able to find any such mark in Evie. He had often thought that those who dealt in espionage, in the betrayal of their own country, were some of the coldest people ever born. They lacked the depth of emotion that others had. That lack of feeling wasn't evident in Evie; if anything, he would say that she felt far too much.

She hadn't hesitated at all in going into the river after Jason. That in itself wasn't unusual; any number of strangers would have done the same thing, much less a relative. But, knowing that every second counted, she had stayed down far too long herself in the effort to find the boy. He knew as surely as he knew the sun was in the sky that she would not have been able to make it back to the surface without his help...and that she had been willing to die rather than release Jason and save herself. Even now, the memory made his bones turn cold.

He had gone inside to work at the computer, but now he got up and restlessly walked out onto the deck, where the burning sun could dispel his sudden chill.

Only a person of deep emotion was capable of that kind of sacrifice.

He braced his hands on the top railing and stared out at the river. It wasn't green today, but rather a rich blue, reflecting the deep blue of the cloudless sky. There was little, if any, breeze, and the water's surface was calm. It lapped gently against the dock and the bank with a sound that tugged at something deep within him. All life had originated in the sea; perhaps it was an echo of that ancient time that made people respond so to water. But this river, peaceful as it was now, had almost taken Evie's life.

He shivered from another chill. He couldn't remember, he thought absently, when he had been so enraged...or so afraid. He had ruthlessly controlled both emotions, allowing no hint of them to surface, but they had roiled deep within him. It hadn't been an intellectual anger, but rather a gut-level rage at fate, at chance, which had seemed to be snatching Evie out of his grasp before he could...what? Have her indicted? He snorted mirthlessly at that idea. The thought hadn't entered his mind. No, he had been furious that he wouldn't be able to hold her, make love to her, that the endless stretch of his days wouldn't have her in them.

Was Evie the type of person who could betray her country? He was beginning to doubt his own information.

Indecision wasn't normally part of Robert's makeup, and he was impatient with himself now. He couldn't allow his doubts about Evie's guilt to alter his plans. If she was innocent, then she wouldn't be harmed. She would have some uncomfortable moments, she would be worried, but in the end he would take care of the situation, and she would be okay.

Thinking about her made him edgy. He glanced at his watch; it was a little after noon. She should be at the marina now, and he should already have heard from the tail that he had assigned to follow her every move.

Right on cue, the phone rang, and he stepped inside to pick it up.

"She went to Huntsville this morning," a quiet female voice reported. "Her destination was an office building. The elevator closed before I could get on it with her, so I don't know where she went. I waited, and she returned to the lobby after an hour and twenty-three minutes. She drove straight home, changed clothes and then went to the marina. Mercer was in his office at PowerNet the entire time, and they didn't talk on the phone. There was no contact between them at all."

"What kind of tenants are in the office building?"

"I made a list. There are two insurance firms, a real estate office, four medical doctors, four lawyers, three dentists, an office temp company and two computer programming firms."

Damn, Robert thought bleakly. Aloud he said, "Find out where she went. Concentrate first on the two programming firms."

"Yes, sir."

He swore as he hung up. Why couldn't she have spent the morning shopping, or paying bills?

He wanted to see her. He wanted to shake her until her teeth rattled. He wanted to whisk her away to some secluded place and keep her locked up there until he had this mess settled. He wanted to ride her until she wept with submission. The violence of all those longings was alien to him, but he couldn't deny it. She had definitely gotten under his skin in a way no other woman had ever done.

Temper and frustration merged, and with a muttered curse he gave in. After swiftly dressing, he left the house and climbed in the black Jeep. Damn it, he wanted to see her, so he would.

Virgil was visiting with Evie again that day. His knee was better, he said, and indeed, he was walking with less effort. The day had been fairly busy, with customers in and out on a regular basis, and Virgil had passed the time with several old friends and casual acquaintances.

She was busy ringing up a fisherman's purchase of gas, a soft drink and a pack of crackers when the door opened. Without looking, she knew Robert had entered. Her skin tingled, and she felt an instant of panic. She had hoped, foolishly, that she wouldn't see him that day, that her frazzled nerves would have a chance to recover somewhat before she actually went out with him the next night. On the other hand, she thought wryly, time and distance probably wouldn't help at all. Even if he wasn't there personally, he was in her mind, dominating both her thoughts and dreams.

Her customer taken care of, she allowed herself to look at him as he genially introduced himself to Virgil, who remembered him, of course. Very little got by that old man.

Robert was wearing jeans and a loose, white cotton shirt. A khaki baseball cap covered his black hair, and a pair of expensive sunglasses dangled from one hand. Her blood raced through her veins in excitement; even in such casual dress, there was something elegant and dangerous about him. The jeans were soft and faded with age, and he was as at home in them as he was in his silk shirts.

Then he was touching her on the arm, and it was like being burned with a tiny spark of electricity. "I'm going to take the boat out for a while, run the river and learn something about it."

So he wasn't going to be hanging around the marina all day. She was both relieved and disappointed. "Have you hired a guide?"

"No, but the river channel's marked, isn't it?"

"Yes, there shouldn't be any problem, unless you want to explore out of the channel. I'll give you a map."

"Okay." Thoughtfully Robert looked at Virgil. "Would you like to show me around the lake, Mr. Dodd? That is, if you don't have plans for the afternoon."

Virgil cackled, his faded eyes suddenly gleaming with enthusiasm. "Plans?" he snorted. "I'm ninety-three years old! Who in tarnation makes plans at my age? I could stop breathin' any minute now."

Amusement danced in Robert's eyes, making them look like pale green diamonds. "I'm willing to take the chance if you are, but I warn you, a corpse in the boat would be a real inconvenience."

Virgil hauled himself out of the rocking chair. "Tell you what, son. For the chance to park myself in a boat again, I'll try real hard not to put you to the trouble of havin' to call the coroner."

"It's a deal." Robert winked at Evie as he turned away.

Evie shook her head as she smiled at Virgil. She knew better than to try talking him out of going. Besides, he deserved to enjoy an hour or so on the river he loved, and she had faith that Robert would be as skillful at handling a boat as he was at everything else he did. How had he guessed, on such short acquaintance, that Virgil would dearly love getting out on the water again?

"Both of you be careful," she admonished. "Virgil, don't forget your cap."

"I won't, I won't," he said testily. "Think I'm fool enough to go out without somethin' on my head?"

"I'll bring the boat around to the dock," Robert said, and she was grateful to him for sparing Virgil the longer walk to the boat slip. He reached the door, stopped and came back to her. "I forgot something."

"What?"

He cupped her chin in one hand, leaned down and calmly kissed her. It wasn't a passionate kiss; it was almost leisurely. Still, when he lifted his head, her heart was pounding and her thoughts scattered. "That," he murmured.

She heard Virgil's cracked laughter and became aware of the interested gazes of the two customers who were browsing among the hooks and spinner baits. Her cheeks burned with a blush, and she turned away to fiddle with some papers until she could regain her composure.

Virgil patted her on the arm. Though stooped under the weight of nine decades, he was still taller than she, and he grinned at her. "Heard tell that young feller made hisself useful the other day, when Becky's boy fell in."

She cleared her throat. "Yes. If he hadn't been there, Jason and I both would probably have drowned."

"Fast mover, is he?"

She found herself blushing again and waved Virgil off with shooing motions. Why on earth had Robert kissed her in public? She would never have thought that he was given to public displays of affection; there was something too contained about him. But he had certainly done just that!

She watched out the window as he idled the sleek black boat around to the dock, the powerful motor rumbling like thunder. The sunglasses were in place on the high-bridged nose, giving him a remote, lethal air. She had seen soldiers with that exact expression, and she wondered at it. With a start, she realized how little she knew about Robert Cannon. What did he do for a living? She knew he had to have some money to be able to afford that house, a new boat and the new Jeep. Where was he from? Did he have family, had he been married before, was he married *now,* did he have children? A chill went through her as she thought of all she didn't know about him.

And yet, in a way, she knew the man. He was cool and complicated, a private man who kept a subtle but permanent distance between himself and everyone else. The distance wasn't physical, God knows; he was the most physical, *sensual* man she'd ever met. Emotionally, though, he always held something back, keeping the inner man untouched. Probably most people thought of him as very controlled and unemotional; Evie agreed with the controlled part, but there was a ferocity lurking beneath the control that alarmed her even as it called to her own inner fire. He was ruthless, he was autocratic...and he had seen, almost at a glance, how much an old man would love to take a boat ride on his beloved river once more.

Her breath caught, and there was a pain in her chest. Panic filled her as she watched Virgil hobble out to the dock as Robert brought the boat alongside. Robert held out a strong hand, and Virgil gripped it and stepped aboard the craft. There was a wide smile on his face as he settled onto the seat. Robert handed him a life jacket, and obediently Virgil slipped it on, though Evie was fairly certain he'd never worn one before in his life.

The panic that almost suffocated her was comprised of equal parts terror and tenderness. She *couldn't* feel this much for him, not so soon. You had to know someone for that, and she had just been thinking how little she knew about him. She was fascinated by him, that was all. It was understandable. He was the first man in her life since Matt's death, twelve long, desolate years ago. He had brought passion alive in her again, with his skillful kisses and determined pursuit.

She had never felt so violently attracted to a man before.

With Matt...they had grown up together, they'd been in the same class in school, from first grade through graduation. She had known Matt as well as she knew herself; they'd been like two halves of a whole. The love had grown gradually between them, pure and steady, like a candle flame. Robert...Robert was an inferno, and the heat between them could leave her in ashes.

Robert and Virgil had been gone for over an hour when Landon Mercer strolled into the marina. "Hi, doll," he said jovially. "How's the prettiest woman in this part of the state?"

Evie's expression was impassive as she glanced at him. Unfortunately, business had slowed down and she was there alone. She always preferred to have company around when she had to deal with him. Of course, being alone meant that she would have the opportunity to follow him again. Her thoughts began to hum. "Hello, Mr. Mercer."

"Landon," he said, as he always did. He leaned against the counter in a negligent pose, one designed to show off his physique. Mercer was a good-looking man, she admitted, but he left her cold.

"Do you want to rent a boat today?" she asked, turning to check which ones were available, though she knew without looking. She had quickly discovered that the best way to deflect his attention was to appear oblivious to it.

"Sure do. It's been a while since I've done any fishing, so I decided to play hooky from work this afternoon." He laughed at his own pun.

Evie managed a polite smile. He had brought in a small tackle box and one rod and reel, the same rig he always carried. The same lure was tied to the line.

"Do you want any particular boat?"

"No, any of them will do." He leaned closer. "When I get back, why don't we go out to dinner tonight? Not anywhere here. We'll go someplace nice, maybe in Birmingham."

"Thanks, but I'm busy tonight," she replied, her tone conveying no interest at all. Unfortunately, he was so taken with his own charm that he was oblivious to her lack of response to him.

"Tomorrow night, then. It's Saturday night. We can even go to Atlanta for some real fun, since we wouldn't have to be back for work."

"The marina's open seven days a week."

"Oh. Okay, we'll go to Birmingham."

"No, thank you, Mr. Mercer. I'm busy tomorrow night, too."

"C'mon, how busy can you be? Whatever it is, you can put it off."

Her teeth were on edge. She barely managed to be polite as she said, "I have a date tomorrow night."

"Now I'm jealous. Who's the lucky man?"

"No one you know." She took an ignition key from the pegboard and slid it across the counter to him. "There you go. Number five, the one at the end of the dock."

He took out his wallet and extracted a couple of twenties. "I'll have it back in two hours." He picked up the ignition key.

"Fine." She mustered a smile. "Have a good time. Hope you catch a lot."

"I never do, but it's fun to try," he said breezily as he picked up his tackle and went out the door.

Evie put the money into the cash drawer and locked it, all the while eyeing Mercer as he walked down the dock. He was looking around, studying the parking lot and the traffic on the street out front, as well as on the bisecting causeway.

Swiftly she picked up the phone and buzzed Burt in the maintenance building. He picked up just as Mercer was getting into the boat.

"Burt, I'm taking the boat out for a while," Evie said swiftly. "I'm locking the store, but keep an eye on the gas pumps while I'm gone."

"Sure," he said, as unquestioning as ever. Burt Mardis didn't have a curious bone in his body.

Mercer was idling away from the dock. Evie jammed a ball cap on her head, grabbed her sunglasses and hurried from the building. She locked the door behind her, then sprinted for her own boat.

He was beyond the wave breakers by the time she reached her boat, and she heard the roar as he opened up the throttle. She all but threw herself into the boat and turned the key in the ignition. The motor coughed to life with a satisfying roar. Her boat was faster than any of the rentals, but on the water, and at speed, it was difficult to distinguish one vessel from another.

She had to idle away from the marina, because a fast takeoff would make waves large enough to violently rock the boats in their slips, possibly damaging them. Swearing at every lost second, she waited until she was past the wave breakers before pushing the throttle forward. The motor roared, and the front end of the boat lifted in the air as the vessel shot forward. It planed off almost immediately, the nose dropping into the running position.

She scanned the water for Mercer; unfortunately, he had gained enough distance that she couldn't positively identify him, and there were three boats speeding away from her, small specks that bobbed slightly as they cut through the waves. Which one was Mercer?

The sun wasn't far past its apex, and the glare turned the lake into a mirror. Hot air hit her, pulling tendrils of hair loose around her face. The scent of the river filled her head and lungs, and a quiet exultation spread through her. This was a part of her life that she loved—the wind in her face, the sense of speed, the feel of the boat as it glided over calm water and bumped over waves. Though there were other boats on the lake, and houses visible all along the shoreline, when she was speeding across the water it was like being alone with God. She would have been perfectly content, if only she knew what Mercer was up to.

After a minute one boat slowed and turned toward another marina. As she neared, she could tell that it held two passengers.

That left two. The throttle was full forward, and she was gaining on one, while the other, probably a speedy bass boat, was pulling away. Since her boat was faster than the rental, the one she was overtaking had to be Mercer. Cautiously she throttled back, enough to stay at a pace with him but not so close that he would see and identify her. Just about everyone on the water would be wearing a ball cap and sunglasses, and her hair was pulled back in a braid rather than flying loose, so she felt fairly confident that he wouldn't recognize her.

He was heading toward the same area, where there were a lot of small islands dotting the lake. She wouldn't be able to get very close, because once he cut his speed he would be able to hear other boats. Her best bet, she thought, was to stop some distance away and pretend to be fishing.

The boat ahead slowed and cut between two islands. Evie kept her speed steady and cruised on past. There was a distance of over two hundred yards between them, but she could tell that now he was idling closer to the bank of the island on the right.

She turned in the opposite direction, away from him. A barge was coming downriver, heavily loaded and settled deep into the water, pushing out a wave as it plowed forward. If she let the barge come between her and Mercer, it would block his activities for almost half a minute, plenty long enough for her to lose him. But if she moved inside the barge's path, it would put her closer to him than she wanted to be.

There was no help for it. She tucked her long braid inside her shirt to hide that identifying detail and turned the boat to angle back across the river ahead of the barge.

"Guntersville Lake's easy to learn," Virgil stated. "'Course, I was fishin' the river back before the TVA built the dam, so I knowed the lay of the land before the water backed up and covered it. Not many of us around now remembers the way it used to be. River used to flood a lot. So Roosevelt's boys decided we needed us a dam, so there wouldn't be no more floods. Well, hell, 'course there ain't, 'cause now the land that flooded ever now an' then is permanently under water. The government calls it flood control. They throwed around words like eminent domain, but what they did is take people's land, turn them off their farms, and put a lot of good land under water."

"The TVA brought electricity to the Tennessee River Valley, didn't it?" Robert asked. He was holding the boat to around twenty miles an hour, not much more than idling speed to the powerful motor behind them, but the slow speed made conversation possible. They had to raise their voices, but they could hear each other.

Virgil snorted. "Sure it did. Glad to have it, too. But nobody ever thought the TVA built that dam to make our lives easier. Hell, we knew what was goin' on. It was the Depression, and Roosevelt would have built the second Tower of Babel to make jobs for folks, for all the good it did to the economy. It took the war to kick-start things again."

"Did you fight in the war?"

"Too old for that one." Virgil cackled with glee. "Imagine that! Over fifty years ago, they said I was too old! But I was in the first one. Lied about my age to get in. Not that they checked too close, 'cause they needed men could hit the broad side of a barn with a rifle slug. During the second one, I volunteered to help train the younger fellers with their rifles, but that was all stateside. Suited me. My wife weren't none too pleased with me, anyway, leavin' her to handle five young'uns on her own. She'd have been mad as hell if I'd gone overseas. Our oldest boy, John Edward, was seventeen when it all started, and he joined the navy.

It fretted her enough that he was gone. He made it back fine, though. Imagine that. The boy went through a war in the Pacific without a scratch, then come home and died two years later with the pneumonia. Life's got a lotta strange turns in it. Don't guess I'll see too many more of them, but then, I didn't plan on hangin' around this long to begin with.''

The old man lapsed into silence, perhaps remembering all the people who had come and gone through his life. After a minute he roused himself. "Got a lot of creeks emptyin' into the lake. We passed Short Creek a ways back. This here's Town Creek.''

Robert had studied maps of the lake, so when Virgil identified the creeks he was able to pinpoint their location. Since the river channel was marked, staying in safely deep water was no problem. It was when he ventured out of the river channel that Virgil's expertise came in handy, because he knew where it was shallow, where the hidden stump rows were lurking just under the surface, ready to tear the bottom out of a boat if the driver wasn't careful. For several more minutes, Virgil devoted himself to his appointed task, pointing out quirks of the lake.

Then he said, "I've lost a lot of folks over the years. My own mama and pa, of course, and all my brothers and sisters. There were sixteen of us, and I'm the only one left. Got a piss pot full of nieces and nephews, though, and all of their kids, and their kids' kids. My wife passed on in sixty-four. Lord, it don't seem like it's been that long. I've lost three of my own kids. Parents ought not to outlive their kids. It ain't right. And all my friends that I growed up with, they're long gone.

"Yep, I've had to bury many a loved one, so I get right protective of the ones I got left.'' Faded blue eyes were suddenly piercing as he turned them on Robert. "Evie's a special woman. She's had enough sorrow in her young life, so if you don't mean to do right by her, it would be a kindness if you'd leave her alone and haul your ass back up north.''

Robert's face was impassive. "Evie's related to you?'' he asked neutrally, ignoring Virgil's rather combative statement. He wasn't about to get into an argument with a ninety-three-year-old man.

Virgil snorted. "Not by blood. But I've knowed her all her life, watched her grow up, and there's not a finer woman in this town. Now, I watch television, so I know times have changed from when I was young enough to court a woman. Back then we had enough respect for womenfolk not to do nothing to cause them harm. But, like I said, times have changed. I know young folks now get serious about things without tyin' the knot proper, and that ain't what I'm talkin' about. Thing is, if you're just lookin' for a good time, then find some other woman. Evie ain't like that."

Robert had to struggle with several conflicting emotions. Foremost was his cold, instinctive anger at Virgil's scolding interference. In neither his business nor his personal life was he accustomed to being taken to task. Right after that, though, was amusement. He was thirty-six and, moreover, an extremely wealthy man who wielded a great deal of power in both financial and political circles. He almost smiled at Virgil lumping him in with "young folks."

What took most of his attention, though, was this second warning that Evie wasn't a good-time girl. Evie herself had issued the first warning: *Don't kiss me unless it's for real.* After Virgil's little speech, the underlying meaning of those warnings was clear, though the reason wasn't.

"I don't usually discuss my relationships," he finally said in a faintly distant tone, just enough to signal his displeasure. "But my interest in Evie isn't casual." *In any way.* "What did you mean, she's had enough sorrow in her life?" Because that had been the basis of the talk: *Don't hurt her.*

"I mean, life ain't been easy on her. Grief comes to everybody, if they live long enough. Some folks, though, it hits harder than others. Losin' Matt the way she did, the day after they got married...well, it changed her. There ain't no sunshine in her eyes now, the way there used to be. She never looked at another man since Matt died, until you. So don't disappoint her, is what I'm sayin'."

Robert was knocked off balance by the surge of jealousy that seared through him. Jealousy? He'd never been jealous in his life, especially where a woman was concerned. Either his women were faithful to him or the relationship ended. Period. How could he be jealous of a boy who had been dead for a dozen years? But Evie still wore Matt Shaw's wedding ring on her finger and had evidently remained faithful to him even after all this time. Forget Mercer; that had obviously been an error. An understandable one, but still an error. He was both glad that she wasn't involved with Mercer, at least on that level, and furious that she was determined to waste herself on a memory. *I don't want to sleep with you,* she'd said. She was still trying to be faithful to a dead husband.

"What kind of person was Matt?" he asked. He didn't want to know, didn't want to talk about the boy, but he felt compelled to find out.

"He was a fine boy. Would have been a good man, if he'd had the chance. Good-natured, honest. Kindhearted, too. Can't say that about too many folks, but Matt didn't have a mean bone in his body. He never dated anybody but Evie, and it was the same with her. They planned to marry each other from the time they started high school together. Never saw two kids love each other the way they did. It was a shame that they didn't have no more time together than what they had. She didn't even have his child to keep part of him alive. Damn shame. She needed somthing to live for, back then."

Robert had had enough. He couldn't listen to much more about how wonderful Matt Shaw had been, and how much Evie had loved him, without losing his temper. He couldn't remember the last time he had lost control, but there was a deep-seated fury in him now that was surging forward. He didn't try to analyze his anger; he simply and ruthlessly contained it, shoving it down as he turned the boat downriver and headed back toward the marina. He eased the throttle forward so the noise would make conversation impossible.

Fifteen minutes later they were idling up to the docks. At the sound of the motor, a man wearing grease-covered coveralls came out of the maintenance building and walked out on the dock. He nodded a greeting to Robert and said to Virgil, "Come in outta the sun and keep me company for a while. Evie closed the office and took her boat out for a while.'' As he talked, he extended a muscular arm to steady Virgil as he climbed out of the boat onto the dock.

"When was this?" Robert asked sharply.

The mechanic shrugged. "An hour, maybe. I didn't pay no attention to the time."

She had refused to close the marina early one rainy late afternoon, when there had been no customers, but now she had closed it not long after lunch on a beautiful, sunny, *busy* day. Robert's eyes narrowed. He looked at the parking lot. He knew the make, model and color of Mercer's car, and there it sat.

Damn her. She had left to meet with the traitorous bastard.

Chapter Eight

Robert was standing on the dock when Evie eased her boat into its regular slip. He was wearing those extra dark sunglasses that completely hid his eyes, but she didn't need to see them to know that they were icy with rage. Maybe it was the way he moved, very deliberately, every action contained, that alerted her to his mood. An uncontrollable shiver ran over her, despite the heat. There was something far more alarming about that cold, ruthless control than if he had been violent. Again she had the thought that he was the most dangerous man she'd ever seen. But what had put him in such a menacing mood?

She tied off and leapt up onto the dock. "Did Virgil enjoy himself?" she asked as she stepped around Robert, heading toward the office. He wasn't the only one who had self-control. Right now she had other concerns besides dealing with his temper. She could hear the roar of a boat coming closer; that might or might not be Mercer, but she wasn't taking any more chances. When Mercer returned to the marina, she intended to be inside the office building, doing business as usual.

"Just a minute," Robert said, his tone clipped, and reached for her.

Evie evaded his grasp. "Later," she said, and hurried up the dock.

He was right behind her when she unlocked the door, but he didn't have a chance to say anything. Virgil had seen her boat and was slowly making his way across the lot. Robert eyed the old man's progress; he wouldn't have time to get any answers out of her before Virgil was there, so it would be better to wait, as she'd said, until later. Once more he controlled his anger and frustration, but the fury in him remained hot. If anything, he was becoming even angrier.

Virgil reached the doorway and gave a sigh of pleasure as the cool air-conditioning washed over him. "Got spoiled in my old age," he griped. "The heat didn't used to bother me none."

"No point in letting it bother you back then," Evie pointed out, smiling at him. "There wasn't any air-conditioning, so we all had to put up with it."

The old man eased into the rocking chair. "Spoiled," he repeated contentedly.

She went over to a vending machine and fed in the change for three soft drinks. She kept the machine's temperatre set low enough to form ice crystals in the drinks, to the delight of her customers. She popped the tops off the bottles and thrust one into Robert's hands, then gave another to Virgil. The third she drank herself, turning up the bottle for a long, cold swallow of the crisp, biting liquid.

She saw Robert eye the hourglass bottle in his hand with a less-than-thrilled expression; then he, too, took a drink. His tastes were probably too sophisticated to run to soft drinks, she thought, but if he was going to live here for the summer, he should do as the natives did. One of the front lines of defense against the heat was to consume cola every day as coolant for the insides.

A boat was idling in past the wave breakers. A quick glance told Evie that it was the rental boat. Mercer had seen her, she knew, but she didn't think he had recognized her. Wearing the universal ball cap and sunglasses, with her hair tucked in, she could have been anyone. It was doubtful that he had even been able to tell she was a woman.

Robert hitched one hip onto the counter, a sockless, docksider-clad foot swinging as he nursed the soft drink. His expression didn't give anything away, but she had the strong impression that he was…waiting. Until they could talk? No. It was more immediate than that.

She watched Mercer tie up the boat and walk jauntily along the dock, tackle box in one hand and useless tackle in the other. Then the door opened and he breezed in, all ego and self-satisfaction. "Nothing today, doll," he said in his obnoxious, too-hearty manner. "Maybe I'd have better luck if you went along. What do you say?"

"I'm not much for fishing," she lied without compunction, causing Virgil to almost choke on his drink.

Robert's back, as he sat on the counter, had been half-turned toward Mercer. Now he shifted around to face the other man. "Hello, Landon," he said coolly. "I'd like to go fishing with you the next time you take the afternoon off."

Evie was startled to hear Robert call Mercer by his first name, and a mental alarm began clanging. *How did Robert know the man?*

But if she was startled, the effect on Mercer was electric. He froze in place, his face draining of color as he gaped at Robert. "M-Mr. Cannon," he shuttered. "I—uh, how—w-what are you doing here?"

The black slashes of Robert's eyebrows rose in that sardonic way of his. Mercer was totally aghast at having run into him, Evie saw, and the tension in her relaxed. Whatever the connection, Robert wasn't in league with Mercer, or the other man wouldn't have been so taken aback at his presence.

The most obvious answer to Mercer's question would have been that he kept his boat here; that wasn't, however, what Robert said. Instead he looked deliberately at Evie and said, "The place has a certain attraction."

She felt silly, but she couldn't stop the color from heating her face. Mercer looked even more aghast, for some reason.

"Oh," he mumbled. "Yeah, sure." With an effort, he regained a bit of control and managed a sickly smile. "It's getting late. I should be going. Call me when you're free, Mr. Cannon, and we'll get in that game of golf we talked about."

"Or some fishing," Robert suggested, his voice like silk.

"Uh...yeah. Yes, we'll do that. Anytime." Mercer tossed the boat keys onto the counter and hastily left.

"Wonder what set his britches on fire," Virgil mused.

"Perhaps it was his bad luck in taking an afternoon off from

work to go fishing and running into his employer at the marina,"
Robert suggested, his eyes hooded.

Virgil leaned back in the rocker, wheezing with laughter.
"Well, I'll be! He works for you, eh? Bet that ruined his fun for
the day."

"I'm certain it did."

Evie stood motionless, absorbing all the nuances of the brief
scene with Mercer, and also the silkiness of Robert's murmured
reply. He had taken a great deal of pleasure in watching Mercer
squirm. He had also made that remark about her being the reason
for his presence for the same reason: to make Mercer squirm.
After all, what man would feel comfortable to find out he had
just come on to the boss's woman...in front of the boss? This
was in addition to being caught playing hooky from work.

Mercer probably didn't realize it, but it had been plain to Evie
that Robert disliked him. He had been perfectly cordial, but the
dislike had been there, underlying every word. She was enor-
mously relieved. For a horrible moment she had been afraid that
Robert was involved with whatever crooked deal Mercer had going on, but Mercer's manner certainly hadn't been that of someone who had met a friend. She was worried, though, to find that
Mercer worked for Robert. Just as she didn't want his dirty waves
to touch the marina, she also didn't want him to somehow harm
Robert.

She hadn't been successful in finding out any more about what
Mercer was up to; he had idled a twisting path around several of
the islands, finally stopping for a moment on the back side of one
of the larger ones. She hadn't been able to see what, if anything,
he was doing. If she had had a trolling motor, she would have
been able to get much closer without him hearing her, but her
boat wasn't equipped with one. Then Mercer had started his motor
again and resumed his weaving in and out of the islands. She had
watched him as best she could, but there was no way to keep him
in sight all the time. When he had finally left the islands, it had
taken all the speed her boat was capable of to outpace him and
reach the marina far enough in advance that he wouldn't see her.

So she still had nothing but suspicion. While she was wondering whether or not to confide in Robert when she had nothing of substance to tell him, Virgil's great-granddaughter came in. This time she was carrying a wide-eyed, eleven-month-old girl on her hip, and was followed by two towheaded boys, ages four and six. "PawPaw, PawPaw," both boys yelled. They ran toward the rocking chair, climbing up on Virgil's lap with a naturalness that suggested they had been doing it all their lives.

"Well, how'd it go?" Virgil asked, gathering both small bodies against him. "Did the dentist give you a sucker?"

"Yep," said the oldest one, pulling a bright red lollipop from his pocket. "Mom says it's okay, because it's sugarless. You want it?" His expression said that he was disappointed by the sugarless state of the candy.

"It's tempting," Virgil allowed, "but you keep it."

Evie smiled as she watched Virgil with his great-great-grandchildren, then turned back to their mother. "Sherry, this is Robert Cannon. He and Virgil have been out running the river today. Robert, Virgil's great-granddaughter, Sherry Ferguson."

"Pleased to meet you," Sherry said with her friendly smile. She obviously remembered Robert from the first time he had come to the marina. She shifted the baby onto her other hip and held out her hand.

Robert reached to shake Sherry's hand, and the baby evidently thought he was reaching for her; with a gurgle of pleasure she released her grip on Sherry's blouse and lunged forward, both dimpled little arms outstretched. Sherry made a startled grab for the child, but Robert was faster, scooping the baby into his arms almost before she had left the safety of her mother's.

"Allison Rose!" Sherry gasped, staring at the baby. "I'm sorry," she apologized to Robert as she reached to retrieve her child. "I don't know what got into her. She's never gone to a stranger like that before."

Allison Rose wouldn't have any of it; she shrieked and turned away from her mother's hands, clinging to Robert's shirt with all her might.

"She's all right," Robert said, his wonderful deep voice now holding a soothing tone to calm both mother and daughter. One powerful hand steadied the baby's back as his eyes smiled at Sherry. "I've always had a way with women."

That was nothing less than the truth, Evie thought, her blood moving in a slow throb through her veins as she watched him cradle the baby as comfortably as if he had a dozen of his own. Was there anything the man couldn't do? Sherry was all but melting under that smiling look, and tiny Allison was in heaven.

Perched on his arm, Allison looked around with a beatific expression, as if she were a queen surveying her subjects. Robert bent his head to brush his nose against the soft blond curls and reflected that girls were different from boys even at this young age. He had rocked Madelyn's two boys when they were infants and played with them as toddlers, but they hadn't been quite as soft as the baby girl in his arms, and her scent was indefinably sweeter. He found himself enchanted by the tiny sandals on her feet and the ruffled sundress she wore. The feel of her chubby, dimpled arms clinging to him was strangely satisfying.

Oh God, Evie thought. Her chest was so tight she could barely breathe. She had to turn away to hide the shattered look in her eyes. Why couldn't he have been uncomfortable with babies? Why did he have to cradle Allison so tenderly and close his eyes with delight at her sweet baby scent? The emotion swelling in her was so overwhelming that she couldn't think, couldn't function.

For the rest of her life she would remember the exact moment when she fell in love with Robert Cannon.

She busied herself fiddling with papers, though she couldn't have said what those papers were. As if from a distance, she could hear Sherry asking about Virgil's excursion on the river, could hear the enthusiasm in Virgil's reply and Robert's comments. The calm, soothing tone was still there, she noticed. How could Sherry fail to be reassured about the safety of the outing when his utter placidity and self-confidence said that he had taken every care without appearing to fuss over Virgil's safety?

He did it deliberately, she realized as she listened to them talk. She felt oddly detached, not really hearing words, but rather the way things were said, the underlying emotion. Robert was a master at reading people, then using his voice and manner with uncanny accuracy to manipulate them into the response he desired. It was almost as if he were a puppeteer, pulling everyone's strings so subtly that they never noticed they were being directed by his will.

And if he manipulated *them*, then it followed that he manipulated *her*.

There was a dull roaring in her ears, as if she might faint. Evie flatly refused to do something that silly and concentrated on breathing deeply. As she sucked in the first breath, she discovered that it was the first time she had done so for some time, judging by the acute relief in her lungs. She had simply stopped breathing, probably about the time Robert had rubbed his face against Allison's curls. No wonder she had felt faint.

Emotionally she had been groping for solid ground, had felt her fingers finally brush against something to which she had thought she could hold. Now she felt as if that lifeline had been jerked away from her and she was lost again, swirling away. Had anything Robert said to her been the truth, or had every word been a subtle manipulation, designed to…what? Get her into his bed? Was the thrill, for him, in the chase? The problem was that he could just as easily be sincere. How was she to tell the difference?

The answer, she thought painfully, was that she couldn't. Only time would tell if she could depend on him, entrust her heart to him, and she doubted that the time was there. He'd said he was here for the rest of the summer, and summer was half-over. He would be here another six, maybe seven, weeks.

"Evie." Her name was spoken quietly, almost in her ear. She felt his heat against her back, smelled the fresh, clean sweat on his body. His hand touched her arm. "Sherry and Virgil are leaving."

She turned, summoning both a smile and self-control. No one else had noticed her preoccupation, she saw, but Robert had, another disturbing example of his acute perception. Allison had been enticed, with one of the red suckers as bait, back into Sherry's arms, where she was engrossed with turning the cellophane-wrapped candy around and around, trying to find access. Finally she simply popped it into her mouth, cellophane and all. Virgil was standing, and the boys were already at the door, shouting that they wanted a Blizzard before they went home, while Sherry insisted that she wasn't driving all the way to Boaz to get one, at which Virgil added that he wouldn't mind having a Blizzard, himself. That, of course, settled the issue.

Evie added her voice to all the rowdy commotion, telling them goodbye, telling Virgil to take care. The boys raced out the door and headed toward the docks. Sherry stepped out and said, ''Y'all get back here, *now!*'' in a tone that stopped them in their tracks and brought them, pouting, back to her. It took another few minutes to get everyone settled in the station wagon, and through it all Evie was acutely aware of Robert standing very close behind her, his hand on the small of her back. Neither Sherry nor Virgil would have missed the body language, much less the touch, that stated his claim on her.

The silence after their departure was almost deafening. She closed the door and tried to slide past him, but his hands closed on her waist, and, with a dizzy whirl, she found herself plunked down on the counter with him standing between her legs to prevent her from getting down. She stared at the center of his chest, refusing to look up at him. She didn't want this, didn't want to confront him when she was still reeling from the jolting realization that she loved him and could trust him even less than she had thought.

''Damn it,'' he said very softly. Then, ''Look at me.''

''Why?''

''Because I don't want to talk to the top of your head.''

''I can hear you just fine the way I am.''

He hissed a curse just under his breath and caught her face between his hands, tilting it up. He was careful not to hurt her, but there was no resisting the easy strength of that grip. She tried to concentrate on his nose, but the pale green glitter of his eyes dominated his face, drawing her attention. There was no way *not* to see the cold fury there.

''Where did you go?''

The question was deceptively calm, almost idle. If she hadn't been able to see his eyes, if she hadn't been able to feel the roiling anger in him, she might have been fooled. ''I had an errand to run.''

''Ah.'' His hands tightened on her face. ''Were you meeting Landon Mercer?'' he asked abruptly. ''Are you having an affair with him?''

She stared at him, stupefied. For several moments she was unable to formulate a single thought, her mind a total blank. How on earth had he managed to link her to Mercer? He had been gone when she had left, and she and Mercer had not come back at the same time. But she *had* left because of Mercer, even though she hadn't been with him. She could feel her cheeks heating and knew that she looked guilty, but she still couldn't seem to manage a coherent reply. Then the last question sank in, and she snapped, ''No, I'm not having an affair with him! I *detest* the man!''

Robert's lips were thin. ''Then why did you sneak off to meet with him?''

''I didn't sneak anywhere,'' she flared. ''And I did *not* meet him!''

''But you closed the office in the middle of a busy day,'' he said relentlessly. ''When you wouldn't close it a little early on a rainy afternoon when there weren't any customers at all.''

''I told you, I had an errand.''

''So you went in a boat?''

''I live on the water,'' she pointed out, light brown eyes glowing more golden by the second. ''I can cross the lake faster than I can drive to my house. Sometimes, if the weather is good and I'm in the mood, I use the boat, anyway, rather than driving.''

The dangerous look hadn't faded from his eyes. ''Are you saying that you went home?''

Very deliberately she caught his wrists and removed his hands from her face. ''I had an errand,'' she repeated. ''I didn't meet Mercer. I'm not having an affair with him. And what in hell makes you think you have the right to interrogate me?'' The last sentence was shouted as she tried to shove him away.

He didn't move, not an inch. "This," he said in a stifled tone, then moved forward as he bent his head to her.

She caught her breath at the heat of his mouth, the ravaging pressure. His movement had forced her thighs even wider, and he settled his hips in the notch. Evie quivered at the hard thrust of his sex against the vulnerable softness of her private body, alarmed by the contact even through several layers of cloth. The passion in him was as overwhelming as his anger had been, buffeting her, bending her under his will. His arms were painfully tight, and she tried to push him away once more, with the same result. "Stop it," he muttered against her mouth, and one arm dropped to encircle her bottom and pull her closer against him, rubbing her against the ridge beneath his jeans.

Unexpected, acute, the pleasure that shot through her loins made her cry out, the sound muffled by his lips. He repeated the motion, rocking his pelvis against her in a fury of jealousy and desire. The jolt was even stronger, and she arched in his arms, her hands lifting to cling to his shoulders. The transition from anger to desire was so swift that she couldn't control it, and the current of pleasure leaped within her. Every move he made increased the sensation, pushed her higher, as if she were being forced up a mountain and the purpose, once she reached the peak, was to hurl her over. The dizzying, panicked sensation was the same, and she clutched at him as the only anchor.

It had never been like this with Matt, she thought dimly. Their youthful passion had been shy, untutored, sweet but hesitant. Robert was a man who knew exactly what he was doing.

Though he hadn't touched them, her breasts were throbbing, the nipples tightly drawn and aching. She arched again, a soft, frantic sound in her throat as she tried to ease the ache by rubbing them against his chest. He knew, and whispered, "Easy," just as his hand closed over one firm, jutting mound.

She whimpered at the heat, the delicious pressure. She knew she should stop him, but putting an end to this ecstasy was the last thing she wanted to do. Her body was pliant, voluptuous with need, glowing with heat. He put his hand under her shirt and deftly opened the front snap of her bra. The cups slid apart, and then his fingers were on her naked flesh. He stroked the satin curves, then circled the tight nipples until she writhed in an agony of unfulfillment. "Is this what you want?" he murmured, and lightly pinched the distended tips. She moaned as a river of heat ran through her, gathering moisture to deposit between her thighs.

He bent her backward over his arm, the position thrusting her breasts upward. Her shirt was pulled up to completely bare them, she realized, wondering when that had happened. She saw her nipples, as red as berries; then his mouth closed over one, and her eyes closed as her head fell back.

He was going to take her right here, on the counter. She felt his determination, his own rampant desire. Panic surged through her, combating the heat that undermined her own will and common sense. He would take her here, where anyone could walk in and see them. He would take her without any thought for birth control. And she, besides risking her reputation and the chance of pregnancy, would lose the last bit of protection she retained for her heart.

His mouth was tugging at her nipple, drawing strongly on it before moving to the other one. And his hands were working at the waistband of her jeans, unsnapping and unzipping.

Desperately she wedged her arms between their bodies and stiffened them. "No," she said. The word was hoarse, barely audible. "Robert, no! Stop it!"

He froze, his muscled body taut as he held himself motionless for a long moment. Then, very slowly, he lifted his hands from her and moved back, one step, then two. His breathing was fast and audible.

Evie couldn't look at him as she slid from the counter and hastily fumbled her clothing back into presentable shape, fastening her bra, smoothing her shirt down, snapping and zipping her jeans. Her own breath was coming light and fast.

"Don't look so scared," he said calmly. "I gave you my word that I'd stop, and I did."

No, the problem wasn't with his willpower, she thought wildly, but with hers. Had they been anywhere else but in the marina, she didn't know if she could have made herself say no.

"Nothing to say?" he asked a moment later, when she remained silent.

She cleared her throat. "Not yet."

"All right." He still sounded far too calm and in control. "We'll talk tomorrow. I'll pick you up at seven o'clock."

"Seven," she echoed as he left.

Robert was on the secure mobile phone in the Jeep by the time he had pulled out of the marina's parking lot. "Did you follow him from the time he left work?" he asked as soon as the phone was answered.

"Yes, sir, we did. We saw your Jeep at the marina and pulled back."

"Damn. I was out in my boat. He rented a boat and met someone out on the lake, possibly Evie, because she left the marina in her boat, too. Was he carrying anything when he left work?"

"Not that we could tell, but he could easily have had a disk in his coat pocket."

"He didn't fish in his suit. Where did he change clothes?"

"At his house. He was there for not quite five minutes, then came out carrying a tackle box and a fishing rod."

"If he had a disk at all, it would have been in the tackle box."

"Yes, sir. We didn't have a chance to get to it."

"I know. It wasn't your fault. First thing, though, I'm going to have a secure phone put in the boat. That way, if I'm out on the water, you can get in touch with me."

"Good idea. We went through his house again while we had the chance. Nothing."

"Damn. Okay, continue to watch him. And send someone out to Evie's house tonight."

"The matter we discussed?"

"Yes," Robert replied. It was time for the pressure to begin.

Chapter Nine

The next morning was awful. Evie hadn't slept well—had scarcely slept at all. She had set the alarm for four-thirty, and when it went off she had been asleep for less than two hours. Dreaming about Robert was one thing, but she had been wide-awake and hadn't been able to get him out of her mind. Her thoughts had darted from the seething passion of his lovemaking, incomplete as it had been, to the unease she felt every time she thought of how he so skillfully manipulated people. She tried to analyze what he did and couldn't find any time when he had been malicious, but that didn't reassure her.

Sometime after midnight, lying in the darkness and staring at the ceiling, she realized what it was that so bothered her. It was as if Robert allowed people to see and know only a part of him; the other part, probably the closest to being the real man, was standing back, inviolate, carefully watching and analyzing, gauging reactions, deciding which subtle pressures to apply to gain the results he wanted. Everyone was shut away from that inner man, the razor-sharp intelligence functioning almost like a computer, isolated in a sterile environment. What was most upsetting was to realize that this was how he wanted it, that he had deliberately fashioned that inner isolation and wasn't about to invite anyone inside.

What place could she hope to have in his life? He desired her; he would be perfectly willing to make her the center of his attention for a time, in order to gain what he wanted: a carnal relationship. But unless she could break through into that fiercely guarded inner core, she would never reach his emotions. He would be fine, but she would break her heart battering against his defenses.

She, better than others, knew how important emotional barriers were. She had propped herself up with her own defenses for many years, until she had slowly healed to the point where she could stand on her own. How could she condemn him for staying within his own fortress? She didn't know if she should even try to get inside.

The thing was, she didn't know if she had a choice any longer. For better or worse, this afternoon he had slipped through her defenses. Such a little thing: playing with a baby. But it was the little things, rather than the watershed events, on which love was built. She had softened toward him when he had saved her and Jason's lives, but her heart had remained her own. Today she had fallen in love; it wasn't something she could back away from and ignore. It might be impossible to breach Robert's defenses and reach his heart, but she had to try.

Finally she drifted into sleep, but the alarm too soon urged her out of bed. Heavy-eyed, she put on the coffee and showered while it was brewing. Then, as she absently munched on a bowl of cereal and poured in the caffeine, a dull cramp knotted her lower belly. "Damn it," she muttered. Just what she needed; she was going out with Robert for the first time that night, and her period was starting. She had thought she had another couple of days before it was due. She made a mental note that in a few days she should begin taking the birth-control pills the doctor had just prescribed.

Normally her period didn't bother her, but the timing of this one, added to lack of sleep, made her cranky as she left the house in the predawn darkness and climbed into the truck.

The sturdy pickup, usually so reliable despite its high mileage, made some unfamiliar noises as she drove along the dark, deserted side road. "Don't you dare break down on me now," she warned it. She was just getting on a firm financial footing; a major repair job right now was just what she didn't need.

She reached U.S. 431 and turned onto it. The truck shuddered and began making loud clanging noises. Startled, she slowed and swept the gauges with a quick glance. The temperature was fine, the oil— Oh God, the oil gauge was red-lining. She slammed on the brakes and started to veer toward the shoulder, and that was when the engine blew. There were more clanging and grinding noises, and smoke boiled up around the hood, obscuring her vision. She steered the truck off the highway, fighting the heavy wheel as, deprived of power, the vehicle lurched to a halt.

Evie got out and stood looking at the smoking corpse as it pinged and rattled, the sounds of mechanical death. Her language was usually mild, but there were some occasions that called for swear words, and this was one of them. She used every curse word she had ever heard, stringing them together in rather innovative ways. That didn't bring life back to the motor, and it didn't make her bank account any healthier, but it relieved some of her frustration. When she ran out of new ways to say things, she stopped, took a deep breath and looked up and down the highway. Dawn was lightening the sky, and traffic was picking up; maybe someone she knew would come by and she wouldn't have to walk the full two miles to a pay phone. With a sigh she got the pistol out from under the truck seat, slipped it into her purse, then locked the truck—though obviously anyone who stole it would have to haul it away—and began walking.

It was less than a minute when another pickup rolled to a stop beside her. She glanced around and saw the boat hitched up behind. Two men were in the truck, and the one on the passenger side rolled down his window. "Havin' trouble?" Then he said, a bit uncertainly, "Miss Evie?"

With relief she recognized Russ McElroy and Jim Haynes, two area fisherman whom she had known casually for several years. "Hi, Russ. Jim. The motor in my truck just blew."

Russ opened the door and hopped out. "Come on, we'll give you a ride to the marina. You don't need to be out by yourself like this. There's too much meanness goin' on these days."

Gratefully she climbed into the cab of the truck and slid to the middle of the seat. Russ got back in and closed the door, and Jim eased the rig onto the highway. "You got a good mechanic?" Jim asked.

"I thought I'd have Burt, the mechanic at the marina, take a look at it. He's good with motors."

Jim nodded. "Yeah, I know Burt Mardis. He's real good. But if he can't get to it, there's another guy, owns a shop just off Blount, who's just as good. His name's Roy Simms. Just look it up in the phone book, Simms' Automotive Repair."

"Thanks, I'll remember that."

Jim and Russ launched into a discussion of other good mechanics in the area, and soon they reached the marina. She thanked them, and Russ got out again to let her out. They probably hadn't intended to put in at her marina, but since they were there they decided they might as well. As she unlocked the gate that blocked the launch ramp, Jim began to maneuver the truck so he could back the boat into the water. Next she unlocked the office and turned on the lights. Just as Jim and Russ were idling away from the dock, Burt drove up, and she went to tell him about the demise of her truck.

It wasn't long after dawn when the phone rang. Robert opened one eye and examined the golden rose of the sky as he reached for the receiver. "Yes."

"The truck didn't make it into town. It blew just as she reached the highway. She caught a ride to the marina."

Robert sat up in bed. He could feel the fine hairs on the back of his neck prickling with mingled anger and alarm. "Damn it, she hitchhiked?"

"Yeah, I was a little worried about that, so I followed to make certain she didn't have any trouble. No problem. It was a couple of fishermen who picked her up. I guess she knew them."

That wasn't much better. Guntersville wasn't exactly a hotbed of crime, but anything could happen to a woman alone. Neither did it soothe him that she had been followed, that help was right behind if she'd needed it. The situation shouldn't have arisen in the first place. "Why was the timing off?"

"The hole in the oil line must have been bigger than West thought. Probably there's a big oil puddle in her driveway. She

would have seen it if it hadn't still been dark when she left the
house.''

In a very calm, remote voice Robert said, ''If anything had
happened to her because of his mistake, I wouldn't have liked
it.''

There was a pause on the other end of the line. Then, ''I understand. It won't happen again.''

Having made his point, Robert didn't belabor it. He moved on.
''Be careful when you're in the house tonight. I don't want her
to notice anything out of place.''

''She won't. I'll see to it myself.''

After hanging up the phone, Robert lay back down and hooked
his hands behind his head as he watched the sun peek over the
mountains. The day before had made him more uncertain than
ever of Evie's connection with Mercer. He was fairly certain she
had rendezvoused with Mercer out on the water, but either she
hadn't told Mercer of his presence, or she had been unaware of
his own connection with PowerNet. This appeared to be an efficient espionage ring, to have escaped notice and capture for as
long as they had; given that, Evie should have known of him. At
the very least, Mercer should have notified her of his presence.
What reason could they have had for keeping her in the dark
about his identity, unless her participation was very peripheral
and no one had thought she needed to know?

The other possibility was that Evie had indeed recognized his
name, or been notified, but for reasons of her own had chosen
not to pass on the information that he had leased a slip at her
marina and appeared to have formed an intense personal interest
in her.

Either way, it followed that Evie wasn't on good terms with
the others in the espionage ring. On the one hand, it gave him a
weakness he could exploit. On the other, her life could be in
danger.

Evie made arrangements to have a wrecker tow the truck to
the marina. That accomplished, Burt stuck his head under the
hood to begin the examination. Next he lay down on a dolly and

rolled underneath for another view. When he emerged, he wasn't optimistic about rebuilding the motor. "Too much damage," he said. "You'd be better off just buying another motor."

She had been expecting that, and she had already been mentally juggling her finances. The payment on the bank loan for the marina would be late this month, and then she would have to put off other payments to make the one on the loan. She could get by without transportation for a few days by using the boat to go back and forth from home to the marina. If she absolutely needed to go somewhere, she could borrow Becky's car, though she didn't like to.

"I'll call around and try to find one," she said. "Will you have time to put it in for me?"

"Sure," Burt said easily. "It's a little slow right now, anyway."

By the time Craig arrived to relieve her, it was all arranged. She had located an engine, and Burt would begin work putting it in as soon as it arrived. Depending on how much marina work came in, she might be driving home the next afternoon.

In Evie's experience, things didn't generally work that well. She wouldn't be surprised if Burt was suddenly flooded with a lot of boats needing attention.

The trip across the lake was enjoyable, despite her worries. The water was green, the surrounding mountains a misty blue, and fat, fluffy clouds drifted lazily across the sky, offering an occasional brief respite from the blazing sun. Gulls wheeled lazily over the water, and an eagle soared high in the distance. It was the kind of day when being inside was almost intolerable.

With that thought in mind, once she arrived home she put her financial worries on hold and got out the lawn mower to give her yard a trimming. She glared at the big black oil stain on the driveway where the truck had been parked. If it had been daylight when she'd left this morning, if she hadn't swapped shifts with Craig, she would have seen the oil and not have driven the truck; the motor would still be intact, and the repair bill would be much smaller.

Just simple bad timing.

The yard work finished, she went inside to cool off and tackle the housework, which was minimal. By three o'clock she was back outside, sitting on the dock with her feet in the water and a sweat-dewed glass of ice tea beside her. Fretting about the truck wouldn't accomplish anything. She would handle this just as she had handled every other money crisis that had arisen over the years, by strict economizing until all bills were paid. She couldn't do anything more than that, since it wasn't likely a good fairy would drop the money into her lap. Though there might be the possibility of taking a part-time job in the mornings at one of the fast-food restaurants serving breakfast. Forty dollars a week was a hundred and sixty dollars a month, enough to pay the power bill, with a little left over for the gas bill. But for now all she wanted was to sit on the dock with her feet in the water and gaze at the mountains, feeling contentment spread through her.

That was how Robert found her. He came around the side of the house and paused when he saw her sitting on the weathered dock, her eyes closed, face lifted to the sun. The long, thick, golden braid had been pulled forward over one shoulder, revealing the enticing, delicate furrow of her nape. She was wearing faded denim shorts and a white chemise top, hardly a sophisticated outfit, but his pulse began to throb as he studied the graceful curve of her shoulders, the delectable roundness of her slender arms, the shapeliness of her legs. Her skin glowed with a warm, pale gold luminescence, like a succulent peach. His eyes, his entire body, burned as he stared at her. His mouth was literally watering, and he had to swallow. He had never felt such urgent lust for any other woman. What he wanted was to simply throw himself on her and have her right here, right now, without thought or finesse.

She was unaware of his presence until the dock vibrated when he stepped onto it. There was no alarm in her eyes as she turned her head to see who had come visiting, only lazy curiosity followed by a warm look of welcome. Even the average five-year-old in a large city was more wary than the people around here, he thought as he sat down beside her and began taking off his shoes.

"Hi," she said, a sort of smiling serenity in that one word, which was drawled so that it took twice as long for her to say than it did for him.

He found himself smiling back, actually smiling, his mouth curved into a tender line as his heart pounded inside his chest. He had wanted her from the moment he'd first seen her; he'd been, several times, unexpectedly charmed by her. Both reactions were acute at this moment, but even more, he was enchanted.

He had whirled across countless dance floors with countless beautiful women in his arms, women who could afford to pamper themselves and wear the most expensive gowns and jewelry, women whom he had genuinely liked. He had made love to those women gently, slowly, in luxurious surroundings. He had taken women when the added fillip of danger made each encounter more intense. But never had he felt more enthralled than he was right now, sitting beside Evie on a weathered old dock, with a blazing afternoon sun, almost brutal in its clarity, bathing everything in pure light. Sweat trickled down his back and chest from the steamy heat, and his entire body pulsed with life. Even his fingertips throbbed. It took all of his formidable self-control to prevent himself from pushing her down on the dock and spreading her legs for his entry.

And yet, for all the intensity of his desire, he was oddly content to wait. He would have her. For now he was caught in the enchantment of her slow smile, in the luminous sheen of her skin, in her warm, female scent that no perfume could match. Simply to sit beside her was to be seduced, and he was more than willing.

Having removed his shoes, he rolled up the legs of his khaki pants and stuck his feet into the water. The water was tepid, but refreshing in contrast to the heat of his skin. It made him feel almost comfortable.

"It isn't seven o'clock yet," she pointed out, but she was smiling.

"I wanted to make sure you hadn't chickened out."

"Not yet. Give me a couple of hours."

Despite the teasing, he was certain she wouldn't have stood him up. She might be nervous, even a little reluctant, but she had agreed, and she would keep her word. Her lack of enthusiasm in going out with him might have been insulting if he hadn't known how potent her physical reaction to him was. Whatever reasons she had for being wary of him, her body was oblivious to them.

She lazily moved her feet back and forth, watching the water swirl around her ankles. After a minute of wondering about the advisability of bringing up the subject that had been bothering her so much, she decided to do so, anyway. "Robert, have you ever let anyone really get close to you? Has anyone ever truly known you?"

She felt his stillness, just for a split second. Then he said in a light tone, "I've been trying to get close to you from the moment I first saw you."

She turned her head and found him watching her, his ice-green eyes cool and unreadable. "That was a nice evasion, but you just demonstrated what I meant."

"I did? What was that?" he murmured indulgently, leaning forward to press his lips to her bare shoulder.

She didn't let that burning little caress distract her. "How you deflect personal questions without answering them. How you keep everyone at arm's length. How you watch and manipulate and never give away anything of your real thoughts or feelings."

He looked amused. "You're accusing *me* of being difficult to get to know, when you're as open as the Sphinx?"

"We both have our defenses," she admitted readily.

"Suppose I turn your questions around?" he said, watching her intently. "Have you ever let anyone get close to you and really get to know you?"

A pang went through her. "Of course. My family...and Matt."

She lapsed into silence then, and Robert saw the sadness move over her face, like a cloud passing over the sun. Matt again! What had been so special about an eighteen-year-old boy that twelve years later just the mention of his name could make her grieve? He didn't like himself for the way he felt, violently jealous and resentful of a dead boy. But at least Matt's memory had diverted Evie from her uncomfortable line of questioning.

She seemed content to sit in silence now, dabbling her feet in the water and watching the sunlight change patterns as it moved lower in the sky. Robert left her to her thoughts, suddenly preoccupied with his own.

Her perception was disturbing. She had, unfortunately, been dead on the money. He had always felt it necessary to keep a large part of himself private; the persona he presented to the world, that of a wealthy, urbane businessman, was not false. It was merely a small part of the whole, the part that he chose to display. It worked very well; it was perfect for doing business, for courting and seducing the women he wanted, and was an entrée into those parts of the world where his business was not quite what it seemed.

None of his closest associates suspected that he was anything other than the cool, controlled executive. They didn't know about his taste for adventure, or the way he relished danger. They didn't know about the extremely risky favors he had done, out of sheer patriotism, for various government departments and agencies. They didn't know about all the ongoing, specialized training he did to keep himself in shape and his skills sharp. They didn't know about his volcanic temper, because he kept it under ruthless control. Robert knew himself well, knew his own lethal capabilities. It had always seemed better to keep the intense aspects of his personality to himself, to never unleash the sheer battering force of which he was capable. If that meant no one ever really *knew* him, he was content with that. There was a certain safety in it.

No woman had ever reached the seething core of his emotions, had ever made him lose control. He never wanted to truly love a woman in the romantic sense, to find himself open to her, vulnerable to her. He planned to marry someday, and his wife would be supremely happy. He would treat her with every care and consideration, pleasing her in bed and cosseting her out of it. She would never want for anything. He would be a tender, affectionate husband and father. And she would never know that she had never truly reached him, that his heart remained whole, in his isolated core.

Madelyn, of course, knew that there were fiercely guarded

depths to him, but she had never probed. She had known herself to be loved, and that was enough for her. His sister was a formidable person in her own right, her lazy manner masking an almost frightening determination, as her husband had discovered to his great surprise.

But how could Evie, on such short acquaintance, so clearly see what others never did? It made him feel exposed, and he didn't like it one damn bit. He would have to be more careful around her.

The sun was shining full on his back now, and his spine was prickling with sweat. Deciding that the silence had gone on long enough, he asked in an idle tone, "Where's your truck?"

"I'm having a new motor put in it," she replied. "I might have it back by tomorrow afternoon, but until then I'm using the boat to get to the marina and back."

He waited, but there was no additional explanation. Surprised, he realized that she wasn't going to tell him about the motor blowing, wasn't going to broadcast her troubles in any way. He was accustomed to people bringing their problems to him for deft handling. He had also thought it possible that Evie would ask him for a loan to cover the repairs. They hadn't discussed his financial status, but she had seen the new boat, the new Jeep, the house on the waterfront, and she was far from stupid; she had to know he had money. He wouldn't have given her a loan, of course, because that would have defeated his subtle maneuvering to put financial pressure on her, but still, he wouldn't have been surprised if she'd asked. Instead, she hadn't even planned to tell him that her truck had broken down.

"If you need to go anywhere, call me," he finally offered.

"Thanks, but I don't have any errands that can't be put off until I get the truck back."

"There's no need to put them off," he insisted gently. "Just call me."

She smiled and let the subject drop, but he knew she wouldn't call. Even if he installed himself at the marina until her truck was repaired, she wouldn't tell him if she needed anything.

He took her hand and gently stroked her fingers. "You haven't asked me where we're going tonight."

She gave him a surprised look. "I hadn't thought about it." That was the truth. Where they went was inconsequential; the fact that she would be with *him* was what had occupied her mind.

"That isn't very flattering," he said with a faint smile.

"I didn't say I hadn't thought about going out with you. It's just that the *where* never entered my mind."

The sophisticated socialites he normally squired about New York and the world's other major cities would never have made such an artless confession. Or rather, if they had, it would have been in an intimately flirtatious manner. Evie wasn't flirting. She had simply stated the truth and let him take it as he would. He wanted to kiss her for it but refrained for now. She would be more relaxed if she didn't have to deal with a seduction attempt every time she saw him.

Then she turned to him, brown eyes grave and steady. "I answered your question," she said. "Now answer mine."

"Ah." So she had been delayed but not diverted. Swiftly he decided on an answer that would satisfy her but not leave him open. It had the advantage of being the truth, as far as it went. "I'm a private person," he said quietly. "I don't blurt out my life story to anyone who asks. You don't either, so you should understand that."

Those golden brown eyes studied him for another long moment; then, with a sigh, she turned away. He sensed that his answer hadn't satisfied her, but that she wasn't going to ask again. The sensation of being given up on wasn't a pleasant one, but he didn't want her to keep prying, either.

He checked his watch. There were a few calls he had to make before picking her up for the evening, not to mention showering and changing clothes. He kissed her shoulder again and got to his feet. "I have to leave or I'll be late to an appointment. Don't stay out much longer or you'll get a sunburn. Your shoulders are already hot."

"All right. I'll see you at seven." She remained sitting on the dock, and Robert looked down at her streaked tawny head with stifled frustration. Just when he thought he was finally making serious progress with her, she mentally retreated again, like a turtle withdrawing into its shell. But this afternoon's mood was an odd blend of contentment, melancholy and resignation. Maybe she was worried about the truck; maybe she was nervous about their first date, though why she should be, when he'd already had her half-naked, was beyond his comprehension.

The truth was that she was as opaque to him as he was to others. He had always had the ability to read people, but Evie's mind was either closed to him or she reacted in a totally unexpected way. He couldn't predict what she would do or tell what she was thinking, and it was slowly driving him mad. He forced himself to walk away, rather than stand there waiting for her to look up at him. What would that accomplish? It was likely that she would figure out why he was waiting and look up just to get it over with, so he would go. Little mind games were only for the insecure, and Robert didn't have an insecure bone in his body. Nevertheless, he was reluctant to leave her. The only time he wasn't worried about what she was doing was when he was with her.

As he climbed into the Jeep, he wryly reflected that it was a sad state of affairs when he was so obsessed with a woman he couldn't trust out of his sight.

Evie remained where she was until long after the sound of the Jeep's engine had faded in the distance. Robert had stonewalled her questions, and sadly she realized that he simply wasn't going to allow her to get close to him. She supposed she could make a pest of herself and keep yammering at him, but that would only make him close up more. No, if she wanted a relationship with him, she would have to content herself with the litte he was comfortable in giving. She had known Matt to the bone and loved him as deeply. How ironic it was that now she had fallen in love with a man who allowed her to touch only the surface.

Finally she pulled her feet out of the water and stood. This had been a day of fretting, though she had tried not to. She would be better off getting ready for her big date. She had the feeling she would need every bit of preparation she could manage.

Chapter Ten

A woman couldn't have asked for a more perfect escort, she realized about halfway through the evening. For all his sophistication, or perhaps because of it, there was something very old-fashioned in the courtesy and protectiveness with which he treated her. Everything was arranged for *her* pleasure, *her* comfort, and she herself was old-fashioned enough, Southern enough, to accept it as the way things should be. Robert Cannon was courting her, so of course he should make certain she was pleased by the evening.

His attention was solely on her. He didn't eye other women, though she noticed other women watching him. He held her chair for her whenever she got up or sat down, poured wine for her and asked the maitre d' to turn up the thermostat when he noticed her shivering. It was a matter of his own presence that his request was instantly honored. Whenever they walked, his hand rested warmly on the small of her back in a protective, possessive touch.

In no time, he had put her at ease. It was only natural that she had been nervous about the evening; after all, she hadn't been on a date in twelve years, and there was a great deal of difference between eighteen and thirty. Back then a date had been a hamburger and a movie, or just getting together with a bunch of friends at the skating rink. She wasn't at all certain what one did on a date with a man who was used to the most cosmopolitan of entertainments.

As she watched his dark, lean face, she realized how truly sophisticated he was. He had brought her to a very nice restaurant in Huntsville, but she was well aware that it didn't compare to the sort of establishments available in New York or Paris or New

Orleans. Not by even a hint, though, did he indicate that the standards were less than those to which he was accustomed. Others, worldly but less sophisticated—and certainly less polite—would have subtly tried to impress by describing the *truly* good restaurants where they'd eaten. Not Robert. She doubted that he even thought of it, for he had the true sophisticate's knack of being at home in any surrounding. He didn't rate or compare; he simply enjoyed. He would have been as happy eating barbecue with his fingers as he was dining with gold flatware and blotting his mouth with a starched linen napkin.

Oh, God. Not only did he play with babies, he was totally comfortable in her world. Just one more thing to love.

He waved his fingers in front of her face. "You've been watching me and smiling for about five minutes," he said with amusement coloring his tone. "Ordinarily I'd be flattered, but somehow it makes me uneasy."

Her mouth quirked as she picked up her fork. "It shouldn't, because actually it was flattering. I was thinking how comfortable you are down here, despite how different things are."

He shrugged and said gently, "The differences are mostly good ones, though I admit I wasn't prepared for the heat. Somehow, ninety degrees in New York is different from ninety degrees here."

Her brows lifted delicately. "Ninety degrees isn't all that hot."

He chuckled and again wondered briefly at her ability to amuse him. It wasn't anything overt, just the subtle differences in her outlook and the way she phrased it. "That's the difference, one of attitude. Though, of course, it gets hotter than that occasionally, to a New Yorker ninety degrees is *hot*. To you, it's a nice day."

"Not exactly. Ninety degrees is hot to us, too. It's just that, compared to a hundred degrees, it isn't bad."

"Like I said, attitude." He sipped his wine. "I like New York for what it is. I like it down here for the same reason. In New York there's an air of excitement and energy, the opera and ballet and museums. Here, you have clean air, no overcrowding, no traffic jams. No one seems to hurry. People smile at strangers." His eyes lingered on her face, and when he continued his voice was a little deeper. "Though I admit I've been disappointed that I haven't heard you say 'y'all' at all. In fact, I've heard it very few times since I've been here."

She hid her smile. "Why would I say it to you? Y'all is plural. You're singular."

"Is it? That minor detail had escaped me."

"That you're singular?" She paused, aware that she was trespassing into his private life and that he might well shut down as he had that afternoon. "Have you ever been married?"

He sipped his wine again, and his eyes glittered at her over the rim of the glass. "No," he replied easily. "I was engaged once, when I was in college, but we both realized in time that getting married—particularly to each other—would have been a stupid thing to do."

"How old are you?"

"Thirty-six. To satisfy any other pertinent questions you may have, my sexual interest is exclusively in women. I've never done drugs, and I don't have any communicable diseases. My parents are dead, but I have a sister, Madelyn, who lives in Montana with her husband and two sons. There are a few distant cousins, but we don't keep in touch."

She regarded him calmly. He was totally relaxed, telling her that he didn't regard those details of his life as being particularly revealing. They were simply facts. She listened, though, because such minutiae made up the skeleton of his life. "Becky and I have relatives scattered all over the state," she said. "One of my uncles has a huge farm down around Montgomery, and every June we get together there for a family reunion. We aren't a close family, but we're friendly, and it's a way to stay in touch. If it wasn't for the reunion, Jason and Paige would never know Becky's side of the family, only their father's, so we make an effort to go every year."

"Your parents are dead?" He knew they were, for that had been in the supplementary report he had received.

"Yes." The golden glow in her eyes dimmed. "Becky is the only immediate family I have. When Mom died, I lived with

Becky and Paul until Matt and I married.'' Her voice faltered, just a little, at the end.

''What about afterward?'' he asked gently.

''Then I lived with Matt's parents.'' The words were soft, almost soundless. ''Where I live now. It was their house. The marina was theirs, too. Matt was their only child, and when they died, they left everything to me.''

Robert was pierced by another arrow of jealousy. She was still living in the house where Matt had grown up; there was no way she could walk into that house without being reminded of him at every turn. ''Have you ever thought of moving? Of buying a more modern house?''

She shook her head. ''Home is important to me. I lost my home when Mom died, and though Becky and Paul made me welcome, I was always aware that it was their home and not mine. Matt and I were going to live in a trailer, at first, but after he died I couldn't.... Anyway, his parents asked me to live with them, and they needed me as much as I needed company. Maybe because they needed me, I felt comfortable there, more like it really was my own home. And now,'' she said simply, ''it is.''

He regarded her thoughtfully. He had never felt that sort of attachment for a place, never felt the tug of roots. There had been a large country estate in Connecticut, when he was growing up, but it had simply been the place where he lived. Now his penthouse served the same emotionless function. Evie wouldn't like it, though it was spacious and impeccably decorated. Still, he was comfortable there, and the security was excellent.

The restaurant featured a live band, and they were really very good. In keeping with the image of the place, they played old standards, meant for real dancing rather than solitary gyrations. He held out his hand to Evie. ''Would you like to dance?''

A glowing smile touched her face as she placed her hand in his, but then she hesitated, and a look of uncertainty replaced the pleasure. ''It's been so long,'' she said honestly, ''that I don't know if I can.''

''Trust me,'' he said, soothing her worries. ''I won't let you come to grief. It's like riding a bicycle.''

She went into his arms. She was stiff at first, but after several turns she relaxed and let the pleasure of the music and the movement sweep through her. Robert was an expert dancer, but then, she hadn't expected anything else. He held her closely enough that she felt secure, but not so close as to touch intimately. More of those exquisite manners, she thought.

As the music continued, she realized that he didn't have to be blatant. Dancing was its own seduction. There was the tender way he clasped her hand, the warm firmness of his other hand on her back. His breath brushed her hair; the clean scent of his skin teased her nostrils. This close, she could see the closely shaven stubble of his beard, dark against his olive skin. Occasionally her breasts brushed against his chest or arm, or their thighs slid together. It was stylized, unconsummated lovemaking, and she wasn't immune to it.

They left at midnight. During the forty-minute drive back to Guntersville, Evie sat silently beside him as he competently handled the black Renegade. They didn't speak until he pulled into her driveway and turned off the ignition, flooding the sudden darkness with silence. As their eyes adjusted, they could see the river stretching, soundless and glistening, behind her house.

"Tomorrow night?" he asked, turning toward her and draping one arm over the steering wheel.

She shook her head. "I can't. I haven't arranged for Craig to take over my shift, so he'll open the marina in the morning as usual. I wouldn't, anyway. That isn't the deal we made."

He sighed. "All right, we'll compromise. How about swapping shifts with him once a week? Would that be acceptable to your strange scruples? He works for you, rather than the other way around, you know."

"He's also a friend, and he does a lot of favors for me. I won't take advantage of him." The coolness in her voice told him that he had offended her.

He got out and walked around to open the door for her. As he lifted her to the ground, he said with a touch of whimsy, "Will you try to make a little time for me, anyway?"

"I'll talk to Craig about it," she replied noncommittally.

"Please."

She extracted her house key from her purse, and Robert deftly lifted it out of her fingers. He unlocked the door, reached inside to turn on a light, then stepped back. "Thank you," she said.

He delayed her with his hand on her arm as she started to go inside. "Good night, sweetheart," he murmured, and placed his mouth over hers.

The kiss was slow and warm and relatively undemanding. He didn't touch her, except for his hand on her arm and his lips moving over hers. Unconsciously she sighed with pleasure, opening her mouth to the warmth of his breath and the leisurely penetration of his tongue.

When he lifted his head, her breasts were tingling, her body was warm, and she was breathing faster than normal. It gratified her to notice that his breath, too, was a little rough. "I'll see you tomorrow," he said. Then he kissed her again and walked back to the Jeep.

She closed the door, locked it and leaned against it until she heard the sound of the Jeep fade in the distance. Her chest felt tight, her heart swollen and tender. She wanted to weep, and she wanted to sing.

Instead, she kicked off her shoes and walked into the kitchen to get a drink of water. Her left foot landed solidly in something wet and cold, and she jumped in alarm. Quickly she turned on the kitchen light and stared in dismay at the puddle around the bottom of the refrigerator. Even more ominously, there was no faint humming sound coming from the appliance. She jerked the door open, but no little light came on. The interior remained dark.

"Oh no, not now," she moaned. What a time for the refrigerator to die! She simply couldn't afford to get it repaired now. She supposed she could buy a new one on credit, but she hated to add another payment to the monthly load. The refrigerator had been elderly, but why couldn't it have lasted another year? By then she would have paid off a couple of debts and had more ready cash. Another six months would have made a difference.

There was nothing, however, that she could do about the refrigerator at nearly one in the morning. She was drooping with fatigue, but she mopped up the water and put down towels to catch any additional leaks.

When she finally got into bed, she couldn't sleep. That part-time job she had thought about during the afternoon now looked like a necessity, rather than an option. Her lower abdomen was dully aching. The evening with Robert, about which she had been so nervous, had turned out to be the best part of the day.

At seven o'clock she was on the phone to Becky. While Becky was calling around to her friends, Evie began systematically calling in response to every Refrigerator For Sale ad in the paper. As she had suspected, even at that early hour there were a number of calls that weren't answered. One, which had seemed the most promising, had sold the refrigerator as soon as the ad appeared.

By nine o'clock, she and Becky had located a good refrigerator for sale. At a hundred dollars, it was more than she could readily afford, but considerably less than a new one would cost. Becky came to get her, and they drove out together to look at it.

"It's ten years old, so it probably has another five to seven years," the woman said cheerfully as she showed them into the kitchen. "There isn't anything wrong with it, but we're building a new house, and I wanted a big side-by-side refrigerator. We were getting one, anyway, but last week I found just what I wanted, on sale at that, so I didn't wait. As soon as I get this one sold, I can have the new one delivered."

"It's sold," Evie said.

"How are you going to get it home?" asked Becky practically. "Until your truck is fixed, you don't have any way to haul it." Having stated the problem, she set about trying to solve it, running down the list of everyone she knew who owned a pickup truck and might be available.

Evie's own list was formidable. After all, she knew a lot of fishermen. Half an hour later, Sonny, a friend who worked second shift and had his mornings free, was on his way.

Time was running short for Evie by the time they got the refrigerator to her house. She called Craig to let him know what was going on and that she might be a few minutes late. "No sweat," was his easygoing reply.

Sonny hooked up the ice maker while Evie and Becky hurriedly transferred what food had survived from the old refrigerator into the new one. The frozen stuff was okay, and since she hadn't opened the door, most of the food in the other compartment was still cool and salvageable. She threw away the eggs and milk, just to be on the safe side.

"Do you want me to haul off the old one?" Sonny asked.

"No, you need to go to work. Let's just push it out onto the deck, and I'll take care of getting rid of it when I get my truck back. Thanks, Sonny. I don't know what I'd have done without you today."

"Anytime," he said genially, and bent his muscles to the job of getting the old refrigerator outside.

After that was accomplished and Sonny had left, Becky grinned at her sister "I know you're in a hurry to get to the marina, so I'll call you tonight. I can't wait to hear all the juicy details about your evening with Robert."

Evie blew a wisp of hair out of her face. "It was fine," she said, smiling because she knew the answer would disappoint Becky. "I was worried for nothing. He was a perfect gentleman all night long."

"Well, damn," muttered her once-protective big sister.

With Murphy's Law in full effect, when Evie arrived at the marina she found that the afternoon before had indeed brought Burt several repair jobs on boats that had to be done before he could get to her truck. Because the people who used the marina were her livelihood, she didn't protest the delay. Financially, it would be better for her if even more repair jobs came in. Enough of them would pay for fixing her truck.

Craig met her at the dock, took one look at her and said, with his tongue firmly planted in his cheek, "Boss, you need to stop all this carousing and get a good night's sleep."

"That bad, huh?"

"Not really. Dark circles are in this month."

"If one more thing tears up," she said direly, "I'm going to shoot it."

He put his brawny young arm around her shoulders. "Aw, everything will be okay. Chin up, boss. You're just tired. If you want to take a nap, I'll hang around for another couple of hours. I've got a date tonight, but I'm free this afternoon."

She smiled at him, touched by his offer. "No, I'm fine. You go on home, and I'll see about getting a morning job to help pay for all this stuff that's going kablooey."

"What stuff?" asked a deep voice behind them. She and Craig turned. A boat had been idling outside, and the noise had masked the sound of Robert's arrival. Unlike her, he looked well rested. His expression didn't give anything away, but she sensed that he didn't like Craig putting his arm around her.

"My refrigerator died last night," she replied. "I spent the morning locating a good used one and getting it home."

That seemed to give him pause, for some reason. Then he gave her a considering look and said, "You didn't get much sleep, did you?"

"A few hours. I'll sleep like a log tonight, though."

Craig said, "If you're sure you don't want me to stay for a while...?"

"I'm sure. I'll see you tomorrow."

"Okay." He took off, whistling. Robert turned to watch him go, a tall, well-built boy who gave the promise of being an outstanding man.

"You don't have any reason to be jealous of Craig," Evie said coolly as she brushed by him, heading toward the office and the promise of air-conditioning.

Robert's eyebrows climbed as he followed her. When they were inside, he murmured, "I don't recall saying anything."

"You didn't, but it was plain what what you were thinking."

He was taken aback. God, her perception was expanding into mind reading. He didn't like the feeling of transparency.

"I've known Craig since he was a child. There's absolutely nothing sexual in our relationship."

"Maybe not from your perspective," he said calmly, "but I was a teenage boy once myself."

"I don't want to hear about raging hormones. If all you can do is criticize, then leave. I'm too tired to deal with it right now."

"So you are." He took her in his arms and tucked her head into the hollow of his shoulder. With one hand he stroked her sun-warmed hair, which was restricted into its usual braid. The night before, she had worn it in an elegant twist. One day soon— or rather, one night—he was going to see it down and spread across his pillow.

Gently he swayed, rocking her. The support of his hard, warm body was so delicious that Evie felt her eyes drifting shut. When she realized that she actually was dozing off, she forced herself to lift her head and step away. "Enough of that or I'll be asleep in your arms."

"You'll sleep there eventually," he said. "But in different surroundings."

Her heart gave a great thump. What he so effortlessly did to her simply wasn't fair. Unbidden, she thought of the one night she had slept in Matt's arms, the sweetness that had so shortly been overlaid with bitterness and regret when his life had ended the next day. Sleeping with Robert wouldn't be anything like that long-ago night....

He saw the sadness darken her eyes again, and he felt like swearing savagely. Every time he thought he was making progress, he slammed into Matt Shaw's ghost, standing like an ethereal wall between Evie and any other man. As unlikely—as damned *ridiculous*—as it seemed, he couldn't doubt that she'd been entirely chaste during her widowhood. Her connection with Landon Mercer, whatever else it was, certainly wasn't physical.

Her relationship with *him*, on the other hand, certainly would be.

"Did you come by for any particular reason?" she asked.

"Just to see you for a moment. Would you like to get a quick bite to eat tonight before you go home?"

"I don't think so. I'm so tired I just want to go home and get some sleep."

"All right." Gently he touched her cheek. "I'll see you tomorrow, then. Take care going across the lake tonight."

"I will. The days are so long, I'll be home before it gets dark."

"Take care, anyway." He leaned over and kissed her, then left.

As soon as he was out of her sight, his black brows pulled together in a frown. Last night's ploy hadn't worked all that well because of something he simply hadn't considered, and he was impatient with himself. He'd been born into money and had made even more, so the option of buying a second-hand refrigerator hadn't occurred to him. He had no idea what she'd paid for it, but he assumed that it was considerably less than a new one, even the cheapest model, would have cost. Though a little more financial pressure had been brought to bear on her, it hadn't been as much as he'd planned.

Mercer was beginning to find the financial waters a little choppy these days, too. It wasn't anything for him to worry about...yet. Soon he would find himself in a pinch with a growing need for ready cash. The next time he made a move, Robert would be ready for him. The net was slowly closing.

He estimated another two weeks, three at the most. He could make things move faster, but he was oddly reluctant to bring everything to a close just yet. If Mercer tried to make another sale, of course he would have to act, but until then, he intended to use the time to complete Evie's seduction.

That was, if he could keep her mind off her dead husband. Robert's jealous fury was banked, but glowing hotly under the restraint. It was ironic that he, of all people, should be jealous. It wasn't an emotion that he'd ever felt before, and he'd been coolly contemptuous of those who allowed someone to become that important to them. But he had never wanted a woman so violently, nor found himself up against such a formidable rival. That, too, was a new experience for him. If a woman had been interested in another man, he had simply moved on, on the theory that battling for her affections was too much trouble and complicated what was, for him, a fairly simple issue.

But then he'd met Evangeline. Her name whispered through

his mind, as musical and elegant as the wind sighing in the trees Evangeline. A poetic name, associated with undying love.

He couldn't accept that she was Matt Shaw's forever, that he might never have her.

Damn it, what was this appeal that teenage boys had for her? He had wanted to punch Craig in the jaw for daring to touch her, but his own sense of fair play had restrained him. Craig looked to be as strong as a young ox, but Robert knew his own capabilities. He could easily have killed the boy without meaning to.

Because Matt had died so young, was Evie's taste forever frozen at that age? The idea was distasteful. He was disgusted with himself for even thinking it. He had no basis for the ugly speculation; he knew very well that there was nothing sexual between Evie and Craig. It was his own jealousy that had spurred the thought.

He had to have her. Soon.

Chapter Eleven

Evie slept soundly for ten hours that night, from nine until seven the following morning. She woke feeling much better, though she was groggy from sleeping so hard. She stumbled through the house toward the kitchen, keeping her fingers crossed that nothing else had gone on the fritz during the night, especially the coffee-maker. Everything seemed to be in working order, though, so she put on a pot of coffee and headed back toward the bathroom while it was brewing.

Fifteen minutes later, semidressed and with hair and teeth brushed, she was contentedly curled in a chair on the deck, sipping her first cup of coffee. She closed her eyes as the morning sun bathed her with soothing heat. It was a perfect morning, clear and still and fragrant. The birds were singing madly, and the temperature was still comfortable, probably in the high seventies.

She heard tires singing on the road, the particular note that meant four-wheel drive, and a few seconds later Robert pulled into her driveway. Though she couldn't see either the driveway or the road from the deck, and though she knew any number of people who had four-wheel-drive vehicles, she had no doubt of her visitor's identity. Her blood had started moving faster, her skin tingled, and a subtle heat that had nothing to do with either the sun or the coffee had begun spreading through her body.

How many women had loved him? Instinct told her that she was far from the first. Poor creatures. They, like her, had been unable to resist that gentle, ruthless charm. She knew just as certainly that he had never loved any of them in return.

Through the open patio door she heard the knock at the front. ''Robert?'' she called. ''I'm on the deck.''

His footsteps in the grass were silent as he walked around, but in fifteen seconds he was coming up the three shallow steps onto the deck. He stopped, his eyes kindling as he stared at her.

Surprised, she curled a little tighter in the chair. "What have I done now?"

His expression relaxed as he moved to take the chair beside her. "You mistake the matter. That was lust, not anger."

"Ah." She used the cup to hide her face as she took another sip. "That should tell you something."

"Should it?"

"That I see anger from you more often than I do lust." Her heart was pounding even harder. My God, she was *flirting*. She was stunned by the realization. She had never in her life engaged in suggestive banter with a man, especially not to discuss his lust for her. She didn't think she had ever even flirted with Matt; somehow things had always seemed settled between them, and they hadn't gone through that dizzying, intense stage of courtship before commitment. They had grown up committed to each other.

"Again you mistake the matter," Robert said idly.

"In what way?"

"The lust is always there, Evangeline."

The quiet, almost casual, statement left her breathless. This time she took refuge in good manners, unwinding her legs to stand up as she said, "Would you like a cup of coffee?"

"I'll get it," he said, stopping her with a hand on her shoulder. His touch lingered, his fingertips lightly caressing the curve of the joint. "You look as contented as a cat. Just tell me where the cups are."

"In the cabinet directly over the coffeemaker. I don't have any cream, only skim milk—"

"It doesn't matter. I drink it black, like you. While I'm in there, would you like a refill?"

Silently she handed him her cup, and he disappeared into the house.

As Robert got a cup from the cabinet, he noticed that his hand was shaking slightly. He was both amused and amazed at the force of his reaction to her, though he had gotten used to being

t least semi-aroused whenever he was in her company. But when
e had first seen her this morning…well, he had wanted to see
her with her hair down, and now he had gotten his wish.

He just hadn't expected the potency of his response, hadn't
expected that thick, tawny-gold, streaky mantle flowing halfway
down her back, the sunlight glinting along the strands like precious metal. Only the ends curled, frothing in delight at having
been released from the confines of her habitual braid. One lock
hung over her shoulder and breast, the curl wrapping around her
nipple as perfectly as if it had been created to do just that. It had
taken only a glance for him to tell that she wasn't wearing a bra
under the pale peach camisole top with the tiny tucks down the
front that she probably thought disguised her braless state.

He should have become accustomed by now to the luminosity
of her skin. He hadn't. Every time he saw her anew, he was struck
by the way she seemed to glow. This morning the effect had been
particularly acute. She had been curled in the chair like a cat,
sleepy and slightly tousled, her shapely legs and delicate feet bare,
the bright sunlight somehow lighting her from within.

He wanted to pick her up and carry her back into the dim
coolness of her bedroom, strip her naked and sate himself on the
golden pearl of her flesh. But he remembered, with an unpleasant
jolt, that this was the house where Matt had grown up. He didn't
want to take her here, where the memories of the boy abounded.

"Robert?" Her tone was questioning at his long delay.

"I'm just reading your coffee cups," he called back, and heard
her chuckle in reply.

He chose the cup that said, "I'm forty-nine percent sweet. It's
the other fifty-one percent you have to worry about," and poured
coffee into it, then refilled her cup. He carried both of them out
onto the deck and carefully gave hers to her, not wanting even a
drop of the hot liquid to spill on her bare legs.

"That's quite a collection of cups."

"Isn't it? Jason and Paige are the culprits. Every birthday,
every Christmas, they give me a cup as a gag gift. It's become
tradition. They put so much time and effort into picking the cup
that it's gotten to where unwrapping it is the highlight of the

occasion. They don't let Becky or Paul see it beforehand, so it' always a surprise to them, too.''

"Some of them are rather suggestive.''

She grinned. "Paige's doing. She's an expert at finding them.'

He raised his eyebrows. "That delicate, innocent child?''

"That precocious, inventive child. Don't let the shyness foo you.''

"She didn't seem shy to me. She started talking to me righ away when I first met her.''

"Blame your own charm. She isn't that open with most people But considering the way Sherry's baby took to you,'' she said judiciously, "it seems that little girls have an affinity for you.''

"That's all well and good,'' he replied, watching her calmly over the rim of his cup, "but what about the grown-up ones?''

"I'll bring you a big stick tomorrow so you can keep them beat off.'' Very calmly he leaned over to place his cup on the deck, then took her cup from her hand and put it beside his. She eyed him warily. "What are you doing?''

"This.'' With one swift, deft movement, he scooped her out of her chair, and settled down in his again with her on his lap. She sat stunned, stiffly erect, her eyes big with surprise. He retrieved her cup and placed it in her hands, then shifted her so she was off balance and had to relax against his chest.

"Robert,'' she said in a weak protest.

"Evangeline.'' His voice lingered over the long *i*.

She couldn't think of anything else to say. She sat there wrapped by his strength, his warmth, his scent. She could feel the steady thumping of his heart. She had known that he was tall, but even now, with her sitting on his lap, her head wasn't as high as his. She felt physically overwhelmed and remarkably safe. Not from him, but from the rest of the world.

His thighs were hard under her, and something else was, too.

"Finish your coffee,'' he said, and unthinkingly she raised the cup to her lips.

They sat there in peaceful silence as the heat grew and the traffic on the river increased. When their cups were empty, he set them aside, then caught her face in his hand and turned it up for his slow, deep kiss.

Like a flower turning toward the sun, she shifted toward him, fitting herself more firmly against him. The taste of coffee was in his mouth and hers. His tongue gently explored, and she trembled, her arms lifting to encircle his neck. How long he drank from her mouth she didn't know; time was measured only by the heavy pulse of her blood, throbbing through every inch of her body.

His hand brushed across her breast, pushing her hair aside, then returned to firmly cup the soft mound. Evie stiffened slightly, but he soothed her with a deep murmur, not really a word, only a calming sound. He had had his hands and his mouth on her breasts before, but he could sense that she was still uncertain about allowing the caress. He petted her, gently circling her nipples with one fingertip until they stood temptingly erect, stroking the lush curves with tender care. He wanted her to relax, but instead the tension in her changed, became more finely charged, and he knew that he was arousing her instead.

Deliberately he unbuttoned the first three buttons of the camisole and slid his hand inside. With a sharply indrawn breath, she turned her face into his neck, but she didn't say the one word that would stop him. Her satiny flesh was cool to his touch, the small nipples puckered and tight. He played with them, rubbing them between his fingers, lightly pinching as he watched her with acute attention to learn exactly what she liked. Slowly her breasts grew warm from his touch, the paleness taking on a pinkish glow.

Evie held herself very still, barely breathing, her eyes closed as she tried to deal with the delicate, exquisite pleasure sweeping through her. She knew she was playing with fire, but she couldn't seem to make herself stop. What if he carried her inside? She would have to call a halt then, because she was still having her period, and she was neither sophisticated nor experienced enough to either let him proceed or tell him, without embarrassment, why he couldn't.

"Shall I stop?" he asked, the sound very low.

She swallowed. "I think you should." But she didn't lift her face, and that wasn't the agreed signal. He shifted her, lifted her, and the shocking heat of his mouth closed over the distended nipple of her exposed breast. She cried out, her nipple prickling at the sensation, and fire shot straight through to her loins.

Then, incredibly, his mouth left her body and he was sitting her up on his lap. "We have to stop," he was saying with gentle regret. "I don't think you're ready to give me the go-ahead, and I don't want to push my self-control much further."

Evie bent her head, struggling with a mixture of relief and chagrin as she fumbled with her buttons, restoring her clothing to order. He was right, of course. She didn't want their intimacy to go any further than it already had, though she intended to be prepared if it did.

She managed to smile at him as she scrambled out of his lap and bent down to get the coffee cups. "Thank you," she said, and carried the cups inside.

Robert rubbed his hand over his eyes. God, that had been closer than he'd let on, at least for him. Would she have let him make love to her, after all? Somehow he didn't think so; he could still sense reluctance in her. In a few more minutes she would have said no, and the way he felt now, the strain might well have killed him. Even if she had said yes, he didn't want to make love to her in this house, so it was just as well he'd had the sense to stop.

They spent the morning together without a repeat of the scene on the deck. He'd already had enough frustration for one day, he decided. When it was time for her to cross the lake to work, he kissed her goodbye and left.

The wind blowing in her face helped clear Evie's mind as she sped across the water. What did he do for most of the day? she wondered. He'd said that he was on vacation, but a person, especially a man like Robert, could take only so much relaxation.

To her relief, Burt had made real progress on the marina jobs and thought he would be able to get started on her truck that afternoon. The prospect of having a vehicle to drive home the next day made her cheerful. Perhaps the run of bad luck was over.

She called the local fast-food restaurants to ask about a part-time job in the mornings, but with school out for the summer, none of them needed any help, all of the part-time jobs being filled by teenagers. Call again after school starts, she was told.

"Well, that was a dead end," she muttered to herself as she hung up from the last call. It looked as if the pendulum of luck hadn't swung back her way, after all.

On the other hand, she had the knack of existing on practically nothing when she had to. Over the next few days Evie cut operating expenses where she could and her personal expenses to the bone. She ate oatmeal or cold cereal for breakfast, and allowed herself one sandwich for lunch and one for supper. There were no snacks, no soft drinks, nothing extra. She turned off the air-conditioning at home, making do with the ceiling fans and drinking a lot of ice water. She was pragmatic enough that she didn't feel particularly deprived by these cost-cutting measures. It was simply something that had to be done, so she did it and didn't think much about it one way or the other.

For one thing, Robert occupied a great deal of her thoughts. If he didn't drop by the house in the morning, he came by the marina in the afternoon. He often kissed her, whenever they were alone, but he didn't pressure her for sex. The more he refrained, the more confused she became about whether she wanted to make love with him or not. She had never bemoaned her lack of practical experience before, but now she did; she needed every bit of help she could muster in handling her feelings for him. With every passing day she wanted him more physically, but caution kept warning her away from letting him become more important to her than he already was. She loved him, but somehow, if she didn't make love with him, some small part of her heart remained hers. If he claimed her body, he would claim all of her, and she would have no reserve to fall back on when the end came.

Still, she was acutely aware of how gradually and skillfully he was undermining her resolve. Every day she became more accustomed to his kisses, to the touch of those lean hands, until he had only to look at her and her breasts would tighten in anticipation. Frightened of the consequences if her willpower faltered, she began taking the birth-control pills on schedule, and as she did so, she wondered if she wasn't actually weakening her own position, for knowing that she was protected might make her less inclined to say no. She was well and truly caught on the horns of that particular dilemma, afraid not to take the pills and afraid of what would happen if she did. In the end, the deciding factor had been that she would rather gamble with her own well-being than that of a helpless baby.

When the next weekend came, Robert once again asked her to swap shifts with Craig so they could have an evening out. Remembering with pleasure the first time she'd had dinner with him, and the dancing afterward, she quickly agreed.

When he picked her up the next night, a slow fire lit the green of his eyes as he looked her up and down. Evie felt a very female gratification at his response. She knew she was looking particularly good, her hair and makeup just as she had wanted, and her dress was very flattering. It was the only cocktail dress she owned, purchased three years before, when the chamber of commerce had organized a party for the local businessmen and women to meet some manufacturing representatives who were thinking about locating in Guntersville.

The deal had fallen through, but the cocktail dress was still smashing. It was teal green, a shade that did wonders for her complexion. There was a full, flirty skirt that swirled just above her knees, a sweetheart bodice supported by thin straps, and it was very low-cut in the back. She had pinned up her hair in a loose twist, with several tendrils left around her ears. Simple gold hoop earrings and her wedding band were the only jewelry she wore, but she had never liked a lot of jewelry weighing her down, so she was satisfied.

Robert was wearing an impeccable black suit with a snowy white silk shirt, but with the heat so oppressive, she wondered how he could stand it. Not that he looked hot; on the contrary, he was as cool and imperturbable as ever, except for the expression in his eyes.

"You're lovely," he said, touching her cheek and watching her bloom at the compliment.

"Thank you." She accepted his verbal appreciation with serene dignity as he drew her outside and locked the door behind them.

He helped her into the Jeep, and as he got in on the other side he said, "I think you'll like the club we're going go. It's quiet, has good food and a wonderful patio for dancing."

"Is it in Huntsville?"

"No, it's here. It's a private club."

She didn't ask how, if it were private, he had managed to get reservations for them. Robert didn't make a show of being wealthy and influential, but he obviously was, given the quality of his clothing, the things he'd bought. Any local bigwig worth his salt would be more than willing to extend an invitation for Robert to join his club.

There was no place in Guntersville that couldn't be gotten to rather quickly. Robert turned the Jeep off of the highway onto a small private road that wound toward the river and soon was parking in a paved lot. The club was a sprawling one-story cedar-and-rock affair, with manicured grounds and a soothing atmosphere. She had seen it before only from the water which glistened just beyond the club. It was only seven-thirty, still daylight, but already the parking lot was crowded.

Robert's hand was firm and very warm on Evie's bare back as he ushered her inside, where they were met by a smiling, very correct maitre d'. They were seated in a small horseshoe booth, upholstered in buttery soft leather.

They ordered their meals, and Robert requested champagne. Evie didn't know anything about wines, period, but his choice brought a spark to the waiter's eyes.

The only time she had tasted champagne had been at her wedding, and that had been an inexpensive brand. The pale gold wine that Robert poured into her glass had nothing in common with that long-ago liquid except its wetness. The taste was dry and delicious, the bubbles dancing in her mouth and exploding with flavor. She was careful to only sip it, not knowing what effect it would have on her.

As before, the evening was wonderful, so wonderful that it was half-over before Evie realized that Robert was herding her toward some swiftly nearing conclusion as implacably as a stallion herded the mare he had chosen to breed, keeping after her, blocking all retreat, until she was cornered. Robert was unfailingly gentle and courteous, but nevertheless relentless. She could see it in those pale eyes, in which a fire smoldered. He intended to have her before the evening was finished.

It was evident in the way he touched her almost constantly, small touches that looked casual but were not. They were seductive touches, light caresses that both gentled her and accustomed her to his hand on her body, while at the same time patiently beginning the process of arousing her.

When they danced, his fingertips moved over her bare back, leaving a trail of heat behind and making her shiver in response. His body moved against hers in rhythm with the music, with her heartbeat, until it seemed as if the music flowed through her. And when they returned to their booth, he was close beside her. Several times she shifted uncomfortably, putting more distance between them, but he was inexorable; he would move closer, so that she could feel the heat of his body, smell the faint, spicy scent of his cologne and the muskiness of his skin. He would lightly stroke her arm, or trace the line of her jaw with one long finger, or rub his thumb over the curve of her collarbone. His leg would slide along hers, and then she would feel the hard curve of his arm behind her back, the firm clasp of his hand at her waist. With every move he made her more aware of him and at the same time broadcast his posession of her to any male in the vicinity who might be thinking of poaching.

Evie was both alarmed and excited, and therefore couldn't get her thoughts in order. She managed to retain an outward calm, but inside she was quietly panicking. Robert had always presented the image of an urbane, eminently civilized man, but from the beginning she had seen beneath the cosmopolitan surface to a far more primitive man, a man of swift and ruthless passion. Now she saw that she had underestimated that volatile streak. He meant to take her to bed with him that very night, and she didn't know if she could stop him.

She didn't even know if she *wanted* to stop him. Was it the champagne, or the fever of desire he had been expertly feeding, not just tonight, but from the moment he'd first kissed her? Her usually clear thought processes kept getting tangled by the slowly increasing heat and hunger of her own body. She tried to think why she should say no, why he was so dangerous for her, but all she could bring to mind was his mouth on her breasts, the way it felt when he touched her.

Physically...oh God, physically he had destroyed all the years of control, of peaceful solitude. She had wanted no man since Matt—until Robert—and she had never wanted Matt this much. Matt had died on the verge of manhood and was forever frozen in her memory as a laughing, wonderful boy. Robert was a man, in the purest sense of the word. He knew the power of the flesh. He knew that, in the taking of her body, he would also be forging a claim, a possession as old as time. His experience far exceeded hers, and he wanted all of her. She would never be able to hold herself, her inner self, inviolate against his taking. A small voice in her cried out in abject fear, and she struggled toward control.

But he seemed to sense whenever that clear inner voice would gather itself, whenever she would panic as she realized anew what he was doing, and with a warm, lingering touch and the brush of his hard body against her soft curves, he would fan the flames of physical desire to overcome the voice of sanity. He was too good at seduction; even though she recognized it, she couldn't stop it. She had the bitter realization that he could have had her any time he'd wanted, that her will was proving no match for his expertise. He had held back only for some reason of his own, and now he had decided that he wasn't waiting any longer.

He asked her to dance again, and helplessly she went into his arms. She felt too warm, her skin too sensitive. She could feel the fabric of her dress sliding over her body, rasping her nipples, caressing her belly and thighs. Whenever he touched her, her entire body seemed to clench. They moved across the dance floor on the patio, and he held her close while his powerful legs slid against hers, sometimes thrusting his thigh between hers, and she began to throb with a hollow ache between her legs. In the distance, heat flashes lit the sky over the mountains with flickers of purple and gold. There was a sullen rumble of thunder, and the air was humid and still, waiting.

She felt weak, physically weak. She hadn't known that desire robbed the muscles of power. She melted against him, flowed against him, until she felt as if only his arm around her was holding her up.

He brushed his hard mouth over the fragile skin at her temple, his warm breath stirring her hair, touching her ear. "Shall we go home?"

A last, small vestige of caution cried, "No!" but she was so caught in his sensual web that she could only nod her head, and the cry remained unvoiced. She leaned against him as he walked her out to the Jeep.

Not even on the way home did he ease the relentless pressure. After he had shifted gears, he put his right hand on her thigh, sliding it up under her skirt, and the heat of his palm on her naked flesh almost made her moan aloud. She didn't even realize where he was taking her until he parked in front of his house, rather than hers.

"This isn't—" she blurted.

"No," he said quietly. "It isn't. Come inside, Evie."

She could say no. Even now, she could say no. She could insist that he take her home. But even if she did, she suspected, the outcome would be the same. All she would be changing was the location.

He held out his hand. The intent behind it was ruthless. She could feel the heavy arousal and hunger that tightened his lean, powerful frame. He was going to take her.

She put her hand in his.

Even though she sensed his savage satisfaction at her tacit surrender, he remained gentle. If he had not, perhaps her common sense would have won after all. But he was too experienced to make that mistake, and she found herself standing in his moonlit bedroom with his big bed looming behind her. She looked out the French doors to the lake, a black mirror reflecting the cool, pale moon. Another low rumble of thunder reached her ears, and she knew that the heat flashes were continuing, bright bursts of light that teased with their promise of rain but never delivered.

Robert put his hands on her waist and turned her to him. Her heart thudded painfully against her ribs as he bent his head and his mouth claimed hers. His kisses were slow, so slow, and devastatingly thorough. His tongue probed, and his mouth drank deeply from hers as his hands leisurely moved over her body, unzipping, loosening, removing. The bodice of her dress fell to her waist, and beyond. He paused a moment to caress her smooth back, the inward curve of her waist; then he gently removed the dress and tossed it aside.

She stood before him wearing only high heels and panties. He caught her to him for more kisses, his tongue stroking deeply within. His hands moved over her breasts, molding them under his lean fingers. Desperately Evie clung to his broad, muscled shoulders, trying to steady her spinning senses. His silk shirt slid across her tightly budded nipples, making her whimper. He murmured soothingly as he unbuttoned his shirt and shrugged out of it, dropping it, too, to the floor. Then her naked breasts were pressed full against his bare chest, nestled into the curly black hair, and she heard herself make a low, hungry sound.

"Easy, darling," he whispered. He kicked out of his shoes and unfastened his pants, letting them drop. His thick sex extended the front of his short, snug boxers. She arched against him, blindly thrusting her pelvis forward to nestle that rigid length. His breath hissed inward, and his control cracked. Fiercely he crushed her to him, his arms tightening until pain made her cry out, the sound stifled against his shoulder.

He lowered her to the bed, the sheets cool against her heated flesh. In a swift movement he divested himself of his shorts. Evie's eyes flared as she saw him totally naked, aroused, the muscles in his body taut with desire and the strain of control. His leanness was dangerously deceptive, for it was all steely muscle, the graceful strength of a panther rather than the bulk of a lion. He lowered himself beside her, one arm cradling her head, while his other hand efficiently removed her shoes and panties. Her total nudity was suddenly startling; she made a brief movement to cover herself, a movement that he halted by catching her wrists and pinning them on each side of her head. Then, very deliberately, he mounted her.

Evie couldn't catch her breath. He was heavier, much heavier, than she had imagined. The sensations were alarming, jarring through her consciousness, coming too swiftly on waves of pleasure that both panicked and beguiled. She was violently aware of his muscled thighs pushing between hers, holding them apart, of his furry, ridged abdomen rubbing against her much softer belly, of the hard press of his chest on her breasts. Between her legs, on her bare loins, she could feel the insistent push of his naked sex against her. Her own sex felt swollen and hot, throbbing in rhythm to her own heartbeat.

He loomed over her in the darkness, much bigger, much stronger. The moonlight was sufficient for her to see the pale glitter of his eyes, the hard planes of his face. His expression was stamped with savage male triumph.

Then he released her wrists and cupped her jaw in one hard, hot hand, turning her face up to him. He held her for the deep thrust of his tongue, the blatant domination of his mouth. Helplessly she responded, caught in the heated madness.

He suckled her breasts, lingering over them and making her writhe with pleasure, and all the while she could feel that hard length impatiently nudging her softest flesh.

The moment came too soon, and not fast enough. He braced himself over her on one arm and reached between their bodies with the other. She felt his lean fingers on her sex, gently parting the folds, finding and stroking her soft, wet entrance. Her hips strained instinctively upward. Her entire body was throbbing. "Robert," she whispered. The single word was taut with strain.

He guided his rigid shaft to her, leaning over and into her as he tightened his buttocks and increased the pressure against the tender opening, forcing it to widen and admit him.

Evie stiffened, her breath quickening. The pressure swiftly became burning pain, real pain. He rocked against her, forcing himself fractionally deeper with every controlled thrust. Her fists knotted the sheet beneath her. She turned her head away, closing her eyes against the hot tears that seeped out beneath her lashes.

He froze as realization hit him.

He turned her head so that she faced him. Her eyes flew open, brilliant with tears in the silver moonlight, and then she couldn't look away. His chest was heaving with the force of his breathing, the sound loud in the quiet, still bedroom. There was nothing of the urbane sophisticate in the man who leaned over her, his face hard with desire. For a split second she saw straight into his soul, into the frighteningly intense, primitive core of him. He held her, forced her to look at him, and with a guttural, explosive sound of control breaking, thrust hard into the depths of her silky body, forcing his way past the barrier of her virginity. She cried out, her body arching under the deep lash of pain. Beyond the pain was the stunning shock of invasion, worse than she had imagined, her delicate inner tissues shivering as they tried to adjust to and accommodate the hard bulk of the intruder.

A rough, deep growl sounded in his throat as he gripped her hips, pulling her more tightly into his possession.

He rode her hard, thrusting heavily, his hips hammering and recoiling as he imprinted his physical brand on her flesh. He had never before been less than gentle with a woman, but with Evie he was ferocious in his need. He couldn't be gentle, not with his head and heart reeling, his entire body exploding with savage pleasure. She was hot and tight, silky, wet...and his. No one else's. Ever. *His.*

He shuddered, gasping, convulsing, and she felt the hot wash of his seed deep inside her. Then he slowly collapsed, shaking in every muscle, blindly groping for support. His heavy weight settled over her, pressing her into the mattress.

Dazed, Evie lay beneath him. She felt shattered, unable to form a coherent thought.

And then she found that it wasn't over.

_____ *Chapter Twelve*

Slowly Robert surfaced from the depths of pure physical sensation, his mind sluggishly beginning to function once more. The power of what he had experienced left him shaken, with a sense of being outside himself, not quite connected. He was intensely aware of his own body in a way he never had been before. He could feel the warmth of his blood pumping through his veins with the heavy, slowly calming beats of his heart. He could feel the harsh bellowing of his lungs decreasing to a more normal pace, feel the intense sexual satisfaction relaxing his muscles, feel the hot, delicious clasp of Evie's body as he remained firmly inside her, satisfied but not yet sated. She was naked beneath him, just the way he had wanted.

Then, with an abrupt shift, the sluggishness was gone from his brain and reality settled in with ruthless clarity. Robert tensed, appalled at himself. He had lost control, something that had never happened before. Gentleness on his part had never been more needed, and instead he had taken her like a marauder, intent only on his own pleasure, on the conquest and possession of her silky flesh.

She lay motionless beneath him, holding herself in a sort of desperate stillness, as if to avoid attracting his attention again. His heart squeezed painfully. Robert shoved aside the matter of her virginity—he would know the answer to that puzzle later—and concentrated instead on the task of reassuring her. His mind was racing. If he let her escape him now, he would have a hell of a time getting anywhere near her again, and he couldn't blame her for being wary. Wary, hell. She would probably be downright scared, and with good reason.

He had shown her the relentless drive of passion but none of the pleasure. She had known nothing but pain, and the scale was dangerously tilted; unless he could balance the pain with pleasure, he was afraid he would lose her. It was the first time Robert had felt that sort of fear, but a sensation of panic seized him and mixed with his determination. A part of his brain remained blindingly clear. He knew exactly how to bring a woman to climax in a variety of ways: fast or slow, using his mouth or hands or body. He could gently take her to ecstasy with his mouth, and that way would perhaps be the kindest, but his instinct rejected it. He had to do it fast, before she recovered enough to begin fighting—God, he couldn't bear that—and he had to do it the same way that had caused her the pain to begin with. He wanted her to find pleasure in his body rather than dread the thrust that brought their flesh together.

He was still hard, and once more he began moving, slowly, within her. She tensed, and her hands flattened against his chest as if she would try to shove him off. "No," he said harshly, forestalling her resistance. "I won't stop. I know I'm hurting you now, but before I'm finished I'm going to make you like having me inside you."

She stared up at him, her eyes darkened with distress. But she didn't say anything, and he gathered her close, adjusting their positions so she would have the maximum sensation. He could feel her thighs quivering alongside his hips.

He took a deep breath and gentled his voice, wanting to reassure her. "I can make it good for you," he promised, brushing her soft mouth with kisses and feeling it tremble beneath his. "Will you trust me, Evangeline? Will you?"

Still she didn't say anything, hadn't spoken a word since whispering his name at the beginning. Robert hesitated for half a heartbeat, then lifted her hands and put them around his neck. After a moment her fingers shifted slightly to press against him, and relief shuddered through him at that small gesture of permission.

Evie closed her eyes again, gathering herself to once more endure this painful use of her body. At the moment, that was the limit of her capability; she couldn't act, couldn't think, could only endure. She wanted to curl herself into a protective ball and weep in shock and pain and disappointment, but she couldn't do that, either. She was helpless, her body penetrated; she was dependent on his mercy, and he seemed to have none.

At first there was only more pain. But then, abruptly, the twisting thrust of his hips made her arch off the bed with something that wasn't pain, but was just as sharp. There was no warning, no gradual lessening of pain and buildup of pleasure, only that jolt of sensation that made her cry out. He did it again, and with a strangled moan she discovered that her body was even less under her control than she had thought.

She had been cold, but now she was suffused with heat, great waves of it, rolling up from her toes until she felt as if her entire body glowed. It concentrated between her legs, increasing with each inward thrust. Her hands slid from his neck to his shoulders, clinging now, her nails biting into the hard layer of muscle. He was gripping her buttocks, lifting her up to meet him, moving her, rocking her subtly back and forth, and each tiny movement set off new explosions of pleasure within her. She had the sensation of being relentlessly driven up an internal mountain toward some point she couldn't see, but now she was straining to reach it. He pushed her further with each hard recoil of his hips until she was panting and desperate, sobbing as she arched tightly into him. And then he forced her over the edge, and Evie screamed as her senses shattered.

She shuddered and bucked, trying to meld into his flesh, as devastated by the paroxysms of pleasure as she had been by the pain that went before. Robert held himself still and deep, gritting his teeth, but the frantic milking of her internal muscles was more than he could stand, and with a groan he gave himself over, pulsing with release. Somehow he forced himself not to thrust, to let her take her pleasure and not intrude with his, and that only intensified the sensation. From a distance he heard himself groan again as he dissolved, collapsing heavily in her arms.

If Evie had been dazed before, she was even more so now. She lay limply beneath him, drifting in and out of a haze. The demands he'd made on her body, the roller-coaster succession of pain and shock and ecstasy, had left her with neither mind nor body functioning. Perhaps she dozed; she knew she dreamed, flickering images that faded too swiftly to grasp as she surfaced into foggy consciousness once more. She felt him separate himself from her, knew he was trying to be careful, but couldn't prevent a moan at the pain of his withdrawal. She didn't open her eyes as he paused, then murmured softly, a soothing sound that also held a note of apology, and completed the motion. She felt instantly bereft, cold in the air-conditioned darkness. She would have curled protectively on her side, but her limbs were too heavy. The next moment the dark fog closed about her again.

A light snapped on, blindingly bright against her eyelids. She flinched away from it, but he stilled her with a touch. The mattress shifted as he sat down beside her and firmly parted her thighs. Evie made a faint sound of protest and tried to struggle upward, but again the effort was too much.

"Shh," he whispered, a mere rustle of reassurance. "Let me make you more comfortable, sweetheart. You'll sleep better."

A cool wet cloth touched her between her legs. Deftly, tenderly, he cleaned away the evidence of their lovemaking, then dried her with a soft towel. Evie gave a soft sigh of pleasure. He returned the washcloth and towel to the bathroom, and when he came back to turn out the lamp and slide into bed beside her, she was asleep. She didn't rouse even when he turned her into his arms, cradling her protectively against him.

Evie woke in the still, dark silence before dawn. The moon had long since set, and even the stars seemed to have given up their twinkling efforts. The darkness that pressed against the patio doors was more complete than at any other time of night, in the last moments before being dispelled by the first graying that heralded the approach of the sun. She was still sleepy, exhausted by the tumultuous night in Robert's arms. It was as if her body was no longer hers, the way he called forth and controlled her responses. He had seduced her past caring about fear, about pain, so that her body arched eagerly into his possessive thrusts.

Robert lay beside her, his breathing slow and deep. One arm

was curled under her head, the other lay heavily across her waist. His heat enveloped her, welcome in the cool night. The strangeness of his presence beside her made her breath catch.

She didn't want to think about the night that had just passed, or the things that had happened between them. She was too tired, too off balance, to handle the riot of impressions and thoughts that whirled in her brain, but she was also too tired to fend them off. She gave up the effort and instead tried to make sense of what she was feeling.

She had never thought that giving herself to the man she loved would prove so traumatic, but it had. The physical pain, oddly, was the least of it, the most understandable. She had known that, under his urbane manner, Robert had the soul of a conqueror. She had also known that he had been sexually frustrated from the time they'd met. It would have made her very uneasy if, under those circumstances, his control *hadn't* wavered. She hadn't expected such a complete collapse, but then, to be perfectly fair, he hadn't expected everything that had happened, either.

She should have told him that she was a virgin, she knew, but the telling would have required an explanation that she simply hadn't been able to give. Talking about Matt, reliving those brief hours of their marriage, was too painful. Her throat tightened with dread, knowing that Robert would demand that explanation soon. She had hoped—foolishly—that he wouldn't be able to tell, that her first time would provide no more than a momentary discomfort that she could easily disguise or ignore. She felt like weeping and laughing at the same time. Had she told him, that might well have been the extent of her pain. As it was, she had paid dearly for keeping her secret, only to have it known, anyway.

The two most difficult things for her to deal with, however, were mingled grief and terror. She had known that sleeping with Robert would destroy her defenses, but she hadn't known how panicked she would feel, or that giving herself to him would call up such poignant memories of Matt. She couldn't distance herself from the grief; loving Matt, and losing him the way she had, had shaped her life and her soul. He had, in effect, made her into the woman she was now.

For twelve years she had been faithful to him, and his memory had wrapped around her like an invisible shield, protecting her. But now she had given herself irrevocably to another man, in both heart and body, and there was no going back. She loved Robert with an intensity that swelled in her chest and made her breath catch. For better or worse, *he* filled her life now. She would have to let Matt go, surrender his memory so that it became only a small, indelible part of her, rather than a bulwark between her and the world. It was like losing him twice.

''Goodbye, Matt,'' she whispered in her mind to the image of the laughing, dark-haired boy she carried there. ''I loved you…but I'm his now, and I love him, too, so much.'' The image stilled, then nodded gravely, and she saw a smile, a blessing, move across the young face as it faded away.

She couldn't bear it. With a low, keening sound of grief she surged out of bed, awakening Robert. He shot out a hand to catch her, but she evaded it and stood in the middle of the floor, looking wildly around the dark bedroom, her fist pressed to her mouth to stop the sobs that pressed for release.

''What's wrong?'' he asked softly, every muscle in his body tense and alert. ''Come back to bed, sweetheart.''

''I—I have to go home.'' She didn't want to turn on a light, feeling unable to bear his too-discerning gaze, not now, with her emotions stripped bare. But she needed to find her clothes, get dressed…. There was a dark heap on the carpet, and she snatched it up, touch telling her that it was her dress. Oh God, her muscles protested every move she made, his lovemaking during the night echoing now in her flesh. A deep internal ache marked where he had been.

''Why?'' His voice remained soft, compelling. ''It's early yet. We have time.''

Time for what? she wanted to ask, but she knew, anyway. If she got back into that bed, he would make love to her again. And again. Shaking with grief, caught in the transition between the old love and the new, she thought she would break into pieces if he touched her. She was irrevocably passing from one phase of her life into another, traumatic enough under any circumstances, but she had the sensation of leaving a secure fortress and plunging headlong into unknown danger. She needed to be alone to deal with what she was feeling, to get herself back.

"I have to go," she repeated in a ghostly voice, tight with suppressed tears.

He got out of bed, his naked body pale in the shadowy darkness. "All right," he said gently. "I'll take you home." She watched in bewilderment as he stripped the top sheet from the bed. His next movement was a blur, so swift that she couldn't tell what he was doing until it was too late. With two quick steps he was beside her. He swathed the sheet tightly around her, then lifted her in his arms. "Later," he added as he opened the patio doors and stepped outside with her.

The early morning was silent, as if all God's creatures were holding their breath, waiting for first light. Not even a cricket chirped. The water lapped at the bank with only a slight rustling sound, like silk petticoats. Robert sat down in one of the deck chairs and held her cradled on his lap, the sheet protecting her from the cool, damp air.

Evie tried to hold herself tight, all emotion contained. She managed for a few minutes. Robert simply held her, not saying anything, looking out over the dark water as if he, too, were waiting for the dawn. It was his silence that defeated her; if he had talked, she could have concentrated on her replies. Faced with nothing but her own thoughts, she lost the battle.

She turned her face into his neck as hot tears ran down her cheeks and her body shook with sobs.

He didn't try to hush her, didn't try to talk to her, simply held her more closely to him and gave her the comfort of his body. It was, despite her chaotic emotions, a considerable comfort. The bonds of the flesh that he had forged during the night were fresh and strong, her senses so attuned to him that it was as if his breath were hers, her jerky inhalations gradually slowing and taking on the steady rhythm of his.

When she had calmed, he used a corner of the sheet to dry her face. He didn't bother to wipe her tears from his neck.

Exhausted, empty of emotion, her eyes burning and grainy feeling, she stared out at the lake. In a tree close by, a bird gave a tentative chirp, and as if that were a signal, in the next moment hundreds of birds began singing madly, delirious with joy at the new day. In the time while she had wept, the morning had grown perceptibly lighter, the darkness fading to a dim gray that gave new mystery to details that had been hidden before. That dark hump out in the water—was that a stump, a rock or a magical sea creature that would vanish with the light?

Robert was very warm, the heat of his powerful, naked body seeping through the sheet in animal comfort. She felt the steely columns of his thighs beneath her, the solid support of his chest, the secure grasp of his arms. She rested her head against that wide, smoothly muscled shoulder and felt as if she had come home.

"I love you," she said quietly.

Foolish of her to admit it; how many other women had told him the same thing, especially after a night in his arms? It must be nothing new to him. But what would she gain by holding it back? It would allow a pretense, when he left, that he had been nothing more than a summer affair, but she couldn't fool herself with a sop to her pride. Probably she couldn't even fool him, though he would be gentleman enough to allow her the pretense.

All the same, she was glad of his self-possession. He didn't parrot the words back to her; she would have known he was lying, and she would have hated that. Nor did he act uncomfortable or nervous. He merely gave her a searching look and asked in a level tone, "Then why the tears?"

Evie sighed and returned to staring at the water. He was due some explanation, would probably insist on one, but even though she loved him, she simply couldn't strip her soul bare and blurt out everything. She had a deeply private core, and even if she remained Robert's lover for years, there would be some things she wouldn't be able to tell him, memories that brought up too much pain.

"Evie." It wasn't a prompt but a gentle, implacable demand.

Sadness haunted her eyes and trembled around her mouth. She was very familiar with it, had walked with it for twelve years, gone to bed with it at night, awakened with it on countless mornings. Sadness and a deep lonelines that neither friends nor family had been able to dispel had been her constant, invisible companions. But Robert wanted an answer. A man who had held a woman through such a bout of bitter weeping should at least know the reason for her tears.

"I realized," she finally said in a low, shaking voice, "that Matt is truly gone now."

Cradled against him as she was, she felt the way his muscled body tightened. His words, however, were still controlled. "He's been gone for a long time."

"Yes, he has." Only she knew exactly how long those twelve years had been. "But until last night, I was still his wife."

"No," he said flatly. "You weren't." He put one finger under her chin and tilted it up, forcing her to look at him. It was light enough now for her to see those pale eyes glittering. "You were never his wife. You never slept with him. I hope you aren't going to try to pretend you weren't a virgin, because I'm not a fool, and the stain on the sheet isn't because you're having your period."

Evie flinched. "No," she whispered. God, it was eerie how he had gone straight to the secret she had kept for so long.

"You married him," he continued relentlessly. "How is it that I'm the only man who's ever had you?"

Sadness still darkened her eyes, but she said, "I had a June wedding," and a wealth of grief and irony lay in those brief words.

He didn't understand, but he lifted his dark brows, inviting her to continue.

"It's impossible to book a church for a wedding in June unless you do it about a year in advance," she explained. "Matt and I picked the day when we were still juniors in high school. But there's no way to do any personal planning that far ahead of time." Evie turned her head away from him once more, toward her private solace, the water. "It was a beautiful wedding. The weather was perfect, the decorations were perfect, the cake was perfect. Everything went off without a hitch. And my period started that morning.''

Robert was silent, still waiting. Evie swallowed, aching inside as she looked back at the innocent girl she had been. "I was so embarrassed that night, when I had to tell Matt that we couldn't make love. We were both miserable."

"Why didn't you—" he began, but then stopped as he realized that two teenagers wouldn't have the ease and experience of two adults.

"Exactly," Evie said, as if he had put his thoughts into words. "We had never made love, obviously. Matt didn't have any more experience than I did. What experience we had, we'd gotten together, but we'd both wanted to wait until after we were married. So there we were, two eighteen-year-olds on our wedding night, and all we could do was neck and hold hands. Matt was so miserable that we didn't even do much of that.

"But he was basically such a cheerful person that nothing depressed him for long. He was making jokes about it the next morning, making me laugh, but we both agreed that it was something we'd *never* tell our kids when we got old." Her voice wavered and faded until it was almost soundless. "He died that day."

Gently Robert pushed a strand of hair away from her face. So she had never made love with her young husband, but for over a decade had kept herself untouched for him. With an acuteness of insight that often made people uncomfortable, he saw exactly how it had been. Traumatized by Matt's death, she had doubly mourned the fact that they had never been able to make love and had sealed herself off from other men. If her first time couldn't be with Matt, it would be with no one. She had existed ever since as an animated Sleeping Beauty whose body had kept on functioning while her emotions had been suspended.

Robert felt a deep, savage satisfaction. Despite that enormous barrier, he had succeeded where others hadn't even been able to begin. Her first time had been *his*. She was *his*.

He had always despised promiscuity but hadn't prized virginity. It had seemed to him the height of hypocrisy to demand something from a woman that he himself lacked. All of his sophisticated affairs, however, had nothing in common with the powerful, primitive sense of jealous possessiveness that had swept over him the moment he had realized that he was the only man ever to make love to Evie.

Her association with Landon Mercer, whatever it was, was certainly not romantic in any sense. Sitting there in the early dawn, with Evie cradled on his lap, Robert made a swift decision. He wouldn't stop the investigation, wouldn't warn her in any way, because the espionage had to be halted before it did irreparable harm to both the space station and national security. But when the net was tightened and all the traitorous little fish caught, he would step in and use his influence to shield Evie from prosecution. She wouldn't escape punishment, but the punishment would be his, and his alone, to mete out. The simple truth was that he couldn't bear for her to go to prison. He was astonished at himself, but there it was.

He didn't know why she was involved in something so vile. He was a very good judge of people, and he would have sworn that honor was a cornerstone of her character. Therefore, she had to be doing it for what she considered a good reason, though he couldn't imagine what that could be. It was possible she didn't realize exactly what was going on; that explanation fit better than any other, and made him all the more determined to protect her. As he had told her once, he was good at taking care of his own, and last night Evie had become his in the most basic of ways.

He was fiercely glad that nature's rhythm had interfered with her wedding night all those years ago. Poor Matt. A lot of his jealousy for the boy faded away, and a rather poignant pity took its place. Matt Shaw had died without ever tasting the perfection of his young wife's body.

Robert remembered the moment the night before when he had removed her last garment and seen her totally naked, nothing left to his imagination any longer. To his numb surprise, his imagination had fallen short. He had seen her breasts before, but each time he had marveled at how firm and round they were, delightfully upright, the nipples small and a delectable shade of dark pink. Her body curved in to a lithe waist, then flared again to very womanly hips. Her skin, in the silver moonlight, had glowed like alabaster. Instead of being model thin, like the women he had been accustomed to, her curves had been lush and sensual. He hadn't been able to wait but had mounted her immediately.

A gentleman would have been far more considerate of her than he had been, but he had always been wryly aware that, despite what all his acquaintances thought, he was definitely *not* a gentleman. He was controlled and intelligent and not a cruel man, but that wasn't the same thing as being gentlemanly. Where Evie was concerned, though, his control went right out the window. His mouth took on a grim line as he remembered the wild rush of passion, the primitive instinct to make her his, that had blotted out all reason. Not only had he hurt her, he hadn't used a condom. He, who had never before neglected to make certain some form of protection was used, hadn't even given a thought to birth control.

She might be pregnant. He allowed the possibility to seep into his mind just as the golden light began to seep over the ridge of mountains. To his surprise, he didn't feel any panic or disgust at his stupidity. Rather, he felt pleased—and intrigued.

He put his hand inside the sheet, resting it on her cool, flat belly. "We may be parents. I didn't wear a condom."

"It's all right." She gave him a composed look. The tears and grief were now well under control. "I went to my doctor in Huntsville and got a prescription for birth-control pills."

He felt a not altogether pleasant jolt. He should have been relieved, but instead he was strangely disappointed. Common sense prevailed however. "When?"

"Not long after meeting you," she said wryly.

Robert almost snorted at the amount of work he'd had his people doing, trying to find out what she had been doing, whom she had seen, that day in Huntsville. He would pull them off that particular job now, but he would be damned if he'd tell them what she *had* been doing.

He lifted his eyebrows at her, a sardonic look on his face. "I distinctly remember you saying that you didn't intend to sleep with me."

"I didn't. But that doesn't mean I'd leave something that important to chance, because you were determined, and I wasn't entirely sure of my willpower."

"Your willpower would have been fine," he said, "if you hadn't wanted me, too."

"I know," she admitted softly.

Dawn was well and truly upon them now, golden light spilling across the water. The roar of outboard motors broke the serene hush of the morning, and soon the river would be crowded with fishermen and pleasure boaters. Though Evie's position on his lap would keep anyone from seeing he was naked, Robert thought it best not to chance shocking the locals. After all, she ran a business here, and she might be recognized. He stood up easily, still cradling her securely in his arms, and carried her back through the open patio doors.

He had never been more content than he was at this moment. Evie probably didn't know what was really going on with Mercer and was involved only peripherally; he would be able to protect her without much problem. He had taken her to bed, and now he knew what had lain beneath her mysterious sadness. He doubted that Evie would ever completely stop thinking about Matt, but that was okay now, because Matt Shaw's ghost had been banished and she had emerged from her emotional deep freeze. She had said that she loved him, and he knew instinctively that she hadn't been mouthing the words merely to rationalize their lovemaking. If she hadn't already loved him, he would never have been able to seduce her.

Some of the women who had come before had also told him that they loved him—most of them, in fact. The declarations had never elicited more from him than a rather tender pity for their vulnerability. Though he had liked and enjoyed all his lovers, none of them had ever managed to pierce his shell; he doubted any of them had even known the shell existed.

Evie's simple statement, though, had filled him with a satisfaction so fierce that his blood had thrummed through his veins. She hadn't expected him to respond. Now that he thought about it, she expected less from him than anyone else ever had. It was a startling realization to a man accustomed to having people come to him with their problems, expecting him to make decisions that would affect thousands of workers and millions of dollars. Evie expected nothing. How was it, then, that she gave so much?

He carried her into the bathroom and stood her on her feet, then unwrapped her from the sheet. The sight of her creamy golden flesh aroused him again, drew his hands to cup her breasts and feel the cool, silky weight of them. His thumbs rubbed across her nipples, making them tighten. Evie's eyes were wide with alarm as she stared at him.

His mouth quirked into a crooked smile. "Don't look so worried," he said as he bent down to press his lips to her forehead. "I'll restrain myself until you've had time to heal. Get in the tub, sweetheart, while I put on the coffee. A bath will relieve some of the soreness."

"Good idea," she said with absolute sincerity.

He chuckled as he left her there. The feeling of contentment was even deeper. She was *his*.

Chapter Thirteen

How could experiencing such a night not leave an imprint on her face? Evie wondered as she got ready for work. After her leisurely soak in the soothing hot water and an equally leisurely breakfast, which Robert had cooked with the same easy competence with which he handled everything else, he had driven her home and reluctantly kissed her goodbye for the day, saying that he had some business to attend to in Huntsville but would try to get back before she closed the marina. If not, he would come to her house.

She had forced herself to do the normal things, but she felt as if her entire life had been turned upside down, as if nothing were the same. *She* wasn't the same. Robert had turned her into a woman who actively longed for his possession, despite the discomfort of her newly initiated body. She hadn't known, hadn't even suspected, that passion could be so savage and all-encompassing, that the pain would be as nothing before the need to link her body with his.

She wanted him even more now than before. He had brought up the long-buried sensuality of her nature and made it his, so that she responded to the lightest touch of his hand. When she thought of him, her body throbbed with the need to wrap her legs around him and take him inside her, to cradle his heavy weight, accept and tame the driving need of his masculinity. The scent of his skin, warm and musky, aroused her. Her memory was filled now with details that she hadn't known before, like the guttural growl of his words and the way his neck corded when he threw his head back in the arching frenzy of satisfaction.

She stared at her face in the mirror as she swiftly braided her hair. Her eyes had shadows under them, but she didn't look tired. She simply looked...like herself. If there was any change at all, it was in the expression in her eyes, as if there was a spark that had been missing before.

But if her face was the same, her body bore the signs of his lovemaking. Her breasts were pink and slightly raw from contact with his beard stubble, her nipples so sensitive from his mouth that the soft fabric of her bra rasped them. There were several small bruises on her hips, where he had gripped her during his climax, and her thighs ached. She was sore enough that every step reminded her of his possession and awakened echoes of sensation that made her acutely aware of her body.

It was much earlier than usual when she drove to the marina, but she needed the distraction to take her mind off Robert. If she was lucky, Sherry would bring Virgil by to spend the day with her.

Craig was gassing up a boat when she arrived. When he had finished, he came in and rang up the sale, putting the money in the cash drawer. "How come you're in so early? Have a nice time last night?"

Her nerves jumped, but she managed a composed smile. "Yes, we did. We went to a private club for dinner and dancing. And I came in early...just because."

"That's a good enough reason for me." He brushed his dark hair out of his eyes and gave her an urchin's grin. "I'm glad you're going out with him. You deserve some fun, after the way you've worked to build up this place."

"Thanks for swapping shifts with me."

"You bet."

Another customer idled up to the docks, and Craig went out again. Evie picked up the morning mail and began sorting through it. The junk mail and sales papers went into the trash. The bills went to one side, to be juggled later. One letter was from a New York bank she'd never heard of, probably wanting her to apply for a credit card. She started to toss it without opening it, but on second thought decided to see what it was about. She picked up the penknife she used as a letter opener and slit the envelope.

Thirty seconds later, her brows knit in puzzlement, she let the single sheet of paper drop to the desk. Somehow this bank had gotten her confused with someone else, though she couldn't think how they had gotten her name on one of their files when she had never done business with them. The letter stated, in brisk terms, that due to a poor payment record they would be forced to foreclose on her loan unless it was paid in full within thirty days.

She would have ignored it except that the amount noted was the same as what she owed her bank for the loan against the marina. She knew that figure well, had struggled to get it down to that amount. Each payment brought it even lower. She didn't know how, but obviously her file had gotten into this other bank's computers, and they wanted her to pay fifteen thousand, two hundred and sixty-two dollars within thirty days.

Well, it was obviously something she would have to clear up before it got even more tangled. Evie called her bank, gave her name and asked for her loan officer, Tommy Fowler, who was also an old school friend.

The line clicked, and Tommy's voice said, "Hi, Evie. How're you doing?"

"Just fine. How are you and Karen doing, and the kids?"

"We're doing okay, though Karen says the kids are driving her crazy, and if school doesn't start soon she's going to get herself arrested, so she can have some peace and quiet."

Evie chuckled. The Fowler kids were known for their frenetic energy.

"What can I help you with today?" Tommy asked.

"There's been a really strange mix-up, and I need to know how to straighten it out. I got a letter today from a bank in New York, asking for payment in full on a loan, and it's the same amount as the one I took out from you, on the marina."

"Is that so? Wonder what's going on. Do you have your account number handy?"

"Not with me, no. I'm at work, and all my bookkeeping is at home."

"That's okay, I'll pull it up under your name. Just a minute."

She could hear the tapping of computer keys as he hummed

softly to himself. Then he stopped humming and silence reigned, stretching out for so long that Evie wondered if he'd left the room. Finally a few more keys were tapped, then more silence.

He fumbled with the receiver. "Evie, I—" Reluctance was heavy in his voice.

"What's wrong? What's happened?"

"There's a problem, all right, hon. A big one. Your loan was bought by that bank."

Evie's mind went blank. "What do you mean, bought?"

"I mean we sold off some of our loans. It's a common practice. Banks do it to reduce their debt load. Other financial institutions buy them to diversify their own debt load. According to the records, this transaction took place ten days ago."

"Ten days! Just ten days, and already they're demanding payment in full? Tommy, can they do that?"

"Not if you've fulfilled the terms of the loan. Have you...ah...were you late with the payment?"

She knew he must have her payment record there in front of him, showing that she had been late several times, though she had never fallen a full month behind and had always gotten back on schedule. "It's late now," she said numbly. "I had an unexpected expense, and it'll be next week before I can."

She heard him exhale heavily. "Then they're legally within their rights, though the normal procedure would be to make an effort at collecting the payment, rather than the full amount."

"What do I do?"

"Call them. It should be fairly easy to straighten out. After all, you're a good risk. But be sure to follow up by letter, so you'll have a record in writing."

"Okay. Thanks for the advice, Tommy."

"You're welcome. I'm sorry about this, hon. It never would have happened if we'd still held the loan."

"I know. I'll see what I can do."

"Call me if there's anything I can do to help."

"Thanks," she said again and hung up.

Her heart was pounding as she dialed the number on the letterhead. An impersonal voice answered and nasally requested her business. Evie gave the name of the man who had signed the letter, and the connection was made before she could even say please.

The call was brief. Mr. Borowitz was as brisk as his letter had been and as impersonal as the operator. There was nothing he could do, nor did he sound interested in trying. The outstanding amount was due in full by the time limit set forth in the letter, or the loan would be foreclosed and the property forfeit.

Slowly she hung up and sat there staring out the window at the blindingly bright day. The lake was crowded with boaters, people laughing, having fun. The marina was busy, with owners cleaning their craft, others using her ramps to launch their boats, still others idling in for gas. If she didn't somehow come up with over fifteen thousand dollars within the next thirty days, she would lose it all.

She loved the marina. Because she and Matt had been playmates before they had become sweethearts, she had spent a lot of time here even as a child. She had spent hours playing on the docks, had grown up with the smell of the water in her nostrils. The rhythms of the marina were as much a part of her as her own heartbeat. She had helped Matt work here, and later, after his death, had taken over the lion's share of the work from his parents. When they had left the marina to her, she had channeled all her energy and efforts into making it prosperous, but it had been a labor of love. The marina, as much as her family, had given her a reason for going on when she had been doubtful that she wanted to even try.

This was her kingdom, her home, as much or more than the house in which she lived. She couldn't bear to lose it. Some way, any way, she would find the money to pay off the loan.

The most obvious solution was to borrow against the house. The amount of the debt would be the same, but it would be stretched out over a longer period of time, and that would actually lower the payments. She felt giddy for a moment as the shock and horror lifted from her shoulders. She would be in even better shape than before, with more free cash every month.

She called Tommy again and got the ball rolling. He agreed that a mortgage was the perfect solution. He would have to get an okay on the loan, but he didn't foresee any problems and promised to call her as soon as permission came through.

When she hung up, Evie sat with her head in her hands for a long moment. She felt as if she had just survived combat. She was shaky, but elated at her victory. If she had lost the marina... She couldn't let herself imagine it.

When she finally lifted her head and looked out the window, driven by a need to see her domain still safe and secure, still hers, her face broke into a smile. Business was good today. So good, in fact, that Craig desperately needed a hand and was probably wondering why she wasn't out there helping him. Evie bounded to her feet, energy restored, and rushed out to help him with the sudden glut of customers.

Robert arrived at the marina just after seven that evening. It had been busy all day, and she was on the dock selling gas and oil to yet another happy, sun-roasted boater. Alerted by a sensitivity to her lover's presence, Evie looked around and saw him standing just outside the door, watching her. She lifted her hand. "I'll be there in a few minutes."

He nodded and stepped inside, and she turned her attention back to her customer.

Robert watched her through the big window as he stepped behind the counter. He had been notified that she had received the letter and called the bank that he had arranged to buy her loan, and that, as instructed, they had been totally unwilling to cooperate on the matter. Glancing down, he saw the letter lying on top of the stack of mail, the single sheet of paper neatly folded and stuffed back into the envelope.

She had to be uspet. He regretted the need for it, but he had decided to see the plan through. Though he was almost certain she didn't know exactly what Mercer was doing, that she was more of an unwitting accomplice than anything else, there was still the small chance that she was involved up to her pretty neck. Because of that, he couldn't relent in his financial pressure. If she *was* involved, she would be forced into another sale just to raise the money to pay the loan. If she wasn't involved, he would take care of her money problems just as soon as he had Mercer in jail. There were others, and he would get them, too. But Evie was his, one way or the other.

Since he had left her that morning, he had several times been struck with amazement that he wouldn't see her sent to jail, even if she was guilty. This was his country's security at stake, something he took very seriously indeed. He had risked his life more than once for the same principle. He had relished the adventure, but the underlying reason for taking those risks had been a simple, rock-solid love of country. If Evie had betrayed it, she deserved prison. But acknowledging that in no way changed his decision. He would protect her from prosecution.

The sunburned customer and his trio of friends, all young men in their early twenties, were obviously in no hurry to stop chatting with Evie. Robert scowled out the window, but he couldn't blame them. Only a dead man wouldn't respond to her curvy, glowing femininity.

He slipped the letter out of the envelope and unfolded it. There was no reason for doing so, except a meticulous attention to detail. He wanted to know exactly what it said. Swiftly he scanned the contents, satisfied with the way it had been handled. Then he read Evie's notes, hastily scribbled in the margin.

She had written down the name "Tommy Fowler," with a phone number beside it. Underneath she had written "mortgage house" and circled that.

A smile tugged at his mouth. She was certainly a resourceful, common-sense woman. Relief welled up in him. If she was truly involved in stealing the NASA computer programs, she wouldn't be trying to mortgage her house to pay the loan; she would simply arrange another buy. In his experience, criminals didn't think of things like honest work to pay off debts; they were leeches, living off the effort of others, and would simply steal again.

Robert returned the letter to the envelope. More than ever, he regretted the need to play out what he had begun, but he never left anything to chance, certainly not in a matter this serious. He would have to squash any attempt to mortgage the house, of course. Evie would be worried sick, but he would make it up to her afterward.

He sat down on the high stool and watched her as she finally got rid of the four admiring young men. She was dressed much as she had been the first time he'd seen her, in jeans and a T-shirt with her tawny blond hair in a thick, loose braid. His reaction, too, was almost the same: he was poleaxed with lust. The only difference was that it was more intense now, and he hadn't thought that possible. But now he knew exactly how she looked naked, knew all the delectable textures and curves of her body, and the hot, tight clasp of being sheathed deep inside her. He shivered with desire, his burning gaze locked on her as she walked up the dock. He knew the sounds she made at the peak of pleasure, knew how she clung to him, the way her legs locked convulsively around him, and how her nipples hardened to tight little raspberries. He knew the taste of her, the scent, and wanted to have it again.

She came inside, glanced at him and froze in place. He saw the shudder of awareness that rippled over her as she sensed his arousal. God, was she even more attuned to him than she had been before? The thought was unsettling.

''Come here,'' he said softly, and she blindly walked into his arms.

He didn't rise from the stool but pulled her between his thighs. Her arms circled his shoulders as he bent his mouth to hers. He kissed her for a long time, so hungry for her that he couldn't be gentle. Evie moved against him, her hips rolling in a languorous, wanton manner that made his heart almost stop in his chest. Kissing her when her response was reluctant had been intoxicating enough; now that she was willing, her mouth clung to his in a way that made him forget about Mercer and the stolen computer programs, about the mess she was embroiled in, even where he was, everything but the hot joy of holding her.

But she would be too sore for any more lovemaking today, and reluctantly he eased away from her mouth, trailing kisses across her temple and the curve of her jaw. He would have to restrain himself for a while yet.

"How did your day go?" he murmured, opening the door for her to tell him about the problem with the bank loan.

"It was as busy today as I've ever seen it," she replied, leaning back in the circle of his arms. Her eyes were soft and sleepy. "How about yours?"

"Tedious. I had some boring details to handle." That was a lie. No detail was boring to him.

"I wish you had been here today, I'd have put you to work. I think everyone who owns a boat was on the water today." She glanced over his shoulder. "There's another one," she said as she slipped out his arms.

This group didn't need any gas but trooped inside in search of some snacks and cold drinks. They had the ruddiness of people who had been out in the sun and wind all day, and brought with them the coconut scent of sunscreen lotion. Once inside, they seemed reluctant to leave the air-conditioning and milled around looking at the fishing tackle. Evie didn't try to hurry them, instead chatting pleasantly. They were two couples about her age, out for a day of relaxation on the lake. One of the women mentioned how nice it was to have a day away from the kids, and for a while the conversation centered on the antics of their children. When the group finally left, it was with friendly goodbyes.

"Alone at last," Robert said, glancing at his watch. "It's closing time, anyway."

"Thank goodness." Evie stretched and yawned, catching herself in midstretch with a wince that she quickly covered, but not quickly enough. He saw that slight hesitation. He would indeed have to exercise self-control.

He helped her to close up, then sent her home while he stopped for takeout. They ate dinner together, then sat out on the deck in the cooling night, talking softly about routine things. But Evie soon became sleepy, a direct result of not sleeping much the night before. On her third yawn, Robert stood up and held out his hand. "That's it, sleepyhead. Bedtime."

She put her hand in his and let him pull her to her feet. He led her to the bedroom and gently began undressing her.

"Robert, wait," she said uneasily, trying to draw away from him. "I can't—"

"I know," he said, and kissed her forehead. "I told you I'd give you time to heal. I didn't say anything about not sleeping together, but *sleep* is the operative word."

She relaxed into his arms again, and he finished the task of undressing both of them. It was too warm in the house for him to be comfortable, but when they were both naked and lying on the bed, the ceiling fan wafted a cooling breeze over them, and he began to get drowsy, anyway. They lay nestled spoon fashion, his hard thighs under her round bottom, one hand possessively covering a breast.

He lay quietly. She was already asleep, her breathing slow and even. All his objections to staying in this house had faded when he had found that Evie had never truly been Matt's wife. He would still have preferred being in his own house; the bed was much bigger, for one thing. But Evie would be more comfortable in her own home, and that was the most important thing. He had notified his people where he would be, just as he had notified them that Evie would be staying with him the night before.

He had given her every opportunity to tell him about the bank loan, but she hadn't said a word about it. Just as she had with the blown motor in her truck, she kept her trouble to herself rather than running to him for help or even emotional support. For someone who was so open and friendly, Evie was a very solitary person, accustomed to handling everything on her own. Though he would have had to turn her down if she'd asked for help, he wanted her to confide in him, to let him far enough into her life that he knew about the problems as well as the pleasures. When they were married, he would make damn certain he knew every time she stubbed her toe.

Until that moment, he hadn't let his plans for the future progress that far, but suddenly it seemed the thing to do. He had never wanted any other woman the way he wanted Evie, and he sincerely doubted that he ever would. After this mess was settled, he intended to keep her close by, which would mean taking her to New York with him. And he knew Evie. Though she had given herself to him, she was essentially a conventional soul. She would want the security of marriage; therefore, he would marry her. Other women had wanted marriage from him, but this was the first time in his life he'd been willing to give it. He couldn't imagine ever becoming bored with Evie, which had always happened with other lovers. Even more, he couldn't imagine letting any other man have the chance to marry her.

He didn't regret the impending loss of freedom. He thought of dressing her in silk gowns and expensive jewelry, of settling her in the lap of luxury—his—so that she wouldn't have to work seven days a week or worry about paying bills. She wouldn't have to make do with a secondhand refrigerator or drive around in a beat-up old truck. She wouldn't be so tired that dark smudges lay under her eyes. He would take her with him on his business trips, show her Paris and London and Rome, and they would take vacations on the ranch in Montana. Madelyn, he suspected, would gloat because he had finally been caught, but she would like Evie. Evie, despite that glowing sensuality, wasn't the type of woman that other women disliked on sight. She was friendly and courteous and unselfconscious about her looks. He had seen a lot of women who were far more vain than Evie, and with a lot less reason.

Within a month, perhaps even sooner, all of this would be behind them and they would be in New York. He fell asleep, thinking with pleasure of having her all to himself.

As usual, Evie woke at dawn. Robert lay close beside her, his body heat bathing her in warmth, despite the fact that the sheet had been kicked completely off the bed. He had done that, she supposed, because he wasn't accustomed to doing without air-conditioning. His arm was draped heavily across her hips, and his breath stirred the hair at the back of her neck.

She had slept with him for two nights in a row now and wondered how she would be able to bear the desolation when he was no longer there.

She turned within the circle of that enveloping arm and rose up on one elbow. He woke immediately. "Is anything wrong?"

he asked, and just for a moment there was something feral and frightening in his eyes, and an instant tension in his muscles, as if he were poised to attack.

Quickly she shook her head to reassure him. "No. I just wanted to see you."

He relaxed at her words, lying back on the pillows. His olive-toned skin was dark against the whiteness. His thick black hair was tousled, and his jaw darkened by a heavy stubble. She was entranced by his sheer, uncomplicated masculinity, not yet smoothed over with grooming and clothes that somewhat obscured his true nature. Lying there with his iron-hard body naked and relaxed, he looked like what he was, a warrior honed down and redefined by years of battle.

She put her hand on his chest, and he lay quietly, watching her from beneath lowered lids but content to let her do as she wished. She didn't whisper her love to him; she had already told him how she felt and didn't intend to badger him about it. She concentrated, instead, on learning as much as she could about him. She had spent the first eighteen years of her life gathering memories about Matt, but she would have a much shorter time with Robert, and she didn't want to waste a minute.

She bent over him, her long hair trailing across his chest and shoulder as she planted a line of gentle kisses down his body. He smelled delicious in the morning, she thought, all warm and sleepy. The crispy curls of black hair on his chest invited her to rub her cheek against them, catlike. His nipples, tiny and brown, were almost hidden in the hair. She sought them out, tickled by the minute points that stood out when she rubbed her fingertip across them. Robert flexed restlessly on the sheet as desire tightened his muscles, then forced himself to relax again to better enjoy her attentions.

"I wonder if that's the same expression a pasha would have, lying back and letting his favorite concubine pleasure him," she murmured.

"Probably." He put his hands on her head, fingers sliding beneath the heavy fall of hair to massage her scalp. "You do pleasure me, Evangeline."

She continued her dreamy exploration, down the furry ridged abdomen toward his hips and thighs, detouring around his early morning erection. Something high on the inside of his left thigh caught her eye, and she bent closer to examine the mark. The morning sunlight clearly revealed a stylized outline of an eagle, or perhaps a phoenix, with upswept wings. The tattoo was small, not even an inch in length, but so finely made that she could see the fierceness of the raptor.

She was startled by the tattoo—not the design, but its very presence. Lightly she traced her finger over it, wondering why he had it. After all, Robert hardly seemed the type of man who would have a tattoo; he was too polished and sophisticated. But for all that sophistication, he wasn't quite civilized, and the tattoo matched that part of him. This was perhaps the only overt signal he permitted himself that he was more than what he seemed.

"How long have you had it?" she asked, looking up at him.

He was watching her with piercingly intent eyes. "Quite a while."

It was a very inexact answer, but she sensed that it was all she would get from him, at least for now. Slowly she leaned down and licked the tattoo, her tongue gently caressing the sign in his flesh that signaled the presence of the inner man.

A low, rough sound vibrated in his throat, and his entire body tightened.

"Do you want me?" she whispered, licking him again. She felt very warm, and slightly drunk with her feminine power. Desire was unfurling inside her, opening like a flower. Her breasts throbbed, and she rubbed them against his leg.

He gave a strangled laugh, almost undone by her natural sensuality. "Look a few inches to your right and tell me what you think."

She did, turning her head with slow deliberation to survey the straining, pulsing length of his sex. "I believe you do."

"The sixty-four-thousand-dollar question is, how do *you* feel?"

Evie gave him a slow, luminous smile of desire that promised him more than he thought he could survive. "I feel...willing," she purred, crawling up the length of his body to lie on him as she wound her arms around his neck.

His face was strained as he rolled, placing her beneath him. "I'll be careful," he promised in a rough whisper.

She reached up to touch his beard-roughened cheek and opened her thighs to clasp them around him. Her heart was in her eyes as he began slowly, with almost agonizing care, to enter her. "I trust you," she said, giving him her body as surely as she had given him her heart.

Chapter Fourteen

Landon Mercer caught himself wearing a habitually worried expression whenever he glanced into a mirror. Nothing was going right, for no particular reason that he could tell. One day he had been feeling pretty damn good about himself and the way everything was going, and the next it all began to go to hell. It was just little things at first, like that bastard Cannon showing up and nearly giving him a heart attack, though it turned out that Cannon had been the least of his worries. The big boss's reputation had been vastly overstated; he was nothing more than another lazy playboy, born into money, without any real idea of what it was like to get out and hustle for what he had.

Sometimes, though, Cannon had a cold look in his eyes that was downright spooky, as if he could see right through flesh. Mercer wouldn't soon forget the panic he'd felt when Cannon had caught him in Shaw's Marina. For one terror-stricken minute, Mercer had thought he was caught, that they'd somehow managed to find out what he was doing. But all Cannon had seemed interested in was that he'd taken off from work for the afternoon, something he'd been careful not to do again. Of all the damn luck! There were plenty of marinas in Guntersville; why had Cannon picked Shaw's? It wasn't the biggest, or the best run. In fact, for him, its major attraction was that it was small, a bit out of the way and basically a one-horse outfit. Evie Shaw didn't have time to pay attention to everything going on around her.

Of course, once Cannon had seen Evie, it was understandable why he kept hanging around. Mercer had been trying for months to get her to go out with him, but she was as standoffish as she was stacked. He just didn't have enough money, he supposed; she had latched on to Cannon fast enough.

Of course, if things had worked out, he *would* have had enough money to interest her. He wasn't stupid. He hadn't blown the payoffs; he'd invested them. The ventures he'd picked had all seemed sound. He'd stayed away from the high-interest but volatile money markets and opted for slower but more secure returns. In a few years, he'd figured, he would have enough money invested to be on easy street.

But stocks that had looked good one day went sour the next, prices going on a steady slide as other investors dumped their shares. In one terrible week the tidy little nest egg he'd built up had decreased in value to less than half of what it had been before. He had sold out, taking a loss, and in a desperate move to recoup his money had invested it all in the money markets. The money market had promptly plummeted, almost wiping him out. He felt like King Midas in reverse; everything he touched turned to dross.

When he was contacted about another sale, he was so relieved that he almost thanked them for calling. If his bank account didn't get a cash transfusion soon, he wouldn't be able to make his car payment, or the payments on all his credit cards. Mercer was horrified at the thought of losing his beloved Mercedes. There were more expensive cars, and he intended to have them eventually, but the Mercedes was the first car he'd had that said he was *somebody,* a man on the way up. He couldn't bear to go back to being nothing.

Evie felt as if she had been split into two separate beings. Half of her was deliriously happy, overwhelmed by the intoxication of having Robert for a lover. She had never dreamed she could be so happy again, or feel so whole, but the great emptiness that had lurked in her heart for so long had been filled. Robert was both passionate and considerate, paying her so much attention that she felt as if she were the center of his universe. He never ignored her, never took anything about her for granted, always made her feel as if she were the most desirable woman he'd ever seen. Whenever they went out, his attention never wandered to other women, though she was well aware of other women looking at him.

She saw him every day, slept with him almost every night. As she became more at ease with her own body and the passion he aroused, their lovemaking became more leisurely, and even more intense, until sometimes she screamed with the force of it. He was a sophisticated lover, leading her into new positions, new variations, new sensations, and he was so skilled that he didn't make her feel awkward or ignorant. He made love to her almost every night. Only once, but that once was long and complete, leaving her sated and sleepy. Then, in the morning when they woke, they would make love again, silently, drifting in that half-awake state when dreams still shadow consciousness.

His mastery of her body was so complete that thoughts of him were always with her, lurking just under the surface, ready to come to the fore and bringing desire with them. She didn't know which she enjoyed most, the intense sessions at night or the dreamy ones of early morning. It was amazing how quickly her body had learned to crave sexual pleasure with him, so that, as the afternoon hours advanced, she would become jittery with anticipation and need. He knew it, surely. She could see him watching her, as if gauging her readiness. Sometimes she had a violent desire to pin him to the floor and have her way with him, but she always restrained herself, because the buildup of desire, though maddening, was equally delicious.

She had become accustomed to containing her thoughts and emotions, guarding them behind a wall of reserve, but Robert drew her out. They had long, involved discussions about a wide variety of subjects. Sitting out on the deck at night, staring up at the stars, they would discuss astronomy and various theories, from the big bang to black holes, dark matter and the relativity of time. His intelligence and the scope of his interests were almost frightening. Without giving any indication of restlessness, his mind was always working, looking for new facts to absorb or arranging those he already had. They would trade sections of the newspaper, and debate politics and national events. They swapped childhood stories, she telling him about growing up with an older sister as

bossy as Becky, he making her laugh with stories of his indom-
itable younger sister, Madelyn. He told her about the ranch in
Montana, which he owned in partnership with Reese Duncan,
Madelyn's husband, and about their two rowdy little boys.

The sense of closeness with Robert was at once seductive and
terrifying. There was a powerful lure that drew her to him, creating an intimacy as much of the mind as of the body, so that
she was no longer a solitary creature but half of a *couple,* her
entire sense of being altering to include him. Sometimes, in the
back of her mind, she wondered how she would survive if he
were to leave—she had to think of it as *if* now, rather than *when*—
and the thought of losing him made her almost sick with terror.

She couldn't let herself worry about that. Loving him now, in
the present, demanded all her attention. She couldn't hold anything back; she was helpless to even try.

At the same time, the other part of her, the part that wasn't
preoccupied with Robert, worried incessantly about the bank loan
and the mortgage on the house. Tommy hadn't called her back.
She had called the bank twice; the first time he said that permission simply hadn't come through yet, but he didn't think there
was any problem and that she should just be patient. The second
time she called, he was out of town.

She couldn't wait much longer. It had already been eleven
days, leaving just nineteen until the loan had to be paid. If her
bank couldn't give her a loan, she would have to find a bank that
would, and if all banks moved so slowly, she could find herself
running out of time. Just thinking of the possibility was enough
to make her break out in a cold sweat.

She tried to think of other options, of some way to quickly
raise the money in case the loan didn't go through fast enough.
She could put her boat up for sale, but it wasn't worth even half
the amount that she needed and might not sell in time, anyway.
Asking Becky and Paul for a loan was out of the question; they
had their own financial responsibilities, and supporting two teenagers was expensive.

She could sell the rental boats, which would raise enough
money but deprive her of a surprisingly tidy bit of income. Of

course, with the loan paid, and if she didn't have to take out another one, she would have much more available cash and would soon be able to acquire more boats for rent. The only problem with that was time—again. In her experience, people took their time buying boats. Boats, even in a town like Guntersville that was geared toward the river, weren't a necessity of life. People looked at them, thought about it, discussed it over the dinner table, checked and double-checked their finances. It was possible, but unlikely, that she would be able to sell enough of them to raise the money she needed in the time she had.

Of the limited options available to her, however, that was the best one. She put a sign that read Used Boats For Sale in front of the marina and posted other notices in the area tackle stores. Even if she sold only one, that would lower the amount of money she would need to borrow.

Robert noticed the sign immediately. He walked in late that afternoon, removed his sunglasses and pinned her with a pale, oddly intense look. ''That sign out front—which boats are for sale?''

''The rental boats,'' she calmly replied and returned her attention to waiting on a customer. Once she had made the decision to sell the boats, she hadn't allowed herself any regrets.

He moved behind the counter and stood in front of the window with his hands in his pockets, looking out at the marina. As she had known he would, he waited until the customer had left before turning to ask, ''Why are you selling them?''

She hesitated for a moment. She hadn't told him anything about her financial worries and didn't intend to do so now, for a variety of reasons. One was simply that she was reticent about personal problems, disinclined to broadcast her woes to the world. Another was that she was fiercely possessive about the marina, and she didn't want word to get around that it was on shaky financial ground. Yet another was that she didn't want Robert to think she was obliquely asking for a loan, and she would be distressed if he offered one. He was obviously wealthy, but she didn't want the issue of money to become a part of their relationship. If it did, would he ever be certain, in his own mind, that her attraction to him wasn't based on his wealth? Still another reason was that she didn't want anyone else to have a share, and thus a say-so, in the marina. Banks were one thing, individuals another. The marina was *hers,* the base on which she had rebuilt the ruins of her life. She simply couldn't give up any part of it.

So when she answered, she merely said, "They're getting old, less reliable. I need to buy newer ones."

Robert regarded her silently. He didn't know whether to hug her or shake her, and in fact he could do neither. It was obvious that she was trying to raise money by any means available, and he wanted to put his arms around her and tell her it would be all right. But his instinct to protect his own had to be stifled, at least for now. Despite his decision that she was largely innocent in Mercer's espionage dealings, the small chance that he was wrong about her wouldn't let him relent. Soon he would know for certain, one way or the other. But if she sold the rental boats, what means would Mercer use to deliver the goods? Every one of those rental boats was now equipped with tiny electronic bugs that would allow them to be tracked; if Mercer was forced to use some other boat, or even change his method of delivery entirely, Robert would lose his control of the situation.

On the plus side, he was certain Mercer would act soon. They had intercepted a very suspicious phone call, putting them on the alert. It didn't matter if Evie managed to sell a couple of boats, or even most of them, so long as she had one remaining when Mercer made his move. He would simply have to monitor the situation and step in to prevent a sale if it looked as if she would manage to unload all of them.

Aloud he asked, "Have you had any offers yet?"

She shook her head, a wry smile curving her mouth. "I just put the sign up this morning."

"Have you put an ad in any of the newspapers?"

"Not yet, but I will."

That might bring in more customers than he could block, he thought with a sigh. The easiest way would be to stop the ads from being printed; there weren't that many area newspapers. The phones both here and at her house were being monitored, so he would know which papers she called. Somehow he hadn't expected to have so much trouble keeping abreast of her maneuvers. Evie was a surprisingly resourceful woman.

Five days later, Evie rushed in from overseeing a delivery of gas to answer the phone. She pushed a wisp of hair out of her face as she lifted the receiver. "Shaw's Marina."

"Evie? This is Tommy Fowler."

As soon as she heard his voice, she knew. Slowly she sank down onto the stool, her legs so weak that she needed the support. "What's the verdict?" she asked, though she knew the answer.

He sighed. "I'm sorry, hon. The board of directors says we already have too many real-estate loans. They won't okay the mortgage."

Her lips felt numb. "It isn't your fault," she said. "Thanks, anyway."

"It isn't a lost cause. Just because we aren't making that type of loan right now doesn't mean other banks aren't."

"I know, but I have a deadline, and it's down to fourteen days. It's taken you longer than that to tell me no. How long would it take to process a loan at any other bank?"

"Well, we took longer than usual. I'm sorry as hell about it, Evie, but I had no idea the okay wouldn't go through. Go to another bank. Today, if possible. An appraiser will have to make an estimate of the house's value, but it's waterfront property and in good shape, so it's worth a lot more than the amount you want to mortgage. Getting an appraiser out there is what will take so much time, so get started as soon as you can."

"I will," she said. "Thanks, Tommy."

"Don't thank me," he said glumly. "I couldn't do anything. Bye, hon."

She sat there on the stool for a long time after she hung up the phone, trying to deal with her disappointment and sense of impending disaster. Though she had been worried, the worry had been manageable, because even though she had been making contingency plans, she had been certain the mortgage would go through.

She hadn't sold a single boat.

Time was of the essence, and she didn't have a lot of faith in getting a loan through any other bank. It was as if an evil genie was suddenly in control of things, inflicting her with malfunctioning machinery and uncooperative banks.

Still, she had to try. She couldn't give up and perhaps lose the marina from lack of effort. She *wouldn't* lose the marina. No matter what, she simply refused to let it go. If she couldn't get a mortgage, if she couldn't sell the boats, she had one other option. It was strictly last-resort, but it was there.

She picked out a bank with a good reputation and called to make an appointment with a loan officer for the next morning.

The heat was already intense the next day when she was getting ready. Despite the ceiling fans, her skin was damp with perspiration, making her clothes cling to her. Robert hadn't asked why her house was so hot, but the past three nights he had insisted on taking her to his home and bringing her back after breakfast. This morning she had showered at his house as she usually did, then asked him to bring her home earlier than usual because she had a business appointment at nine. He hadn't asked any questions about that, either.

She retrieved her copy of the deed from the fireproof security box under the bed and braced herself like a soldier going to war. If this bank wouldn't give her a loan, she wasn't going to waste any more time going to another one. Time was too short. She would rather be too hasty than take the chance of losing the marina.

She rolled the truck window down, and the wind blowing in her face cooled her as she drove to the bank. The heat was building every day, and soon it would be unbearable in the house if she didn't turn on the air-conditioning. She smiled grimly. She might as well turn it on; one way or the other, she would have the money to pay the power bill.

Her appointment was with a Mr. Waldrop, who turned out to be a stocky, sandy-haired man in his late forties. He gave her a strangely curious look as he led her into his small office. Evie took one of the two comfortable chairs arranged in front of the desk, and he settled into the big chair behind it.

"Now then, Mrs. Shaw, what can we do for you today?"

Concisely, Evie told him what she needed, then pulled the copy of the deed from her purse and placed it on his desk. He unfolded it and looked it over, pursing his lips as he read.

"It looks straightforward enough." He opened his desk and extracted a sheet of paper. "Fill out this financial statement, and we'll see what we can do."

Evie took the sheet of paper and went out to one of the small seating areas off the lobby. While she was answering the multitude of questions, her pen scratching across the paper, someone else came in to see Mr. Waldrop. She glanced up automatically, then realized she knew the newcomer, not an unusual occurrence in a small town like Guntersville. He was Kyle Brewster, a slightly shady businessman who owned a small discount store, dealing in seconds and salvage material. He was also known as a gambler and had been arrested once, several years back, when the back room of a pool hall had been raided on the information that an illegal game was being conducted there. Evie supposed that Kyle was fairly successful in his gambling; his style of living was considerably higher than the income from the discount store could provide.

The door to Mr. Waldrop's office was left open. She couldn't hear what Kyle was saying, only the indistinct drawl of his voice, but Mr. Waldrop's voice was more carrying. "I have the check right here," he was saying cheerfully. "Do you want to cash it, or deposit it into your account?"

Evie returned her attention to the form, feeling slightly heartened. If the bank would lend money to Kyle Brewster, she saw no reason why it wouldn't lend money to her. Her business was more profitable, and her character was certainly better.

Kyle left a few minutes later. When Evie completed the form, someone else had come in and was with Mr. Waldrop. She sat patiently, watching the hour hand on the clock inch to ten o'clock, then beyond. At ten-thirty, the other customer left and she carried the form in to Mr. Waldrop.

"Have a seat," he invited as he looked over the information she had provided. "I'll be back in a few minutes." He carried the form out with him.

Evie crossed her fingers, hoping the loan would be okayed that morning, pending an appraisal of the property. She would get the bank's appraiser out to the house if she had to call him ten times a day and hound him until he appeared.

More time ticked by. She shifted restlessly in the chair, wondering what was taking so long. But the bank seemed busy this morning, so perhaps the person Mr. Waldrop had taken the form to was also tied up, and Mr. Waldrop was having to wait.

Forty-five minutes later Mr. Waldrop returned to his office. He settled into his chair and tapped his fingertips together. "I'm sorry, Mrs. Shaw," he said with real regret. "We simply aren't making this type of loan right now. With the economy the way it is..."

Evie sat up straight. She could feel the blood draining from her face, leaving the skin tight. Enough was enough. "The economy is fine," she interrupted sharply. "The recession didn't hit down here the way it did in other parts of the country. And your bank is one of the strongest in the country. There was an article in one of the Birmingham papers just last week about this bank buying another one in Florida. What I want to know is why you would lend money to someone like Kyle Brewster, a known gambler with a police record, but you won't make a loan on a property worth five or six times that amount."

Mr. Waldrop flushed guiltily. A distressed look came into his eyes. "I can't discuss Mr. Brewster's business, Mrs. Shaw. I'm sorry. I don't make the decisions on whether or not to okay a loan."

"I realize that, Mr. Waldrop." She also realized something else, something so farfetched she could hardly believe it, but it was the only thing that made any sense. "I didn't have a chance of getting the loan, did I? Having me fill out that form was just for show. Someone is stepping in to block the loan, someone with a lot of influence, and I want to know who it is."

His flush turned even darker. "I'm sorry," he mumbled. "There's nothing I can tell you."

She stood and retrieved the deed from his desk. "No, I don't suppose you can. It would mean your job, wouldn't it? Goodbye, Mr. Waldrop."

She was almost dizzy with fury as she went out to the truck. The heat slammed into her like a blow, but she ignored it, just as she ignored the scorching heat of the truck's upholstery. She sat in the parking lot, tapping her finger against the steering wheel as she stared unblinkingly at the traffic streaming by on U.S. 431.

Someone wanted the marina. No one had made an offer to buy it, so that meant whoever it was knew she wasn't likely to sell. This mysterious someone was powerful enough, well-connected enough with the local bankers, to block her attempts to get a loan. Not only that, the original transfer of the loan from her bank to the New York bank had probably been arranged by this person, though she couldn't think of anyone she knew with that kind of power.

She couldn't think why anyone would want her little marina enough to go to such an extreme. Granted, she had made a lot of improvements in it, and business was better every year. When she paid off the outstanding debt, the marina would turn a healthy profit, but it wouldn't be the kind of money that would warrant such actions from her unknown enemy.

Why didn't matter, she thought with the stark clarity that comes in moments of crisis. Neither did *who*. The only thing that mattered was that she kept the marina.

There was one move she could make that wouldn't be blocked, because she wouldn't be the one obtaining the loan. She wouldn't breathe a word about this to anyone, not even Becky, until it was a done deal.

Numbly she started the truck and pulled out into traffic, then almost immediately pulled off again when she spotted a pay phone outside a convenience store. Her heart was thudding with slow, sickening power against her ribs. If she let herself think about it, she might not have the nerve to do it. If she waited until she got back home, she might look around at the dear, familiar surroundings and not be able to make the call. She had to do it now. It was a simple choice. If she lost the marina, she stood to lose everything, but if she sacrificed the house now, she would be able to keep the marina.

She slid out of the truck and walked to the pay phone. Her legs seemed to be functioning without any direction from her brain. There was no phone book. She called Information and got the number she wanted, then fed in another quarter and punched the required numbers. Turning her back on the traffic, she put her finger in her other ear to block out noise as she listened to the ringing on the other end of the line.

"Walter, this is Evie. Do you and Helene still want to buy my place on the river?"

"She stopped at a convenience store immediately after leaving the bank and made a call from a pay phone," the deep voice reported to Robert.

"Could you tell what number she called?"

"No, sir. Her position blocked the numbers from view."

"Could you hear anything she was saying?"

"No, sir. I'm sorry. She kept her back turned, and the traffic was noisy."

Robert rubbed his jaw. "Have you checked to see if it was the marina she called?"

"First thing. No such luck. She didn't call Mercer, either."

"Okay. It worries me, but there isn't anything we can do about it. Where is she now?"

"She drove straight home from the convenience store."

"Let me know if she makes any more calls."

"Yes, sir."

Robert hung up and stared thoughtfully out at the lake as he tried to imagine who she had called, and why. He didn't like the angry little suspicion that was growing. Had she called the unknown third party to whom Mercer had been selling the stolen computer programs? Was she involved up to her pretty little neck after all? He had backed her up against a financial wall, just to find out for certain, but he had a sudden cold, furious feeling that he wasn't going to like the results worth a damn.

Chapter Fifteen

"Would you like to go fishing this morning?" Robert asked lazily, his voice even deeper than usual. "We've never been out in a boat together."

It was six-thirty. The heat wave was continuing, each day seeing temperatures in the high nineties, and it was supposed to reach the hundred mark for the next few days, at least. Even at that early hour, Evie could feel the heat pressing against the windows.

It was difficult to think. Robert had just finished making love to her, and her mind was still sluggish with a surfeit of pleasure. He had awakened her before dawn and prolonged their loving even more than usual. Her entire body still throbbed from his touch, the echoes of pleasure still resounding in her flesh. The sensation of having him inside her lingered, though he had withdrawn and moved to lie beside her. Her head was cradled on one muscled arm, while his other arm lay heavily across her lower abdomen. She would have liked nothing better than to snuggle against him and doze for a while, then wake to even more love-making. It was only when she was sleeping, or when Robert was making love to her, that she was able to forget what she was doing.

But the throb of pleasure was lessening, and a dull ache resumed its normal place in her chest. "I can't," she said. "I have some errands to run." Errands such as finding a place to live. Walter and Helene Campbell had jumped at the chance to buy her house. They had wanted it for years and had decided to pay cash for it and worry about the financing later, afraid she would change her mind if she had a chance to think about it. Evie had promised she would be out within two weeks.

She couldn't bring herself to tell Robert, at least, not yet. She was afraid he would feel pressured to ask her to live with him, when he seemed perfectly satisfied with things the way they were now. It was difficult to think of anyone pressuring Robert to do anything he didn't want to do, and he might not offer, but neither did she want him to think she was hinting that he should. It would be best to find an apartment or house for rent first, then tell him about it.

For that matter, she hadn't told Becky, either. She hadn't told anyone. She had made her decision, but hadn't managed to come to terms with it yet. Every time she thought about moving, tears burned in her eyes. She couldn't bear to go into the explanations and listen to the arguments.

She didn't let herself think about who was behind all these financial maneuverings. First she had to concentrate on saving the marina and finding a place to live. After that was settled, she would try to find out who had been doing this to her.

"What kind of errands?" Robert asked, nuzzling her ear. His hand stroked warmly over her stomach, then covered her left breast. Her nipple, still sensitized from the strong suckling he had subjected it to a short while ago, twinged with a sharp sensation and immediately puckered against his palm. Her breathing deepened. Rather than becoming less intense with familiarity, his sensual power over her body seemed to increase each time he took her.

"I have to pay a few bills and do some shopping," she lied, and wondered why he'd asked. He had no compunction about taking over every facet of her private life but seldom inquired about what she did when they weren't together.

"Why not put it off until tomorrow?" His nuzzling was growing a bit more purposeful, and she closed her eyes as pleasure began to warm throughout her body again.

"I can't," she repeated regretfully. He rolled her nipple between this thumb and forefinger, making it even harder. She caught her breath at the tug of desire, as if the nerves of her nipples were directly connected to those in her loins.

"Are you certain?" he murmured, pressing his open mouth against the rapid pulse at the base of her throat.

Going fishing didn't tempt her, at least not in this heat. Lying in bed with him all morning, though, was so tempting it took all of her willpower to resist. "I'm certain," she forced herself to say. "It has to be done today."

Another man might have turned surly at having his advances refused, but Robert only sighed as he rested his head once again on the pillow. "I suppose we should get up, then."

"I suppose." She turned into him, pressing her face against his chest. "Hold me, just for a minute."

His arms tightened around her, satisfyingly tight. "What's wrong?"

"Nothing," she whispered. "I just like for you to hold me."

She felt his muscles tense. Abruptly he rolled on top of her, his hair-roughened thighs pushing hers apart. Startled, she looked up into slitted green eyes, glittering beneath those heavy black lashes. She couldn't read his expression but sensed his tightly contained violence.

"What—" she began to ask.

He thrust heavily into her, the power of his penetration making her body arch and shudder. He had had her only a little while before, but he was as hard as if that had never happened, so hard that she felt bruised by the impact of his flesh against hers. She gasped and clutched his shoulders for support. Not since the first time he'd taken her had he moved so powerfully. A primal feminine fear beat upward on tiny wings and mingled with an equally primitive sense of excitement. He wasn't hurting her, but the threat was there, and the challenge was whether she could handle him in this dangerous mood, all raw, demanding masculinity.

Desire flooded through her. She dug her nails into his muscular buttocks, pulling him deeper, arching her hips higher to take all of him. He grunted, his teeth clenched against the sound. Evie locked him to her, as fiercely female as he was dominatingly male, not only accepting his thrusts but demanding them. The sensation spiraled rapidly inside her, burning out of control, and she bit his shoulder. He cursed, the word low and hoarse, then slid his arms under her bottom to lift her even more tightly against him. All of his heavy weight bore her into the mattress as they strained together.

The sensation peaked, and Evie cried out as she shuddered wildly in the throes of pleasure. His hips hammered three more times; then he stiffened and began to shake as satisfaction took him, too. He ground his body against hers, as if he could meld their flesh.

The room slowly stopped spinning about her. She heard the twin rhythms of their panting breaths begin to calm. His heartbeat seemed to be thudding through her body, until it was in sync with her own. Their bodies were sealed together with sweat, heat rolling off them in waves.

Their first lovemaking of the morning had lasted an hour. This time, it hadn't taken even five minutes. The fury and speed of it, the raw power, left her even more exhausted than she'd been before.

What had aroused him so violently? After their first night Robert had been a slow, considerate lover, but he had just taken her like a marauder.

He was very heavy on top of her, making breathing difficult. She gasped, and he shifted his weight to the side. Pale green eyes opened, the expression still shuttered. His mouth had a ruthless line to it. "Stay with me today," he demanded.

Regret pierced her, sharp and poignant. "I can't," she said. "Not today."

For a split second something frightening flickered in his eyes, then was gone. "I tried," he said with rueful ease, rolling off her and sitting up. He stretched, rolling his shoulders and lifting his muscled arms over his head. Evie eyed his long, powerful back with pleasure and approval. The layered muscles were tight and hard, the deep hollow of his spine inviting kisses, or clutching hands. He was wide at the shoulders, his body tapering in a lean vee to his hips. She reached out and ran a lingering hand over the round curve of his buttocks, loving the cool resilience of his flesh.

He looked at her over his shoulder, and she saw a smile come into those green eyes. He leaned over to kiss her, his mouth lingering warmly for a moment; then with a yawn he was off the bed and heading toward the shower. She watched him until he closed the bathroom door behind him, drinking in his tall, naked body. She felt like smacking her lips, like a child drooling after a tasty treat. He was a fine figure of a man, all right. Sometimes, when she saw him sprawled naked and sleepy beside her, it was all she could do to keep from attacking him. She lay in bed for a while, listening to the shower run and entertaining a wicked, delicious fantasy in which he was tied to the bed and totally at her mercy.

But a glance at the clock told her that time was still ticking away. Sighing, she got out of bed and slipped into his shirt, then went to the kitchen to make coffee.

When she returned, he was just coming out of the bathroom, a towel draped around his neck but otherwise still completely naked. His skin was glowing from the shower, his black hair wet and slicked back.

"I put on the coffee," she said as she went to take her turn in the shower.

"I'll start breakfast. What do you want this morning?"

The thought of what she had to do that day killed her appetite. "I'm not hungry. I'll just have coffee."

But when she had showered and dressed, she went into the kitchen to find that he had his own ideas about what she was having for breakfast. A bowl of cereal, as well as a glass of orange juice and the requested coffee, was sitting at her customary place at the table. "I'm really not hungry," she repeated, lifting the coffee cup and inhaling the fragrant steam before sipping.

"Just a few bites," he cajoled, taking his own place beside her. "You need to keep up your strength for tonight."

She gave him a heated, slumberous look, remembering her fantasy. "Why? Are you planning something special?"

"I suppose I am," he said consideringly. "It's special every time we make love."

Her heart swelled in her chest, making it impossible for her to speak. She simply looked at him, her golden brown eyes glowing.

He picked up the spoon and put it into her hand. "Eat. I've noticed you haven't been eating much while it's been so hot, and you're losing weight."

"Most people would consider that a good thing," she pointed out.

His black eyebrows lifted. "I happen to like your butt as round as it is now, and your breasts perfectly fit my hands. I don't want to sleep with a stick. Eat."

She laughed, amused by his description of her rear end, and dipped the spoon into the cereal. It was her favorite brand, of course; once he had seen the box in her cabinets, a box of the same cereal had taken up residence in his.

She managed to choke down a few bites, more than she wanted and not enough to satisfy him, which was a reasonable compromise. The cereal felt like a lump in her stomach.

Less than an hour later he kissed her goodbye at her door. "I'll see you tonight, sweetheart. Take care."

As she entered the house, she thought it a little odd for him to have added that last admonition. What on earth did he think she would be doing?

Sadly she dressed for work, so she wouldn't have to come back to the house before going to the marina. She wouldn't be braiding her hair in front of this mirror very many more times, she thought. After this afternoon, the house would no longer belong to her. Walter and Helene were getting a real estate agent, a friend of theirs, to handle the transaction immediately. They were supposed to bring all the paperwork to the marina this afternoon, along with a cashier's check in the specified amount. Evie was taking the deed to the property, the surveyor's report that she had had done when she inherited the house, as well as the certification of the title search that had also been done at that time. It was a measure of their trust in her that they were willing to forgo another title search, probably against their agent friend's advice.

She addressed an envelope to the bank in New York, stamped it and added it to her stack of papers. She would take the cashier's check immediately to her bank, desposit it and have another cashier's check made out in the amount of the outstanding loan against the marina. Then she would express-mail that check to New York, to Mr. Borowitz's attention. All her financial troubles would be over.

She wouldn't have her home any longer, but she could live anywhere, she told herself. The marina was more important, the means of her support. With it, she could someday buy another house. It wouldn't hold the memories this one did, but she would make it into a home.

She took a last look in the mirror. "Standing here won't get anything done," she said softly to herself and turned away.

She spent the morning driving around Guntersville. She had checked a few of the rental ads in the newspaper but didn't want to call them yet, preferring to see the houses and the neighborhoods before calling. She knew she was just stalling, despite the urgency of the situation, but somehow actually making contact was beyond her at the moment. She gave herself a stern talking-to, but it didn't help much. She didn't like any of the houses she saw.

It was almost noon when she came to a decision. She made an abrupt turn, causing a car behind her to squeal its tires and the irate driver to lean on the horn. Muttering an apology, she cut through a shopping-center parking lot and back onto the highway, but in the opposite direction.

The apartment complex she had chosen was new, less than two years old, incongruously known as the Chalet Apartments. She stopped the truck outside the office and went inside. Twenty minutes later she was the new resident of apartment 17, which consisted of a living room and combination dining room/kitchen downstairs, along with a tiny laundry area just big enough to hold a washer and dryer, and two bedrooms upstairs. There were no one-bedroom apartments available. She paid a deposit, collected two sets of keys and went back out to the truck.

It was done. She doubted she would be happy there, but at least she would have a roof over her head while she took her time looking for a house.

The cellular phone beeped, and Robert answered it as he threaded his way through the traffic on Gunter Avenue, the one-way street that bisected Guntersville's downtown area and also ran through a neighborhood of grand old houses that looked turn-of-the-century.

"I think she spotted me."

"What happened?" he asked in a clipped tone.

"First she just drove around, all over town. I had to hang back so I wouldn't be as easy to spot. She slowed down several times but didn't stop anywhere. Maybe she was looking for something. Then she got on the highway, going south toward Albertville. She was on the inside lane, I was on the outside. All of a sudden, without a turn signal, she whipped the truck into a parking lot and nearly got hit doing it. I was in the wrong lane and couldn't follow her. By the time I got turned around, she'd vanished."

"Damn." Robert felt both tired and angry. Just when he'd been convinced of Evie's innocence, she was suddenly doing some very suspicious things. She was obviously worried about the marina, but there was something else on her mind, something she was trying to keep hidden. This mornng, in bed, he had been seized by the urgent need to keep her with him all day, thereby preventing her from doing anything foolish. He wasn't used to women refusing any request he made, but Evie didn't appear to have any trouble doing it. She had said no with insulting ease.

Furious, he had even tried to seduce her into staying with him, only to lose his control, something he'd sworn wouldn't happen again. And afterward she'd still said no.

"I'll pick her up again when she comes to the marina," the man said in his ear. "I'm sorry, sir."

"It wasn't your fault. No tail's perfect."

"No, sir, but I should have been more careful about letting her see me."

"Have two cars next time, so you can swap."

"Yes, sir."

Robert ended the call and replaced the receiver. It took all his self-control to keep from driving to the marina to wait for her so he could shake some sense into her as soon as he saw her. But he had to play this through to the end.

As mundane as it was, he had his own errand to run that day: grocery shopping. It wasn't something he normally did for himself, but it wasn't an onerous duty. Despite its strangeness, or perhaps because of it, he didn't mind doing it. Southerners imbued grocery shopping with the same casualness that characterized almost everything else they did. Shoppers ambled down the aisles, stopping to talk with chance-met acquaintances or to strike up conversations with strangers. The first time he had gone into the big grocery store, he had been amused by the thought that a New Yorker relaxed in the park with more energy than Southerners shopped. But when in Rome... He had learned to slow his own pace, to keep from smashing into old ladies who had stopped to pass the time of day.

Today, though, he wasn't in the mood to be amused. It went against his protective, controlling nature to leave Evie to hang herself with all the evidential rope he was feeding to both her and Mercer. He wanted to snatch her away from here, kidnap her if necessary. But if she *were* involved with Mercer, that would scare off the others and they might never be caught. Not knowing for certain, one way or the other, was driving him crazy with frustration.

Two more days. From the telephone calls they had intercepted, they knew that Mercer would transfer more stolen data the day after tomorrow. Evie hadn't been able to sell any of the rental boats, so that was one less problem for Robert. It didn't matter which boat Mercer took, since they were all wired. As a precaution, he had also had Evie's boat wired. In two days it would all be over except for the cleanup. In three days, if all went on schedule, he would be back in New York, and Evie would be with him.

He wouldn't need many groceries, just enough for three days, but he was completely out of coffee and almost out of food, and he didn't want to eat in restaurants for three days. He strode through the aisles of the grocery store, his expression remote as he planned the damage-control measures he would use. Operating with his usual efficiency, he was in and out of the store within fifteen minutes. As he walked out the automatic doors with a grocery bag in his arms, though, the woman just entering through the other set of doors stopped and stared at him.

"Robert."

He paused, immediately recognizing Evie's sister, Becky. Another shopper was exiting behind him, and he stepped out of the way. "Hello, Becky. How are you?" He smiled faintly. "And how's Jason? I haven't seem him at the marina again."

"Didn't Evie tell you? He can't come back to the marina for the rest of the summer. That's a real punishment to him," Becky said dryly. "The marina's one of his favorite places." She too, stepped away from the doors. "There's no sense standing here blocking traffic. I'll walk you to your car."

They strolled across the hot, sticky pavement. The heat was smothering, and sweat began to gather almost immediately on his skin. Wryly he waited, seeing Becky's determination plain on her face. The protective older sister wanted to have a heart-to-heart talk with him, to make certain he didn't hurt Evie.

They reached the Jeep, and he stored the groceries inside, leaving the door open so some of the heat inside could dissipate. He leaned against the vehicle and calmly eyed her. "You worried about Evie?" he prompted.

She flashed him a rueful look. "Am I that easy to read?"

"She mentioned that you're a bit protective," he murmured.

Becky laughed and pushed her hair out of her face. Her hair was darker than Evie's, but in that moment Robert saw a flash of resemblance, a similarity in expression and in the husky tone of their voices. "The big-sister syndrome," she said. "I didn't use to be this bad, only since—"

She stopped, and Robert felt his curiosity stir. "Since when?"

Becky didn't answer immediately, instead turning her gaze to the traffic on the highway. It was a delaying tactic, to give her time to think and organize her answer. He waited patiently.

"Are you serious about her?" she asked abruptly.

He wasn't accustomed to being interrogated about his intentions, serious or otherwise, but he quelled his surge of irritation. Becky was asking only out of concern for Evie, an emotion he shared. In a very level tone he said, "I intend to marry her."

Becky closed her eyes on a sigh of relief. "Thank God," she said.

"I didn't realize the state of our relationship was so critical," he said, still in that cool, dead-level tone.

Becky's eyes opened, and she gave him a considering look. "You can be very intimidating, can't you?"

He almost smiled. If he could, it obviously wasn't working on her. He'd never managed to intimidate Evie, either.

Becky sighed and looked again at the traffic. "I was worried. I didn't know how important Evie is to you, and...well, the success of your relationship *is* critical to her."

His curiosity became intense. "In what way?"

Becky didn't answer that directly, either. Instead she asked, "Has she told you about Matt?"

Robert's eyes glittered suddenly. "Probably more than even you know," he said, his voice deepening as he remembered the first time he'd made love to Evie.

"About how he died?"

Sweat trickled down his back, but suddenly nothing could have moved him from the scorching asphalt parking lot. "He died in a car accident, didn't he?" He couldn't remember if Evie had told him that, or if it had been in the report he'd requested on Matt Shaw.

"Yes, the day after they married." She paused, organizing her thoughts, and again she made what appeared to be a shift in topic. "Our father died when Evie was fifteen. I was twenty, already married, already about to be a mother. A year later our mother died. Can you understand the difference in the way losing our parents affected us?" she asked, her voice strained. "I loved them both dearly, but I had built my home with Paul. I had him, I had my son, I had an entire life away from my parents. But losing Daddy shook Evie's foundations, and then when Mother died...Evie didn't just lose Mother, she lost her home, too. She came to live with Paul and me, and we loved having her, but it wasn't the same for her. She was still just a kid, and she had lost the basis of her life."

Robert stood silently, all his attention on this insight into Evie's past life. She didn't talk about her childhood much, he realized. They had talked about a lot of things, sitting on the deck at night with all the lights off and the starry sky spread like a quilt overhead, but it was as if Evie had closed a mental door on her life before Matt's death.

"But she had Matt," Becky said softly. "He was a great kid. We'd known him all his life, and I can't remember when they hadn't been inseparable, first as buddies, then as sweethearts. They were the same age, but even as young as he was, when Daddy died, Matt was right there beside Evie. He was there with her when Mother died. I think he was her one constant, the only person other than me who had been there for as long as she could remember. But I had my own family, and Evie had Matt. He put a smile back in her eyes, and because she had him, she weathered the loss of our parents. I remember what she was like back then, a giggling teenager as rowdy as Jason is now, and full of mischief."

"I can't picture Evie as rowdy," he commented, because Becky's voice had become strained, and he wanted to give her a moment to compose herself. "There's something so solemn about her."

"Yes, there is," Becky agreed. "Now."

The jealousy he thought he had banished swelled to life again. "Because of Matt's death."

Becky nodded. "She was in the car with him." Tears welled in her eyes. "For the rest of my life, I'll carry two pictures of Evie in my mind. One is of her on her wedding day. She was so young and beautiful—so *glowing*—that it hurt to look at her. Matt couldn't take his eyes off her. The next time I saw her, she was in a hospital bed, lying there like a broken doll, her eyes so empty that—" She stopped, shuddering.

"They had spent the night in Montgomery and were going on to Panama City the next morning. It was raining. It was Sunday, and they were in a rural area. There wasn't much traffic. A dog ran out into the highway, and they hit it, and Matt lost control of the car. The car left the road and rolled at least twice, then came to a stop, on its right side, in a stand of trees. Evie was pinned on the bottom. Matt was hanging in his seat belt above her. She couldn't get out, couldn't get to him, and he b-bled to death in front of her, his blood dripping down on her. He was conscious, she said.'' Furiously Becky dashed the tears from her cheeks. ''No one saw the car for a long time, what with the rain and the trees blocking the view. He knew he was dying. He told her he loved her. He told her goodbye. He'd been dead for over an hour before anyone saw the car and came to help.''

Robert turned to stone, his eyes burning as he pictured, far too clearly, what a young girl had gone through that rainy Sunday. Then he reached out automatically and took Becky in his arms, holding her head against his shoulder while she wept.

''I'm sorry,'' she finally managed, lifting her head and wiping her eyes yet again. ''It's just that, when I let myself think about it, it tears my heart out all over again.''

''Yes,'' he said. Still holding her with one arm, he fished his handkerchief out of his pocket and gently wiped her face.

''She's never let herself love anyone else,'' she said fiercely. ''Do you understand? She hasn't risked letting anyone else get close to her. She's stuck with the people she already loved, before the accident—Paul and me, Jason and Paige, and a few, very few, special friends, but no one else. If you hadn't pulled her and Jason out of the river, she would have drowned rather than let him go, because she couldn't have stood to lose anyone else she loves. She's been so…so *solitary,* keeping everyone a safe distance from her heart.''

''Until me,'' he said.

Becky nodded and managed a wavery little smile. ''Until you. I didn't know whether to be glad or terrified, so I've been both. I want her to have what I've got, a husband I love, kids I love, a family that will give her a reason to go on living when someone else dies.'' She saw the sudden flare in Robert's eyes and said quickly, ''No, she never said anything about suicide, not even right after Matt died. That isn't what I meant. She recovered from her injuries—both legs were broken, some ribs, and she had a concussion—and did exactly what the doctors told her, but you could see that she wasn't interested. For *years,* life for her was just going through the motions, and every day was an effort. It took a long time, but finally she found a sort of peace. Evie's incredibly strong. In her place, I don't know if I could have managed it.''

Robert kissed Becky's forehead, touched and pleased by this fiercely competent woman's concern for her sister. He would, he realized, like having her for a sister-in-law. ''You can put down your shield and sword, and rest,'' he said gently. ''I'll take care of her now.''

''You'd better,'' Becky said, her fierceness not one bit abated. ''Because she's already paid too much for loving people. God only knows where she found the courage to love you. I've been terrified that you didn't care about her, because if you waltzed out of here at the end of the summer, it might well destroy her.''

Robert's eyes glittered. ''When I waltz out of here,'' he said, ''I'm taking her with me.''

Chapter Sixteen

Walter and Helene Campbell were in their mid-sixties, retired, comfortable but not wealthy. Evie's house was just what they wanted, well-built and maintained, but old enough and small enough that her asking price was much less than what they would have paid for a new house on the lakefront. They were both thrilled to the point of giddiness at their unexpected good fortune, for though they had asked several times if she would sell, they had long since given up hope that she would.

They arrived at the marina over half an hour early, their estate agent in tow and bearing a huge sheaf of papers. Having never bought or sold a house before, Evie was struck by the amount of paperwork it evidently required and amazed that the agent had managed to get it all prepared in less than a day.

There weren't sufficient chairs for everyone to sit down, so they stood grouped around the counter. The agent explained the purpose of each document as he presented it first for her signature, then the Campbells'. After an hour of dedicated document-signing, it was finished. Evie had sold her house, and the check was in her hand.

She managed a smile to send the joyous Campbells on their way, but as soon as the door had closed behind them, her smile collapsed. She closed her eyes and shuddered in an effort to control the grief that had been growing since she had made the phone call the day before. No matter that she had told herself it was just a house and she could live anywhere, it was her _home,_ and she had just lost part of herself. No, not lost it—sold it.

But the marina was a more important part of her foundation, and the green cashier's check in her hand had just saved it.

She wiped the betraying moisture from her eyes and braced her shoulders. She called Burt and told him she had to go to the bank and would be back in about half an hour. "Okay," he said, as laconic as ever, when she asked him to watch for customers.

The transaction at the bank took very little time. The Campbells' cashier's check was deposited and a new cashier's check cut in the amount she owed on the loan. Tommy Fowler saw her standing at the counter and came out to speak to her, his eyes anxious.

"How're you doing, Evie?"

She heard the worry in his tone and managed a version of the same smile she had given the Campbells. "I'm okay. I have the money to pay the loan."

Relief flooded his face. "Great! That didn't take long. So another bank gave you the mortgage?"

"No, I sold my house."

The relief faded, and he stared at her, aghast. "Sold your house? But, Evie...God, why?"

She wasn't about to tell him, with the teller and other customers listening, that she suspected someone of blocking the mortgage. "It was something I'd been thinking about," she lied. "Now my bank account is healthy, the marina is out of debt and will turn a pure profit, and I can take my time looking for another house."

Varying expressions were flickering across Tommy's face like slides. The final one, a rather uneasy relief, was testament to his belief in her pragmatic lie. "I guess it's worked out, then," he said.

She kept her smile intact with an effort. "Yeah, I guess it has."

The teller handed the check over the counter to her, and she slipped it into the envelope. "I'm getting this mailed today," she said to Tommy. "Thanks for all you did."

"I didn't manage to do anything," he replied.

"Well, no, but you tried."

She left the bank and drove straight to the post office, where the precious envelope was dispatched by express mail. She felt a sense of finality. It was done; she had gotten past this. It hadn't been easy, but now she could move on.

Robert was waiting at the marina when she got back. "Where have you been?" he demanded, striding up as she slid out of the truck.

She blinked at the unguarded fierceness of his tone. Robert was seldom overt in his reactions, except in bed. "The bank and the post office. Why?"

He didn't answer but caught her shoulders in a hard grasp and pulled her to him. His mouth was heavy and hungry, demanding rather than seducing a response from her. Evie made a muffled sound of surprise, her hands lifting to rest against his chest, but she gave him what he wanted, her mouth opening to admit the thrust of his tongue, her lips shaping to the pressure of his.

Passion rose sharply between them, strong and heady. She hadn't recovered her balance after the difficult events of the day and she melted against him, drawn irresistibly to the whipcord strength of his body. Although a whirlwind was tossing the rest of her life about, he wasn't swayed but remained solidly on his feet and in control. Though she had bitterly resisted—and feared—coming to depend on him, his very presence now made her feel better. She was both aroused and comforted by the familiarity of his body, his warm animal scent, all the subtle details by which she knew her mate.

He drew back, hampered by the public nature of the parking lot. Inside wouldn't be much better, with people coming and going. He threaded his hands through her hair, tilting her face back so he could read every nuance of her expression. He must have been pleased by the drowning look of desire he saw there, for his fingers tightened on her scalp. "Not here, damn it. But as soon as I get you home..." He didn't have to finish the sentence. Raw lust was on his face and in his voice, violent and intense.

Recalled to where she was, Evie cast a half-embarrassed look around and touched his hand as she slipped from his grasp. How many hours until they could go home? She didn't know if she could wait that long. Her body was throbbing.

The long afternoon was an exercise in self-control, and she wished the summer days weren't quite so long. She needed Robert, needed his driving presence within her, taking her into oblivion so she could forget everything but the almost narcotic pleasure of making love with him. She felt raw, her emotions sharp and too near the surface.

It was difficult, when she was finally able to close the marina that night, to hold to the schedule they had established. Robert wanted to take her straight to his house, but she resisted. "I don't want to leave my truck here overnight," she said. "You'd either have to bring me to pick it up in the morning or waste your morning hanging around so you could drive me to work."

"It wouldn't be a waste," he growled, his lean face taut, and she knew what he envisioned them doing to pass the time.

Temptation weakened her, but she shook her head again. "It would be so blatant, if my truck was still here and you brought me to work. Craig—"

"You're worried about Craig knowing that we sleep together?" he asked, amusement lighting his eyes. "He's seventeen, sweetheart, not seven."

"I know, but...this isn't New York. We're more conventional down here."

He was still smiling, but he gave in with good grace. "All right, protect his tender sensibilities, though I have to tell you that most teenage boys have the sensibility of a rhino in heat."

She laughed, and it felt good, her heart lightening. "Then let's just say that *I* wouldn't feel comfortable."

He kissed her forehead. "Then go home, sweetheart. I bought some fillets this afternoon, and I'll get them ready to grill before I pick you up."

"I have a better idea," she said. "You start grilling, and I'll drive over. That will save even more time."

He smiled again as he rubbed his thumb over her lower lip in a gentle caress. "You make me feel like a teenage rhino myself," he murmured, and she blushed.

Anticipation heated her blood as she drove home, preoccupying her so much that she showered and dressed without more than a twinge of sadness. Her heartbeat pounded in the rhythm of his name.

It was still hot, so hot that she couldn't bear the idea of encasing her legs in clothing, but she didn't want to wear shorts. She opted instead for a gauzy blue skirt and a sleeveless, scoop-necked chemise, with her breasts unconfined beneath. The floaty skirt was virtually transparent, clearly showing her legs, but allowed air to filter through the flimsy fabric and cool her skin. She would never have worn it out in public, but to Robert's house…yes, definitely.

He came to the door when he heard the truck in his driveway. His face tightened as he watched her walk toward him. "God," he muttered. As soon as she was inside, he slammed the door and caught her arm, pulling her rapidly down the hall to the bedroom.

"What about the steaks?" she cried, startled by his haste despite the pleasant frustration of the afternoon.

"Screw the steaks," he said bluntly, wrapping his arms around her and falling across the bed. His heavy weight crushed her into the mattress. With a quick motion he flipped the skirt to her waist and caught the waistband of her panties, tugging them down her legs. When her feet were free, he tossed her underwear aside and pulled her thighs apart, kneeling between them.

Evie laughed, the sound low and provocative. He hadn't even kissed her, and her entire body was throbbing. He was tearing at his belt buckle with impatient fingers, and she added her hands to the confusion, trying to find the tab of his zipper and pull it down. She could feel the hard, swollen ridge of his sex, pushing at his clothing. He grunted as his length sprang free and lowered himself between her legs.

No matter how many times he took her, she always felt a small sense of surprise at his size and heat, and a flutter of uncertainty at the stretching sensation that followed the initial pressure as he sank deep within. She gasped, her entire body lifting to the impact. She was tender from the unbridled lovemaking of the morning, his thrusting sex rasping against inner tissues that were sensitive to the least touch. Intense pleasure rippled through her, tossing her unprepared into paroxysms of satisfaction. She cried out, her hands digging into his back as the shivery delight went on and on, past bearing, until she thought she would die if he didn't let the pleasure ebb. He was muttering hotly in her ear, sex words, the sound indistinct but the meaning clear.

And then he shuddered, too, holding himself deep as the spasms took him. Afterward, he lay heavily on her, both of them breathing deeply in the exhausted aftermath. Drowsily she let her eyes drift shut, only to open them again as he suddenly chuckled, the small movement shaking them both. "Definitely like a teenager," he murmured, nuzzling the lobe of her ear before taking it between his teeth and gently biting it. "No matter how often I have you, I want you again almost as soon as I move off you. The only time I'm satisfied is when we're like this." He thrust lazily, their bodies still linked.

"Then let's stay like this." She ran her hands down his muscular back, feeling the heat of him through the fabric of his shirt. "Someone will find us in a couple of weeks."

He laughed and kissed her. "They'd probably think, wow, what a way to go, but I'd prefer both of us being warm and pliable. If I want to keep you that way, I suppose I'd better feed you, hadn't I?" He kissed her again and rolled away to sit up.

She stretched, replete, the afternoon's aching frustration relieved. Even the hollowness in her chest had faded, though by no means vanished. She had never had this before, she thought dimly, this bone-deep sense of connection. And she wouldn't have it now if Robert had been less ruthlessly determined to have his way.

They spent the next couple of hours grilling the steaks, then sitting out on the deck after they had eaten and cleaned the kitchen. The night was thick and warm, the temperature still in the high eighties. Robert stretched out on a chaise longue and pulled Evie down on top of him. There were no lights on in the house, and the concealing darkness was like a blanket. They lay there in the heavy, peaceful silence, with his hand slowly moving over her back. Slowly his caresses grew more purposeful, and Evie melted against him. Her chemise top was lifted off over her head and dropped to the deck. She hadn't put her underwear back on, so when his hand moved under the gauzy skirt, he touched only the bare flesh of her thighs and buttocks. He cupped the twin mounds in his hands and held her hard against him, nestling his arousal in the soft junction of her thighs.

"You have on too many clothes," she murmured, kissing the underside of his jaw.

"You, on the other hand, hardly have on any."

"Whose fault is that?" Her wandering mouth nibbled down his neck. "I was completely dressed when I arrived here."

"I wouldn't say that, sweetheart. Even if your nipples hadn't been sticking out like little berries, the delicious jiggle of your breasts when you walked made it obvious you weren't wearing anything under your top. And this thing," he continued lazily, grasping a handful of material, "doesn't qualify as a skirt." Tiring of her mouth being on his throat rather than his own mouth, he pulled her up for a long kiss, during which his own clothing was opened and removed. Sighing with pleasure, she lifted the skirt out of the way and settled over him, gasping a little as he slid inside her.

Then they lay quietly again, bodies linked, content with the sensation as it was. The lights of a night fisherman drifted by on the lake, but they were shielded by the darkness. Sometime later it became difficult to lie still. Hidden impulses twinged deep inside, inviting undulating movement. She resisted, but knew he was feeling the same compulsion. He was growing even harder, reaching deeper into her, and a fine tension invaded his muscles as he lay motionless beneath her.

She pressed her forehead hard against his jaw, fighting not to move. He throbbed inside her, and she moaned softly. Her inner muscles clenched in helpless delight on his invading length, then did so again, and her soft cries floated in the night air as the moment took her. In an effort to control his own reaction, Robert gripped her bottom hard, his teeth clenched against the almost overwhelming need to give in. He won, but sweat beaded on his forehead from the struggle.

When she stilled, he lifted her from him and bent her over the end of the chaise. He knelt behind her, his thighs cupping hers, and thrust heavily into her moist, relaxed sheath. She clung to the chaise, unable to stifle her moans of pleasure as his rhythmic motion increased in speed and power. He convulsed, flooding her with warmth, and lay heavily over her for a long time, while his breathing slowed and his heartbeat returned to normal.

Recovered, he gathered their scattered clothing and pushed it into her arms, then lifted her and carried her inside, to the big bed that awaited them.

They slept late the next morning, until after nine o'clock. She yawned and stretched like a sleepy cat, and Robert held her close, stroking her tangled hair away from her face. As usual, he had awakened her at dawn with silent, drowsy lovemaking; then they had both gone back to sleep.

With a quick kiss and a lingering pat on her bare bottom, he left the bed and headed toward his shower. Evie yawned again and got up herself. She slipped into his shirt as she went to the kitchen to make coffee. "Robert, you need an automatic timer on your coffeemaker," she muttered to herself as she scooped the coffee into the round filter. Not that they would ever remember to prepare the coffee and set the timer before they went to bed.

Standing there in the sun-drenched kitchen, listening to the coffeemaker pop and hiss, she became aware that she felt strangely light, almost carefree. She hugged herself in an effort to contain the elusive feeling. She was happy, she thought with some surprise. Despite selling the house, she was happy. She had saved the marina, and she had Robert. Most of all, she had Robert.

Her love for him quietly grew each time she was with him. He was such a complicated, controlled, private man; no matter how often he made love to her, he still kept that inner core of himself inviolate, not allowing her or anyone else inside. Knowing that had no effect on the way she felt about him. He hadn't opened his heart to her, but that in no way made him less worthy of love. He might never love her, she realized. But if this was all he could give a woman, then she would take it.

A ringing interrupted the quiet. It sounded like a telephone, but the phone there in the kitchen definitely wasn't ringing, and this sound was muffled, as if it were in a different room. The line in Robert's office must be a different number, she realized. He was in the shower and wouldn't be able to hear it. It rang only once, though, and she realized that the answering machine there must have picked up the call.

She walked down the hall to the office and opened the door. The whirring sound of the fax machine greeted her. So it hadn't been a call, after all, but a fax.

The machine stopped whirring and lapsed into silence after having spat out only one sheet of paper. As she turned to go, her eye was caught by a name on the page, and curiously she turned back.

It was her name that had caught her attention.

The message was brief. "Mr. Borowitz just reported that a cashier's check from E. Shaw, in full payment of the outstanding amount, was delivered by express mail and received by him. His hands are tied. Further instructions?" The scrawled signature looked like "F. Koury."

Evie picked up the page and read it again. At first she was merely puzzled. Why would this F. Koury be telling Robert that she had paid the loan? And why would Mr. Borowitz be reporting it at all? Robert didn't even know about the loan, much less the threat of foreclosure.

Her mind stopped, along with her breathing. She hung there, paralyzed by a sickening realization. Robert knew all about it because he was the one who had been blocking her efforts to mortgage the house. He was also the reason why her loan had been bought, and why Mr. Borowitz had been so intractable in demanding full payment. He had been instructed to give her no cooperation at all, instructed by Robert Cannon. Her lover was her enemy.

Her chest was hurting. She gasped and resumed breathing, but the pain remained, a cold, heavy lump in her chest. The sense of betrayal was suffocating.

Obviously Robert was far wealthier and more powerful than she had imagined, to have this much influence, she thought with detached calm. She didn't know why he wanted her marina, but he obviously did. There were a lot of why's she couldn't comprehend, particularly right now. Maybe later, when she could think better, some of this would make sense.

Right now, all she could think was that Robert had tried to take over her marina and had cost her her home.

That distance she had sensed in him had been all too real. He hadn't committed his heart because, for him, it had all been business. Had he seduced her simply so he could stay close and keep tabs on what she was doing? Given what else he had done, that seemed to her like a reasonable assumption.

Her lips felt numb, and her legs moved like an automaton's as she left the office, carefully closing the door behind her. The damning fax was still in her hand as she returned to the kitchen.

The hopeless enormity of the situation overwhelmed her. How ironic that she had fallen in love with the man who was coolly trying to destroy her! Oh, she doubted he looked at it in such melodramatic terms, but then, he probably saw the whole thing as a successful business takeover, rather than a love affair.

She heard the shower cut off. With slow, achingly precise movements, she folded the fax and dropped it into the trash, then poured a cup of coffee. She desperately needed the caffeine, or anything, to bolster her. Her hands were shaking slightly as she lifted the cup to her lips.

She was standing in front of the window when Robert came into the kitchen a few moments later, wearing only a pair of jeans and still rubbing a towel across his chest. He stopped, his entire body clenching at the sight of her. God, she was breathtaking, with her mane of tawny gold hair loose and tousled. She was wearing only his shirt, and it was unbuttoned. There had never been another garment invented, he thought with a surge of desire, that looked better on a woman than a man's shirt. She was sipping coffee and looking out the window, lost in thought, her expression as calm and remote as a statue's.

He dropped the towel and went to her, sliding one arm around her as he took the cup and lifted it to his own lips. He imagined he could taste her on the rim, but then, his senses were so attuned to her that he could pick her out of a crowd blindfolded.

No woman had ever responded to him the way Evie did. She

was pure fire in his arms, reveling in every thrust, tempting more from him. If he was gentle, she melted. If he was rough in his passion, she clung to him, clawed at him, her soaring desire feeding his own until they were both frenzied with need. He wanted her incessantly.

He smoothed his hand over the curve of her bottom, delighting in the silky texture of her flesh. "The shower's all yours, sweetheart."

"All right," she said automatically, but he had the impression she didn't really hear him. She was still looking out the window.

He tipped his head to see if he could tell what had her so interested. He saw only a wide expanse of lake, dotted with a few boats. "What are you looking at?"

"Nothing. Just the lake." She turned away from his embrace and left the kitchen.

Robert's brows briefly knit in puzzlement, but he was hungry, and breakfast took precedence at the moment. He had scarcely gotten the bacon started when Evie reappeared in the kitchen, fully dressed, and with her keys in her hand.

"A fax came in while you were in the shower," she said quietly.

He turned, going still at what he saw in her face—or rather, what he didn't see. She was pale and expressionless, her eyes empty. With a chill, he remembered how Becky had described the look in Evie's eyes after the accident and he knew it must have been something like this. She looked so terribly remote, as if she had somehow already left.

"Who was it from?" he asked, keeping his voice gentle while his mind raced, sorting through the possibilities, all of them damning. The worst-case scenario was if she was indeed working with Mercer and had found out that the trap was closing tight about them.

"An F. Koury."

"Ah." He nodded, concealing a sense of relief. "My secretary." Probably it had nothing to do with Mercer, then, but why was Evie looking so frozen?

"It's there in the trash, if you want to read it, but I can tell you what it said."

He leaned against the cabinet and crossed his arms, eyeing her carefully. "All right. Tell me."

"Mr. Borowitz notified your secretary that he'd received a cashier's check from E. Shaw for payment in full of the loan, and that his hands were tied. She asked for further instructions."

Robert's expression didn't change, but inwardly he was swearing viciously. Of all the things for Evie to stumble onto! It was less damaging, from a security standpoint, than anything connected with Mercer would have been, but a hell of a thing to try to explain to a lover. He'd never intended her to know about it. The pressure had been real, but he would never have let it go to foreclosure. He didn't rush into explanations but waited for her reaction so he could better gauge what to say to her. And how in hell had she managed to get the money to pay the loan?

"You're the reason I couldn't get a mortgage on my house," she said, her voice so strained it was almost soundless.

She'd put it together quickly, he thought. But then, from the beginning, she'd proven herself to be uncomfortably astute. "Yes," he said, disdaining to lie.

"You're behind the loan being sold to another bank in the first place."

He inclined his head and waited.

She was gripping the keys so tightly that her fingers were white. He noted that small giveaway of emotion held in check. She took several shallow breaths, then managed to speak again. "I want your boat gone from my marina by the end of the day. I'll refund the balance of the rent."

"No," he said gently, implacably. "I'm holding you to the agreement."

She didn't waste her breath on an argument she couldn't win. She had hoped he would have the decency to do as she asked, but given his ruthless streak, she hadn't really expected it.

"Then leave it there," she said, her voice as empty as her eyes. "But don't call me again, because I don't want to talk to you. Don't come by, because I don't want to see you."

Sharply he searched her expression, looking for a way to penetrate the wall she had thrown up between them. "You won't get rid of me that easily. I know you're angry, but—"

She laughed, but it was raw and hollow, not a sound of amusement. Robert winced. "Is that how you've decided to 'handle' me? I can see you watching me, trying to decide which angle to take to calm me down," she said. "You never just react, do you? You watch and weigh other people's reactions so you can manipulate them." She heard the strain in her voice and paused to regain control of it. "No, I'm not angry. Maybe in fifty years or so, it'll just be anger." She turned on her heel and started for the door.

"Evie!" His voice cracked like a whiplash, and despite herself, she stopped, shivering at the force of will he commanded. This wasn't the cool strategist speaking but the ruthless conqueror.

"How did you pay off the loan?" The words were still sharp.

Slowly she looked at him over her shoulder, her eyes dark and unguarded for a moment, stark with pain. "I sold my house," she said, and walked out.

R̲obert started to go after her, then stopped. Instead he swore and hit the countertop with his fist. He couldn't explain anything to her, not yet. Every instinct in his body screamed for him to stop her, but he forced himself to let her go. He stood rigidly, listening as the truck door slammed and the motor started. She didn't spin the wheels or anything like that; she simply backed out of the driveway and drove away without histrionics.

God! *She had sold her house.* The desperation of the action staggered him, and with sudden, blinding clarity he knew, beyond the faintest doubt, that she wasn't involved with Mercer in any way. A woman who could make money by espionage would never have sold her home to pay a debt. She had appeared to be leaving the marina and meeting with Mercer on the lake, but it must have been nothing more than damnable coincidence. Evie was totally innocent, and his machinations had cost her her home.

She wouldn't listen to anything he said right now, but after he had the espionage ring broken up and Mercer safely behind bars, he would force her to understand why he had threatened foreclosure on her loan. That he had suspected her of espionage was another rocky shoal he would have to navigate with care. He didn't imagine it would be easy to get back into her good graces, but in the end he would have her, because he didn't take no for an answer when he really wanted something. And he wanted Evie as he had never wanted anything or anyone else in his life.

He would have to make amends, of course, far beyond apologies and explanations. Evie was the least mercenary person he'd ever met, but she had a strong sense of justice, and an offer of reparation would strike a chord with her. He could buy her house from the new owners—they probably wouldn't be willing to sell at first, but he cynically suspected that doubling the price would change their minds—and present her with the deed, but he far preferred that she have a newer, bigger house. The simplest thing would be to deed over his own house to her. It meant nothing to him, he could buy a house anywhere he wanted, but Evie needed a base that was hers and hers alone. It would be a vacation home, a getaway when they needed a break from the hubbub of New York, a place for her to stay when she wanted to visit Becky.

He fished the damning fax out of the trash and read it. Three concise sentences, Felice at her most efficient. There was nothing more he could do about the loan; realizing that, she had de-prioritized it and sent the information by fax so he could have it immediately but respond at his leisure, rather than calling and wasting both his time and hers. Felice was a genius at whittling precious seconds here and there so she would have more time to devote to the truly important matters. In this instance, however, her knack for superefficiency had worked against him and perhaps cost him Evie.

No. No matter what, he wouldn't let Evie go.

Evie drove automatically, holding herself together with desperate control. She tried to empty her mind, but it wasn't possible. How could she be so numb but hurt so much at the same time? She literally ached, as if she had been beaten, yet felt somehow divorced from her body. She had never felt as remote as she did now, or as cold and hollow. The heat of the sun washed over her, but it didn't touch her. Even her bones felt cold and empty.

Why? She hadn't asked him that and couldn't think of a reason that would matter. The why of it wasn't important. The hard fact was that he had sought her out for a reason that had nothing to do with love or even attraction, used the intimacy he had deliberately sought as a means to gather information that he wanted, and then turned that knowledge against her. How had he known about the loan in the first place? She supposed it was possible a credit report would have given him the information, but a far more likely explanation was that he had simply taken a look through the papers in her desk at home. There had been ample opportunity for him to do so; the very first time he had been in her house, she remembered, was when he had brought her home to change clothes after Jason had fallen in the water, and she had left him alone while she showered and changed.

She didn't know why he had targeted her marina, and she didn't care. She marked it down to simple avarice, the greedy impulse to take what belonged to others.

She hadn't known him at all.

She was still calm and dry-eyed when she reached her house. No—not her house any longer, but the Campbells'. Dazed, she unlocked the door and walked inside, looked at the familiar form and content of her home, and bolted for the bathroom. She hung over the toilet and vomited up the little coffee she had swallowed, but the dry, painful heaves continued long after her stomach was emptied.

When the spasms finally stopped, she slumped breathless to the floor. She had no idea how long she lay there, in a stupor of exhaustion and pain, but after a while she began to cry. She curled into a ball, tucking her legs up in an effort to make herself as small as possible, and shuddered with the violent, rasping sobs that tore through her. She cried until she made herself sick and vomited again.

It was a long time before she climbed shakily to her feet. Her eyelids were swollen and sore, but she was calm, so calm and remote that she wondered if she would ever be able to feel anything again. God, she hoped not!

She stripped, dropping her clothes to the floor. She would throw them out later; she never wanted to see that skirt again, or any other garment she had worn that night. She was shivering as she climbed into the shower, where she stood for a long time, letting the hot water beat down on her, but the heat sluiced off her skin just like the water, none of it soaking in to thaw the bone-deep cold that shook her.

She would have stood there all day, paralyzed by the mind-numbing pain, but at last the hot water began to go and the chill forced her out. She wanted nothing more than to crawl into bed, close her eyes and forget, but that wasn't an option. She wouldn't forget. She would never forget. She could stay in the shower forever, but it wouldn't wash his touch off her flesh or his image out of her mind.

He had never wanted her at all. He had wanted the marina.

The marina. Her mind fastened on it with desperate gratitude. She still had the marina, had salvaged something from the ruin Robert Cannon had made of her life. No matter how much damage he had done, he hadn't won.

The habits of years took over as she moved slowly about, getting ready to go to work. After towel-drying her hair, she stood in front of the bathroom mirror to brush out the tangles and braid it. Her own face looked back at her, white and blank, her eyes dark, empty pools. Losing Matt had been devastating, but she had carried the knowledge of his love deep inside. This time she had nothing. The care Robert had shown her had been an illusion, carefully fostered to deceive her. The passion between them, at least on his part, had been nothing more than a combination of mere sex and his own labyrinthine plotting. The man could give lessons to Machiavelli.

He had destroyed the protective shield that had encased her for so many years. She had thought she couldn't bear any more pain, but now she was learning that her capacity for pain went far beyond imagination. She wouldn't die from it, after all; she would simply rebuild the shield, stronger than before, so that it could never be penetrated again. It would take time, but she had time; she had the rest of her life to remember Robert Cannon and how he had used her.

She hid her sore, swollen eyes behind a pair of sunglasses and carefully drove to the marina, not wanting to have an accident because she wasn't paying attention. She refused to die in a car accident and give Cannon the satisfaction of winning.

When she drove up to the marina, everything looked strangely normal. She sat in the truck, staring at it for a few seconds, bewildered by the sameness of it. So much had happened in such a short time that it seemed as if she had been gone for weeks, rather than overnight.

No matter what, she still had this.

Robert prowled the house like a caged panther, enraged by the need to wait. Waiting was alien to him; his instinct was to make a cold, incisive decision and act on it. The knowledge of the pain Evie must be feeling, and what she must be thinking, ate at him like acid. He could make it up to her for the house, but could he heal the hurt? Every hour he was away from her, every hour that passed with her thinking he had betrayed her, would deepen the wound. Only the certainty that she would refuse to listen to him now kept him from going after her. When Mercer was in jail, when he had the proof of what he'd been doing and could tell her the why, then she would listen to him. She might slap his face, but she would listen.

It was almost three o'clock when the phone rang. "Mercer's moving early," his operative barked. "He panicked and called them from the office. No dead drop this time. He told them that he needed the money immediately. It's a live handoff, sir. We can catch the bastards red-handed!"

"Where is he now?"

"About halfway to Guntersville, the way he was driving. We have a tail on him. I'm on the way, but it'll take me another twenty-five minutes to get there."

"All right. Use the tracking device and get there as fast as you can. I'll go to the marina now and get ahead of him. He's never seen my boat, so he won't spot me."

"Be careful, sir. You'll be outnumbered until we can get there."

Robert smiled grimly as he hung up the phone. Everything he needed was in the boat: weapons, camera, binoculars and tape recorder. Mercer's ass was in a sling now.

He drove to the marina, ignoring the speed laws. He only hoped Evie wouldn't come out when she saw him and do something foolish like cause a scene. He didn't have time for it, and he sure as hell didn't want to attract any attention. He tried to imagine Evie causing a scene, but the idea was incongruous. No, she wouldn't do that; it wasn't her style at all. She would simply look through him as if he didn't exist. But when he reached the marina, he didn't take any chances. He went straight to the dock where his boat was moored, not even glancing at the office.

Evie heard him drive up. She knew the sound of that Jeep as intimately as she knew her own heartbeat. She froze, trying to brace herself for the unbearable, but the seconds ticked past and the door didn't open. When she forced herself to turn and look out the window, she caught a glimpse of his tall, lean figure striding purposefully down the dock toward his boat. A minute later she heard the deep cough of the powerful motor, and the sleek black boat eased out of its slip. As soon as he was out of the Idle Speed Only zone, he shoved the throttle forward, and the nose of the boat rose like a rearing stallion as the craft shot over the water, gaining speed with every second.

She couldn't believe how much it hurt just to see him.

Landon Mercer walked in ten minutes later. Loathing rose in her throat, choking her, and it was all she could do to keep from screaming at him. Today, though, there was none of the slimy come-on attitude he thought was so irresistible; he was pale, his face strained. He was wearing slacks and a white dress shirt, the collar unbuttoned. Sweat beaded on his forehead and upper lip. He carried the same tackle box, but no rod and reel.

"Got a boat for me, Evie?" he asked, trying to smile, but it was little more than a grimace.

She chose a key and gave it to him. "Use the one on the end."

"Thanks. I'll pay you when I get back, okay?" He was already going out the door when he spoke.

Something in her snapped. It was a quiet snap, but suddenly she had had enough. Mercer was definitely up to no good, and today he hadn't even made the pretense of going fishing. The marina was all she had left, and if that bastard was dealing drugs and dragged her into it by using her boats, she might lose the marina after all.

Over her dead body.

It was too much, all the events of the day piling on top of her. She wasn't thinking when she strode out to the truck and retrieved her pistol from under the seat, then hurried to her own boat. If she had been thinking, she would have called the police or the water patrol, but none of that came to mind. Still reeling from shock, she could focus on only one thing—stopping Mercer.

Robert had positioned his boat where he could see Mercer leave the marina and fall in behind him without attracting his notice. The tracking device was working perfectly, the beeping increasing in speed as Mercer approached his position, then decreasing as the rental boat sped past. Not wanting to get too close and scare off the people Mercer was meeting, he started the motor and began idling forward, letting Mercer put more distance between them.

Another boat was coming up fast on the left, intersecting his path at a right angle. There was enough space that Robert didn't have to back off his speed, and he kept his eye on the diminishing dot on Mercer's boat. Then the other boat flashed across his line of vision, and he saw a long blond braid bouncing as the boat took the waves.

Evie! His heart leapt into his throat, almost choking him. Her appearance stunned him; then, suddenly, he knew. *She was following Mercer!* That was what she'd been doing all along. With that unsettling intuition of hers, she had known that Mercer was up to no good and had taken it upon herself to try to find out what it was. He even knew her reasoning: by using one of her boats, Mercer was involving her marina. Robert knew better than most to what lengths she would go to protect that place. She would give up her home, and she would risk her life.

Swearing savagely, he picked up the secure phone and punched in the number even as he pushed the throttle forward. "Evie is following Mercer," he snarled when the call was answered on half a ring. "She's on our side. Pass the word and make damn sure no one fires on her by mistake!"

His blood ran cold at the thought. None of his people would shoot at her, but what about the others?

* * *

Mercer was heading toward the islands again, as she had known he would. She kept about five hundred yards between them, enough distance that her presence wouldn't worry him, at least not yet. She would close the gap in a hurry when he reached the islands and slowed down.

The pistol lay in her lap. It was a long-barreled .45 caliber, very accurate, and she not only had a license to carry it, she knew how to use it. Whatever Mercer was doing, it was going to stop today.

There was another boat anchored between two of the smaller islands, two men inside it. Mercer didn't take his usual circuitous route around and through the islands, but headed straight toward the other boat. Grimly Evie increased her speed and followed.

Mercer pulled up alongside the other boat and immediately passed the tackle box over. Evie saw one of the men point to her as she neared, and Mercer turned to look. She wasn't wearing a hat or sunglasses, and though her hair was braided, she knew she was easily recognizable as a woman. But she didn't care if Mercer recognized her, because the time for stealth was past.

The fact that she was a woman, and alone, made them less cautious than they should have been. Mercer was standing, his feet braced against the gentle rocking of the boat. Confident that they hadn't been caught doing anything suspicious, he said something in a low tone to the two other men, then raised his voice to call to her. "Evie, is something wrong?"

She waved to allay any suspicions. She was still twenty yards away. She eased the throttle into neutral, knowing that the boat would continue nosing forward for several yards even without power. Then, very calmly, she lifted the pistol and pointed it at the man holding the tackle box.

"Don't make me nervous," she said. "Put the tackle box down."

The man hesitated, darting a petrified look at his partner, who was still behind the wheel of the boat. Mercer was frozen, staring at her and the huge pistol in her hand.

"Evie," he said, his voice shaking a little. "Listen, we'll cut you in. There's a hell of a lot of money—"

She ignored him. "I told you to put the box down," she said to the man who was holding it. Her mind still wasn't functioning clearly. All she could think was that if he dropped the tackle box into the river, the evidence would sink and there wouldn't be any way of proving what he was doing. She had no idea how she would manage to get three men and three different boats to the authorities, but there was a lot of boat traffic on the river this afternoon, and eventually someone would come over this way.

Another boat was coming up behind her already, way too fast. Mercer's attention switched to it, and a sick look spread over his face, but Evie didn't let her attention waver from the man holding the tackle box. A sleek black boat appeared in her peripheral vision, nosing up to the side of the boat holding the two men. Robert rose from the seat, holding the steering wheel steady with his knee as he leveled a pistol on the three men, his two-fisted grip holding the weapon dead level despite the rocking of the boat.

"Don't even twitch a muscle," he said, and the tone of his voice made Evie risk a quick glance at him. The facade of urbanity had fallen completely away, and he made no attempt now to disguise his true nature. The lethal pistol in his hand looked like a natural extension of his arm, as if he had handled weapons so often it was automatic to him now. His face was hard and set, and his eyes held the cold ferocity of a hunting panther.

The waves made by Robert's boat were washing the others closer together, inexorably sweeping Evie's boat forward to collide with them. "Look out," she warned sharply, dropping one hand to the throttle to put her motor into reverse, to counteract the force of the waves. The two other boats bumped together with staggering force, sending Mercer plunging into the river. The man holding the tackle box cursed and flailed his arms, fighting for balance, and dropped the box. It fell into the bottom of the boat. Robert's attention was splintered, and in that instant the driver of the boat reached beneath the console and pulled out his own weapon, firing as soon as he had it clear. Evie screamed, her heart stopping as she tried to bring her pistol around. Robert ducked to the side, and the bullet tore a long gouge out of the fiberglass hull. Going down on one knee, he fired once, and the driver fell back, screaming in pain.

The second man dived sideways into the rental boat. Mercer was clinging to the side, screaming in panic as the man hunched low in the boat and turned the ignition key. The motor coughed into life, and the boat leapt forward. Knowing she couldn't get a good shot at a moving target, especially with her own boat still rocking, Evie dropped the pistol and shoved the throttle back into forward gear. The two boats collided with a grinding force that splintered the fiberglass of both craft, her more powerful motor shoving her boat on top of the other. The impact tossed her out of the seat, and she hit the water with a force that knocked her senseless.

She recovered consciousness almost immediately but was dazed by the shock. She was underwater, the surface only a lighter shade of murky green. There was a great roaring in her ears, and a vibration that seemed to go straight through her. Boats, she thought dimly, and terror shot through her as she realized how much danger she was in. If the drivers couldn't see her, they might drive right over her, and the propeller would cut her to pieces.

She clawed desperately for the surface, kicking for all she was worth. Her head cleared the water, and she gulped in air, but there was a boat almost on top of her, and she threw herself to the side. Someone in the boat yelled, and she heard Robert's deep voice roaring, but she couldn't understand his words. Her ears were full of water, and dizziness made everything dim. If she passed out, she thought, she would drown. She blinked the water out of her eyes and saw the wreckage of the two boats, not five yards away. She struggled toward it and shakily hooked her arm over the side of the rental boat. It was very low in the water and would probably sink within half an hour, but for now it was afloat, and that was all that mattered.

The boat that had almost hit her was idling closer. Two men were in it, dressed in jeans and T-shirts. The driver brought the boat around sideways to her, and the other man leaned out, his arm outstretched to her. The sunlight glinted off a badge pinned to the waistband of his jeans. Evie released the rental boat and swam the few feet to the other craft. The man caught her arms, and she was hauled out of the water and into the boat.

She sank down onto the floor. The man knelt beside her. His voice was anxious. "Are you all right, Mrs. Shaw?"

She was panting from exertion, gulping air in huge quantities, so she merely nodded. She wasn't hurt, just dazed from the impact, so dazed that it was a minute before she could wonder how he knew her name.

"She's okay!" she heard him yell.

Gradually her confusion faded, and things began to sort themselves out. She remained quietly in the bottom of the boat, propped against one of the seats, and watched as the two men in the water were hauled out and roughly handcuffed, and the man Robert had shot was given medical aid. Though pale and hunched over, he was still upright and conscious, so Evie assumed he would live.

Four more boats had arrived, each of them carrying a team of two men, and all of those men wore badges, either pinned to their jeans or hung around their necks. She heard one of them briskly identify himself to Mercer as FBI and assumed that they all were.

Other boats who had seen the commotion on the water were approaching but stopped at a short distance when they noticed the badges. "Y'all need any help with those boats?" one fisherman called. "We can keep 'em afloat and haul 'em to a marina, if you want."

She saw one agent glance at Robert, as if for permission, then say, "Thanks, we'd appreciate your help." Several of the fishermen idled foward and added their boats to the snarl.

Evie resisted the urge to look at Robert, though she could feel his hard, glittering gaze on her several times. For the rest of her life she would remember the cold terror she'd felt when that man had shot at him and she had thought she would have to watch another man she loved die in front of her. The devastation she'd been feeling all day, bad as it was, paled in comparison to that horror. Robert didn't want her, had used her, but at least he was alive. Reaction was setting in, and fine tremors were starting to ripple through her body.

The mopping-up seemed to take forever, so long that her sopping clothes began to dry, as stiff as cardboard from the river water. The wounded man was placed in another boat and taken for further medical attention, with two agents in attendance. Mercer and the other man were taken away next, both of them handcuffed. There was a lot of maneuvering around the two wrecked boats as the salvaging continued. Gathering her strength, she took control of the boat she was in, while the driver added his efforts to the job. Finally, though, it all seemed to be winding down. Robert brought his boat alongside the one Evie was handling.

"Are you all right?" he asked sharply.

She didn't look at him. "I'm fine."

He raised his voice. "Lee, get this boat. I'm taking Evie back to the marina."

Immediately the agent clambered back into the boat, and Evie relinquished her place behind the wheel. She didn't want to go anywhere with Robert, however, and looked around for anyone else she knew.

"Get in the boat," he said, his voice steely, and rather than make a fool of herself, she did. There was no way to avoid him, if he was determined to force the issue. If he wanted to discuss private matters, then she would prefer that they were private when he did.

Nothing was said on the ride back to the marina. The black boat moved like oiled silk over the choppy waves, but still every small bump jolted her head. She closed her eyes, trying to contain the nausea rising in her throat.

As Robert throttled down to enter the marina, he glanced over at her and swore as he took in her closed eyes and pale, strained face. "Damn it, you *are* hurt!"

Immediately she opened her eyes and stared resolutely ahead. "It's just reaction."

Coming down off an adrenaline high could leave a person feeling weak and sick, so he accepted the explanation for now but made a mental note to keep an eye on her for a while.

He idled the boat into his slip, and Evie climbed onto the dock before he could get out and assist her. True daughter of the river that she was, she automatically tied the lines to the hooks set in the wood, the habits of a lifetime taking precedence over her emotions. The boat secured, she turned without a word and headed toward the office.

Burt was behind the counter when she entered, and a look of intense relief crossed his lined face, followed by surprise and then concern when he saw her condition. It went against his grain to ask personal questions, so the words came reluctantly out of his throat, as if he were forcing them. "Did the boat flip? Are you all right?"

Two questions in a row from Burt? She needed to mark this date on her calendar. "I'm all right, just a little shaken up," she said, wondering how many more times that day she would have to say those words. "The boat's wrecked, though. Some guys are bringing it in."

Robert opened the door behind her, and Burt's expression went full cycle, back to relief. "I'll get back to the shop, then. How long do you reckon it'll take 'em to get the boat here?"

"About an hour," Robert answered for her. "They'll have to idle in." He went to the soft-drink machine and fed in quarters, then pushed the button. With a clatter, the bottle rolled down into the slot, and he deftly popped off the top.

"Well, don't make no difference. I reckon I'll stay until they get here." Burt left the unnatural surroundings of the office and headed back to where he felt most comfortable, leaving the oily smell of grease behind.

Evie walked behind the counter and sat down, wanting to put something between herself and Robert. It didn't work, of course; he knew all the moves, all the stratagems. He came behind the counter, too, and propped himself against it with his long legs outstretched and crossed at the ankle.

He held out the Coke. "Drink this. You're a little shocky and need the sugar."

He was probably right. She shrugged and took the bottle, re-membering another time when she'd been fished out of the water, and how he had insisted she drink very sweet coffee. The last thing she wanted to do was faint at his feet, so she tilted the bottle and drank.

He watched until he was satisfied that she was going to follow his orders, then said, "Mercer was manager of my computer programming firm in Huntsville. We've been working on programs for the space station, as well as other things, and the programs are classified. They began turning up where they shouldn't. We figured out that Mercer was the one who was stealing them, but we hadn't managed to catch him at it, so we didn't have any proof."

"So that's what was in the tackle box," she said, startled. "Not dope. Computer disks."

His dark eyebrows rose. "You thought he was a drug dealer?"

"That seemed as plausible as anything. You can't sneak up on anyone in the middle of the river. He must have been weighting the package and dropping it in a shallow spot between the islands, and the others were picking it up later."

"Exactly. But if you thought he was a drug dealer," he said, his voice going dangerously smooth, "why in hell did you follow him today?"

"The federal seizure law," she replied simply. "He was in my boat. I could have lost everything. At the very least, he could have given the marina a bad reputation and driven away business."

And she would do anything to protect the marina, he thought furiously, including sell her house. Of course she hadn't balked at following a man she suspected of being a drug dealer! She had been armed, but his blood ran cold at the thought of what could have happened. She had been outnumbered three to one. In all honesty, however, she had had the situation under control until the waves from his boat had washed them all together.

"You could have killed yourself, deliberately ramming the boat like that."

"There wasn't much speed involved," she said. "And my boat was bigger. I was more afraid of the gas tanks exploding, but they're in the rear, so I figured they'd be okay."

She hadn't had time to consider all that, he thought; her reaction had been instantaneous and had nearly given him a heart attack. But a lifetime spent around boats had given her the knowledge needed to make such a judgment call. She hadn't known that reinforcements were almost there, she had simply seen that one of them was about to escape, and she had stopped him. Robert didn't know if she was courageous or foolhardy or both.

She still hadn't so much as glanced at him, and he knew he had his work cut out for him. Carefully choosing his words, he said, "I've been working with the FBI and some of my own surveillance people to set a trap for Mercer. I soured some deals he had made, put some financial pressure on him, to force him to make a move."

It didn't take more explanation than that. Watching her face, he saw her sort through the implications and the nuances of what he had just said, and he knew the exact moment when she realized he had also suspected her. A blank shield descended over her features. "Just like you did with me," she murmured. "You thought I was working with him, because he was using my boats, and because I'd been following him, trying to find out what he was doing."

"It didn't take me long to decide that if you were involved at all, you probably didn't realize what was going on. But you kept doing suspicious things, just enough that I didn't dare relax my pressure on you."

"What sort of suspicious things?" she asked, a note of disbelief entering her flat tone.

"Leaving the marina in the middle of the day to follow him. The day before yesterday, when you left the bank, you immediately stopped at a pay phone and made a call that we couldn't monitor. Yesterday you led the guy following you all over Guntersville, then ditched him by making an abrupt turn across traffic, and we weren't able to find you again until you came to work."

Evie laughed, but the sound was bitter and disbelieving. "All that! It's amazing how a suspicious mind can see suspicious actions everywhere. When the mortgage was turned down a second time, I realized there had to be someone behind it, someone who was blocking the loans. I couldn't lose the marina. The only thing left to do was sell the house, and I knew if I didn't make the call right then, I'd lose my nerve. So I stopped at the first pay phone I came to and called some people who have tried several times to buy the house, to see if they were still interested. They were so interested that they decided to pay me immediately rather than take a chance that I'd change my mind.

"Yesterday," she said softly, "I was looking for a place to live. But I knew I was just dithering, and that the longer I put it off, the worse it would be. So I made a quick turn, drove to an apartment complex and rented an apartment."

Yes, he thought, watching her colorless face. A quick, sharp pain was better than endless agony. Innocent actions based on desperate decisions.

She shrugged. "I thought you wanted the marina. I couldn't figure out why. It means a lot to me, but if you were looking for a business investment, there are bigger, more profitable ones around. Instead, you thought I was a traitor, and what better way to keep tabs on me than to start a bogus relationship and push it until we were practically living together?"

This was the tricky part, he thought. "It wasn't bogus."

"The moon isn't round, either," she replied, and turned to look out the windows at her kingdom, saved at such cost to herself.

"I wasn't going to go through with the foreclosure," he said. "It was just a means of pressure. Even if you'd been guilty, I'd already decided to prevent them from prosecuting you."

"How kind of you," she murmured.

He uncrossed his ankles and left the support of the counter, moving until he was directly in front of her. He put his hands on her shoulders, warmly squeezing. "I know you're hurt and angry, but until Mercer was caught, I didn't dare ease up on the pressure."

"I understand."

"Do you? Thank God," he said, closing his eyes in relief.

She shrugged, her shoulders moving under his hands. "National security is more important than hurt feelings. You couldn't have done anything else."

The flat note was still in her voice. He opened his eyes and saw that he hadn't cleared all the hurdles. The issue of the house was still between them.

"I'm sorry about your house," he said gently. "I would never have let you sell it if I'd known that was what you were planning." He cupped her cheek with one hand, feeling the warm silkiness of her skin under his fingers. "I can't get your house back, but I can give you mine. I'm having the deed made over in your name."

She stiffened and jerked her face away from his hand. "No, thank you," she said coldly, standing up and turning to stare out the window, her back to him.

Of course she had jumped to the wrong conclusion, he thought, annoyed with himself that he had brought up the house before settling the other issue. "It isn't charity," he said in a soothing tone, putting his hand on the nape of her neck and gently rubbing the tense muscles he found there. "It isn't even much of a gesture, come to that, since it will be staying in the family. Evie, sweetheart, will you marry me? I know you love it here, but we can compromise. I won't take you completely away from your family. We can use the house for vacations. We'll come down every summer for a long vacation, and of course we'll visit several times during the year."

She pulled away from him and turned to face him. If she had been white before, she was deathly pale now. Her golden brown eyes were flat and lusterless, and with a chill he remembered how Becky had said she'd looked after Matt had died. What he saw in Evie's eyes was an emotional wasteland, and it froze him to the bone.

"Just like everything else, your *compromises* are heavily in your favor," she said, a rawness in her voice that made him flinch. "I have a better one than that. Why don't you stay in New York, and I'll stay here, and that way we'll both be a lot happier."

"Evie..." He paused, forced himself to take a deep breath and reached for control. She was wildly off balance, of course, with everything that had happened today. She loved him, and he had hurt her. Somehow he had to convince her to trust him again.

"No!" she said violently. "Don't try to decide. how you're going to manipulate me into doing what you want. You're too intelligent for your own good, and too damn subtle. Nothing really reaches you, does it?" She spread her hands far apart and gestured. "You're over here, and everyone else is way over here, and never the twain shall meet. Nobody and nothing gets close to you. You're willing to marry me, but nothing would change. You'd still keep yourself closed off, watching from the distance and pulling strings to make all the puppets do what you want. What I had with Matt was *real,* a relationship with a person instead of a facade! What makes you think I'd settle for what you're offering?" She stopped, shuddering, and it was a moment before she could speak again. "Go away, Robert."

_____ *Chapter Eighteen*

Evie's absence left a great, gaping hole in his life. Robert had never before in his life missed a woman or let one assume enough importance to him that he was lonely without her, but that was the predicament he found himself in now. After her flat rejection of his marriage proposal, he'd returned to New York the next day and immediately taken up the threads of his business concerns, but the social whirl he had enjoyed before seemed simultaneously too frantic and too boring. He didn't want to attend the opera or the endless parade of dinner parties; he wanted to sit out on the deck in the warm, fragrant night, listening to the murmur of the river and enjoying the array of stars scattered across the black sky. He wanted to lie naked on the chaise with Evie, motionless, their bodies linked, until their very stillness was unbearably erotic and they both shattered with pleasure.

Sex had always been a controlled but extremely important part of his life, but now he found himself unresponsive to the lures cast his way. His sex drive hadn't abated; it was driving him crazy. But he didn't want the controlled pleasure he'd known before, his mind staying remote from his body. He hadn't been remote when he'd made love with Evie, and several times he hadn't been controlled, either. Having her naked under him, thrusting into her tight, unbelievably hot sheath, and feeling her turn into pure flame in his arms...

The carnal image brought him to full arousal, and he lunged to his feet to prowl restlessly around the apartment, swearing between his teeth with every step. Nothing else made him hard these days, but just the thought of Evie could do it. He wanted her, and her absence was like acid, eating away at his soul.

He still couldn't decide what had gone wrong. He sensed the answer, but it was an ethereal thing, always floating just beyond his comprehension. His inability to understand the problem was as frustrating, in its own way, as his hunger for Evie. He had always been able to grasp nuances, see clearly to the crux of any problem, with a speed that left others in the dust. Now it was as if his brain had failed him, and the thought infuriated him.

It wasn't the house. As much as that had hurt her, she had understood his explanation; he had seen that in her eyes. Balanced against national security, her house was nothing, and she had believed him when he'd told her that he'd never intended to go through with the foreclosure. It was a dreadful miscalculation on his part, and though it chafed that he had made such a mistake, Evie had made a move that no one could have anticipated. Mortgage the house, yes, but not *sell* it. He was still stunned by the solution she had chosen.

But she had forgiven him for that, had even forgiven him for suspecting that she might be a traitor.

Why in hell, then, had she refused to marry him? The expression in her eyes still haunted him, and he lay awake nights aching with the need to put the glow back into her face. His golden, radiant Evie had looked like...ashes.

She loved him. He knew that as surely as he knew his heart beat in his chest. And still she had turned him down. "Go away, Robert," she'd said, and the finality in her voice had stunned him. So he had gone away, and he felt as if, every day away from her, he died a little more.

Madelyn had called several times, and she was becoming insistent that he come to Montana for a visit. Knowing his sister as he did, he was ruefully aware that he had maybe two more days to get out there before she turned up on his doorstep, holding one toddler by the hand and the other balanced on her hip, a ruthless expression in those lazy gray eyes. She knew him well enough to sense that something was wrong, and she wouldn't rest until she knew what it was. Her determination had been a fearsome thing when she'd been a child, and it had gotten worse as she'd grown older.

Robert swore in frustration, then made a swift decision. Other than Evie, Madelyn was the most astute woman he knew. Maybe, as a woman, she could put her finger on the reason that was eluding him. He called Madelyn to let her know he was coming.

With the time difference, it was still early the next morning when his plane landed in Billings. The ranch was another hundred and twenty miles, and had its own airstrip, so he had long since developed the habit of renting a small plane and flying the rest of the way, rather than making the long drive. As he banked to align the Cessna with the runway, he saw Madelyn's four-wheel drive Explorer below; she was leaning against the hood, her long hair lifting in the breeze. The color of her hair was lighter and cooler than Evie's tawny-blond mane, but still his heart squeezed at the similarity.

He landed the plane and taxied it close to the vehicle. As he cut the engine, he could see the two lively little boys bouncing in the cargo area, and a rueful smile touched his eyes. He had missed the little hooligans. He wanted some of his own.

As he crossed the pavement, Madelyn came to meet him, her lazy stroll fluid and provocative. ''Thank God you're here,'' she said. ''The imps of Satan have been driving me crazy since I told them you were coming. Did you know that when a one-year-old says Uncle Robert, it sounds remarkably like Ali Baba? I've heard it fifteen thousand times in the past hour, so I'm an expert.''

''Dear God,'' he murmured, looking past her to where the two imps of Satan were shrieking what was undoubtedly their version of his name.

She went up on tiptoe to kiss his cheek and he hugged her to him. Something guarded inside him always relaxed when he set foot on the ranch. The sense of nature was much closer here, just as it had been in Alabama.

Madelyn waited until after lunch before broaching the subject he knew had been eating her alive with curiosity. The boys had been put down for their afternoon naps, and he and Reese were sitting at the table, relaxing over coffee. Madelyn came back into the dining room, sat down and said, ''All right, what's wrong?''

He gave her a wry smile. "I knew you couldn't wait much longer. You've always been as curious as a cat."

"Agreed. Talk."

So he did. It felt strange. He couldn't remember ever needing help before in deciding what to do. He concisely outlined the situation with Mercer, explaining Evie's suspected involvement and the method he had used to force them into action. He described Evie, unaware of the aching hunger in his eyes as he did so. He told them everything—how Evie had sold her house to stop the foreclosure on the marina, how she had discovered that he was behind it all, and how Mercer had been caught. And how she had turned down his marriage proposal.

He was aware that Madelyn had stiffened during his recital of events, but she was looking down at the table, and he couldn't read her expression. When he finished, however, she lifted her head, and he was startled to see the molten fury in her eyes.

"Are you that dense?" she shouted, jumping to her feet with a force that overturned her chair. "I don't blame her for not marrying you! I wouldn't have, either!" Infuriated, she stomped out of the dining room.

Bemused, Robert turned to stare after her. "I didn't know she could move that fast," he murmured.

Reese gave a startled shout of laughter. "I know. It took me by surprise the first time I made her lose her temper, too."

Robert turned back to his brother-in-law, a big, tough rancher as tall as himself, with dark hair and hazel-green eyes, coloring that he had passed on to his two sons.

"What set her off?"

"Probably the same thing that set her off when I was being that dense, too," Reese explained, amusement in his eyes.

"Would someone please explain it to me?" Robert asked with strained politeness. On the surface he was still in complete control, but inside he was dying by inches. He didn't know what to do, and that had never happened to him before. He was at a complete loss.

Reese leaned back in his chair, toying with the handle of his cup. "I almost lost Madelyn once," he said abruptly, looking down. "She probably never told you, but she left me. She didn't go far, just into town, but it might as well have been a million miles, the way I felt."

"When was this?" Robert asked, his eyes narrowing. He didn't like knowing that Madelyn had had problems and hadn't told him about them.

"When she was pregnant with Ty. I tried everything I could think of to convince her to come back, but I was too stupid to give her the one reason that mattered."

Reese was going somewhere with this, Robert realized. He was a private man and not normally this talkative. "Which reason was that?"

Reese lifted his gaze to meet Robert's, and hazel-green eyes met ice-green ones, both stark with emotion.

"It isn't easy to give someone else that kind of power over you," Reese said abruptly. "Hell, it wasn't easy to even admit it to myself, and you're twice as bad as I ever was. You're a tough son of a bitch, more dangerous than you want people to know, so you keep it all under control. You're used to controlling everything around you, but you can't control this, can you? You probably don't even know what it is. I practically had to be hit in the head before I saw the light. You love her, don't you?"

Robert froze, and his eyes went blank with shock. Love? He'd never even thought the word. He wanted Evie, wanted to marry her, wanted to have children with her. God, he wanted all of that with a fierce passion that threatened to destory him if he didn't get it. But everything in him rebelled at the thought of being in *love*. It would mean a terrible helplessness; he wouldn't be able to hold himself apart from her, to keep uncompromised the basic invulnerability that was at the core of him. He was well aware of his true nature, knew the savage inside. He didn't want to unleash that kind of raw passion, didn't want anyone to even know it existed.

But Evie knew, anyway, he realized, and felt another shock. She had seen through him right from the beginning. With that maddening intuition of hers, she sometimes went straight into his thoughts. He could shut everyone else out, but he had never been able to shut out Evie, and he had spent the entire time they were together trying to regain control over himself, over the situation, over her. She knew him for what he was, and she loved him, anyway.

He swore, running a shaking hand over his face, blinding truth staring him in the eye. Evie wouldn't have loved him if that savage intensity hadn't been there. She had known real love with Matt, and lost it; only something incredibly powerful could take her beyond that. Loving Evangeline couldn't be a civilized, controlled affair; she would want him heart and soul, nothing held back.

The house hadn't been the issue. Neither had suspecting her of a crime. He could offer her a hundred houses, all the power his wealth could bring, and none of that would tempt her. What she wanted was the one thing he hadn't offered: his love.

"It was that simple," Reese said softly. "I told Maddie that I love her. More importantly, I admitted it to myself."

Robert was still stunned, still turned inward. "How do you know?" he murmured.

Reese made a low, harsh sound. "Do you feel as if you can never get enough of her? Do you want to make love to her so much that the ache never quite leaves your gut? Do you want to protect her, carry her around on a satin cushion, give her everything in the world? Are you content just being with her, listening to her, smelling her, touching her hand? Do you feel as if someone's torn your guts out, you miss her so much? When Maddie left me, it hurt so damn bad I could barely function. There was a big empty hole in me, and it ached so much I couldn't sleep, couldn't eat. The only thing that could make it better was seeing her. Is that the way it feels?"

Robert's green eyes were stark. "Like I'm bleeding to death inside."

"Yep, that's love," Reese said, shaking his head in sympathy.

Robert got to his feet, his lean face setting in lines of determination. "Kiss Madelyn goodbye for me. Tell her I'll call her."

"You can't wait for morning?"

"No," Robert said as he took the stairs two at a time. He couldn't wait another minute. He was on his way to Alabama.

Evie didn't like her new home. She felt hemmed in, though she had a corner apartment and neighbors on only one side. When she looked out the window, she saw another apartment building, rather than the river sweeping endlessly past. She could hear her neighbors through the thin walls, hear them arguing, hear their two small children whining and crying. They were out until all hours, children in tow, and came dragging the poor little tykes in at one or two in the morning. The commotion inevitably woke her, and she would lie in bed staring at the dark ceiling for hours.

She could look for another place, she knew, but she couldn't muster enough energy or interest to do it. She forced herself to go to the marina every day, and that was the limit of what she could do. She was going through the motions, but each day it took more and more effort, and soon she would collapse under the strain.

She felt cold, and she couldn't get warm. It was an internal cold, spreading out from the vast emptiness inside, and no amount of heat could get past it. Just thinking his name was like having a knife jabbed into her, shards of pain splintering in all directions, but she couldn't get him out of her mind. A glimpse of black hair brought her head snapping around; a certain deep tone of voice made her heart stop for an instant—a precious instant—as uncontrollable joy shot through her and she thought, *He's back!* But he never was, and the joy would turn to ashes, leaving her more desolate than before.

The sun burned down, the heat wave continuing, but she couldn't feel its heat or see its bright light. The world was colored in tones of cold gray.

I got through this before, she would think on those mornings when there didn't seem to be any reason to get out of bed. *I can do it again.* But the fact was, doing it before had nearly killed her, and the depression that sucked all the spirit out of her was getting deeper every day. She didn't know if she had the strength to fight it.

Becky had gone ballistic when she found out Robert had left town. "He told me he was going to ask you to marry him," she'd roared, so enraged her hair had practicallly been standing on end.

"He did," Evie had said listlessly. "I said no." And she had refused to answer any more questions; she hadn't even told Becky why she'd sold the house.

Summer was coming to an end, burning itself out. It was almost time for school to start. The calendar said that fall was a month away, but the scent of it was in the air, crisp and fresh, without the redolent perfumes of summer. She was burning herself out, too, Evie thought, and didn't much care.

She went to bed as soon as it was dark, hoping to get a few hours' sleep before her noisy neighbors came home. It was usually a useless effort. Whenever she stopped, she couldn't keep the memories at bay; they swarmed at her from all the corners of her mind. Lying in bed, she would remember Robert's warm presence beside her, feel his weight compressing the mattress, and the memory was so real that it was almost as if she could reach out and touch him. Her body throbbed, needing his touch, the exquisite relief of having him inside her. She would relive every time he had made love to her, and her breasts would grow heavy with desire.

He was gone, but she wasn't free of him.

That night was no different; if anything, it was worse. She tossed about, trying to ignore the fever in her flesh and the misery in her heart. The T-shirt she wore rasped her aching nipples, tempting her to remove it, but she knew better. When she had tried to sleep nude, her skin had become even more sensitive.

Someone banged on the door, startling her so much that she bolted upright in bed. She glanced at the clock. It was after ten.

She got up and slipped on a robe. The banging came again, as thunderous as if someone was trying to beat down her door. She paused to turn on a lamp in the living room. "Who is it?"

"Robert. Open the door, Evie."

She froze, her hand on the knob, all the blood draining from her face. For a moment she thought she would faint. "What do you want?'' she managed, the words so low that she wasn't sure he could hear them, but he did.

''I want to talk to you. Open the door.''

The deep, rich voice was the same, the tone as controlled as ever. She leaned her head against the door facing, wondering if she had the strength to send him away again. What remained to be said? Was he going to try to make her accept the house? She couldn't live there; the memories of him were too strong.

''Evangeline, *open the door.*''

She fumbled with the lock and opened the door. He stepped in immediately, tall and overwhelming. She was swamped by her reactions as she fell back a pace. The scent of him was the same, the leashed vitality of his tall, lean body slamming against her like a blow. He closed the door and locked it, and when he turned back to her she saw that his black hair was tousled, and a dark shadow of beard covered his cheeks. His eyes were glittering like green fire as they fastened on her. He didn't give the apartment a glance.

''I'm only going to ask you once more,'' he said abruptly. ''Will you marry me?''

Evie shuddered with the strain, but slowly shook her head. She could have married him before, when she'd thought he cared for her at least a little, but when she had realized he'd only been using her... No, she couldn't do it.

A muscle clenched in his jaw. She could feel the tension in him, like some great beast coiled to jump, and she took another step back. When he spoke, however, his voice was almost mild. ''Why not?''

The contrast of his voice to the energy she could feel pulsing in him was maddening. All the misery of the past weeks congealed inside her, and she felt herself splintering inside. ''Why not?'' she cried incredulously, her voice shaking. ''My God, look at yourself! Nothing touches you, does it? You'd take everything I have to give, but you'd never let me inside where you really live, where I could reach the real man. You keep yourself behind a cold wall, and I'm tired of bruising myself against it!''

His nostrils flared. ''Do you love me?''

"Is that what you came for?" Tears welled in her eyes, rolled slowly down her cheeks. "A sop to your ego? Yes, I love you. Now *get out!*"

She saw his powerful muscles tense, saw his eyes flare with something savage. Her heart leapt, and too late she saw the danger. She turned to run, but Robert grabbed her, whirling her to face him. Confused, Evie thought at first it was one of his carefully gauged actions, designed to impress upon her how serious he was, but then she saw his eyes. The pupils were contracted to tiny black points, the irises huge and glittering like pale fire. His face was tight and pale, except for two spots of color high on the blades of his cheekbones. Not even Robert, she thought dazedly, could control those physical reactions.

His hands tightened on her waist until his fingers dug painfully into her soft flesh, a grip that she knew would leave bruises. "You're right," he said almost soundlessly. "I've never wanted anyone to get close to me. I've never wanted to care this much for anyone, to let you or anyone else have this kind of power over me." His lips drew back over his teeth, and he was breathing hard. "Shut you out? My God, I've tried to, but I can't. You want the real man, sweetheart? All right, I'm yours. I love you so much it's tearing me apart. But there's a flip side to it," he continued harshly. "I'll give you more than I've ever given any other human being, but by God, I'll take more, too. You don't get to pick and choose which qualities you like the best. It's a package deal. You get all the bad with the good, and I warn you now, I'm not a gentleman."

"No," she whispered, "you're not." She hung in his grip, her eyes fastened on his face, seeing the sheen of sweat on his forehead and the ferocity of his expression. Her heart thundered at what he had just said, her mind reeling with joy. He loved her? She almost couldn't take it in, couldn't believe he'd actually said it. She stared up into those fiery eyes, too dazed to say anything else.

"I'm jealous," he muttered, still in that tone of stifled violence. "I don't want you even looking at another man, and if any fool tries to come on to you, he'll be lucky if I only break his arm." He shook her with enough force to make her teeth snap together.

"I want you all the time, and now, damn it, I'll take you. I'll be on you so often, four and five times a day, that you'll forget what it's like not to have me inside you. No more being a gentleman and restricting myself to twice a day."

Her golden brown eyes widened. "No," she said faintly. "I wouldn't want you to restrict yourself." There were no controls on him now; she could feel the passion surging through him, a wild and savage force that caught her up in its tide and swept her along with him.

"I'll want you at my beck and call. I can't ignore the business, so I'll expect you to fit your schedule around mine, to be available whenever I'm home." As he talked, he moved her backward and roughly pushed her against the wall. His hands tugged at her panties, stripping them down her legs. He leaned against her, his heavy weight pinning her to the wall as he tore his pants open. She gave a brief, incoherent prayer of thanks that her neighbors were gone, then clung to his shoulders as he hooked one arm under her bottom and lifted her. Her heart pounding, her blood rushing through her veins on a giddy tide of joy, she parted her thighs, and he shoved himself between them. His penetration was fast and rough. She bit back a cry and buried her face against his neck. She could feel his own heartbeat thudding against her breast.

They were both motionless, overwhelmed by the stunning relief and pleasure of their bodies being joined once more, she trying to adjust to the hard fullness of him, he groaning at the tightness of her inner clasp on his sex. Then, still caught in the savage exaltation of emotional freedom, he drove mercilessly into her.

"I don't want to wear a condom," he said fiercely, his breath hot against her ear. "I don't want you to take birth-control pills. I don't want you to act like my semen is some hostile marauder that you have to protect yourself against. I want to give it to you. I want you to want it. I want you to have my babies. I want a house full of kids." With each word he thrust, pushing himself deeper and deeper into her.

She moaned, shuddering around him with the force of her plea-sure. "Yes." She had unleashed a monster of passion, a total dictator, but she could meet his power with her own. This was the real man, the one who made her feel alive again, who sent heat throbbing through every cell of her body. She wasn't cold any longer, but radiant with vibrant life.

"I want marriage." His teeth were ground together, and a drop of sweat ran down his temple. "I want you tied to me—legally, financially, every way I can devise. I want you to take my name, Evangeline, do you understand?"

"Yes," she said, and splintered with joy. "Robert, *yes!*"

He bucked violently against her with his climax, flooding her with moisture and heat. Evie locked her legs around him and took him deep within, her senses whirling and fading, all consciousness gone except for the primal awareness of him inside her.

Some endless time later, she realized that she was on the bed and he was stretched out naked beside her. She hadn't fainted, but neither had she been aware of anything else but him. He hadn't released her during the entire time he had stripped both her and himself, struggling out of clothing while still keeping her in his grasp. She turned to snuggle closer, and the lure of his body, after the long deprivation, was too great. She found herself on top of him, wriggling to find the right contact and nestle his sex against the soft heat between her legs. He caught his breath, and she felt him begin to harden again.

"You might get started on that house full of kids sooner than you thought," she murmured, moving against him again in voluptuous delight. "I stopped taking the birth-control pills the day you left."

"Good." He caressed her bottom and hip, urging her closer to him. "I don't want to hurt you," he said even as he slipped inside her.

She heard the worry in his voice and knew that he was uneasy with releasing all the force he'd kept contained for so long. She kissed him and bit his lip as his subtle movements made her nerve endings riot with pleasure. "You can't hurt me by loving me," she said.

His eyes glittered in the faint light coming from the lamp in the living room. "That's good," he murmured. "Because God knows I do."

_____ *Epilogue*

Evie heard the elevator arrive and crouched down beside the tiny, adorable creature who was clinging unsteadily to the chair in the entrance hall. "There's Daddy," she whispered, and watched her daughter's big eyes go round with delight. She barely restrained herself from gathering the baby into her arms; sometimes the surge of love was so strong that she thought she would burst from the force of it.

The elevator doors slid open, and Robert stepped out, an indescribable light flaring in his pale green eyes as he saw them waiting for him. With a joyous gurgle, the baby let go of the chair and hurled herself toward him, every toddling step teetering on the edge of disaster. Robert turned absolutely white, dropped his briefcase with a thud, and went down on one knee to swoop her into his arms. "My God," he said, shocked. "She's walking!"

"For a couple of hours now," Evie said, smiling as Angel caught her father's silk tie in one tiny, chubby hand and began babbling at him. "It makes my heart stop every time she lurches across the floor."

"She's too young to walk. She's only seven months old." Aghast, he stared down at the small head, covered with downy dark hair, that butted against his chest. He had been just as aghast when she had started crawling at five months. If he could, Robert would have kept his darling offspring as a babe in arms for the first five years of her life. She, however, was blissfully oblivious of his panic at her daring.

Still holding the baby, he hugged Evie close for a long kiss, one that quickly grew heated despite his squirming burden, who tried to poke her fingers between their mouths. They had named her Jennifer Angelina, intending to call her Jenna, but instead she had been Angel from the day she'd been born. She was angelic only when she was asleep, however; during waking hours, she had the fearless spirit of a daredevil.

Evie clung to his mouth for a long time, her hand clenching his hair to hold him in place. She had been waiting all day for him to come home, feeling shivery and excited and a little frightened.

"You were right," she murmured.

He lifted his head, and the green eyes gleamed. "I was, huh?"

She laughed and pinched him. "You knew you were." They had decided to have another baby as soon as possible. Both pregnancy and delivery had been easy for her, and though they had decided that two children would fill the house they were building just fine, they had both wanted to have them close together.

Three weeks ago, they had spent the night locked together, lost in the passion that hadn't faded during the sixteen months of their marriage. When they had awakened at dawn, for their ritual of morning love, Robert had looked down at her with his sleepy green eyes barely open and said, "We made a baby last night."

She had thought so, too, her instincts certain even before the early pregnancy test she'd taken just that morning had confirmed it. Already it was as if she could feel that hot, tiny weight in her womb, pulsing with life.

She leaned her head against his broad shoulder, remembering the sheer terror she'd felt when she had realized that she was pregnant the first time. Taking a chance on loving Robert had required all her courage, but now there was to be someone else to love, someone who was part of her, part of Robert. She would have no defense against this new little person, and she had thought she would shatter from the fear. But Robert had known how she was feeling, had seen the raw fear in her eyes and hadn't left her side all day. He had called Felice and announced that he wouldn't be in, cancel everything, and had spent the day holding Evie on his lap or making love to her. His solution, she thought wryly, had been to overwhelm her with what had gotten her in that condition to begin with; the tactic had been amazingly successful.

Angel was trying to throw herself bodily out of his arms. Sighing, he released Evie to bend down and set the baby on her chubby feet. As soon as he released her, she was off like a wobbly rocket. Evie went back into his arms, but they both kept a weather eye on their precocious daughter as she began investigating a fascinating crack in the hardwood floor.

Evie rested her head on his chest, reassured by the strong, steady thump of his heart beneath her ear. Far from losing himself in his work and demanding that she structure her time around him, as he'd said he would, Robert had instead ruthlessly reorganized his office schedule so he could spend every available moment with her and Angel. She had known that he was a man of alarming intensity, but instead of being frightened when he focused it on her, she had bloomed. Robert wasn't a man who loved lightly; when he loved, it was with every fiber of his being.

His hand moved to Evie's belly and pressed in gentle reassurance. "Are you all right?" he asked softly.

She lifted her head and gave him a luminous smile. His love had renewed her strength, banished the shadows. "I've never been better."

Robert kissed her, savoring her sweet taste and the familiar, delicious tension of desire that quivered in their bodies. "I love you, Evangeline," he said, gathering her close to him. Loving her was the most joyous, satisfying thing he'd ever done. She demanded everything from him and gave him all of herself, and sometimes he was staggered by the richness of the bond between them. He'd been right; loving Evangeline took everything he had, heart and soul.

Celebrating Our Authors

MORE ABOUT THE BOOKS

MORE ABOUT THE AUTHOR

WE RECOMMEND

LINDA HOWARD ON *Raintree: Inferno* and *Loving Evangeline*

Robert Cannon first appeared in "*Duncan's Bride*," and I knew immediately he'd have his own story to tell me. The identity of the perfect woman for him, though, was a mystery. When she finally appeared, Evangeline was the complete opposite of what Robert had always thought he wanted in a woman. She was a woman who had endured so many personal losses, including the death of her childhood sweetheart while on their honeymoon, that she had learned to protect herself by not letting anyone get close to her. Robert was a man used to getting what he wanted, a man used to dominating all his relationships, but Evie was a woman who quietly blocked his every move, who relied on her own strength instead of his, and who was willing to go to extreme lengths to maintain her independence. She was the one woman he couldn't dominate, and, he discovered, the one he couldn't live without.

'...I knew immediately he'd have his own story to tell me...'

Raintree: Inferno was born from a conversation with my long-time friends, Beverly Barton and Linda Winstead Jones, who is also known as "LJ" because I'm older than she is and I got to be the "Linda" in the group. We were playing with the concept of writing a trilogy together, and before we knew it the concept was a plan, and Raintree was formed. We spent almost five years developing the mythology behind the royal family of wizards, but we knew immediately who would write each character. I had Dante, the king; LJ had Gideon, the non-conformist middle brother

Detailed

who became a police detective even though he was backed by the wealth of the royal Raintree family, and Beverly had Mercy, the powerful younger sister who had the biggest secret of all. We had this over-arching plot of the royal family being under attack by the Ansara, a family of evil wizards. The only thing was, if Dante figured out what was going on and didn't tell both his siblings, then he was a fool. The same went for the others. No matter what order the books came in, the first one had to tell the others, but if the others knew then the last two books would have no plot because all of it was about how each character figured it out. The only thing we could do was have the action in all three books take place simultaneously.

We couldn't have thought of anything else that would have caused as much difficulty. Every detail became crucial to the timing. We had to co-ordinate conversations, the timeline of the action…and then we realised the first book couldn't have the resolution of the epic battle with the Ansara. That had to come in the third and final book. That meant *Raintree: Inferno* couldn't have an ending, and neither could *Raintree: Haunted*. The real, final ending had to be in the final book, *Raintree: Sanctuary*. As I said, we could scarcely have made things more difficult for ourselves if we'd sat down and said, "Hey! Let's write a trilogy that will make us beat our heads against the wall!" Despite all that, we loved the characters, and we loved the books.

'…We spent almost five years developing the mythology…'

Celebrating Our Authors

AUTHOR BIOGRAPHY

Linda Howard sold her first book in 1980, and has now written almost forty. She lives in Alabama with her husband of twenty-seven years, Gary, and their two stupendously spoiled golden retrievers. He fishes for a living, she reads and writes, and they both think it's paradise.

LINDA HOWARD ON WRITING

What do you love most about being a writer?

The writing itself. The stories. Getting to know the characters, feeling the plot develop, the joy of losing myself in the lives of the characters. Writing, for me, is like putting a jigsaw puzzle together in the dark. I have to go by feel, and when it feels right, that's an incredible high.

Where do you go for inspiration?

Nowhere. The stories come from inside, not anywhere outside.

Where do your characters come from and do they ever surprise you when you write?

I don't model characters on anyone I know. The characters are themselves, as real to me as anyone else I know. I don't develop them so much as I get to know them, and, yes, they often surprise me as I'm getting to know them.

'...Writing is like putting a jigsaw puzzle together in the dark...'

Do you have a favourite character and what is it you like about that character?

I have many favourite characters. I can't say there's one who stands above all the others, because each of them is unique, and they all have something special. They all walk different paths, want and need different things, and offer different strengths to the world.

When did you start writing?

I was nine years old. I'd already read all the books in my school's small library, I was bored, and I wanted something to read. So I wrote a story myself. It was four pages long. My teacher was astonished, and read it aloud to the class. I thought, "Four pages isn't long enough," and promptly began writing a book. It was terrible, of course, but I wrote and wrote and wrote. I think it was over three hundred pages long before I got bored with it and ended it. I never looked back. Writing was all I ever wanted to do, and a writer was all I ever wanted to be.

What one piece of advice would you give a writer wanting to start a career?

Read a lot, and write what you love. Life's too short to waste it writing things you don't love.

'...*write what you love*...'

LINDA HOWARD'S FUTURE PROJECTS

I have a rough idea of what I *want* to write, but I'm not certain it will be my next book. Sometimes other concerns determine when I'll write any individual book. I'm not the type of writer who can sit down and plot a book, then begin writing on it. The ideas have to grow on me, I have to brood about them, daydream about them, and one day the characters reach what I call critical mass and they're ready to be written. If my publisher doesn't like that idea, then I'm back to square one – and I don't assume that all of my ideas are great. Some of them are real stinkers. So I have to wait and see if my current rough idea makes the cut.

8

Celebrating Our Authors

If you enjoyed *Raintree: Inferno*, we know you'll love these great reads!

Raintree: Haunted
by Linda Winstead Jones and
Raintree: Sanctuary by Beverly Barton

The next two books in the Raintree trilogy are as exciting and romantic as the first. Published over the next two months, you won't want to miss the thrilling conclusion to this epic story.

At His Mercy
by Linda Howard

As part of Mills & Boon's Queens of Romance collection, three of Linda Howard's fabulous stories are brought together in this very special edition, which will be available from September 2008.

'...I love nurseries and art galleries...'

Celebrate 100 years of pure reading pleasure with Mills & Boon®

To mark our centenary, each month we're publishing a special 100th Birthday Edition. These celebratory editions are packed with extra features and include a FREE bonus story.

Now that's worth celebrating!

4th January 2008

The Vanishing Viscountess by Diane Gaston
With FREE story The Mysterious Miss M
This award-winning tale of the Regency Underworld launched Diane Gaston's writing career.

1st February 2008

Cattle Rancher, Secret Son by Margaret Way
With FREE story His Heiress Wife
Margaret Way excels at rugged Outback heroes…

15th February 2008

Raintree: Inferno by Linda Howard
With FREE story Loving Evangeline
A double dose of Linda Howard's heady mix of passion and adventure.

Don't miss out! From February you'll have the chance to enter our fabulous monthly prize draw. See special 100th Birthday Editions for details.

www.millsandboon.co.uk

100ᵗʰ Birthday Prize Draw!

£500 worth of prizes to be won every month. Now that's worth celebrating!

To enter, simply visit **www.millsandboon.co.uk**,
click through to the prize draw entry page and quote
promotional code **CEN08MA03**

Alternatively, complete the entry form below and send to:
**Mills & Boon® 100ᵗʰ Birthday Prize Draw
PO Box 676, Richmond, Surrey, TW9 1WU**

Mills & Boon® 100th Birthday Prize Draw (CEN08MA03)

Name: _____

Address: _____

Post Code: _____

Daytime Telephone No: _____

E-mail Address: _____

❑ I have read the terms and conditions (please tick this box before entering).

❑ Please tick here if you do not wish to receive special offers from
   Harlequin Mills & Boon Ltd.

Closing date for entries is 15ᵗʰ April 2008

Terms & Conditions

1. Draw open to UK and Eire residents aged 18 and over. No purchase necessary. One entry per household per prize draw only. 2. Prizes are non-transferable and no cash alternatives will be offered. 3. All prizes are subject to availability. Should any prize be unavailable, a prize of similar value will be substituted. 4. Employees and immediate family members of Harlequin Mills & Boon Ltd are not eligible to enter. 5. Prize winners will be randomly selected from the eligible entries received. No correspondence will be entered into and no entry returned. 6. To be eligible, all entries must be received by 15ᵗʰ April 2008. 7. Prize winner notification will be made by e-mail or letter no later than 15 days after the deadline for entry. 8. No responsibility can be accepted for entries that are lost, delayed or damaged. Proof of postage cannot be accepted as proof of delivery. 9. If any winner notification or prize is returned as undeliverable, an alternative winner will be drawn from eligible entries. 10. Names of competition winners are available on request. 11. See www.millsandboon.co.uk for full terms and conditions.

FREE!

4 Books
and a surprise gift!

We would like to take this opportunity to thank you for reading this Mills & Boon® book by offering you the chance to take FOUR more specially selected titles from the Intrigue series absolutely FREE! We're also making this offer to introduce you to the benefits of the Mills & Boon® Reader Service™—

- ★ FREE home delivery
- ★ FREE gifts and competitions
- ★ FREE monthly Newsletter
- ★ Exclusive Reader Service offers
- ★ Books available before they're in the shops

Accepting these FREE books and gift places you under no obligation to buy, you may cancel at any time, even after receiving your free shipment. Simply complete your details below and return the entire page to the address below. You don't even need a stamp!

YES! Please send me 4 free Intrigue books and a surprise gift. I understand that unless you hear from me, I will receive 6 superb new titles every month for just £3.15 each, postage and packing free. I am under no obligation to purchase any books and may cancel my subscription at any time. The free books and gift will be mine to keep in any case.

18ZEF

Ms/Mrs/Miss/Mr ....Initials.........................

BLOCK CAPITALS PLEASE

Surname ....

Address...

....

....Postcode ....

Send this whole page to:
UK: FREEPOST CN81, Croydon, CR9 3WZ

Offer valid in UK only and is not available to current Mills & Boon® Reader Service™ subscribers to this series. Overseas and Eire please write for details. We reserve the right to refuse an application and applicants must be aged 18 years or over. Only one application per household. Terms and prices subject to change without notice. Offer expires 31st May 2008. As a result of this application, you may receive offers from Harlequin Mills & Boon and other carefully selected companies. If you would prefer not to share in this opportunity please write to The Data Manager, PO Box 676, Richmond, TW9 1WU.

Mills & Boon® is a registered trademark owned by Harlequin Mills & Boon Limited.
The Mills & Boon® Reader Service™ is being used as a trademark.